**FRANCES PARKINSON KEYES
WRITES OF LOVE AMONG THE ARISTOCRATS
IN HER MOST THRILLING ROMANTIC NOVEL.**

EUNICE HALE
*A beautiful, headstrong heiress who listened only to
her heart—and a faithless love.*

FRANCIS FIELDING
*He used women with charm, grace and utter
ruthlessness.*

EDITH LASTERIE
*A heady Hawaiian diversion, she was enough
to tempt any honeymooning husband.*

CRISPIN WOOD
*At last he met the woman he
couldn't buy—but she was already taken.*

MILLIE STONE
*Dazzling and determined,
she was out to conquer—and divide—every
couple who crossed her path.*

Frances Parkinson Keyes

Fielding's Folly

 AVON PUBLISHERS OF BARD, CAMELOT, DISCUS AND EQUINOX BOOKS

NO WRITER IS A HEROINE TO HER SECRETARY
BUT SOMETIMES HER SECRETARY
IS A HEROINE TO A WRITER.
THIS HAS BEEN TRUE IN MY CASE.
THIS NOVEL IS THEREFORE DEDICATED
TO HARRIET STEARNS WHITFORD
THE SECRETARY WHO THROUGH THICK AND THIN
HAS STOOD BY.

AVON BOOKS
A division of
The Hearst Corporation
959 Eighth Avenue
New York, New York 10019

Copyright 1940 by Frances Parkinson Keyes.
Published by arrangement with Julian Messner, Division of
Simon and Schuster, Inc.

ISBN: 0-380-00241-8

First Printing, September, 1961
Twelfth Printing

Printed in Canada

FOREWORD

BOOKS COME INTO BEING in strange and devious ways.

One day in the early spring of 1939, I received a communication from a friend who conducts the highly successful "Counsel" column entitled, "Mary Haworth's Mail" appearing in the *Washington Post*. "The letter I am enclosing," Mary said, "seems to be down your alley rather than mine. It tells the story and makes the plea of an old house. Is there anything you can do with it? If there is, why don't you answer it?"

I did answer it, and the story of *Fielding's Folly* is the result.

Though I have followed my usual custom of using a name typical of a region, I should be careful to say that no family of Fieldings ever lived in the old house which proved such a treasure trove, nor have any of its real inhabitants borne the slightest resemblance, so far as I know, to those I have created. Eunice and Francis, Mrs. Fielding and the "trundle-bed trash" and their various relatives and friends, are all imaginary characters. Nor is the prototype of Retreat actually located in the vicinity of the Upper and Lower Gardens—Indeed, all three of the southern houses from which I drew my inspiration in these cases are in different counties! Evergreen, on the other hand, is a composite picture which owes its conception to more than one house in New England which is near and dear to me. In this instance I was free to draw more fully on facts, because these facts are an integral part of my own heritage and my own being. It is true that I am a Virginian myself, both by the happy accident of birth and by subsequent deliberate choice. But my ancestral affiliations are in the Upper Connecticut Valley, embracing both Vermont and New Hampshire, and these I can never uproot or transplant.

The good earth in the state of Vermont is literally honeycombed with deposits of marble and granite, and the Spencerville of my story has several prototypes in reality, though, as far as I know, the Spencer family itself has not. I have all my life been familiar in a general way with the regions which produce marble and granite. But I am especially indebted to Mr. Wallace M. Fay of Proctor, Vermont, and to

Mr. Athol R. Bell, of Barre, Vermont, for personal conferences with them which shed much light on the marble and granite industries and for recent delightful visits to the quarries and workrooms of the Vermont Marble Company and The Rock of Ages Corporation. The land where the Rock of Ages granite quarries now stand was actually acquired in the manner which "Grandma Hale" describes, and the successful manufacture of maple sugar by that company, as a by-product, inspired my fictional reference to this wise and pleasing development.

I am indebted to Mrs. Mable Taylor of San Francisco for permission to use certain anecdotes of the Far East founded on her experience.

During the course of a trip around the world which my oldest son made with me, he was stricken with the malady which, in this novel, is given as the cause of Francis Fielding's critical illness. I am glad to be able to pay a tribute to the kindness shown to both my son and myself, at this agonizing period, by the British officials in Singapore and the members of the hospital staff there. But though the scene is real, and the circumstances founded on fact, the characters are all fictitious. In the Hawaiian part of the story, only the geographical scene is real, and only the descriptions of native celebrations, like *luaus* and hulas, founded on fact.

I am indebted to Mr. John W. Gwathmey, the distinguished author of *Legends of Virginia Courthouses, Legends of Virginia Lawyers, Justice John* and various other valuable works in which the Old Dominion forms the background, for permission to use, in fiction form, the stories which appear on pages 210, 307 and 420 of *Fielding's Folly*. The ghost story interwoven with the main plot of my novel owes its origin to a manuscript entrusted to me by Frances Krautter of Kinlock, Anchorage, Kentucky. She vouches for its authenticity, though the scene of the mysterious apparition she describes, while Virginian, has no connection with the real Retreat. This does have a ghost story of its own, but permission to use it came too late for inclusion in the present narrative. I hope, however, to use it at some future time.

Nina Carter Tabb, of Middleburg, the columnist of "The Hunt Country," has been most helpful in facilitating and furthering my own familiarity with the locality.

For the bulk of the Virginian source material in my story, other than that which my own knowledge and experience furnished, I am indebted to Mrs. John Aldridge of Lyells and to her aunt, the late Miss Evelyn D. Ward. Miss Ward died before my story was completed, but her co-operation in the early stages of its preparation was invaluable. She was good enough to put into my possession many manuscripts of her own, with full permission to draw on them or adapt them in any way I chose. Most of them were private papers. One article, however, entitled "Aunt Eve: Lest We Forget," had been printed—November 1928—in *The Black Swan*, a periodical published in Richmond, Virginia. Miss Ward and Mrs. Aldridge were good enough to receive me as their guest several times, and the personal conferences I had with them were even more illuminating than the documents with which they supplied me; I listened to all they said with a sense of enthrallment. If my own imagery lacks warmth or vividness, it is not for any want of this in the tales these wise and kindly ladies told.

F.P.K.

"Tradition"
Alexandria,
Virginia

PART I

Trundlebed Trash

~~~~~~

Chapter 1

"I BEG your pardon. Could you tell me how to get to Solomon's Garden from here? I seem to be lost."

The young hunter, whose own tawny figure emerged vividly from the gloom of the autumnal twilight, was not wholly unprepared for the appeal so pleasantly put. He possessed the sensitivity to sound of the country born and bred; he had been alert from the instant the fallen leaves carpeting the driveway had been stirred by more than the gusty breeze and his own leisurely progress; and he knew that this change was wrought by hoofs before he could see either a horse or a rider. So he had stopped and waited with anticipation. Outsiders on the premises were sufficiently rare to be arresting, under almost any circumstances. But as he watched the approach of this one, he found it unexpectedly attractive.

The rider was a girl, mounted sidesaddle on a beautiful black horse. The hunter, who was a good judge of horseflesh, took in the value of the specimen before him in one glance. But his eyes did not linger long on the mount. Instead, they swept swiftly over the face and figure of the rider.

She was very slender and she sat very straight in the saddle, less with the ease of one to whom riding is second nature than with the poise of one to whom horsemanship has become a skilled accomplishment. Her habit was superbly cut, of dark covert cloth, clinging to her small waist and outlining the curves of her breast and hips. Her high stock and her doeskin gloves were both spotless, her boots burnished. A net veil, encircling her beaver hat, confined the smooth coils of her hair and covered her fresh face without concealing it. There was something almost fantastic about the flawless finish of her outfit. It seemed more appropriate for an entry at a metropolitan horseshow than for a casual ride across a lonely landscape. Though the man whose searching glance took in every detail of her appearance had never been to a metropolitan horseshow, he was instinctively aware of this.

The girl's smile, as she spoke, had been a little hesitant; and for all the perfection of her apparel, her manner lacked the complete freedom from embarrassment which characterized the young hunter who wore his leather jacket and corduroy breeches with such grace. He answered her easily and cordially.

"Why, yes. It's only four or five miles from here—that is, the Upper Garden. The Lower Garden is a little farther."

"It's at the Upper Garden I'm staying, with Millie and Freeman Stone. Perhaps you know them."

"They're kinsfolk of mine—that is, Millie is. Her great-grandmother, Mildred Fielding, and my great-grandfather, Hilary Fielding, were brother and sister. That makes us third cousins, doesn't it? Or second cousins once removed? Which is it? I never can remember. Anyway, Millie isn't very proud of the relationship, so I won't try to make it seem any closer than it really is."

The young man smiled in his turn. If his expression had not been so engaging, there might have been a hint of shamelessness about it. As it was, the girl on horseback was conscious only of its charm, as her cool gray eyes met the merry brown ones that were upturned toward her.

"My name is Francis Fielding," he went on, casually and conversationally. "Won't you come on up to the house with me? I live just at the end of this driveway. My mother'd be delighted to see you—not to mention my numerous brothers and sisters. There are six of us altogether—'trundlebed trash,' grandfather used to call us—but heaven knows he had twelve of his own, and most of them were even trashier than we are! Mother'll give you a cup of tea or whatever else you'd like, while I saddle a horse for myself. It won't take me but a minute. Then I'll ride over to the Upper Garden with you and deposit you safely at the entrance to the Great Hall. But I won't disgrace you. I'll fade away into the darkness and distance before any of Millie's fastidious and faithful retainers has time to get to the door."

Francis Fielding's eyes twinkled as he spoke and his engaging smile widened. There was a slight upward tilt to his brows and the same tilt to his lips. He was carrying a gun over his shoulder, and in his left hand were a brace of birds. Nevertheless, the girl had the feeling that he was actually leading her horse as he started down the driveway with her at his side, and a dog, more or less discernible as a pointer, at his heels. Apparently he had taken her acquiescence for granted, since he had not waited for an answer after making his courteous, though casual, suggestion. But

10

though she did not actually draw back, the tone of her voice betrayed her continued hesitancy.

"I didn't realize I was on private property. I'm terribly sorry if I've intruded, if I've put you to any trouble. I'm sure I could get back by myself if you'd just tell me the way."

"Of course you could. But the trouble with this property is that it's a great deal too private. It's so well hidden that hardly anyone ever finds it—on purpose. I'm delighted that you did so accidentally. You've no idea how far removed I live from the world—not to mention the flesh and the devil. As to letting you go back to Solomon's Garden by yourself, you wouldn't be so unkind, would you, as to rob me of the first chance I've had in months to see a girl home?"

"No—no, but—are you sure it won't be inconvenient for your mother to have me drop in on her, from nowhere, like this?"

"Inconvenient? How could it possibly be inconvenient? Except that I shan't know how to present you to her, unless you tell me your name. You haven't done that yet, you know."

"Oh, I'm so sorry! I'm—I'm just a little upset—at getting lost and all, you know. I didn't mean to be rude or thoughtless. It's Hale. Eunice Hale."

"I don't see how you could keep a nice name like that to yourself all this time. You're not a Virginian, are you?"

"Oh no. I'm a Vermonter. That is, I was born in Vermont, and my own people are all Vermonters. But after my father died, my mother married again, a New Yorker. I live with them part of the time and with my grandmother part of the time. My stepfather owns a big place near Middleburg—Tivoli, the name of it is. Perhaps you've heard of it."

"Yes, I've heard of it. I used to visit there when I was a kid. I know the Taliaferros who owned it before it was sold. They're kinsfolk of mine too."

"Oh, are they? I've always felt so sorry for them—sorry that they had to lose a lovely place like Tivoli, I mean. Of course, in a way, my stepfather's improved it a lot. The house fairly gleams, its columns are so white and its wings are so yellow. The stone vases on the balustrade around the terrace have been scraped and filled with neat plants, and the garden is all spruced up too. The dirt and disorder are all gone. But something else is gone too. The place doesn't seem the same as it did beforehand."

"Old places never do. Their spirit survives everything better than alien prosperity. You'll see one in a few minutes that hasn't been sold—or improved either for that matter— So Millie and Freeman were lucky enough to find you in Middleburg? I know they go over there a lot for the races."

11

"Yes. I met them at the fall Hunter Show last year. They've been awfully kind and cordial to me. They've asked me several times to come to Solomon's Garden. But somehow I never could, before this."

"I've heard that the New Yorkers who've taken over Middleburg are simply rooted to the spot— But then, you're not really a New Yorker, are you? Anyway, it's a pity that the first time you venture into the wilds of King George County you should get lost. I mean, it's a pity as far as you're concerned. But think what a godsend it's been to me!"

Again he spoke with a lightness that robbed his words of impudence. Secretly, he was inclined to discredit Miss Eunice Hale's story of being lost in the woods, or at least to accept it with reservations. It was contrary to the custom of the county to turn strangers out alone in the wide fields and deep woods. His guess was that the lovely Vermonter had not left Solomon's Garden for a solitary sylvan ride, but that she had parted, voluntarily and perhaps abruptly, from the escort with whom she had set out. After that she might well have become confused as to direction, especially if she had already been "upset," as she put it. Millie's house parties were locally reputed to be pretty wild; the male guests probably "took liberties" with their feminine companions almost as a matter of course; and unless he had sized her up incorrectly, the girl beside him was a puritan by instinct as well as by breeding. As he glanced up at her again, he was momentarily almost abashed at the chaste beauty of line revealed by her profile; he had never seen a girl before with just that look. There was a quality about it that shamed him. But the moment of humility passed, and another thought passed across his mind. Was she indeed inaccessible? Was there no way of breaking down her barriers? Would it not be intriguing to try, not only for the satisfaction of succeeding where others had failed, but also for the sake of the guarded treasure itself?

The dry leaves rustled about his feet as he strode forward, more quickly now. There was no other sound, except the thud of the beautiful black horse's hoofs. The girl herself seemed undisposed to talk. She was shaken as well as shy— there was no doubt of that. The driveway was so rough that she had doubtless mistaken it for a misused logging road when she had come upon it by chance. It needed draining, grading, resurfacing. Francis Fielding's laughing lips stiffened into a straight line as he thought of it. But how was it possible to put money into a road when there was none to put into shingles for a roof or brick for a chimney? As far as that went, if he had not shot four quail and two wild ducks that afternoon, what would there have been for dinner

12

the next day? While he was thinking about money, which he did as seldom as possible, why not wonder where the cash was coming from for flour and sugar and coffee, and what he would do without cash, since credit was getting increasingly hard to come by?

He continued to glance from time to time at the girl beside him. Since she had ceased to apologize and explain, her face had taken on a look of repose that was as remarkable as its purity. Trifles might trouble her; but Francis Fielding could visualize her as calm in calamity. He doubted if she had ever been touched by such turmoil as now possessed him. After all, why should she be? Her stepfather must be a multimillionaire; he could not recall the man's name, but he remembered that the price demanded for Tivoli had been fantastic, that the Taliaferros had been pried from their ancestral property on a premium basis. Doubtless Eunice Hale had money in her own right besides. Everything about her bespoke the undisputed possession of wealth—her horse, her habit, her own essential elegance. Again an involuntary thought flashed across his mind. Was she an heiress as well as a beauty? Was the guarded treasure which she innocently tempted him to uncover a gilded one? Quickly the conviction began to crystallize that the answer to both these questions was yes, and with it the knowledge that he must walk warily. It was one thing to take a citadel by storm. It was quite another to keep its value intact for permanent possession——

The audacity of his sudden vision amazed him; but he made no effort to dismiss it. The forest was very still, and in its mysterious depths, permeated with the unreal and the romantic, the dusk deepened into portentous darkness. The strange girl on the black horse was only a part of their imagery. Inevitably, she dared him to dream——

"Once I read a story called *The Heart of the Ancient Wood*. I really feel as if I were penetrating into its pages. Have we much farther to go?"

Now that she had spoken at last, of her own accord, the tone of Eunice Hale's voice revealed a recaptured composure at the same time that it broke the spell of silence. It was a clear voice, free from affectation and from the slight sharpness characteristic of the average Northerner's tones. It fell pleasantly on Francis Fielding's ears.

"No, not much. But the house was built a long distance from the highway. The original name of it was 'Retreat.' I hope these overhanging branches don't bother you. They ought to be cut back."

"No, they don't bother me. I think it's very beautiful here. But it's an eerie kind of beauty, isn't it?"

"Yes. Our negroes think the place is peopled with ghosts.

But I've never seen any. So I hope you won't let their superstitions frighten you away."

"Indeed I shan't. . . . You say the original name of the place was Retreat. Has it been changed?"

"Not officially. But colloquially, for a long time, it's been called 'Fielding's Folly.' "

"Fielding's Folly! Why?"

"The first Fielding was a fool to build as he did and where he did. He came here with a grievance instead of a purpose, like most of the colonists; and he wanted to bury himself, not to build up a settlement in a wilderness. His retreat was dramatic; but it wasn't practical from any point of view; and none of his descendants have shown much better sense or much more initiative. Not that he didn't build beautifully. Occasionally a stray architect comes along and raves about our walnut wainscoting and our heaven-and-hell hinges and the star-shaped catches that hold back our shutters. One of them even went so far as to say that the house meant as much to him as a Beethoven manuscript to a musician. That was when he discovered that the ends were 'brick-nogged.' He stood and fondled them as if they were alive. It was all Mother could do to get him out into the garden to see the arborvitae and hundred-leafed roses that are her own special pride. Some of these fancy features date back to seventeen hundred. In fact, I believe Retreat is one of the oldest plantations on this continent. But it's going to rack and ruin now."

"Can't you do something to save it?"

"I've never tried—I told you Millie Stone wasn't proud of her relationship with us. She never was, and now that she's married into America's Royal Family, she'd like to forget all about us. Me especially. I'm the black sheep of a flock that's dingy gray at best—like our Retreat. If that was ever painted, it's so long ago no one would ever know it. Look ahead of you. You'll see it for yourself in a minute."

The woods were beginning to open. Beyond them, Eunice Hale could see a clearing, dotted here and there with trees, which might conceivably be called a lawn. On the farther side of it a dim façade began to gradually assume shape and substance. The house of which it was a part formed a huge rectangle, from which a high roof perforated with a long row of dormer windows sloped loftily away. It had dignity of dimension and sturdiness of style; but the dignity was decadent, the sturdiness shaken. Above the weather-beaten clapboards, splintered shingles folded down under an overlay of moss and lichen. Fantastically, a denuded vine waved back and forth above a crumbling chimney from which it protruded. Great unkempt clumps of box and holly flanked the sides, and beyond these crouched a cabin, with a thin wisp of smoke curling over it and a faint light gleaming from behind its windows. The rich husky sound of negroes' voices came from this cabin, mingled with children's laughter and the strumming of a banjo. But from Retreat itself came neither smoke nor sound nor any light. It loomed still and somber through the dusk, as if it were itself only an apparition of the past, and not an enduring creation of wood and brick, iron and mortar.

"The trundlebed trash must all be over in the cabin listening to Uncle Nixon's songs and stories. They love to do that, at dusk. And when she's rid of them, my mother lies down to rest for a little while, before she lights the lamps. I'll go and call her, if you'll wait just a minute. And keep your horse reined in. I'd hate to have him stumble on these pesky Osage oranges. The ground is covered with them."

"Osage oranges? I don't think I know what they are."

"You don't? Then I must show you. Grandfather used to say the best bows were always made from the wood of the Osage orange trees— People used to practice archery on the lawn at Fielding's Folly when he was a boy, and there were quantities of peacocks strutting about, to add to the picture. The bows are broken and the peacocks are dead and the picture's faded—as you can see for yourself. But the branches of the trees have a strange grace. They divide and subdivide into semicircles, like bows themselves, to the very tips. And there are more and more oranges every year."

Francis Fielding placed his gun against the wall of the house, laid the game he had shot on the stoop, and bending over, gathered up two or three ball-shaped objects from the shaggy grass on which they lay. As he did so, Eunice was conscious of the grace which characterized all of his movements, of the extreme litheness of his figure and the supple strength of his fingers. It was at these that she looked, involuntarily, instead of at the "oranges," covered with warty green rind, which he handed her. There was a fresh spicy scent to the balls, and she raised them to her face and smelled them, partly to cover the slight confusion she feared she had betrayed, and partly because their fragrance really delighted her.

"Are they good to eat?" she inquired with interest.

Francis Fielding laughed, a trifle bitterly. Then he flung one of the oranges against the stone step of the stoop. When he picked it up, it was a battered mass of hairy pith and slimy seeds, unredeemed by pulp or juice. This time, when Eunice's eyes met his, she saw no merriment there.

"They're not good for anything," he said tersely. "They're not fit for you to touch. Throw them away."

Chapter 2

EUNICE NEVER forgot the suddenness with which the dark and silent house, seemingly so deserted, began to glow with radiance and teem with activity. The tensity of the moment which followed Francis Fielding's unexpected outburst over the oranges was almost instantly eased. A faint glimmer, appearing first in an upper window, swelled swiftly in size, as if emanating from a lamp whose unseen bearer lighted other lamps in the course of rapid progress from story to story and from room to room. The heavy door, pulled hard two or three times from within, swung creakingly open on its hinges, disclosing a spacious hallway; and in the embrasure appeared a woman of gracious aspect, dressed in faded plum silk fastened at the throat with a pansy pin. Her greeting was simple and spontaneous.

"Good evenin'. I'm glad to see a visitor, 'deed I am. I've been pinin' for company all the afternoon. Is this a new neighbor of ours you brought to see me, Frank? That sho'ly was thoughtful of you, and of her too!"

"It's Miss Eunice Hale, of Vermont, Mother. She's visiting Millie and Freeman and she lost her way in the woods. I persuaded her to come home with me. I told her you'd give her a cup of tea while I saddled myself a horse. Then I'll restore her to Solomon's Garden, where she belongs temporarily."

"Well now, I'm right sorry she can't stay just where she is, and spend the night with us at Retreat. Come in, honey chile. There's a fire in the back parlor and the kettle's singin' on the hob already, just like it knew you were comin'. Would you care to rest your wraps? Soon as I see you-all settled, I'm goin' to call Blanche. I can't say for certain, but I think she has some ash cakes, fresh made."

Eunice had slid lightly from the saddle, avoiding, as far as possible, Francis Fielding's proffered assistance. Since the mere sight of his hands had stirred her so unexpectedly, she shrank slightly from his touch; and momentary as this was, a queer little quiver crept through her as her gloves brushed his fingers. But the quiet warmth of her hostess's greeting was comforting. She followed Mrs. Fielding into the house with a mounting sense of reassurance.

The hall through which she was ushered ran straight to the rear, separating the rooms on either side of it. Its unpainted floor and its unpapered walls gave it a bare look, as if it had never been wholly finished. The one picture breaking the blankness was a steel engraving of General Latané's funeral.

Only one of the paneled doors leading from it was open, and these shut surfaces added an aspect of secrecy. But Mrs. Fielding explained this away as they went along.

"We never did get 'round to have a furnace put in Retreat," she said, so casually as to infer that the cause of this delay was unhurried leisure rather than insufficient funds. "And I declare right now we seem to be short of wood for the fireplaces. One of Blanche's boys died a while back and another's been in the lockup and Frank just naturally can't see to everything himself. So I keep most of our rooms closed up, come fall. But I've got a right smart blaze goin' in the back parlor anyway, like I told you. Come in, honey chile, come in."

Eunice did not need a second bidding. She was glad to get out of the cold and into the warmth. There were pictures on the walls and a rug on the floor in the parlor which relieved it somewhat of the blank unfinished look which characterized the hall; and the chimney piece itself was indeed a center of good cheer. A log fire burned brightly behind brass andirons, and the brass kettle which hung close to these on a wrought-iron stand was steaming cozily. A huge bottle-shaped jar made of dark translucent glass stood on one side of the hearthstone and two fluted, pink conch shells stood on the other; the smooth surfaces of all these reflected the color of the flames. The mantel was adorned with a variety of small china ornaments and two tall vases filled with sprays of lunaria, all of which was shining too; and above the shelf was the picturesque portrait of a woman whose comely face had a radiance of its own, and whose resemblance to the present chatelaine of Retreat was very striking.

"Sit down, honey, do," Mrs. Fielding said hospitably. She indicated a large mahogany sofa upholstered in blue velvet, with twin footstools, also made of mahogany and upholstered in blue velvet, placed primly side by side in front of it. "I'm just goin' to speak to Blanche, and then I'm goin' to come right back and take my ease, like I want you-all should. If any of my young ones come in while I'm gone, don't let 'em plague you. They're not triflin' children, but they're powerful pert. I don't know whether you're used to a whole parcel of 'em together, like I am."

She laughed indulgently and stooped to adjust one of the footstools at a more advantageous angle for her visitor. While she was doing so, the front door creaked on its hinges again, and the sound of pulling and pushing which seemed to presage its opening was repeated. As a gust of cold air blew into the room, she looked up with a smile to greet three newcomers whose hurrying footsteps clattered down the hall.

"Now, now," she said in a soothing voice, forestalling their

17

onrush. "We got young lady company. You mustn't act so as to scare her. This is Miss Eunice Hale, of Vermont, children. She's visiting Millie and Freeman, but she got lost. So of co'se, when he met her, Frank brought her home with him. Miss Eunice, this is Purvis, one of my younger sons. Rosa Belle and Sabina are both older than he is. We all call them Bella and Bina, and we'd be mighty pleased if you would too."

The young Fieldings, thus amiably presented, advanced with exuberance toward their visitor. They were all wearing dilapidated clothes and they all looked rather disheveled; but neither of these disadvantages seemed to detract in the least from their high spirits or their great good looks. Rosa Belle, who was evidently the oldest of the three, slid easily into the role of hostess as her mother glanced at her with fond confidence and glided from the room.

"I am so sorry we weren't here to greet you," the young girl said, seating herself on the vacant footstool at Eunice's feet, and flinging her gorgeous mop of auburn hair back from her face. The vagrant locks were confined only by a stringy black ribbon, but she tightened and retied this, achieving a perky little bow over one ear, while she talked. "Of course, if we had only known you were coming, we would have been. But it is so dreary at dusk when there is nothing special to do that we nearly always go over to Blanche's cabin about that time. I don't know whether anyone has told you: Blanche is our cook, I suppose, up North, you'd call her a general maid, because she's the only servant we have. That is, she's the only one we pay. We pay Blanche whenever we have any cash money at all. She's a widow. Her husband dropped dead a few years ago while he was trying to fix the cabin door so that he could keep out the cold. But fortunately she has a very large family. All her sons and daughters and nephews and nieces—Violet and Kate and Orrie and Drew and the rest of them—help her out. Then she has a foster son, Elisha. A well caved in on his father, and his mother was the neighborhood 'bad woman,' so Blanche took him in and raised him. He's what she calls an adapted child. He's in love with Violet but Violet thinks he's too old for her. She's forever flirting with a no-count nigger named Malachi, without any family connections, from down Warsaw way. A nice old man named Uncle Nixon lives with Blanche too. He tells the best stories of any darky around here. We love to listen to him."

"He told us my favorite story today," chimed in Sabina. She was not quite so lovely looking as Rosa Belle. But her great intense eyes, set far apart in her camellia-colored face, made her very striking. "Of course, he's told it to us hundreds of times already, but we like to hear it over and over again. Would *you* like to hear it?" she inquired, drawing up a ladder-back chair and sitting down opposite Eunice.

"Very much."

"It's a sad story. It won't make you cry, will it?"

"No, I don't think so."

"Well, a long time ago, Uncle Nixon was a slave. He and his wife, Aunt Silvie, had a nice little cabin that they kept very neat, and a little boy whom they loved very much. That was before they belonged to my great-grandfather. My great-grandfather never sold his own people, but sometimes he bought them from other plantations, because he knew he could give them a good home and prevent them from being bought by someone else who might treat them badly."

"I see."

"Uncle Nixon and Aunt Silvie were very happy in their little cabin with their little boy. But one day when Uncle Nixon was working in the fields, he saw a strange man driving down the road, a good way off. He was driving a wagon that was filled with plantation negroes, and Uncle Nixon's little boy was with them. Uncle Nixon couldn't understand what it meant, so he dropped his hoe and ran after the wagon. He could hear his little boy calling to him as he ran. And then it dawned on him that the strange white man must be one of those traders that the slaves dreaded to see. He knew that his little boy was sold. He ran and ran, and he called out, too, while he was running; but he couldn't catch up with the wagon. By and by he crumpled up in a heap and fell down by the side of the road. He never saw his little boy again."

"It is a sad story. I'm afraid I am crying a little, after all. Why is such a sad story your favorite?"

"I don't know. Anyway, I don't like it so much because it's sad, but because Uncle Nixon tells it so beautifully. Every now and then he stops, and strums a little on his banjo, and then he goes on. It's always been his dream that someday he'd find the little boy again. Of course he wouldn't be a little boy now, he'd be quite an old man himself. But Uncle Nixon still thinks of him as a little boy. After great-grandfather bought Uncle Nixon and Aunt Silvie, he tried to help with the search. Grandfather did too, and even father. Now they're all dead, except Uncle Nixon, and he's almost blind and very feeble. But still he goes on hoping. He says even if he doesn't find his little boy in this world, he knows the dear child will be standing at the bottom of the golden stairs to help his poor old daddy walk up them into heaven."

"If I ever come to Retreat again, I hope you'll take me over to the cabin and let me listen to Uncle Nixon too. Not that you don't tell the story beautifully yourself, Sabina. But you've made me want to see and hear this old man."

19

"Why, of course you're coming to Retreat again! This is only the first time. You'll be coming right along after this!"

The slim boy who had been busy cleaning and polishing his gun while his sisters talked and who had not spoken before seemed almost to be voicing a protest at the mere suggestion that Eunice Hale had not become an accepted friend of the family. Now he laid the gun down on the square piano, between two lamps with globular glass shades, and came over to the hearthstone.

"If you're going in for sad stories, Bina," he remarked, stretching himself out on the floor with his knees raised and his hands clasped behind his head, "you ought to tell Miss Eunice about the picture over the piano. She's been looking at it all this time."

"Yes, I have been looking at it," she confessed. Eunice looked at the canvas which confronted her again, less covertly than she had before. It represented a dead girl clothed in white, raised high upon her pillows in a great white bed, and a bearded man, holding a palette in his hand and wearing rich garments of deep amber which matched the mellow tones of the background, standing grief-stricken beside her. There was a morbid quality about it which repelled Eunice, and she had shivered a little when her startled gaze had first fallen upon it. At the same time, it fascinated her. She was beginning to wonder if such mixed emotions were to characterize all her contacts with Retreat.

"It's a strange picture, isn't it?" she asked. Privately, she thought it was a very strange picture to place in a cheerful family living room, but she did not wish to hurt anyone's feelings by seeming to infer this, so she went on quickly, "Still, it looks vaguely familiar to me. Is it a copy of a picture I might have seen somewhere else?"

"I reckon so, if you've been abroad," Bella said brightly. "One of my great-aunts copied it from a picture her art teacher, Mr. Nevile, brought home with him from Europe. And *he* copied it from one he saw in Italy. Our encyclopedia says that Tintoretto had two sons and five daughters, and that his favorite was Marietta, who was almost as great a painter as her father, besides being a wonderful musician. When she was a young girl she used to go around with Tintoretto, dressed like a boy, and helped him with his work, as if she had been an apprentice. But by and by she married a jeweler whose name was Mario Augusto. After that she gave up wearing boy's clothes and she did not paint so much. When she was only thirty, she died; and her father, who was simply overwhelmed, tried to make a last picture of her before she was buried. Of course he couldn't do it. His tears

20

kept falling and blinding him. But another artist heard about it, and preserved the scene."

"No, Bella, that isn't the true story at all," broke in Sabina. "You shouldn't tell it that way. Chambers' *Miscellanea* says that Tintoretto forced Marietta to study music against her will, when he knew that she really wanted to paint. So secretly she helped one of her brothers, whom Tintoretto had chosen as his successor, though he did not have half as much talent as his sister. Then after she died this brother confessed that Marietta had done all his best work, and their father was stricken with remorse as well as grief. So he determined to immortalize her by a deathbed portrait that would hold everyone who saw it spellbound."

"Well, anyway, it was a queer picture for a fellow to bring across the ocean and give a girl to copy," Purvis remarked scornfully. "I should think there were lots of others he could have brought instead. I've always thought there was something fishy about Mr. Nevile. And about Great-Aunt Charlotte, too, as far as that goes. Besides, I reckon you've told Miss Eunice enough sad stories for one evening. I hope Blanche comes along pretty soon with the tea."

As if the boy's wish had echoed through to the kitchen, a door in the distance opened and closed, and footsteps sounded through the hallway again. They were slow shuffling ones this time, indicating that the person who was approaching was wearing felt slippers and was proceeding with caution. Purvis leaped lightly to his feet in front of Eunice and moved a pie-crust table that stood against the wall. At the same moment a smiling servant, whose fresh calico apron was set somewhat askew over a soiled and shoddy dress, entered the room and set down a laden tray.

"Good ebenin', little missie," she said amiably. "We sho' is mighty glad you-all done come to see us. I is Blanche. Miss Alice, she'll be back hyah in jes' one minute. She's gettin' some wild pear preserves outen the corner cupboard in the dinin' room. She done lost the key, but it ain't gonna take her long to find it. She thought maybe you moughten like jam with my fresh ash cakes."

Blanche was quite the blackest negress Eunice had ever beheld. The incongruity of her name seemed one more added to the mounting number of those in which Retreat abounded. The tray which she placed before Eunice with such pride and care was incongruous too. It was made of heavy Sheffield plate, but the silver had worn off in places, permitting the copper to show through, and it was in serious need of polishing. The same could be said of the graceful silver teapot and the sugar bowl and cream pitcher which flanked this. The delicate porcelain cups were chipped, the thin pointed tea-

21

spoons dented. The fine linen napkin, heavily embroidered, in which the ash cakes were wrapped, was rent and ragged. The first impression of abundance produced by the elegance of the silver service was a false one. There was nothing to eat on the tray except the ash cakes. Again Eunice hoped that the sharp-eyed youngsters clustered around her had not been able to read her thoughts.

"I'm sure your ash cakes will be delicious, Blanche, whether they have jam on them or not," she said with careful politeness. "But it was very kind of Mrs. Fielding to think of the preserves, too. And nothing could taste better to me now than tea. I was so chilled when I came in that I'm not really warm yet, in spite of this fine fire."

"Purvis, do put on some more wood. I know Miss Eunice is frozen. And don't wait for Ma, please. Drink your tea and eat your ash cakes while they're hot. Blanche makes the best ash cakes of anyone in King George County. Tell Miss Eunice how you make them, Blanche."

"I rakes out my coals real good and den I cubbers 'em all over wid ashes *careful*," Blanche explained proudly. "Afterwards I fixes wetted leaves on top of de ashes. Dey has to be oak leaves or grape leaves, lessen dey's cabbage leaves. *Yassum*. When I gotten dat all fixed I puts in my pone."

"Then she puts more wetted leaves and more ashes and more coals on top of the pone," added Sabina, who seemed to feel that no one's story was complete unless she had a voice in it. "You know what a pone is, don't you, Miss Eunice? It's a cake made of cornmeal dough. Blanche's ash cakes are always just as brown as a berry and ever so much better than those that other people bake in skillets. Sometimes Ma lets us take our snack in the cabin. Maybe you don't know what a snack is, either. You see, when we have breakfast at eight and dinner at three, we get awfully hungry in between, so we have to eat something, and that is our snack, though you can have them at other times also. Blanche always gives us ash cakes and buttermilk when we have our snack with her. Buttermilk is awfully good with ash cakes. Would you like some with yours?"

"No, thank you. I told you this nice hot tea was just what I wanted. And the ash cakes are delicious. Aren't you going to have some with me?"

Without waiting for a second bidding, the three young Fieldings fell avidly on the food before them. Blanche continued to stand near by, her pleased expression becoming more and more intense. When Mrs. Fielding returned with the pear preserve, there were second helpings all around. She explained that the jam had been pushed far back in the cupboard behind the pickles, that she had had trouble finding it even after she had found the key to the cupboard; that was why she had been gone so long. Eunice suspected that she kept these articles carefully hidden, and that possibly she had forgotten herself just where she had put them. At all events, the jam was worthy of hiding and hoarding, rich and sweet and spicy; it added immeasurably to the substance of this particular "snack." As she ate it, Eunice, who had been hungry no less than cold, began to be conscious of deep inner warmth and satisfaction. But she missed Francis Fielding from the cheerful scene; without him it seemed vaguely incomplete. She could not help reflecting how much he would add to it if he were lounging against the mantelpiece, putting in a lazy word here and there, and looking at her with laughter in his eyes. She forced herself not to keep glancing toward the door at every strange creaking sound. But she could not help wondering why he did not come in. It would not take him but a moment to saddle a horse. He could well have waited until after tea to do that——

"If you-all want to smoke, honey chile, you go right ahead," Mrs. Fielding said cordially, when the pile of ash cakes had been demolished and the jam pot scraped empty. "I never did feel to do it, and Bella and Bina don't either. I reckon over Middleburg way all the ladies smoke now, don't they?"

"Yes, most of them. But I don't really belong to Middleburg. I always seem like an outsider there. Anyway, I don't often smoke and I certainly don't feel like doing it just now, any more than you do. I'm almost ready to purr with contentment as it is. I would like to meet the rest of the family though, if I may, before I go. Didn't I understand your oldest son to say he had five brothers and sisters?"

"Now then, of co'se he would tell you that, and likely as not he called 'em trundlebed trash, didn't he? I'd sho'ly like to show you Mamie Love, my baby. She's the sweetest little thing, just ten years old last month. But she's been drowsy all day and now she's asleep. I was sittin' upstairs in the dark with her when you came. I don't rightly know what ails her. If she isn't better tomorrow, I'll have Doctor Tayloe over from Barren Point to have a look at her—seems to me like she's sickenin' for somethin'. I just don't see how I could have the heart to wake her. And Peyton, my other son's, at the University. He won't be home till Christmas."

"Unless he's expelled, the way Frank was," Rosa Belle remarked, without any loss of her characteristic brightness. "If he were expelled, he might be back any day, Ma— One of our kin, who is wealthy, offered to send all of the boys to the University," she explained to Eunice. "But so far he's saved money, because Frank was only there a little while, and

23

Purvis won't try to get in. So that leaves just Peyton, and Peyton plays cards most of the time. Of course he earns a little extra that way, but mostly he drinks it up. He——"

"Bella, your dear brother Peyton is one of the sweetest boys there ever was in this world. You're goin' to give Miss Eunice the wrong idea if you talk about him like that. How do you think he's ever goin' to get along at the University if he don't drink and gamble once in a while? You know how everyone is, over Charlottesville way. And don't you go forgetting that Edgar Allan Poe, the most famouslike man that ever went there, was expelled. It just naturally seems to happen to high-spirited handsome young men to get expelled from the University."

"Ma, Edgar Allan Poe wasn't the most famous man that ever went to the University. Woodrow Wilson was much more famous," objected Sabina. "He wasn't expelled, either."

"No, but everyone found fault with him afterward. He sickened and died because everyone found so much fault with him."

A family dispute appeared to be imminent. Eunice began to feel uncomfortable again. Blanche, who had not once left the room since she brought in the tea tray, now created a diversion by picking this up again.

"Effen you ladies don't need me no mo', I'se goin' to leave de night wid you," she said tactfully. "Virgin, he dun promised to take me into town dis ebenin', to tend to my polishes."

"Virgin!" exclaimed Eunice involuntarily, no longer able to suppress all of her manifold astonishment.

"Yassum. Virgin am my biggest boy. He am a powerful lot of help to me. I don't know what I'd do withouten him, specially now his po' brudder Dewdy dun died of romantics around de heart. It's bouten Dewdy's polishes we aim to drive inter de seat."

"Her oldest son's name really is Virgin," Sabina said to Eunice in a stage whisper. "She had him christened that before Ma and Pa knew what she was about. She said she liked the sound of it, though she didn't rightly know what it meant. The son she calls Dewdy was named for Admiral Dewey, but she never got it just straight. Virgin's about the only one she ever did. She mixes all her words up. She means rheumatic instead of romantic and policies instead of polishes. We don't correct her because we think it's fun to listen to her talk the way she does. Anyway, it wouldn't do any good to tell her she was wrong. She'd forget again straight off."

Blanche had been slowly receding with the tray while this explanation was taking place. Eunice had the feeling that the negress half heard and half understood what was being said, but that she was not displeased at being discussed, that on the contrary it gave her a sense of importance. As the sound of her shuffling footsteps grew fainter and died away in the distance, Eunice herself rose.

"I think I ought to follow the example of Blanche and 'leave the night with you,'" she said. "That is, if it would be convenient for Mr. Fielding to guide me back to Solomon's Garden now. He said it would take him only about five minutes to saddle a horse, and I'm sure I've been here more than an hour. Perhaps he found something else that was important for him to do. If he did——"

Her sense of relaxation and comfort was gone completely. She felt certain that Francis Fielding had remained withdrawn from the family circle on purpose, so that eventually she would be forced to ask for him, and she was shamed and angry because this was so. Yet she could not sit forever waiting for him to appear of his own accord; neither could she set forth in the darkness completely alone. She turned to Rosa Belle, with whom she was captivated.

"Won't you go with us?" she asked. "Or perhaps, if Mr. Fielding *is* busy, you and Sabina and Purvis would all come with me, instead of him. That would relieve my mind of the fear that I'm being a bother to him."

"Don't you have any such fears, honey chile," Mrs. Fielding said reassuringly. "And don't you start suggestin' that all this trundlebed trash should go ridin' along with you and Frank. He wouldn't thank you, and neither would I. He isn't half so busy as the rest. I aim to have Bina sit with Mamie Love when she wakes up so's she can tell my po' baby stories. Bella's goin' to help me get supper by and by, seein' I promised Blanche she could go down to the county seat about Dewdy's life insurance. And Purvis ought to be doin' his sums right now, or he won't ever get to the University, just like his sister says. Frank's waitin' for you out by the stoop, Miss Eunice. He was ready a while back, before I brought in the wild pear preserves. But he didn't want to hurry you, any more than the rest of us did. We all wanted you should feel at home here, like you'd be pleased to stay and pleased to come back. At Christmastime we have half the county in for dinin' day. You'd be more than welcome and you'd see Peyton and Mamie Love both then— And in springtime it sho'ly is sweet pretty at Retreat. Especially here on the south side. The pink puff balls wave up and down against the open windows, and the ruby-throated hummin' birds fly through 'em. And outside, in the gyarden, there's the mimosa, and the crepe myrtle and the white violets——"

"You can catch the humming birds and hold them in your hand," Purvis said eagerly. "They lie still on your palm and play dead. It's fun to watch them. Then you can toss them up in the air and whizz! They're gone so fast you can't see where they've flown!"

"And you can make wreaths out of the white violets," said Sabina. "That is, Bella and I can. Then you could wear them, Miss Eunice. I think she would look lovely with white violets in her black hair, don't you, Ma?"

"I reckon she'd look lovely no matter what she wore, Bina. But you and Bella must make those wreaths for her. That is, if she's here, come spring. You think you will be, don't you, honey chile?"

They had all walked slowly through the hall together while they were talking. Now, reluctantly, Purvis began to pull at the difficult door. It came open slowly, disclosing the darkness outside. Mrs. Fielding raised the lamp she was carrying so that Eunice could see.

Francis Fielding was standing beside the beautiful black horse, holding its bridle. He looked toward the light, and Eunice saw again that his eyes were glad and gay, and that his smile was bold and bright. Then he looked away, as if to indicate that he felt no impatience with the leisurely leave-taking on the stoop, and no eagerness to have his long ride with her begin. His own horse waited quietly near by, without being held. The shaggy grass, strewn with the mock oranges, stretched out behind them. Beyond, on every side, lay the dimness of the woods.

Eunice caught her breath. Another queer little quiver was creeping through her, but this time she did not stiffen or shrink away. Instead she waited expectantly for Francis Fielding to help her on her horse. Instead of springing into her seat, she let him lift her into the saddle.

"Yes—yes indeed," she called back to the group that stood watching in the doorway. She was startled at the sound of joyousness in her own voice, but she went on calling. "Yes —I'll be back in the spring. And at Christmastime too—or before then."

Chapter 3

SHE WAS tingling all over. Her resentment, like her shyness, had been instantly dispelled when she had looked out into the darkness and seen the face and figure of Francis Fielding emerge from the surrounding shadows. In awaiting his support, she had almost invited an embrace. She knew he had sensed this, for he had been slow to withdraw his hands after she was securely seated in her saddle; she could

26

still seem to feel him clasping her waist, first with firmness, then with a lighter but lingering pressure. She began to long for the moment when he would lift her down again— No, not that, for when he lifted her down, they would be back at Solomon's Garden, he would be saying good night, she would be parting from him— For what moment then was she longing?

"So you liked us better than you thought you would? That's always a pleasant surprise—both for the underestimated miscreants and the beneficent patron!"

She was wholly unprepared for his mockery. She had not expected that he would read her mind as easily as he guessed her feelings. She tried to make her retort sound indignant.

"But of course I liked you from the beginning And of course I knew I'd like your family too! If I hadn't—both, I mean—I wouldn't have gone home with you. Surely you must realize that!"

"I realize that something had upset you, and that you were cold and tired and hungry besides. I'm glad the succor providentially provided was so satisfactory to the damsel in distress."

"Now you're making fun of me. I think you're very unjust."

"Really? Come on, tell me the truth. On the whole, hasn't the succor been even more than satisfactory? Actually rather stimulating, into the bargain?"

"I think your mother is lovely," Eunice said with dignity, "and of course the trundlebed trash is simply delightful, and Blanche the most amusing darky I ever saw."

"I'm part of the trundlebed trash myself, you know. Won't you condescend to include me in a general characterization, at least?"

"Well, if you must know, I think you're pleasant, but presuming."

"Pleasant? Not exciting, but pleasant? What a damning thing to say! Almost like remarking that you are sure I mean well—and I don't think you are so sure! And presuming? When I stayed for a whole hour out of the only warm room in the house? When I waited for you so patiently beside the stoop? When I've tried so hard to do your bidding?"

Eunice flushed furiously in the darkness. Everything he said was technically true; she could not deny any of this. He had been "doing her bidding" when, instead of respectfully releasing her, he had continued to stand beside her and clasp her waist. She had willed with all her might that he should do exactly that. But she would never have so far forgotten herself if he had not teased and tempted her first. He was teasing and tempting her now. Unless she were very careful, he would trap her as well. And stirred as she was, she was unready to be ensnared.

"I'd rather not argue with you, if you don't mind. I'd much rather listen to stories about Retreat. I heard two or three, while I was sitting beside the fire, that fascinated me. Won't you tell me some more?"

"Yes, if you will set me a good example first," he answered easily. The mockery was gone from his voice, and it was charmingly deferential again. "You haven't told me any stories at all about the place you come from yourself. Don't you think it would be fairer if you did?"

"There isn't much to tell. None of the Hales, or the Spencers either, ever owned a place like Retreat. My father came from a little village called Hamstead, on the Connecticut River. His family had a farm and timber lots near there. They had moderate means, but they were thrifty. They sent him to Dartmouth and he met my mother at a dance there—a friend of his brought her to a college prom. She came from a bigger place, Belford. There are some big marble quarries near Belford, and her people got control of these and became very prosperous. It was she who had most of the money."

"I see," remarked Francis Fielding, with unfeigned interest. Vermont marble—of course! So Eunice really was a "marble maiden"—in more ways than one! And he himself was no different from the Greek about whom he had read in *Chambers' Miscellanea*—Pygmalion, was that the man's name?—who had wanted to make a statue come to life. He did not recall the details of the myth, only that Pygmalion had succeeded. The remembrance was gratifying. But after all, he did not need to draw on stupid stories buried in musty books for encouragement. As clearly as Eunice had seen his face emerging from the darkness, he had seen hers framed in the doorway—eager, expectant, flushed with warm color that had not been there before. As strongly as she could still feel the pressure of his hands about her waist, he was still conscious of the change from the shrinking stiffness with which she had dismounted to the perfect pliancy with which she had anticipated his assistance afterward.

"They must have lived in some kind of houses," he went on, returning to the amenities of the moment. "Your father and mother, I mean. Surely you can tell me something about them."

"The Spencers built their house in Belford about 1870. They didn't begin to make money until then. It's an enormous Victorian atrocity. It's always half dark, because there are so many plush portieres in it. The chandelier in the dining room is in the shape of a huge bunch of glass grapes, and the sideboard's built into the wall; it's made of golden oak, and so are the leather-seated chairs and the extension table. The library is furnished in dark red, and it leads out of the parlor which is furnished in pale pink. Upstairs the rooms are large and lonely. The beds are made of black walnut with ponderous headpieces and the bureaus have gray stone tops— Were you ever in a house like that?"

"No, never, but you've made me see it very clearly. What's its name?"

"I don't think it has any name. People don't always name houses in Vermont, the way they do in Virginia. My grandmother Hale did name her farm, though. She calls it Evergreen."

"On account of its trees?"

"Yes. Grandma's very fond of evergreens. She says a tree that can keep its color straight through a Vermont winter has a lot of credit coming to it, the same as a woman would. She despises women that wilt and fade, the same way she despises wilting and fading leaves. Besides, she's very proud of the pines. There was a lot of timberland on the farm when the Hales first settled in the Valley; but there was a lot of sandy soil, too. Nothing would ever grow on it until one of my ancestors tried setting out pines. Those grew and throve. So he got all his sons to set out pines too. And they taught their sons. And so on. You can look out of the windows of Grandma's house now and count the generations that have lived on the farm now, by the pines. There isn't an inch of waste land anywhere on the place. And the pines pay. They've been cut carefully, and new ones have always been planted when the old ones have gone. But all the Hale boys have gone to college on those pines. I would have myself, since I didn't have a brother, if my father hadn't married a Spencer. Of course that made it unnecessary."

"Unnecessary to go to college or unnecessary to pay for it with pines?"

"Oh, I went to college. I went to Smith. My mother and my grandmother both had very definite ideas on the subject —definite and different, I mean. It was Grandma who won out. My mother didn't want me to go at all. She wanted to give a big ball for me at Sherry's and a series of house parties at Tivoli. She gave the ball anyway, during Christmas vacation, but there wasn't much time for house parties at Easter and in the summer it's so dreadfully hot in Virginia that I always go to Vermont if I can. Grandma feels that she won quite a victory. She said it was bad enough to have her only son's widow carrying on the way she did, without having her granddaughter forget that she was a New Englander into the bargain. Grandma still talks about my mother as if

29

she were a widow. She's never recognized the existence of my stepfather at all."

"She sounds like a mighty grim old lady to me."

"She is rather grim, especially toward my mother. She always thought that father married beneath him. The money didn't make a bit of difference to her, any more than—well, any more than it often makes in Virginia. She said the Spencers had to start blasting to make anyone notice them in Vermont. She never will stay in that Victorian house I told you about. She says the place for marble is in cemeteries, not on mantlepieces. She is very shrewd and snappy."

"I should say so— I take it the mantels in her farmhouse are all made of wood?"

"Oh, yes— And she burns wood in them too, from her own timber lots. Half the time she carries it in herself. She never could abide having help in the kitchen—she does all her own work and the house is just as clean as a new pin. She does keep a hired man to milk the cows and plow the fields, but she doesn't wait to have him fill the woodbox. She says he is slower than cold molasses. She loves her fireplaces, just as she does her pines. She didn't use airtight stoves, or coal, even when everyone else started doing it; and she never put in a furnace until our doctor, David Noble, asked her whether she'd rather have that down in the cellar, or her only son sick with pneumonia up in the best bedroom. Dr. Noble is the only person I've ever seen that's a match for her."

"You don't think I'd be a match for her, by any chance?"

"No—that is—well, it would be fun to see you and her together!"

For the first time Eunice laughed. The sound of her laughter was pleasant, like the sound of her voice; it had the same qualities of clarity and sincerity. But it was faintly irritating to Francis Fielding. A girl who could laugh like that, spontaneously and heartily, was by no means spellbound. Her silence, even her shyness, was far more advantageous. Tactically, he had made a mistake in urging her to talk about Evergreen instead of encouraging her to listen while he talked about Retreat. It would have been much better if he had followed her suggestion instead of countering with one of his own. His curiosity had been too strong; he should have continued to rely on his charm. He sought to retrieve his mistake by a quick retort.

"Is that a veiled invitation? If it is, I accept with pleasure. I always accept invitations from lovely young ladies—perhaps you guessed that already. When they're veiled, they're doubly alluring."

"The invitations—or the young ladies themselves?"

There was no doubt that she was slipping away from him

fast. It was she who was doing the teasing now. His irritation flared into effrontery.

"Both. Lifting veils is one of my pet pastimes. I can remove them very quickly and painlessly. From invitations— and from young ladies. Would Thanksgiving suit you for my Vermont visit? I am sure I can get there by then. And would tonight suit you—for this?"

He had checked both his horse and her own. Handicapped though he was by both and darkness and distance, his fingers were already on her face, searching out the edge of the light net that covered it. She might still have eluded him; she had only to lean forward in her saddle. But unaccountably she did not. Something stronger than her own will kept her motionless and impelled her quiescence until the moment of instinctive resistance had passed. Then she felt the veil folded back from her forehead and his lips against this, lingering there as his hands had clung to her waist, gently and caressingly. She could not struggle against such a kiss as that; it was too tender. It disarmed her even though she knew its protectiveness was fleeting, that it was merely the forerunner of passion. She could not see and still she closed her eyes. She longed to have her lids so smooth that he would linger over those also; but when he came to them she knew that their white perfection would not detain him long. She tried to raise her arms, to make one last futile gesture toward pushing him away from her. Instead, when she had succeeded in lifting them halfway, they stole of their own accord around his neck, drawing him closer to her, until their lips met. After that she ceased to be sure of anything. Wonder engulfed her, and joy, closing in upon her together.

The embrace ended—as it had begun—so slowly that Eunice never knew how or when it was actually brought to a close. Only after Francis Fielding spoke to her did she realize that she must in some measure have been released, that his mouth was no longer pressed against hers.

"Darling——"

"Yes——"

"I want to lift you off your horse, and put you in front of me, on mine. I want you to ride there, the rest of the way. Will you?"

"Yes."

"Wonderful! Swing your knee back from the pommel and slip your foot out of the stirrup. As quietly as you can. Don't frighten your horse. He's been a marvel so far. I can lead him, and guide my own, and hold you, all at once. It's easy."

She was on the verge of asking him how he knew it was easy, but something restrained her. Instead, she followed his directions, expertly and unquestioningly. Again her perfect pliancy delighted him as he drew her near him once more.

"Darling, you're as light and graceful as a doe! I think you're like a doe in other ways, too—shy and easily startled and still looking out at a wicked world with trustful eyes and a brave heart— Did anyone ever tell you that before, Eunice?"

"No. Not—not exactly that."

"None of this is exactly like anything that ever happened to you before, is it?"

"You know it isn't."

"Would you rather it hadn't happened?"

"You know about that, too. That I'm glad it happened, I mean."

"I wouldn't have chosen to kiss you that way the first time. I'd rather have been holding you in my arms, the way I am now. But I couldn't wait any longer. I was certain, when you came out of the house, that you felt the same way I did. You did, didn't you?"

"Yes."

"Then later on you seemed to be slipping away from me. I couldn't stand that. But I didn't mean to rush my fences so. I meant to wait. Really I did. I hope you believe me."

"Yes, I believe you."

"Then don't hold it against me, will you? I know as well as you do what I ought to have done. I ought to have taken you protectively back to Solomon's Garden and told you good-by from a discreet distance. Then I ought to have gone galloping off to find that grim Grandmother of yours, and said, 'Madam, I have fallen in love with your charming ward at first sight. Have I your permission to address her?'"

"You'll still have to do that, if you want peace in the end."

"Oh, but it'll be different! Because I've addressed you already! Haven't I?"

"If you call what you did addressing. It's not the word I'd use for it."

There was a hint of laughter in her voice again, but he no longer resented it. After all, it could not harm him any more. It was too late for that now. He spoke laughingly also.

"I've addressed you and you've accepted me. Haven't you?"

"More or less."

"It'll have to be more rather than less, Eunice."

"Why?"

"Because it wouldn't work out any other way, for us."

"What do you mean?"

"I mean you could bolt for Vermont tomorrow, but it wouldn't do you any good. You'll never get me out of your mind or your heart again, after this, as long as you live. No matter what you do. No matter what I do either."

"What were you thinking of doing?"

"Nothing, specifically. But I've told you already that it's the habit of my family to stoop to folly. I can't promise that I'll be an exception to the rule. I can't promise much of anything, except that you'll be a lot happier with me than without me from now on. You'll have to take me on trust—if you do take me. Blindly, the way you went home with me, the way you let me kiss you. But you're glad you did that. I believe you'd be gladder still if you'd marry me."

"And you—you'd be very glad too?"

He bent over her again. She could not even see the outline of his face in the profundity of the darkness, but she knew when he came closer, and she was unsurprised when his mouth closed down upon hers again, hard, and with no gentle preliminary caress. Her lips were smarting and her breast bruised when he let her go.

"Do you understand now?" he asked abruptly.

"No— It was lovely the other way. What made you hurt me so?"

"I didn't want to hurt you. Not primarily. But I didn't want you to ask me such a question, either."

"Such a question?" she said, in genuine bewilderment.

"Yes. Whether I'd be glad to marry you. I thought I'd shown you already that I would be. It seemed I hadn't succeeded. I thought perhaps another method might work better. It was worth trying, anyway. That is, it was worth it to me. I won't do it again, if it offends you."

"It doesn't exactly offend me. You did hurt me, but there was a sort of splendor to it too. I can't explain."

"You don't need to, darling. I understand, even if you don't. That was what I hoped you'd find—the splendor. That's what I want to share with you. I will, if you'll only marry me. Can't you do it, Eunice?"

She did not instantly answer. Sitting very still, she made a supreme effort at detachment. With all her might, she strove, one last time, to reason with herself, to say in her soul that she would commit a folly greater than any Fielding's, if she entrusted her love and her life into the keeping of this man whom she had never seen a few short hours before, of whom she knew no good, who stood indeed condemned, by the words of his own mouth, for faults and failings the gravity of which she could not gauge. But her effort was unavailing. As long as he held her in his arms, with her head resting on his shoulder, she could see nothing objectively, she could think of nothing dispassionately. He had told her the truth when he said she would never get him out of her heart or out

33

of her mind again. She could face this fact in all its implications. But she could not force herself to face a future in which he had no part.

"Yes," she said at last. "I can do it." She stopped, forestalling his quick response. "I can't help doing it," she said, and raised her glorified face.

PART II
Lanai

~~~~~~

Chapter 4

LANGUOR WAS a new sensation for Eunice Fielding. She
reveled in it, as she did in every other new sensation that
was a part of her love.

She lay extended at ease on the bamboo chaise longue,
which, together with chairs upholstered in bright chintz to
match it, and the gaily painted little tables scattered over the
straw matting, formed the furnishings of her lanai. Great jars
of flowers, presented to her at the time of sailing with the
typical prodigality of Californians, stood against the softly
tinted wall which flanked the cabin, and the two latticed
sides at right angles to this; the fourth side, except for a narrow railing, was wide open to the sea. Eunice had told Francis their first day out, as they stood watching the receding
skyline, perpendicular and provocative, of San Francisco, that
she would never be satisfied with a New England porch or a
southern stoop again; she would demand a lanai, wherever
they lived. Later on, when the Golden Gate had also vanished
in the splendor of the sunset and she could see only mounting waves crested with whitecaps and gray clouds scurrying
over a dark horizon, she said she felt as if someone had given
her a patch of the Pacific Ocean for her very own as a wedding present.

She still felt that way about it. The patch of ocean fascinated her, though the whitecaps had long since vanished and
the undulant water looked like quicksilver now. She preferred to lie on the lanai, watching the endless swell of the
sea and the endless flight of fleecy white clouds, than to take
part in any of the manifold amusements provided by an alert
and progressive steamship company on a perfectly appointed
liner. It was admittedly stimulating to plunge into the pool
for a short swim before dinner in the silver walled saloon, admittedly thrilling to dance under the fanciful lights in the
bizarre ballroom. The beauty of the smooth turquoise tiles

lining the pool, like the freshness of the foaming water that filled it, was a source of delight to Eunice; so was the many-faceted mica ball, illumined from an unseen source, which swung from the center of the ceiling in the darkened dancing pavilion, scattering globules of rainbow-colored radiance in every direction. But elsewhere there was little which tempted her to leave the lanai. Long idle hours in the bar seemed to her aimless and futile. She did not care for games like bridge and keno, and she seldom smoked and drank very little. The heavy air and the loud voices made her eyes smart and her head ache; the free and easy atmosphere, increasingly bois-terous as the day wore on, repelled her. She hated to see men surreptitiously taking flasks out of their hip pockets, and to hear them bragging about the "prescription" whisky they had procured; she hated the loose laughter and smutty stories of the girls still more. The sports deck was less distasteful to her, for she enjoyed the bright sunshine and the soft breezes, and here the prevailing camaraderie was not based on boot-legged liquor; but she had never excelled at shuffleboard or deck tennis, and she craved no other companionship than that of her husband. She found pretexts whenever she could for remaining on the lanai, or returning to it. Idleness did not seem futile to her there; it left her free to dream. And she felt no resentment because Francis did not stay per-petually at her side. Her love for him filled her life so com-pletely that she was not dependent upon his presence to feel the flood tide of it.

Gazing out at her own particular patch of ocean through half-shut lids, she dwelt drowsily on the series of episodes which lay between her meeting with Francis Fielding and her marriage to him. In every one of them seeds of separa-tion had been sown; but none of these had borne lasting fruit. She had scorned advice and rebelled against control and cast discretion to the winds; and in the end, her will had been stronger than all the misgivings she had met and all the opposition with which she had contended. She had gone through some grueling moments; but she had never once flinched from her purpose or faltered from her course. And she was still dazzled by the results of her persistence. Noth-ing had adequately prepared her for the ecstasy she had achieved against such heavy odds. She still shivered some-times at the thought of what she might have missed——

First, of course, there had been her reception at Solomon's Garden on her return from Retreat. Francis Fielding's orig-inal plan of leaving her at the entrance had naturally been abandoned. They had walked straight into the Great Hall to-gether, to find Millie and Freeman and their guests all as-sembled there, in a pleasant state of post-prandial relaxation.

36

Some of the men, who had been to the Deep Run Meet, were still in their hunting pink; some of the women in tweed skirts and angora sweaters, rather incongruously worn with ropes of pearls; but for the most part they were well turned out in faultless evening clothes. Freeman himself, immaculate in black broadcloth and white linen, was standing with a high-ball in his hand beside a girl in emerald green satin, whose cigarette was tilted aloft from a fantastic jade holder. Millie was seated behind a low table placed near the immense fire-place, serving coffee from a shining silver service.

She was easily the most arresting woman in the room. Her ash-blonde hair was cut like a page boy's, with a long bang across her forehead and a long bob behind which swept back from her ruby-studded ears. Her dress, made of stiff red and gold brocade, had loose sleeves which came to her wrists, and a small standing collar fastened with a magnificent ruby brooch. In spite of her fair coloring, the dress and the jewels gave her the exotic look of an Oriental princess. She had spent several years in Siam, and it was evident that she had profited by them in more ways than one. Although she was the farthest from the door, she was the first to notice the new arrivals. She rose and came toward the door, her brocade brushing the floor and standing out stiffly all around her, her rubies gleaming in the mellow light. She moved beautifully, and the walnut wainscoting of the Great Hall made a rich background for her striking presence.

"Hello, Eunice," she said agreeably. "We were beginning to be worried about you. D'Alessandro said he got separated from you in the woods, he couldn't imagine how. Were you lost, strayed or stolen? Who've you brought back with you? I like all these candles to look at, but not to see by— Oh, hello, Frank."

The tone of her voice had changed completely. Freeman, who had been laughing while he talked to the girl in green, turned toward his wife's kinsman with a look of cold civility.

"Kind of you to bring Miss Hale home, Frank. I hope there wasn't an accident of any kind?"

"It was a mighty happy accident for me— Miss Hale did get lost in the woods. Then she strayed onto my land. And afterward I stole her. So she can answer every part of your question affirmatively, Millie."

"Mr. Fielding very kindly invited me to have tea at Retreat with his family," Eunice interposed quickly. "And he offered to guide me back here. I never could have found the way to Solomon's Garden without his help. It's pitch dark outside."

"I'm surprised that he knew it himself. It's a long time since he's been here— Will you have a drink, Frank, now that you *are* here?"

37

"Neither of us has had any dinner. I hope Barrell Boxen has saved some and that Mr. Fielding will go down to the dining room with me." Eunice had spoken quickly again, and this time her voice was edged with anger. She would not have believed Millie capable of such discourtesy. But the unwelcome interloper was apparently wholly undisturbed by his cool reception. He stood completely at ease, as striking a figure in his leather jacket and corduroy breeches as his kinswoman in her stiff brocade. Freeman Stone, who numbered two Chief Executives among his forebears and countless other statesmen among his relatives, was less outstanding in his broadcloth than this man who had so unaccountably become Eunice's suitor.

"It's kind of you to think of it, Miss Hale," he said. Just how it was he managed to convey that it was Millie who should have thought of it, and spoken of it too, while his voice remained so suave and his lips so smiling, Eunice could not determine. But he did. "It would give me the greatest pleasure to dine with you," he said. "Unfortunately, I can't do so tonight—I'm late for another appointment already. But then, I'm going to have that pleasure tomorrow, at Retreat, I believe? My mother is looking forward so much to your return. I'm sure you won't disappoint her. I'll come for you around two. Let me tell you again how happy I am that your flight through the forest ended with Fielding's Folly. Good night. Good night, Millie. Good night, Free."

He had bowed—deferentially to her, mockingly to Millie—nodded casually to Freeman, and ignored all the others far more effectively than they had ignored him. Then he swung the door of the Great Hall open and stood for an instant on the threshold, looking back on her with an expression of amusement, as if the secret they shared were a great joke on all the rest.

"Good night," he said again. "Good night, Eunice." And disappeared into the darkness.

"How could you be so insulting?" Eunice asked furiously, as the door closed behind him. She had come up very close to Millie, and for the first time in her life she felt as if she would like to lay violent hands on someone. Millie shrugged her shoulders.

"You can't insult Francis Fielding. He's beneath it," she said nonchalantly. "I'm sorry you ran across him, but that can't be helped now. Don't go back to Retreat tomorrow, though. Have a headache or something— Of course there's some dinner saved for you. Why not eat it here, while the rest of us are finishing our coffee? Wouldn't that be pleasanter than having it alone down in the dining room?"

"I don't want any dinner. I'm going to my own room—to pack. I'm leaving in the morning."

"Look here, Eunice." Freeman spoke after the characteristic manner of the Stones, pleasantly, but with authority. It was the manner that had helped to put them in the Cabinet and the White House, and to send them to the Senate and the Court of St. James's. "If you knew more about Francis Fielding, you wouldn't blame Millie. Virginians don't cast out their own kin without grave cause. But he doesn't belong in the pasture. He's a maverick."

"I believe the rest of the Stones called Jerry a maverick at one point. Now lots of people think he's worth all the rest of them put together."

The thrust was a telling one. Jerry Stone was at one and the same time Freeman's distant cousin and his father-in-law. Millie's gifted mother, Honor Bright, had married him in the face of bitter opposition after the death of Millie's father; but her second marriage had proved as successful as her first had been disastrous. Honor and Jerry lived the year round at the Lower Garden and were both immensely popular throughout the county, with which they were much more closely associated than Millie and Freeman who only came and went at certain seasons. It had always been a source of chagrin to Freeman Stone that he had never been "accepted" with the same wholeheartedness as Jerry.

"It might be easier to overlook Francis Fielding's wicked ways if his family were not all so sketchy," remarked Flora Treadway, the girl in green. She had seated herself in the corner of a great sofa when Freeman had become otherwise preoccupied, and had sat there blowing smoke through her long jade holder and looking extremely bored during the explosion that followed. Now it appeared she had been less detached and indifferent than she had sought to seem. "His mother talks just like her own niggers. And I never saw such a shiftless housekeeper. You remember the day we all went over to Retreat for dinner, Millie, years ago, before the split came? Mrs. Fielding had bought a bottle of sherry for the occasion, but she couldn't remember where she had put it. So between each course everyone got up from the table to hunt for it. There wasn't anything else to drink, so we needed it badly. But no one could find it. Finally, after dinner, when we were all in a state of coma because we were so full of heavy food, we were startled almost out of our senses by an unearthly howl. Purvis had been sent to build a fire in the back parlor before we went in there, and he had found the sherry in the woodbox."

"I think Mrs. Fielding is one of the sweetest women I ever saw in my life. I love her accent. It's genuine, it isn't put on like some people's. And she's genuinely hospitable, too. It means a lot more to ask people to dinner when you haven't any too much yourself than when it's a mere matter of telling a butler how many plates to lay. What difference does it make whether the sherry was in the woodbox—or where it was? The point is that she bought it."

A strange hush had fallen on the Great Hall. Nobody broke in on Eunice when she paused for breath. Recklessly she went racing on.

"As for the family being 'sketchy,' " she said, "I think it's delightful. I was fascinated by both the girls I saw. Sabina is a born storyteller, and Rosa Belle is a raving tearing beauty. If they had any sort of a chance, they could make a lot of themselves. Bina could be a *diseuse*, or something of the sort, and Bella could be a movie star. I'm going to talk to Honor about them the next time I see her. She knows all the promoters and agents in New York and she made a great hit with everybody in Hollywood while her latest book was being filmed. I'm sure she could do something to help them."

"If you leave the first thing in the morning, you won't have a chance to see Honor," remarked Millie. She still spoke imperturbably, as if there were much ado about nothing. "Do sit down and drink some coffee, Eunice, if you won't eat any dinner. You must be dead tired, after such an exhausting day."

"Do not discourage her, Mil-lee," remarked D'Alessandro, the young attaché of the Italian Embassy. Like Flora Treadway, he had been watching the scene with an all of sophisticated detachment. Now he spoke smilingly but satirically. "I think it is ver-ee amusing that our marble maiden should show so much fire. I am sure she tells us the truth, that she has found fascination at Retreat. Though I am not so certain its sole source is those two talented young sis-tairs of our recent caller."

Eunice's outspoken fury turned to cold rage. She did not know, then, that Francis Fielding had also thought of her that day as a "marble maiden," for he had not put his thought into words. But she had not forgotten that D'Alessandro had attempted the same sort of advances which Francis had achieved, though so differently that whereas Francis had filled her being with joy, she had fled from the amorous Italian with abhorrence. Later, she could say with sincerity that she bore him no ill will, that she was in a sense grateful to him for his indirect contribution to her boundless happiness. But it was still far too soon for that.

"I believe there is marble in Italy as well as Vermont," she said evenly. "If anything should happen to recall you from your post, you might spend your leave at Cararra."

Tardily, D'Alessandro remembered that the Honorable Aloysius Hogan, the brother of Eunice Hale's stepfather, had recently resigned as congressman from New York to become American Ambassador to Italy. The official connection would not be advantageous to himself, under all the circumstances.

"As for the fascination of Fielding's Folly," Eunice went on, "you're quite right, it was very general. I've never met a man who attracted me as much as Francis Fielding. But Millie is right too. I am exhausted. So I think I'll go to my room now, if you'll all excuse me. I'm still planning to leave in the morning. I'll go to see Honor early. Then when I've been to Retreat for dinner, I'll go on to Tivoli. Good night, everybody."

The waves had turned from quicksilver to sapphire, the sky from pearl gray to turquoise; gazing out upon them, framed by the latticed walls of her lanai, Eunice could still look back on this encounter with supreme satisfaction. Millie herself would have conceded that Eunice had carried off all the honors. But the next episodes on which she dwelt had left more scars.

She had carried out all her plans in regard to leaving. Directly after her breakfast, which she ate as usual in her own room, she had gone over to the Lower Garden to see Honor, whom she found revising a manuscript in the old office which she had transformed into a study. The older woman had received her cordially and listened with courteous attention while Eunice talked about Bina and Bella; but in the end she had answered rather noncommittally.

"I'm sorry I've let myself lose track so completely of that branch of the family," she said with evident sincerity. "I don't feel toward the Fieldings the way Millie and Freeman do, and neither does Jerry, though there have been some things— But I'm so busy with my books and all that I don't seem to take the initiative, any more, in keeping up acquaintances. And Alice Fielding leads a very isolated life. I rather had the impression she preferred to. It may be a wrong impression. She was certainly very cordial to you. She's terribly poor and terribly proud. It's hard to know just how to help her. But I'll go over someday soon, Eunice, I really will—if I can get up that dreadful driveway in this weather."

"The driveway is rough, but it isn't impassable."

"All right then— Now that you speak of it, I do remember that those two girls are both very striking. But that isn't saying I can get them onto the stage and screen. A good school that specializes in elocution is the place for Bina. But I'm not sure she even wants to be educated. The grandfather of this trundlebed trash you've fallen in with really showed

41

a good deal of initiative. He opened up a boarding school at Retreat after the war between the States. He had plenty of room there, and this gave him a chance to have his own children taught free, along with the outsiders who paid. But the next generation didn't do so well, and this one— Families go to seed, you know, sometimes, just like plants. Well— Bella might get a job in Hollywood. I'll look into it, Eunice."

"Right away?"

"No, not right away. Jerry and I are going over to Orange for the Meet tomorrow, and then we're spending Sunday at the White House with Neal and Anne Conrad. And I'm so close to the deadline on this new novel that I ought not to be running around anywhere. I've got to buckle down to it pretty soon. But presently——"

Eunice had left the Lower Garden soothed but discouraged. She was mollified because Honor had spoken so much more leniently of Fielding's Folly than Millie; but she recognized the older woman's preoccupation. Honor was deeply in love with her husband; moreover, her life was filled to overflowing with pleasant and profitable pursuits. Between making official visits and writing best sellers, she had enough to do on her own place without trying to concern herself intensively with estranged and distant relatives who had no valid claims upon her. Eunice felt that she would act, and act efficiently, in her own good time. That was Honor Bright's way. In the meanwhile there was nothing more that she herself could do in that direction.

When she returned to the Upper Garden Francis Fielding was already waiting for her, seated in a carryall drawn up beyond the small arched bridge which led from the smooth lawns to the outlying pasturelands. The carryall had evidently once been an equipage of some style, and he had managed to imbue it with a little of its erstwhile elegance. She did not suggest that he should come into the house, but shook hands with him rather self-consciously, and after a brief pause, during which he looked at her in a way that made her blush, said she would go in and tell Barrell Boxen to bring out her bags. Millie did not accompany her on her return; and when the butler had stowed her luggage into the back of the carryall and they had started on their way, she sat beside him with her downcast eyes fixed on her clasped hands as they rode along.

"I'm glad to have you see Fielding's Folly in the daylight," Francis remarked at length. He had not seemed to feel that the silence which lay between them was in any way awkward, and when he broke it, he did so nonchalantly. "You must have got the idea last night that it was nothing except woods. But there are acres of pasture and meadow too.

They're separated from Solomon's Garden by old fences made of split hickory almost covered with holly. Mighty pretty those fences are, too, especially at this time of year. Watch for them. We'll be coming to them presently."

"Does your land actually adjoin Honor's and Millie's?"

"Yes—a long way from the houses. Solomon's Garden is enormous—and so is Fielding's Folly for that matter." He laughed, as if he relished his own double entendre. "Neither family is conscious of any great propinquity though, as you've already discovered. The feud goes as far as the negroes. Blanche accuses Barrell Boxen of keeping a still in Millie's woods and making bootleg liquor out of 'consecrated lye.' And poor old Dewdy used to say all the time, 'D'ere ain't no compassion between our crops an' dose udders.' I don't know for certain about the still, but Dewdy was right. The lack of compassion isn't limited to the crops, either."

"Why does Millie hate you so, Francis?"

"Do you really want to know?"

"Yes."

"It began when I got expelled from the University. Millie adores her stepfather and it was he who gave me the money to go there."

"Jerry!"

"Why, yes. Is there anything strange about that?"

Eunice did not want to tell him that her call on Jerry's wife that morning had been made specifically in behalf of the trundlebed trash. Besides, she was overwhelmed at the memory of Honor's tactful restraint. She realized how much Honor might have said that she had not, how reluctant she naturally would be to give further aid when that already extended had been squandered. Eunice answered in some confusion.

"No—I suppose not. I know that Jerry and Honor are both very generous."

"Exactly. And Millie felt I abused their generosity because I didn't graduate *summa cum laude,* Phi Beta Kappa and all the rest of it. Not that Millie wanted to go to college herself. She flatly refused to, and went off to Siam with the Freeman Stones when Free's father was appointed financial adviser to the King. But that's neither here nor there. I don't know whether Honor and Jerry felt the same way she did or not. If they did, they never showed it. I'll say that for them. They're financing Peyton now, just as pleasantly as if I'd covered them with vicarious glory."

"Did— Is there any other reason Millie dislikes you, besides this one?"

"You're filled with curiosity this morning, aren't you, darling? Have you forgotten what happened to the poor little

43

kitty that died of it? I wouldn't want your curiosity to be fatal—to anything."

"It won't be."

"Well, Millie didn't approve of an affair I had."

"She wouldn't approve of the one you're having now, if she knew about it."

"She approved of the other still less than she will of this when she does know about it. It wasn't the same kind of affair, Eunice."

She flushed again, so deeply that she felt as if her innermost being were flooded with hot color.

"It's all over, if that's what's worrying you. In fact, the girl's dead— I told you that you must take me on trust, Eunice, if you took me at all. Perhaps you'd better reconsider. It isn't too late yet."

"You told me yourself, last night, that it was too late already."

"And you believed me. Do you still believe me?"

"Yes."

"Then stop asking questions and wringing your hands and look up at me and tell me that you love me. Oh, yes— And you might give me a kiss, now that we're out of sight of Solomon's Garden. That's a grand way to start off a day when you're in love. It brings good luck."

The clouds had become a golden bank over a golden sea; above them a rainbow arched in scintillating glory to the zenith of the heavens. Eunice watched it form and fade as she recalled each detail of the day that brought good luck.

Dinner had been ready when she and Francis reached Retreat; inevitably they had loitered along the way, and the carryall did not represent a rapid means of transportation at best. So they had gone at once to the dining room where a long table was spread with a white cloth and half covered with large platters and steaming dishes. Blanche had cooked the wild ducks to a turn, and the rice that surrounded them rose in light fluffy mounds. There were fried yams besides, and Jerusalem artichokes, richly creamed, and three kinds of pickle, not to mention pile after pile of biscuits, split and buttered in the kitchen and brought in piping hot; and afterward there was seamoss blanc mange with marmalade and poundcake. Forgetting that she had gone supperless to bed and that she had breakfasted on coffee and toast, Eunice had not realized how ravenous she was. Now she ate her fill of the hot and homely fare which gave the illusion of such plenty.

After dinner was over, they all went to the cabin except Mrs. Fielding, who wanted to sit with the still ailing Mamie Love. Eunice joined the circle that sat around Uncle Nixon while he strummed his banjo and told his stories. She would willingly have sat there all evening and half the night, for the old blind minstrel had magic in his voice and in his fingers. But finally Francis whispered to her that he wanted her to come for a walk before it grew too late; last night the skies had been overcast with clouds, the darkness complete; tonight the air was clear as crystal. He would show her something beautiful.

She slipped a sable jacket over her dress of dark tailored cloth and rejoined him. The sky was still streaked with opalescence when they went out; the marshland pools, beyond the woods, reflected its lambency; and as the streaks faded, stars began to prickle through them. Francis and Eunice skirted the marshes and climbed a knoll that rose beside the river. When they reached the top, they could see beyond this a golden glow, bright as a summer sunrise. Little by little its radiance widened, suffusing the horizon like a slowly spreading fire; and from it soared a huge golden ball, so lustrous that it looked like the magnified glory encircling the head of some somber saint whose giant features were dimmed by its radiance.

"The hunters' moon!" Francis whispered. "I feel as if it were my own! Whoever had such good hunting as I've had?"

Eunice did not instantly answer. Once before, and only once, had she seen a moon so splendid. That had been at Rimini, where she was spending a brief vacation in the course of an Italian school year, and where she had watched the moon rise from the sea with all the triumph of a nascent Aphrodite. Looking at it then she had thought she could dimly understand why Francesca had felt the world well lost for love when she trysted with Paolo in such magic light. Now Eunice understood better. Violence and tragedy, death and dishonor, had been inescapable at Rimini, perhaps; but so had joy and glory and the swift hot current of life. Were they inescapable for the lovers of all ages, everywhere?

"A penny for your thoughts, darling! Don't you like my moon? You seem about a thousand miles away!"

"It was about three thousand! May I tell you a story? It's one that's always thrilled and moved me very much, one that's been told by very famous poets—Dante and D'Annunzio, for instance. I can't do justice to it; I can't even tell it as well as Bina would, if she knew it. But I'd like to try. Because you've made me see tonight, for the first time, that it must have been even more wonderful in the living than it ever has been in the telling!"

Eunice told her story and Francis told her what he thought of it. He had read a version of it in Chambers' Encyclopedia already; but this was brief and dry compared to the glowing account he heard now, and he encouraged Eunice to enlarge on it. That was one of several reasons why it was very late when they went back to the house. Purvis and the girls had gone to bed already, and Blanche had left for her cabin; but Mrs. Fielding was waiting up for them, sitting by the cheerful fire in the back parlor, beneath the portrait of her comely grandmother. She showed no surprise because they had been gone so long, and when Eunice told her, spontaneously, that they had been to watch the moon rise over the river and marshes, she nodded with a little reminiscent smile and said, sighing faintly, that she had often done that herself when she had come as a girl to visit at Retreat. This memory led to other reminiscences; she chatted on, amiably and volubly, while Francis and Eunice ate the sandwiches and drank the cocoa she had made for them. Then she led her visitor solicitously to the guest room which had been prepared for her coming.

"I do hope you-all won't be uncomfortable, honey chile," she said, with genuine affection in her voice. "You know we never did get 'round to put a bathroom in Retreat. But I've filled both pitchers in the china chamber set, and there's the jar— I reckon there's plenty of quilts on the bed— It is right cold here though, isn't it? Perhaps I should have kept the fire goin'. I'll remember, next time you come, you're not used to an unheated house. The cupboard's all cleared, you can hang your pretty dress up in there. Sweet dreams, Eunice."

Eunice had assured her hostess that she knew she would have such dreams, as she returned Mrs. Fielding's kindly kiss. Secretly, she was not so sure. The room was certainly very cold. She shivered as she undressed, and crept in under the quilts as soon as possible. But she could not go to sleep. All the eerie elements of Retreat seemed unleashed now that night had come and she was alone. Eunice lay rigid, with wide-open eyes. The moonlight, streaming into the room, turned the bare boards of the floor to glistening planks and transfigured the forms of all the furniture. The chair on which she had thrown down her clothes, the washstand with its "china chamber set," the tall wardrobe standing in one corner—all these had taken on strange and sinister shapes. A board creaked, and she shivered again; the doors of the wardrobe swung slowly ajar, and she shook all over. The night was as still as it was clear—how could doors open like that, when there was no wind? She had hardly asked herself the question when a cold breeze blew across her bed like an icy breath. Before she could suppress her mounting terror, she had screamed. As she did so, she seemed to see a wraith-like figure detach itself from the footboard and flutter across

46

the room toward the blank wall opposite the window. Then it melted into nothingness. At the same moment there was a knock at the door. She had screamed again before she heard a reassuring voice and realized that Francis was standing outside.

"What's the matter, darling? What scared you? May I come in?"

"No—no—of course not! Oh, Francis, I'm frightened to death!"

"Don't be silly, darling. Of course I'm coming in. And of course there isn't anything to be afraid of."

He advanced quietly, carrying in his hand a lighted candle which he placed on the bedside table. Then he himself sat down on the edge of the bed. Although he looked comfortably drowsy, he was still fully dressed. The candle lent the air of luminosity to him which light of any kind always seemed to give him, as if he absorbed part of its rays. He took her trembling hands and patted them gently.

"I fell asleep by the fire after you left the parlor," he said. "I only just waked up. I was coming up the stairs to go to bed myself when I heard you scream. What frightened you, Eunice?"

"There are all kinds of strange sights and sounds in this room."

"Nonsense! Boards always creak in an old house, and the moon always plays tricks with light effects. I can close the shutters, if that will help."

He started to rise. She clutched tightly at his hand.

"That isn't all. A cold breeze blew across this bed, though there isn't an atom of wind. And after that I saw some kind of a—a phantom, leaning against the footboard. When I screamed, it disappeared through that side wall over there, though there isn't any door. You can't explain things like that away."

He did not instantly answer. Then he spoke in an altered voice, tender but teasing.

"I told you there were ghosts at Retreat. You must have had a visit from one. But cheer up, they never call twice the same night. Cuddle down now like a good girl and go to sleep. I'll stay here until you do."

"Francis, you—you know you mustn't do that! What would your mother think if—if she should happen to find you here?"

"She'd figure out the truth—that something frightened you, and that you called, and that I was the first person to hear you. What harm would be done if she did find me here? But she won't. She's sound asleep, with Mamie Love in bed beside her, over in the other part of the house. Bina and Bella

47

and Purvis all sleep at that end too. We believe in letting our guests have privacy. Most of them prefer it—for one reason or another. I'm sorry you don't."

"You make it all sound very plausible, but——"

"Eunice, you better look at this straight. If I'd meant to get into bed with you tonight, I wouldn't have tried to find a pretext, like a ghost, for doing it. I'd have waited until the house was quiet, and then I'd have just done it. You wouldn't have had a chance to scream and risk rousing the house—I'd have taken care of that too. But I hadn't even thought of doing it until you put the idea into my mind. I have my own ideas of the kind of bride I want. They're very different from the kind of ideas I have about a girl I'd only want to sleep with."

"Francis, you—you mustn't say such dreadful things."

"Yes, I must, if you won't be a rational human being as well as a modest maiden and go to sleep. Come now!"

He drew the covers high up on her shoulders, patted these as he had patted her hand, and kissed her on the cheek. Then he drew a straight-backed chair up beside the bed and sat down. He was still sitting there when she went to sleep.

In the morning the room was bright and open and full of sunshine. Mrs. Fielding brought up a breakfast tray to her guest herself. She had decorated it carefully with some sprays of cosmos which had escaped the frost, and had put the sugar in an old-fashioned muffineer, which she divined would prove intriguing to Eunice. It all bespoke kindliness and thoughtfulness. But when Eunice tried to talk to her about ghosts, she betrayed her first signs of evasiveness.

"You must have been dreamin', honey chile. Or maybe Virgin got to talkin' to you when you-all were in the cabin. Virgin says he 'sees de debble frequent in de big woods and dat de debble has a haid wid horns and a tail jes' like de preacher say he hab.' All the darkies are superstitious as they can be, and it doesn't mean a thing."

"I didn't talk to Virgin. I listened to Uncle Nixon all the time I was in the cabin. But right here in this room I saw——"

Mrs. Fielding laughed comfortably. "Once Virgin went up to the county seat with an empty kerosene can," she said. "and the wind got into the spout. The faster he ran, the louder the wind in the spout sounded—as if someone were whisperin' beside him. He came pantin' up the path with his eyes bulgin' right out of his head. He was certain 'de debble' was after him that time. And it was only the wind!"

"Well, this wasn't the wind. There wasn't any wind. But I heard——"

"Honey chile, when you've taken your sponge bath, won't

48

you put on your wrapper and come on into my room? Mamie Love is just plaguin' the life out of me, she's so set on seein' you. Afterward Francis wants to take you down to see the dam his grandfather built. Once there was a dreadful storm and the dam burst. All the water rushed out and the reeds were full of fishes floppin' around in 'em. Blanche and her family just went there and gathered 'em up by hand for a fry. There were big turtles there too— We never got 'round to build up the dam again. I'm sort of sorry, because there used to be a pool there, sweet pretty, with lily pads floatin' on it. The children learned to swim there too, and they had a canoe. That fell to pieces, a while back. But Frank thought you'd like to see where the dam used to be."

Eunice had gone gladly enough to see Mamie Love, who proved to be a quaint little girl with a piquant face, big eyes, and long pigtails. She was not as pretty as her sisters, but she was certainly very lovable, and Eunice thought that she had been felicitously named. After she had read aloud to Mamie Love for half an hour, and answered innumerable questions, she left the house, telling Mrs. Fielding, quite sincerely, that she had supposed Francis would be busy that morning; so she had promised to walk over to the village with Bella and Bina when they went for the mail. It appeared that this had not been procured for a week. Besides, she herself needed to telephone Tivoli for a car. She had neglected to do so before leaving Solomon's Garden the previous day, and since there was no telephone at Retreat, the pay station in the general store represented her only opportunity. Mrs. Fielding watched her depart almost reproachfully; she did not know what she would say to Frank when he came back —he had stepped out for just a minute. Eunice's reply was that it would be just a minute before she was back herself.

She drank in the crisp air, thankful for the sparkling sunlight and for the great stretches of peaceful pasture that lay beyond the deep woods. She walked briskly, much more rapidly than either of her companions; she was obliged to keep stopping and waiting for them, and as she did so, she studied the surrounding landscape. There was a serenity about it that pleased her, and a mellowness; she could understand why it held the hearts of those who dwelt there from one generation to another. But something Honor Bright had said the day before kept running through her mind to trouble her —"Families can run to seed, you know, as well as plants." These fields that lay around her were not as fruitful as they should be, and the fault did not lie in the ground; it lay in the people who failed to plant them and cultivate them. Dependable resources were undeveloped, potential riches wasted. A great longing to improve and perpetuate this neglected heritage swept over her. Here was work for her hands to do, and help that would come from her heart.

"Bina," she said suddenly. Bina was tagging behind again, and she waited eagerly for the young girl to catch up with her. "Bina, wouldn't you like to go to school? I've heard there's a very good school for girls at Tappahannanock. If you don't want to go far from home, you could go there. I'd —I'd like to send you. Just the way Jerry Stone has sent your brothers to the University, you know."

"Oh, Miss Eunice, you do declare, you're too sweet! But I did go to school in Tappahannanock a while back, and somehow I just naturally couldn't stay there. And ma never would let me go farther away. She thinks young girls should stay where their own dear mothers can watch over them. She doesn't think books matter so much as some other things."

"What other things?"

"Why not having beaux too soon, and things like that. You know, Miss Eunice."

"I reckon I better bob my hair," remarked Bella, inconsequentially. Bella was not actually as slow as Bina, but she made no more progress because she kept dancing away from the road and then dancing back to it again, singing snatches of song as she did so. Her slim body swayed blithely to and fro in time to the tunes which she hummed, and her long locks, escaping entirely from their inadequate ribbon, kept blowing over her face. "What do you think, Miss Eunice?"

"I think it would be a crime. That beautiful auburn hair! Most girls would give their eye teeth to have hair like that! There may be a fortune for you in it someday, Bella! Besides, it's your 'crown of glory.' "

"Land sakes, Miss Eunice, you talk just the way Blanche did when her girl Annie Laurie cut her hair! You haven't seen Annie Laurie yet, she's married now and lives down the road aways on Barrack Field. She's smart but mighty uppity, and Ma won't let her on the place any more. She had an engagement child and was bold as brass about it; Ma's never forgiven her for the way she talked before Bina and me. She used to take off all her clothes, too, and prance around in front of the mirror in the guest room where you're sleeping now, when she thought no one would catch her. But I did catch her, twice— She knew how to dance, too. I'd like to be able to dance that way myself. Well, anyway, when she came home from the county seat one night with her hair bobbed, she had to run right out in the yard again. Blanche was after her, hell bent for leather, swearing that if she could get hold of her she'd 'lay her haid on the woodblock and chop it off, same as if it was a rabbit's'— There are lots of rabbits around in the woods at this time of year, Miss Eunice.

50

Have you seen any? Frank snares them, and they make mighty good eating. I shouldn't wonder if he weren't trying to snare some now. There wasn't anything in the larder this morning but the two quail he shot day before yesterday and those won't go far. We'll be hungry when we get back from the store."

"I thought perhaps I could buy a steak at the store. I'd like dinner today to be my treat."

"Why the very idea, Miss Eunice! Ma would never forgive you if you did a thing like that."

Eunice thought there might be some truth in this. Nevertheless, she made the purchase, and though it was protestingly received, the last morsel of it was heartily devoured. She decided this procedure might be typical of Fielding's Folly, and that she might take other risks of the same kind. But for the time being there was no chance to experiment further. The car from Tivoli for which she had telephoned—a large lumbering Rolls Royce, which got stuck twice in the driveway before it finally pulled through—was already waiting for her when she finished her dinner. The chauffeur's manner was disdainful as he climbed out of it and asked whether Miss Hale's bags were ready for him to bring down. Francis, who had gone to the door himself, answered the man curtly.

"You needn't bother. The butler will see to all that."

The chauffeur's manner had changed instantly. Francis had an effect upon servants that galvanized them into action and commanded their utmost respect. He was insolent to them and inconsiderate of them. But they groveled before him. The steward on the ship now— Eunice came back to the present with a start. The steward laid out Francis's dinner clothes every night, changed his studs, pressed his trousers and forestalled his evening order for cocktails on the lanai. The stewardess did not begin to do as much for her, and what she did do was accomplished civilly, but without spontaneity. Eunice did not resent this, and it did not surprise her. She would have served Francis, willingly, herself. In a sense, that was what she did do, and gloried in doing——

It had been true enough that Virgin was hovering close at hand, that day at Retreat, ready to bring down her bags and to receive the lavish tip which he had anticipated. But Francis, after shutting the door in the chauffeur's face, had not called Virgin. He had gone upstairs himself, ostensibly to see to her luggage. But once inside, he had shut the bedroom door and come close to her.

"You ran away from me this morning."

"Not really. I honestly did think you'd be busy."

"You're running away from me now."

"No, I'm not. I'm preparing the way for you. The minute I get to Tivoli, I'm going to tell my mother."

"Tell her what?"

"That I'm engaged to you. Isn't that what you want me to tell her?"

"That depends— What are you going to do next?"

"Next I'm going to Evergreen to tell Grandma I want to marry you right away."

"That's better. Remember I said, night before last, that I could get to Vermont for Thanksgiving. I still think I could. Can you be ready to marry me then?"

"Perhaps."

"Don't say perhaps. Say you can. Otherwise I shan't believe you aren't running away from me."

"I— Yes, I can."

"Grand girl! I suppose I have to let you go then—to pre-pare, as you put it. But I hate like hell to have you. You've done something to me— What kind of kiss have you got for me, darling, if you're bound to tell me good-by?"

Mrs. Fielding had been standing in the upper hallway wait-ing for them when they came out of the guest room. She evinced no astonishment at their appearance together, and if she noticed that the door had been closed, apparently she did not give the matter a passing thought. Mothers felt dif-ferently, Eunice decided, when their sons were concerned rather than their daughters. At all events, Mrs. Fielding's own parting caress had been full of characteristic cordiality. And at the last moment she had slipped a small trinket into Eunice's hand.

"It's nothing much, honey chile. Just a little enameled locket. But I think it's mighty pretty in that maroon color, and there's a spray of rose diamonds on the back. Frank's fa-ther gave it to me when our first dear little boy was born. I've always carried Frank's baby picture in it. I thought maybe you'd like it. Now don't say a word. I despise pryin' women and I'm not askin' any questions. You write to me, Eunice dear, when you feel like it. And I'll be lookin' for you to come back for dinin' day."

Eunice had been deeply touched by the gift of the locket. She had put it on at once and she was still wearing it when she reached Tivoli, where it instantly caught her stepfather's sharp eye. Patrick Hogan was a huge jovial Irishman who had made one immense fortune through the contracting busi-ness which his immigrant father had founded, and another through his advantageous association with Tammany Hall. He still spoke with a brogue and was proud of it; he had a mighty laugh and a robust constitution. In New York he had hundreds of kindred spirits with whom he was hail fellow well met; in Middleburg he had practically none and he was both puzzled and hurt at the lack. Yet he yearned to become a southern country gentleman, and never wholly gave up hope that this role would be in his grasp; he could not conceive that there was anything he coveted that could not be either bought or coaxed into his possession. As Eunice entered the house, she found him standing by the suspended stairway in the paneled hall hung with sporting prints and Troy paintings of prize winning horses, measuring the comparative lengths of some long, tasseled whips, which he fondly imagined were appropriate for use with an ultra-smart four-in-hand.

"Well look who's here!" he exclaimed, dropping the whips with a clatter to the floor and giving her a hearty hug and a loud smack. "Back ahead of time and not a second too soon to suit your old daddy. What's this you've got on—a new pendant?"

"No, Patrick, it's an old locket."

"I wouldn't say it would bring much at auction," he said, lifting it and looking at it appraisingly. "But it's not bad looking at that. And who might be giving you an old locket, mavoureen?"

"A nice lady named Mrs. Fielding."

"And who might be the gossoon's picture that's in it?"

"That's her oldest son, when he was a baby."

"When he was a baby! And how long ago was that?"

"About twenty-five years, I think," Eunice said, laughing in spite of herself.

"Faith, if I didn't know you so well, I should think you were up to some mischief. There's that sort of sleekness about you that comes over a girl who's been carrying on and who's enjoyed it. I'm not sure I shouldn't take one of these whips to you. No one can tell by the looks of a frog how far it will jump. Was it clean out of the old mill pond you went, Eunice?"

"Yes, Patrick. I'll tell you all about it, gladly. But I think I ought to tell Mamma first, don't you?"

"Just suit your fancy, my child. I'll be waiting to listen when you're ready to talk to me. And it's pleased I am to see you so blithe, if you're after asking me!"

Eunice left him reluctantly and went on to her mother's room. She found Mrs. Hogan dressing, which was one of that lady's principal preoccupations. She always patronized the best dressmakers with great prodigality, just as she always went to the best hotels and engaged the most expensive suites to be found. These pleasures served to divert her mind, more or less, from the fact that in spite of them she was never seen wearing her beautiful clothes and installed in her costly quarters with the very best people.

"Well, Eunice," she said, rather less agreeably than Millie Stone had said it two nights earlier. "So you decided to come home? I still don't understand why. Bates couldn't hear you very well over the telephone. Why didn't Millie send you? I thought that was the arrangement when you went to Solomon's Garden."

"It was. But I left Solomon's Garden yesterday and went to another old place near there, named Retreat. The Fieldings, who own it, are distant relatives of Millie's. They don't have a car."

"They don't have a car?" echoed Mrs. Hogan, in the voice of one inquiring why a slum child has no toothbrush. "How on earth do they manage, especially in a place like King George? I've never been able to understand, anyway, how anyone could live down there on the Northern Neck, where there isn't so much as a railroad, much less any other signs of civilization— How do you like this negligee, Eunice? Madame Tremaine sent it on for me to see with two or three others that were in a shipment that just came in on the *Ile de France*."

"It's your style," Eunice said. The comment seemed to satisfy Mrs. Hogan, and Eunice was relieved, for she did not like to hurt her mother's feelings any more than she liked to fib; but secretly she considered the negligee hideous. She herself liked plain straight lines and clean cool colors; the garment in which Mrs. Hogan was pirouetting was made of mauve taffeta, trimmed with tiers of lace ruffles caught up with coquettish bows. It matched the mauve decor which she had superimposed on the chaste colonial elegance of her great rectangular bedroom; but it would have been more becoming to her personally if she had been twenty years younger and thirty pounds lighter.

"It's nice that you got back in time to go to the Hunt Ball at the North Wales Club, anyway," Mrs. Hogan continued. "I don't like to keep nagging you, Eunice, but it really would please me very much to have you take a more prominent part in local activities. Almost everyone around here asks you to parties, but you so seldom go, people get the idea you don't care to, and then they decide the whole family's unsociable. I'm sure that's why Patrick and I aren't asked more. Of course, it's a feather in our caps to own Tivoli. The house is the finest example of Georgian architecture anywhere around here and the terraces are unique. But it's lonely, just the same, and dull, the way things are. Now if you——"

"I'm sorry, Mamma. I'd like to be helpful, if you really

54

think I could be. But I've decided to go home for a few weeks."

"Go *home?* You mean to Hamstead? I wish you wouldn't keep on talking about Hamstead as if it were your home, Eunice. Now that your stepfather and I have gone to all the trouble of buying this enormous place, in the most fashionable part of Virginia———"

"I'm glad you have it, Mamma. I know how much you and Patrick wanted it. But I still like Evergreen better, and after all, Grandma's alone there except when I'm with her. She never complains, but I think the old lady likes company once in a while herself. Besides, this time I have a special reason for wanting to go there. I want to help get Evergreen ready for a wedding."

"A wedding! Whose wedding?"

"Mine, Mamma. I've decided to get married. You know you've been telling me for some time that you wished I would."

"I've said I'd like to see you *suitably* married," Mrs. Hogan said sharply. "I never said I wanted you to dive off the deep end, as you evidently have. You, of all girls! I'm amazed at you, Eunice!"

"I'm amazed at myself. But I've done just what you said. I've dived off the deep end. Or as Patrick put it, I've jumped out of the old mill pond. Anyway, the family similes all seem to be aquatic. I think Patrick is rather amused. He has quite a sense of humor. And as you say, I haven't acted very consistently, in getting engaged. Patrick guessed what I'd done, though, the minute he saw me."

"Well, I'm not amused," Mrs. Hogan retorted, still more sharply. "And I don't see when you've had *time* to get engaged. Who is this young man?"

"His name is Francis Fielding. It's at his family's house that I've been staying. He's very attractive. In fact, the whole family is."

"No doubt. When did you meet this attractive young man and his attractive family?"

"Just a short time ago." In spite of her dislike for prevarication, Eunice could not bring herself to tell her mother how short this time actually was. But she summoned her courage to go on. "I'm going to have a short engagement too. Francis would like to be married on Thanksgiving Day. Of course, Grandma will expect me to have the wedding at Evergreen. I hope it won't be inconvenient for you and Patrick to go north at that time. I'm counting on Patrick to give me away. Grandma will have to recognize his existence if he does."

"Of course it will be inconvenient. Have you forgotten

that the outstanding meet of the year comes on Thanksgiving Day, the one everyone goes to?"

"I'm afraid I did, temporarily. I'm afraid getting engaged has driven other things out of my mind. It's a new experience for me."

"I think it's made you lose your senses entirely. I shan't consent to this mad plan of yours, Eunice."

"I hope you will, Mamma. Because I'm going to carry it through anyway."

Mrs. Hogan stared at her daughter with helpless rage. She had seen Eunice take the bit in her teeth before; it was always hard to deal with her when she did it, and this time it might prove impossible. Eunice was of age, and she was financially independent. Mrs. Hogan had always resented the terms of her first husband's will. He had been made a partner in the Spencer marble works at the time of his marriage and—most ungratefully in her opinion—had left all his stock to his daughter instead of his widow. The reason he had assigned for this was that his widow would be well off in any case, through her father's estate, and that he desired Eunice to enjoy a similar advantage. Eunice had been in complete control of her own fortune for more than a year, and Mrs. Hogan was bound to admit that she had handled it very competently. Now she had lost her head and was about to squander it on some worthless fortune hunter, unless she could be stopped.

"I should think you would be ashamed to have a man marry you for your money," Mrs. Hogan said tauntingly.

"What makes you think he's marrying me for my money? Money hasn't even been mentioned." It was true, yet deep down in her heart, Eunice knew only too well that everything about her bespoke unmistakable wealth and that inevitably Francis must have noticed this. Besides, there had been those questions he had asked—tactful questions, casual questions, but nevertheless questions. She had told him herself there was money in her grandmother's pines. He knew without the telling that there was money in marble. Her pride was touched at the thought that his passionate wooing had been precipitated by such knowledge. "Isn't there any other reason why a man should want to marry me, except for money?" she asked, almost desperately.

"I don't know. I've often wondered. You're pretty, but you're prim. The average man doesn't care for a prude. He's frightened of frigidity."

Her mother's words had cut her to the quick. But the pain had lasted only a moment. She had retorted swiftly, because she could do so sincerely.

"I don't think Francis is much frightened. He hasn't acted

as if he were. He started making love to me about three hours after we first met. It may interest you to know that I was very responsive. I'm just as eager to be married as he is——"

It was true. From the time she left him until he came to Evergreen she had counted off days on her calendar. Her grandmother, to her pleased surprise, had betrayed far less resentment than her mother. Indeed, the old lady, sizing up the situation with her usual shrewdness, had not struggled against it at all; she had even appeared to enjoy it, especially after learning that her despised daughter-in-law did not. She was touched that Eunice should have wished to be married at Evergreen, and she showed this in more ways than one.

"The parlor's real pretty when it's fixed up for a wedding," she said with pride. "I don't know but what the white-painted paneling in it isn't just as handsome as all that walnut wainscoting you say they have down South. Anyway, the Hales have always had their weddings there, and their funerals. It's fitting to carry on the custom— My house plants have done better than ordinary this year. That Star of Bethlehem, now, hanging in the window, looks as if it had bloomed a-purpose for a bride— I don't know what you have in mind, Eunice, but if it's nothing in particular, I'd like to have you wear my wedding dress. I've kept it in good condition, turned inside out, wrapped in a clean sheet. I've a notion it would fit you. You're a mite taller than I am, but the dress has a deep hem. We could let that out. And I presume it would be too tight around the waist, but we could let that out too. You're slim, but you haven't got the figure I had when I was married."

Eunice had already visualized a wedding dress made of heavy white satin, cut on the straight lines she loved, and worn with a lace veil. But she did not have the heart to tell her grandmother so; and when the treasured bridal raiment had been unsheathed and tried on, she was thankful for her forbearance. The grosgrain silk, creamy with age, which Mrs. Hale herself had worn, proved unexpectedly becoming to Eunice. It was made with a plain, tight-fitting bodice, heavily boned inside, which fastened all the way down the front with silk buttons and was finished at the neck with a small standing ruche of lace. The long leg-o'-mutton sleeves closed around the wrists in the same way, and there were loops of lace around the bottom of the full skirt, outstretched over the modified hoops of the late sixties. Except for the details Mrs. Hale had foreseen, the dress might have been made for Eunice.

"You look real nice," the old lady said, with unconcealed admiration. "There's a little pearl breastpin I used to fasten

57

that collar with. I'd just as lieve you had that too. Southerners seem to have the notion nobody but them inherits lace and pearls and houses and the like. We're going to show them different. Eunice. We're going to make it plain to them how things are in Hamstead."

"All right. Don't rub it in, Grandma, that's all. I'd love to wear the dress anyway."

"I don't aim to rub it in, but I'm going to make it plain just the same."

She did make it plain, but she achieved her ends pleasantly. She even kept her surprise to herself upon the arrival of two rattletrap cars, one containing the Fielding family, and the other Blanche, Virgin and Uncle Nixon. She greeted everyone agreeably and a certain strange warmth crept into her face when Francis kissed her. Afterward, she listened politely while Bella lightheartedly explained that the cars had been purchased with the proceeds derived from the sale of a box tree. which a member of Alexandria's "Foreign Legion," who had unaccountably strayed down into King George County, had seen and coveted.

"He bought the hanging lantern in the hall, too," chimed in Sabina. "It had been there ever since the house was built. I was sick of the sight of it myself. We're going to do painting and papering with the money from that. And he wants the two battered old loveseats we have in the attic--rosewood upholstered in horsehair. He says he'll give us a thousand dollars for them. Imagine, a thousand dollars cash money!"

"Oh, Bina, don't think of such a thing! Why, I was counting on using those loveseats myself! And I loved the lantern! We must try to get it back—it's part of Retreat, just like the brick noggings and the heaven-and-hell hinges. You'll have all the 'cash money' you need for everything from now on."

Eunice had not been able to suppress this exclamation of dismay. But Mrs. Hale had given no sign of any kind of disapproval. She showed her guests to the spotless rooms which she had scrubbed with her own hands for their reception, and promised that she would soon have quarters available for their "hired help." It was only after everyone was comfortably installed and she had stood for some time at the parlor window looking out at her pines that she turned to Eunice with a remark which might have been construed as an indirect thrust at thriftlessness.

"Those pines go right on prospering," she said. There was deep satisfaction in her brisk voice as she spoke, and her wiry little figure, always erect, seemed to take on additional straightness. "They bring me in more money than I can use,

58

living all alone like I do now. I've got me quite a sum put by. I've never done anything with the money I meant to send you and your brother to college with, Eunice."

"My brother!"

"Well, of course you never had a brother, but I'd figured you would someday, so I'd started saving money for him. Your mother's been a disappointment to me, Eunice, and I can't deny it. But I'm real proud of you. You've got gumption. I always did like gumption in a girl. Now it would please me if you would take this college pine money, Eunice, that I haven't got a mite of use for; I've got considerable besides. I want you should have a real nice trip with it, you and that young man of yours. He'll take it better that way than if you should keep doling out cash to him for expenses. I'm not such a fool I don't know he's glad you're wealthy, any more than you are. But I can say the same to you that you said to me. Don't rub it in."

"I don't aim to, Grandma."

Mrs. Hale chuckled. "You're kind of saucy, aren't you, Eunice? You're smart-spoken, same as Francis is soft-spoken. I presume you and he may have a misunderstanding, now and again, on that account. On some other accounts, too. People are apt to be considerable like the places they come from, and you and Francis haven't come from the same sort of place. There's a lot of stone and a lot of snow in a Vermont background. Of course, we've got some real nice sap running in our trees; but it takes a spring thaw to bring it out after a hard winter. Even pines aren't easy to raise; you have to keep right after them. Now from all I've heard tell Virginia is different. It has a lot of swampland that's never solid, summer or winter, and the red mud's so rich that if you so much as set a stick into it, flowers start sprouting. I guess it's a sweet pretty country. I guess it comes natural for people to be pleasant and easygoing there. It don't come quite so natural to us. We have to learn."

"Do you think I can learn, Grandma?"

"Yes, if you put your mind to it. I hope you will. You've got a good mind, Eunice, and Francis has too—don't you make any mistake about that. I don't know whether he's got as much character as you have. You may have to make yours do for the two of you. I hope you won't rub that in either. But he has a way with him. In fact, his whole family has. You'll be blessed in your mother-in-law. More than your mother's been in me, when all's said and done. I'm not surprised you acted like you did."

Mrs. Hale's eyes twinkled and then seemed to mist a little. She took off her glasses and wiped them vigorously on her clean apron.

"Francis Fielding puts me in mind of a young fellow I met myself, at a Halloween party," she said, "the winter I went to St. Johnsbury Academy. We weren't through bobbing for apples before he told me he wanted I should elope with him. He was joking then, but he saw me home from Christian Endeavor Meeting the next Thursday, and then he started up the subject again. He meant it that time, too. Of course I couldn't listen to anything of the kind. I was keeping company with your grandfather already. But I haven't forgotten that smooth-speaking scalawag to this day."

"Weren't you ever sorry that you didn't elope with him, Grandma?"

"Well," said Mrs. Hale. "Well—I'd given my word to your grandfather and I never was one to go back on promises. He was a godfearing man and a good provider, too. He made me a faithful husband and I made him a faithful wife. But I'm glad you hadn't been keeping company with anyone else, Eunice, when you met this young man of yours."

"Grandma, I think it's sweet of you to say this to me. It makes me love you more than ever."

Mrs. Hale disengaged herself from her granddaughter's hug and put her glasses back on again. "Mind, now, I haven't said I thought you'd always be happy," she remarked warningly. "But I don't know as many women are, when you come right down to it. You'll be happier than most for a while, anyway, and I guess that's what counts— You save your own money that comes from the Spencer marble works to fix up that rundown old place in Virginia. I judge it hasn't been kept up, like Evergreen has, and that cash is kind of scarce around there besides. Yours will be welcome. I'm not hinting anything against the Fieldings, either, when I say that. Some of the nicest people you'd ever wish to know are just naturally butterfingered."

It was very seldom that Mrs. Hale made such long speeches or such complimentary ones. Eunice looked at her in growing astonishment.

"Grandma, I can't tell you how much I appreciate all this. But I ought not to take your pine money for a trip."

"Now, Eunice, you do like I say. I haven't interfered with you much, so far. But I'm set on this. I always wanted to take a trip myself. I told your grandfather, before we were married, that I'd admire to see Niagara Falls. But it was just haying time then, and after that, it always seemed to be just threshing time, or logging time, or planting time, or something— Since I've been a widow, I've thought now and again of striking out alone. But it doesn't seem the same, somehow, as to go traveling with a man. That other young fellow I told you about, he went to India as a missionary. I guess he livened up the heathen considerably—before he died of cholera."

"Grandma, if it would really make you happy——"

"I've told you more than a dozen times already I want you should take that pine money. Land sakes, how many times do you need to have me say so? I want you should go to India with it. Come to think of it, if you get that far, you might just as well go 'round the world. There's ten thousand dollars I've always kept in a separate savings bank account. I'll never miss it. You and that young man of yours can start looking up steamboat schedules right away. I guess maybe you'd go to Hawaii first, wouldn't you?"

"Well, look at the lazy lady! I've played three sets of tennis and four rubbers of bridge while you've been snoozing. This lanai has you hypnotized all right! Don't forget you'll have another at the Royal Hawaiian and still another at the Kona Inn. It isn't as if this were your only chance to lounge around on one!"

Eunice laughed herself, as she looked up into the teasing face above her. She had not heard Francis come in. She must have been even deeper in dreams than she had realized.

"Perhaps you think I'm like an old lady who used to live in Hamstead," she said. "This old lady saved her money up for years so that she could go to New York. When she got there, she asked the clerk at the hotel she had chosen how much her room was, and he told her it was five dollars a day. She didn't make any objection, but after she was back in Hamstead, and the neighbors came crowding in to hear about what she'd seen, she looked at them in horror. She said she hadn't seen anything, she had just sat in her room. She was paying five dollars a day to do it and she had to get her money's worth!"

"You're getting your money's worth, darling, aren't you—of everything?"

"As if you didn't know!"

She moved over so that he could sit down beside her on the chaise longue. She had thought at first that nothing could ever be so becoming to him as his leather hunting jacket and his corduroy breeches, but he looked even more attractive in a soft shirt open at the throat and white flannel trousers. His skin had turned to a deep golden color in the sun on the sports deck, and his teeth looked dazzling against the tan. He had evidently finished off his outing with a swim, for his tumbled hair was wet around the temples, and the fresh scent of salty water clung to him. She felt his vitality flowing over her as he gave her the lingering kiss with which he invariably greeted her, no matter how brief their parting had been. His lips moved slowly down from her face and throat until they reached the hollow between her breasts; then he buried his face there, leaning over with his arms tightly clasped around her waist. Neither of them spoke for a long time.

"I wish I could always keep you in clothes like this," he murmured, as he raised his head at last. He took the lace-edged border of her chiffon robe between his fingers, felt it appreciatively, and then turned it back still farther from her white neck. "And you have no idea how lovely you look when your hair is loose, the way it is now over your bare shoulders. It makes me think of a cloud resting on alabaster. Very appropriate simile for a marble maiden, don't you think so?" It was no longer a secret that he had called her that, to himself, from the beginning. They jested about it together now. "I wanted to say all that to you—about the cloud and the alabaster, I mean—the night you spent at Fielding's Folly, when you thought there was a ghost around, do you remember? But you were so suspicious of my motives because I'd come into your room at all that I thought the less I said the better. To think those suspicions are all laid at rest —and how! Why you practically invite me to make love to you these days!"

"Francis, you don't mean——"

"I only mean that you're so sweet you're irresistible. And you're a constant source of surprise to me. With your natural reserve, I wasn't prepared for such a prodigal bride. But you've been magnificent, darling. You've acted from the beginning as if you'd chosen to come to me, as if you wanted me to take you quickly and keep you forever."

"I've acted that way because it's true. I don't know how to pretend."

"Well, you were a revelation to me anyway. It changed everything. Of course, I'd coveted you from the moment I saw you. But that was partly because I knew no one else had been able to get you, because I'd made up my mind to sweep you off your feet first and batter down your resistance afterward. Then when I saw how much you cared, when you gave in of your own accord, I fell in love with you all over again, in a different way. I'm more and more in love with you every day. There isn't time to tell you how much!"

He pulled her gently to her feet, and with his arms still around her, walked slowly over to the railing of the lanai. Silver stars were showing in the sky, already sapphire-colored overhead, though rimmed with iridescence still; a sickle moon was rocking radiantly toward the horizon. Beneath these, a lighted ship was passing, so close that it seemed as if they might almost touch it if they stretched out their hands.

Under all, the languorous swell of the ocean went incessantly on.

"There is something about it all that gets you, isn't there?" Francis said. "I see what you mean too by saying a lanai makes a sort of frame. Do you remember, the day we left San Francisco, how the girl who has the next lanai looked, standing on hers? She took some trailing vines that had come with her flowers and twisted them around the railings, so that they blew out over the water in the breeze. They looked mighty pretty, and so did she. That was a picture all right!"

"Yes, I remember. I thought she was exquisite too, at the time. But since then I've changed my mind. I haven't met her but from the sounds on the other side of the partition, I should say she'd had a succession of rather wild parties. I like that quiet little cousin of hers, Ruth Felton, much better."

"Well, after all, I wouldn't hold the parties against her. Life on shipboard is apt to be rather free and easy, isn't it? That's part of the picture too. At least, I've always heard so. I did meet our neighbor this afternoon and I rather liked her. She's really great fun. Her name is Edith Lasterie. I think you'd enjoy meeting her too. In fact, I told her so when she suggested that we should join her crowd for cocktails."

Momentarily, Eunice stiffened. She had encouraged Francis to range around the ship while she rested. But somehow she had not expected— She answered with careful compliance.

"Of course we'll do it if you'd like to, dear. But that means we should be dressing, doesn't it, right away?"

He had been instantly aware of her slight recoil. Now, with equal quickness, he caught the lack of spontaneity in her voice. The soft pressure of his arm around her waist became insistent.

"No, honey, not right away," he answered. "Won't you make up to me now for all this time I've let you spend alone on the lanai?"

PART III
Kona Weather

~~~~~~

Chapter 5

FRANCIS WAS partly right and partly wrong. They did have another lanai, leading from their suite at the Royal Hawaiian and overlooking the dazzling sands and sparkling waters of Waikiki. But Eunice did not have much chance to lounge around on it.

This did not matter because she was less languid than she had been at first. The rapt readiness of her surrender had represented a revolutionary change in every aspect of her life; and in her swift adaptation to this change, she had drawn on all her reserves of stability. Now her strength had begun to flow back, her course was steady again. At night, she was still unwearied when Francis sank at last into satisfied slumber; and every morning she woke refreshed to face the beauty of a new day.

Sometimes she slipped from his side while he was still sleeping and went out on the lanai before daylight. The colors were different here in Honolulu from those she had seen on the ocean, but they fascinated her in the same way. The sky at this early hour was pearl gray overhead, and shaded strangely into pale lemon behind the jagged darkness of Diamond Head; the palms were sharp black silhouettes against a shadowy shore, the sea somber as indigo. She could always dimly discern the forms of men, swimming out to meet the dawn, and these men shouted as they swam; the ringing sound of their voices roused her to a fuller sense of her own joyousness. If it had not been for Francis, still sleeping in the room beyond, she would have rushed out and plunged in the water herself and joined the shouting swimmers. But the thought of Francis held her back. She wanted to swim, but she wanted still more to be waiting for him when he tumbled out of bed in his turn and came to join her on the lanai.

A Chinese boy, dressed in smooth starched white, brought

them pineapple juice when they rang. They drank it by the pitcher instead of by the glass, and according to all the rules, it should have dulled their appetite for breakfast, but it never did. By and by the Chinese boy came padding back again bringing coffee, which he told them came from Kona, where they were planning to go next if they could ever tear themselves away from Waikiki, and crisp toast and *poha* jam and eggs so fresh that Francis swore the hens which laid them must still be cackling. They ate up every scrap in sight, and smoked a few cigarettes. Then they put on their bathing suits and went down to the beach.

Usually they lay down for a while under the shade of a big umbrella, striped in green and orange. The sand was warm underneath them and the sun was warm over them; they both tanned without burning, their skin turning to a deeper shade of amber day by day, as if it were tinged with the golden sun and the golden sand. They lay close together, holding hands; nobody bothered them or noticed them; a great many other couples were doing the same thing. Sometimes they kept their eyes shut, and let their limbs go limp; sometimes they opened their eyes and sat up long enough to watch the buffoonery of the beach boys. It was the habit of these boys to parade along the sand during the intervals between their duties as life guards, dressed in outlandish costumes and indulging in all sorts of pranks. Their own childlike enjoyment of these seemed quite as wholehearted as the amusement they gave to others; there was something very attractive about it. Francis and Eunice knew that several of them were famous characters, that they were point winners in Olympic games and prize winners in lifesaving contests. But somehow this knowledge made the beach boys' artless antics seem doubly appealing.

The small children who were playing all around, scooping up the warm sand in yellow shovelfuls, were appealing too. Eventually these children always seemed to drop their spades and go racing down to the shallow water where the waves came curling gently in around their small pink feet. Small friendly dogs barked at their heels, and youthful parents, clad in abbreviated bathing suits, held out helping hands as they all went into the sea together.

"Maybe the next time we come here we'll have a couple of kids and a family pet," Francis said jestingly. "Would you like that, darling?"

"Yes—if you would. But I like it the way it is now. Just you and me. What do you say we have a swim ourselves, before lunch?"

"Yes, let's."

Eunice was a good swimmer. She had the same natural

ease in the water that Francis had on a horse. It was she who first suggested that they might take lessons in surfboarding. He was less enthusiastic.

"It might be fun. But why not try the outrigger canoes first?"

"All right. Now?"

"Oh, lady, lady! Just because we got married in a hurry doesn't mean we have to hurry over everything. I'm hungry again. I could do with some lunch."

"So could I. Crabmeat and breadfruit and cream pie, like yesterday."

Luncheon was on the tiled terrace that was adorned with great sapphire-blue jars. The sunshine was tempered here, for overhead was a pergola of banyan, and behind were rose-colored stucco walls and ledges. "Dappled sunshine," Eunice called it. After lunch they went through the long lobby into the tropical garden on the western side of the hotel to find the car which they had rented and which they kept parked there. The residential streets, shaded with blossoming trees, were quiet as they drove through them. No discordant sounds came from the vine-sheltered houses standing in the midst of smooth lawns and surrounded with sweet-smelling hedges. Eunice had already noticed this lack of turmoil, remarkable in a thriving city; now she spoke of it.

"It makes me think of Hamstead on a Sunday morning just before the church bells have begun to ring. It's that kind of quiet. Why even the heat here is different from any other heat! There's something fresh and blowy about it."

"No snakes in your paradise?"

"There aren't, you know. No one has ever seen a snake in the Islands. Are there snakes at Retreat?"

"Lord, yes. Hundreds of them. But only the moccasins and the copperheads are poisonous. The big black ones never do any real harm."

"They—they're way off in the woods, though, aren't they?"

" 'Deed they're not. They're in the underbrush and thickets all over the place. Sometimes they even come crawling along the edges of the garden. It's a wonder we never came to grief with them when we were children and went barefoot all the time. We used to kill them and carry them up to the house on sticks to show Mother. One of the worst disappointments I ever had when I was a youngster was caused by a snake. Father was still alive then and once in a great while he used to take me to the Upperville Colt and Horse Show— I was going to enter my own little colt with the mares and foals and I was sure he'd get a prize. Then the very day before we were to start for the show he was bitten by a snake on the hillside back of the barn."

"Did he die?"

"No. But his leg swelled so he couldn't stand on it and he was spoiled for the entry. Of course he suffered, too. He showed it as plainly as a child. I ought to have been sorry for him when I saw him lying on the ground and rolling his eyes around. But I was a heap sorrier for myself. Because I'd spent my prize money about twenty different ways already."

Francis gave a reminiscent chuckle, half rueful, half happy. Eunice knew that he loved to talk about his own little colt, and about horses and shows and racing generally. She wished she could indicate a more intelligent interest in them all. And she wished she had not asked about the snakes, for she had a horror of them that went far deeper than mere timidity. It had never occurred to her that there might be snakes at Retreat. She resolved to have all the underbrush cut away and the garden thoroughly cleared; she would write a letter about it that very evening. Meanwhile, she made a resolute effort to be gay again.

Eunice and Francis were already fairly familiar with the lay of the land. When they had left the city behind them they began to traverse plantations where pineapples grew on the highland and sugar on the lowland, both wafting a peculiar perfume into the warm air. They stopped the car to watch a water buffalo laboring through a sodden field, and at the Pali to see the sun set in fiery glory beyond the great cliff and the little islands which dotted the smooth surface of the water. As darkness closed quickly down on them after the fleeting twilight, Francis suggested they should try a Chinese restaurant they had heard was good——

Lau Yee Chai proved to be most attractive, extending in a succession of courtyards and gardens over a space much more considerable than was evident from the outside. The proprietor, an elderly and dignified Cantonese, clad in somber rich brocade, greeted his patrons personally with a low bow, and after one shrewd glance at Francis and Eunice, he led them to a small private dining room adorned with painted carvings. Presently the table was laid with Cantonware— and a huge melon, cooked to the point of succulency, was brought in and set down before them, followed by countless other delicacies. There were boneless chicken wings mixed with mustard vegetable and chicken livers mixed with olive nuts; there were broiled duck and fried duck, each served with a different seaweed. And finally there were almond tea and litchei tea and rice——

"Do you think you can still stagger out and listen to the beach boys?" Francis inquired, as they swallowed the last of the Chinese sweetmeats that had been set before them. "Talk about dining day in King George County—why, it's nothing but a famine compared to this! Were you ever so full in all your life?"

"No, never. But I wouldn't miss the concert for anything."

"The concert" was a wholly impromptu affair which the beach boys who were not on duty staged almost every evening. They sat in the small wooden pavilion at the end of a long pier, playing on ukuleles and steel guitars, and singing old Island melodies as they did so. Apparently they had no set program. They played and paused, and played again. One of them spontaneously struck up a tune, and the others joined in it. Their voices were sweet and wistful, their music haunting. People came again and again to listen to it. The pier and the surrounding beach were always crowded with listeners.

Francis and Eunice took their places among the many others who were already there. Diamond Head was as black as ebony now. Its outline against the soft, star-spangled sky looked even more jagged than it did in the daylight. The waves rolling in across the sand made a crisp, rushing sound. The voices of the beach boys rose above it:

> *"Aloha means we welcome you, it means more than*
> *words can say,*
> *Aloha means good luck to you, good night at the end*
> *of day.*
> *It's just like a love song with its haunting sweet refrain,*
> *Bringing you joy and bringing you pain,*
> *Aloha means farewell to you, until we meet again."*

On the evenings when there were dances at the Royal Hawaiian, Eunice and Francis did not go to hear the beach boys sing. They dined very late, on the paved terrace, and instead of sitting far back under the pergola as they did at lunchtime, they reserved a table at the very edge of the open-air dance floor beside one of the tall columns which rose in a row at right angles to a double line of palm trees. The white monkey jacket of the tropics was becoming to Francis; and as his bride's eyes rested fondly on him, she began to realize that he would wear everything equally well, that it was his own charm that had given grace and dash to his hunting togs and his sports shirts, and no essential quality in the clothes themselves. Her own evening dresses were as flawless as her riding habits, and every night two fresh *leis* were sent to her room, and she chose between them which she would wear. Her choice was nearly always the same, and she went down to dinner wreathed in white carnations; there were no other flowers that had such a clean, spicy scent,

68

none that still looked so fresh when the evening was over. She took the second *lei*, the one she did not choose to wear, and garlanded the bed with it. There were nearly always several *leis* on every bedpost, for they lasted from one night to another, and Francis often bought her extra ones during the day besides—ginger blossom, plumeria, mauna loa. She loved her *leis*. Often she stood fingering them caressingly the last thing at night. Finally she made up verses about them.

"When you were a little boy," she said to Francis, "did you ever recite that rhyme about the four angels?"

"The four angels? No— I recited one about the three bears and another about the five little pigs, but I don't remember any about four angels."

"It went like this:

> *'Four corners to my bed,*
> *Four angels at my head.*
> *Matthew, Mark, Luke and John*
> *Bless the bed that I lie on.'* "

"And so what?"

"And so now I've made up a new version to it. Listen!

> *'Four corners to my bed,*
> *Four angels at my head.*
> *A blessing comes and a blessing stays,*
> *When my bed is wreathed with leis.'* "

"Very pretty. Were you by any chance thinking of me, when you referred to a blessing? Because I'm coming to bed now, and I'm certainly going to stay there."

Several times Eunice remembered the letters of introduction she had brought with her to Hawaii with strict instructions from her grandmother and her stepfather, respectively, to see that these were promptly delivered. Mrs. Hale had gone to school with the daughter of an outstanding missionary; Patrick Hogan had business affiliations with several steamboat and sugar magnates. But these connections seemed to Eunice inconsequential. She did not want to meet strangers, she did not want to be with anyone but Francis. She was determined to keep him to herself. It was different here, from the boat. He had not once suggested leaving her, so far. When he did—she thought of the inevitable moment with a pang, resolving to postpone it by every means in her power, and redoubling her efforts to please him as he began to give a few signs of restiveness. Tardily, she had almost made up her mind that it might be better to establish some outside contacts after all, when the intrusion upon their solitude, which she had so greatly dreaded, unexpectedly came.

They had nearly finished their dinner when she noticed that Francis was not listening to her with undivided attention. She paused to follow his wandering glance and saw that this was fixed on a couple coming across the dance floor in the direction of their table. The man was powerfully built and very dark; Eunice had heard that there were several distinguished families of Portuguese extraction on the Islands, and the thought crossed her mind that perhaps he belonged to one of these. But her observation of him was only passing, for when she turned from him to look at the girl beside him, she was startled to see that this was Edith Lasterie, dressed in glittering gauze which matched her golden curls, and wearing a double *lei* of gardenias.

As Edith moved forward, the scent of her flowers seemed to float in front of her and perfume the air all around her. She kept looking up over her shoulder at the man who was with her, whose heavy brows and thick hair looked all the blacker beside her yellow locks, and whose size seemed immense in comparison to her dainty figure. She was chattering gaily and smiling archly. But she continued to walk steadily in the direction of the table where Eunice and Francis were sitting; it was her manifest destination. Upon reaching it, with one last languishing look at her escort, she held out both of her fairylike hands to Francis.

"I'm so *thrilled* to see you again!" she exclaimed. "I was *terrified* that you'd go on to Japan before I got back from Maui— I transshipped, you know, the very day we landed, to visit there. What have you been doing all this time? Just the usual tourist things, I suppose—the beach, and the Pali, and Lau Yee Chai. What a pity! If I'd only been here I could have arranged it all so differently for you. Oh—I almost forgot— May I present Mr. Wood? Mr. and Mrs. Fielding."

"Won't you sit down?" Eunice asked. She hated to hear her own voice sounding so cold and formal. But she could not control it. Edith had shaken hands with her belatedly and casually after her effusive greeting of Francis; now, hardly waiting to be asked, she had seated herself beside him, leaning her elbows on the table and commencing a conversation that was as animated as it was frothy. Eunice thought she had never seen a girl as ill-bred as Edith. At the same time, she knew she had never seen one who was so beautiful.

"Would you care to dance?" Edith's escort inquired of Eunice.

She was unprepared for the invitation. It had not occurred to her that she would be asked to dance by anyone but Francis, and courteously as the suggestion had been made, it was unwelcome to her. She answered hesitatingly, her voice still cold and formal.

"It's very kind of you. But I'm a little tired. I think I won't, if you'll excuse me."

"Why, Mrs. Fielding, you can't *mean* it! Every girl who comes to the Islands is simply *dying* for the chance to meet Crispin Wood. They stand in *rows,* waiting, don't they, Penny? And when he asks them to *dance——*"

Edith spread out her exquisite hands as if to indicate that this represented the acme of bliss. Crispin Wood answered with a slight show of impatience.

"You'll give these *malahinis* a bad impression of the Islands. Edith, if you talk like that— I don't want to be insistent. Mrs. Fielding, but I do wish you'd reconsider."

"She has already. Haven't you, Eunice?"

When Francis spoke like that, Eunice knew that she had no choice. She rose, deliberately, and stepped slowly toward the dance floor. It required all her will power not to glance back at Edith Lasterie, whose little pointed white chin was now resting on her small clasped hands, and whose flowerlike face was upturned toward Francis's, just as a few minutes earlier it had been upturned toward Crispin Wood's. They would talk laughingly together, like that, for a moment or two, and then Francis would ask her to dance. That was what he had wanted. He had not cared a rap whether Eunice danced with Crispin Wood or not. But he himself had been eager for the excuse to dance with Edith Lasterie.

It was immaterial to Eunice that Crispin Wood really did dance very well indeed. Like many powerfully built men, he was extremely light on his feet, and it seemed to require no effort on his part to maintain rhythmic motion. It was quite conceivable that many girls might be quite as eager to dance with him as Francis was to dance with Edith Lasterie. He was very good looking, too, in his dark strange way; he had presence and sophistication. Eunice tried to think of something to say to him, wishing that she did not feel like a raw schoolgirl besides feeling angry. She kept asking herself when she had first been jealous of Edith Lasterie, whether the sensation had crept up on her gradually or whether it had begun at some specific moment. She was not sure, but she thought her resentment had arisen from Edith's insistence that she herself should take part in one of those wild shipboard parties. She had been perfectly content to have Francis range around the boat while she rested on the lanai. She had never dreamed— Yes, that was it, she had hated being dragged into the noise and the confusion and the vulgarity

71

of Edith Lasterie's crowd. And Francis had not minded. He had enjoyed it. That had been the worst of all. But since Edith had left for Maui, he had never once spoken of her, and Eunice supposed he had forgotten all about her. She had almost forgotten Edith herself, she had been so happy in Honolulu. And now Edith was back again, deriding everything she had thought so beautiful, sidling up to Francis and babbling baby talk in his ear——

"I'm so glad Edith has presented me to you at last. I saw you and your husband the day you landed when I went down to meet her. But there didn't seem to be a chance to meet you then."

Crispin Wood was taking the lead in conversation as expertly as he took it in dancing. Eunice managed to make a conventional response.

"Are you and she old friends?"

"Oh, yes! She comes out from the Mainland almost every year. She's one of the type that doesn't seem to have any settled abode, that just goes from ship to ship and continent to continent with a trunkful of fluffy clothes and a large assortment of winning ways. I always see a good deal of her when she's here."

Crispin Wood did not speak as if he were madly in love with Edith Lasterie, or even as if she had made a deep impression of any sort upon him. Eunice felt vaguely comforted as he went on talking.

"She's coming down to stay at my place on Kauai next week. I'd be delighted if you and your husband would come too."

"You don't live in Honolulu then?"

"Oh, I have a little shakedown here, too. But next week I'm going to be in Kauai. I think you'd enjoy it there."

"It's very kind of you. But I'm not sure just how soon we'll be leaving for Japan."

"You shouldn't do that until you've seen all the Islands. You haven't any real reason for hurry, have you?"

"No-o-o. But we hadn't thought of going anywhere else except to the Kona Inn."

"You don't need to go to the Kona Inn just now. We're having Kona weather all over the Islands. Not to mention moonlight that can compete with Kona's too!"

He began to hum a gay little song, under his breath, that Eunice had not heard before.

" 'Pretty soon, pretty soon
      The moon will be shining over Kona
      A fairer sight I never hope to see——' "

72

"Does Kona have a special kind of weather and a special moon too? I thought it was just coffee!"

She was beginning to feel better in spite of herself. She had glanced covertly about the dance floor and she had not seen Francis and Edith anywhere. Perhaps she had misjudged Francis, perhaps he had not been so crazy to dance with Edith after all.

"Kona has all kinds of specialties. The weather is one of the most important of all. It is very warm and relaxing —balmy is the word the Tourist Bureau uses, in case you didn't know. We Hawaiians have a saying that almost anything can happen during a spell of Kona weather."

"Do you believe it?"

"Yes, indeed! We're a superstitious lot."

Her interest was fast getting the better of her anger. The way he said "we Hawaiians" piqued her curiosity. Was it possible that he meant this in the literal sense, that he really had Hawaiian blood? She had heard that in the families where an admixture of this existed, there was pride and not shame in the original strain; but she had not believed it before. Now, quietly appraising Crispin Wood, she thought it might be true. It was stupid of her not to have remembered the Hawaiian kings when she thought of the great Portuguese families.

"You haven't answered my question about coming to Kauai. I hope you are not trying to dodge it."

"No, really I'm not. But you see——"

"Well, come to my table for the time being, anyway. We can talk about the other later. Edith's cousin, Ruth Felton, is there with an English friend of mine, Guy Grenville. I told them I'd try to persuade you to join us. I believe Edith is going to bring your husband along too, later."

The remark was unfortunate. It struck the first discordant note. But Eunice had no time to dwell on it, for the music had stopped and Crispin Wood was already guiding her toward his table, halfway across the dance floor from the place where she and Francis had been sitting. It stood apart from all the others, both as to position and as to adornment. Almost the only critical remark that Eunice had been moved to make was in regard to the floral decorations at the hotel. These invariably consisted of several hibiscus flowers, none of which matched, stiffly imbedded in laurel leaves. Once she had gone so far as to ask if it would not be possible to have all pink or all red or all yellow, for a change, instead of an inharmonious mixture. The boy to whom the question was put had stared at her with Oriental impassivity, and without answering. Crispin Wood evidently had other means of management. The loveliest lilies Eunice had ever seen were lightly scattered over a lace cloth amidst ornaments of white jade. The goblets and service plates were made of etched crystal. The silverware was crested. It was indubitably the table set to suit a man whose whim it was to have special service, whose taste was impeccable, and whose means permitted him to gratify both. In her increasing bewilderment over Crispin Wood, Eunice turned to look at Ruth Felton, feeling that this unremarkable person should prove reassuring at such a juncture.

She had never seen Edith's mouselike little cousin look so colorless. The drabness of Ruth's hair, the dullness of her complexion, the dowdiness of her clothes—all these seemed intensified in comparison to the brilliance of her surroundings. A wilted *lei* of purple mauna loa hung limply around her scrawny neck, and Eunice thought pityingly that Ruth could not possibly have chosen a color which would more relentlessly reveal the sallowness of her skin. She had on a dress of printed silk, figured in sprawling flowers, which looked as if it had been made for a much larger woman and then cut down for her. Her thick glasses, as usual, were sliding far down on her shining nose. Nevertheless she was beaming about her with her customary good will, and the unmistakable sincerity of her cordial greeting was soothing to Eunice.

"Mrs. Fielding! I'm so glad to see you again! It seems ages already since we left the ship, doesn't it? I can't believe that it's only a little over a week! You haven't met Mr. Grenville, have you? May I have the pleasure of presenting him to you? He's a visitor in the Islands, like ourselves. I've been comparing notes with him. I'm sure you'll want to do the same."

Eunice achieved an adequate answer and sat down in the chair the blond Englishman pulled out for her. He was very tall, almost as tall as Crispin Wood; but he was slender, like Francis, and his skin was as smooth and rosy as a schoolboy's. This glowing complexion, combined with his slimness, gave him an air of extreme youth, in spite of his small mustache and his finished manner of speaking. Eunice wondered if he were taking a trip around the world too, perhaps as a complement to his studies, and presently she put her mental question into words.

"No, I came down from Oxford four years ago," he said pleasantly. "I'm on my way to the States—beg pardon, Penny, the Mainland—from the Straits Settlements. I live in Singapore."

"I've heard it's a charming city. My husband and I thought we might break our trip there."

"I hope you will, and that you'll let me know when you

74

pass through. I'll surely be back before you get there. I don't expect to be in the States long."

"On the Mainland," corrected Crispin Wood, motioning to a waiter. "What will you take to drink, Mrs. Fielding?"

"Pineapple juice, if I may— Is there a joke about the Mainland?"

"It isn't a joke at all, Mrs. Fielding. These Hawaiians are obsessed with the idea that they must keep impressing you with the fact that the Islands are 'an integral part of the United States.' If you can remember that, without prompting, Penny will be your willing slave."

"I'm that already, of course. I don't care what she calls them, as long as she stays on them. I'm trying to persuade her to come to Kauai with us next week."

"I've a notion you shouldn't miss it, Mrs. Fielding. Penny says the sands bark and the sugar cane rustles, and I don't know what more besides. There's even something about a spouting horn and a rock called the sliding bathtub. And there's a cave— What is it that happens in the cave, Penny? Nymphs have been said to swim there, is that it?"

"Known to swim there," corrected Crispin Wood. "Do you really want pineapple juice, Mrs. Fielding? I've some exceptionally good ginger ale."

He motioned to the waiter again, and the boy came forward and filled Eunice's glass. She lifted it, and began to sip the contents slowly. It was not ginger ale at all, though it had certainly been poured out of a ginger-ale bottle. It was superlatively good champagne. She looked across at her host in astonishment.

"Island magic," he said with a smile. "I told you almost anything might happen during a spell of Kona weather. I might even persuade you to come to Kauai. At all events, I'm going to continue trying, during the next dance."

"During the next but one," remarked Guy Grenville, rising and offering a correction in his turn. "This one, I hope, is mine."

Chapter 6

EUNICE HAD never met a man she liked as much as Guy Grenville. He did not fascinate her like Francis, or puzzle her like Crispin Wood, but she felt he was her friend from the moment she saw him.

There were ample opportunities for the development of this friendship. The tenor of life on Crispin Wood's plantation was unhurried and informal. The ranch house itself was

75

a T-shaped white clapboarded building with a wide paved terrace on one side of it, and a long gallery, from which hanging plants were suspended, extending the full length of the upper story. Its floors were smoothly tiled, with typical Island rugs of closely braided straw resting upon them; and its walls were smoothly paneled, with paintings of typical Island scenes hanging upon them. A dining room which could, and often did, seat more than twenty persons, and a big music room where a grand piano was in constant use, both opened from the spacious hallway. But it was through the so-called "gun room" beyond that most of the leisurely life flowed. The dominating feature of this room was a bed, double the size of a large four-poster, which was made of *koa* wood, and which had formerly belonged to one of the Hawaiian kings; it was equipped with an enormous mattress and innumerable pillows covered with *tapa* cloth, and it served both as an outstanding ornament and a luxurious lounge. Various great vessels, also made of *koa* wood, and several of the stone balls once used for bowling, were among the other decorations in the room. It also contained a big desk and a still bigger fireplace, bookcases that were filled to overflowing, and a tall gun rack full of firearms. Flowers, magazines and cigarette stands were scattered all around it; and a bridge table stood invitingly near a large recessed window which framed the fields beyond it.

Crispin Wood's guests drifted in and out of this room at will. It made surprisingly little difference whether he were actually there in the flesh or not, the imprint which his personality had stamped on the place was so strong. The visitors spent a large part of their time there, returning only intermittently to the guest cottage—slightly separated from the main ranch house—which he had placed completely at their disposal and to which he never came at all, once he had seen them settled in their quarters and assured himself of their comfort. A smiling little Japanese maid, whose gay kimono was belted around her with a wide, stiff-bowed *obi*, and whose white-stockinged feet were thrust into wicker sandals, brought morning coffee and afternoon tea to the cottage, and appeared frequently at other hours with flowers she had arranged and proffers of personal service for the guests. But half the time she found them all gone when she made her careful rounds, and crouched quietly down in a corner awaiting their delayed return without either impatience or resentment.

Edith and Ruth and Guy were already installed in the guest cottage when Francis and Eunice arrived at the ranch. Their rooms were all adjacent, leading in a row from the lanai which they all shared, but where Edith's presence and personality seemed predominant. She fluttered out on it in a filmy negligee before and after her bath. She lay at ease in the swinging seat placed cater-cornered at the end of it, a small slippered foot tapping the floor and keeping the couch in motion. She dropped a sequined scarf when she went in to dinner, a pair of tiny gloves when she returned from riding; they lay indefinitely where she left them, exquisite and unescapable. Her prattle never ceased, and the scent she used lingered in the air. Her appearance was fairylike, her manner melting, her tones coy. But these outer attributes of hers were misleading. Coiled within her daintiness, there was a quality of deadly determination.

Eunice felt that only Crispin Wood's complete self-sufficiency, and his tactful, but conclusive way of drawing attention to this, prevented Edith from insinuating herself into the place left vacant by the absence of a hostess, where her position, as a substitute, would be duly recognized and acknowledged by the other guests, even though it were unofficial. But she made no headway in her efforts, arch, persuasive and untiring as these were. Crispin never failed in courtesy to her; but he paid her no tribute, and he made it clear that he was far from expecting anyone else to do so for his sake.

Ruth Felton was as retiring as Edith was presumptuous. She had never learned to ride and betrayed such fright at the mere suggestion that she should get upon a horse that the effort to include her in morning rides was soon abandoned. She swam puffingly and painfully, with the old-fashioned breast stroke, holding her chin high out of the water; the idea of shooting down the "sliding bathtub" into an abysmal pool was terrifying to her also. She was willing to play tennis, but her game was so poor that nobody cared to take her on. So she was happiest when allowed to sit in a rocking chair on the lawn of resilient grass which mantled the knoll where the ranch house and the guest cottage stood, watching the Japanese gardener who puttered about among the flower beds, the mother turkey which strutted proudly past, and the five setter puppies which tumbled playfully about. Ruth kept yards of needlepoint spread out around her on which she stitched now and then. The work she did on this strained her nearsighted eyes, but it suited her timid spirit.

She always urged the others to leave her behind when they went junketing off to various parts of the island; and Guy Grenville was apt to say that he was not in the mood for violent exercise either, that he would much rather rest and read. As a matter of fact, his reading was almost as desultory as Ruth's embroidery, but he was less absorbed in his immediate surroundings than she was. It was beyond the knoll that he liked best to gaze, at the wide fields overlaid by a vast patchwork, the seams rich earth, the stripes sturdy pine-apple plants. He was a planter of sorts himself, he explained to Ruth, in the course of casual conversation. It was rubber that he knew most about, but he liked to study other products also, and to his mind there was no better method than to sit still and watch them grow.

He did not talk very much. Sometimes he puffed away at a pipe without speaking at all for an entire hour. But he knew how to make silence companionable. Eunice would have been glad to spend more of her own time in such tranquilizing propinquity, instead of in the provocative presence of Crispin Wood. She thought scornfully of Ruth's timidity about horses and water, but she herself was beginning to feel something akin to fear as far as her host was concerned. She had resented his intrusive entrance into her life from the beginning, and she bitterly regretted the weakness she had shown in permitting Francis to win her reluctant consent to the Kauai visit.

For it was Francis, not Crispin, who had done this. She had withstood all Crispin's cajolery; but her objections had melted away under Francis's teasing. She had been both puzzled and pained because he was so eager to accept the invitation. One of his arguments was that he would feel more as if he were at home on a ranch than he did at a hotel. She had not realized that he wanted to feel as if he were at home. She had taken it for granted that the unknown and the unfamiliar had the same fascination for him as they did for her. She was happy when she was at Hamstead, but Evergreen was not an integral part of her being; she had always welcomed an opportunity to travel widely and she found it hard to understand how any man could have such a passionate attachment to one place as Francis had for Retreat. She tried to reason with him that this was provincial and met with a retort that came as a shock to her.

"It may be prehistoric, for all I know. But it's a fact you'll have to accept. I belong at Retreat just the same way my blood and my bones belong in my body. I'd have told you so long ago, if you'd bothered to ask me. I didn't suppose you needed to be told. But another thing you didn't bother to ask me was whether I really hankered to go around the world or not. I didn't like to make an issue of that point either, just then. But if I'd had my way we'd have spent our honeymoon at Retreat."

"With your mother and brothers and sisters! I think that will take enough adjustment later on, without having to do it in the beginning!"

"Perhaps you ought to have thought over that aspect of the case a little more thoroughly then, for you'll certainly have to do it later on. But I didn't mean to ask you to do it in the beginning. There's a little lodge over by the marshes that could have been made quite habitable—and we could have put all the money the trip is costing into the plantation."

She was too hurt to pursue the question any further, too proud to remind him that she had already arranged for the restoration of Retreat at her expense. But she made a final effort to prolong the seclusion she considered so ideal and which she had fondly hoped would satisfy Francis indefinitely also. The futility of her attempt had been a further blow to her pride. Francis had been perfectly pleasant throughout their discussion; he had treated it lightly and laughingly, as he treated everything. But he had not yielded a single point, and Eunice was chagrined that her wishes should carry so little weight, besides being humiliated to find that his contentment alone with her was so ephemeral. There was an element in her silence, as she prepared for departure from the Royal Hawaiian, that was almost sulky; and the fact that Francis blithely disregarded this only intensified her resentment. It was still deep when she reached Kauai after a rough over-night voyage on a small inter-island boat and began to unpack and arrange her possessions in the pleasant room furnished with a high old-fashioned "dresser" and a sleigh bed, which had been assigned to her in Crispin Wood's guest cottage.

It was at this point that the ubiquitous Japanese maid appeared for the first time, balancing a tray in one hand and a box in the other. Perched on top of each, as airily as a white butterfly, was a small envelope containing a short note.

"Your husband called you honey, which is his great prerogative—" the note on the tray ran— "but I can at least send you some. This is made from the blossoms of *keawe* trees on my Molokai ranch. I hope you will enjoy it."

The other note was written in similar vein. "Pansies are for thoughts. Perhaps you knew this. But evidently you did not know they were for *leis* too. At least I have not seen you wearing a pansy *lei*, and I think they are the loveliest of all. It will please me very much if you will wear the one in this box."

"I am very much afraid that I have a rival," Francis observed. He was standing with his arm around Eunice, looking over her shoulder, his chin resting against her hair as she read the note, and he spoke with his usual pleasant raillery. Her reaction to his jesting remark, however, was as serious as if he had made it in all earnestness. She answered him accusingly.

"How can you say such a thing? You know it isn't true!"

" 'Methinks the lady doth protest too much!' Of course it's true. Crispin Wood fell in love with you at first sight, just as

79

I did. And I'm terribly worried. He is supposed to be irresistible."

"You're not insinuating anything, are you, Francis?"

"Certainly not. Insinuations are so pointless. I'm only stating obvious facts. Haven't you discovered even yet, in addition to all his personal attractions, Crispin Wood is the richest man in Hawaii and the most powerful?"

"His personal attractions don't mean anything to me, or his money and his power either, and you know it. I didn't want to come here, and you know that too. It was you who insisted upon it."

"Of course. I was consumed with curiosity to see a sample of his famous establishments. He has one on every island. I thought that might have filtered through to you also. Surely you wouldn't want me to go on to Japan without learning all I could about this 'Paradise of the Pacific?' "

For the first time she shook herself free from him. "Just what do you mean by an establishment?" she asked tersely.

"Why—an enormous ranch and a wonderful house and manservants and maidservants and strangers within the gates. Lavish and luxurious living."

"Is that all?"

"Isn't it enough? Since you press me, however, I'll admit I'd gathered there was usually a lovely lady in residence wherever Crispin Wood happened to be. Not always the same lovely lady. Sometimes several in swift sequence. Sometimes several simultaneously. He would have been delighted to fit you into the picture in either case."

"You insisted on bringing me to a house which you thought would be a sort of seraglio?"

"Of course not. Each lady lives on a different island. The lay of the land here makes tactful separations of that sort very simple."

She stared at him speechlessly. Her anger had amused him. But now that abhorrence was mingled with it, his instinct warned him that he had gone too far. He caught her to him again, so quickly that she had no chance to draw away.

"Eunice, darling, what a funny little sober-sides you are! Of course I was only joking about the lovely ladies. Unless you insist on counting Ruth in, there aren't any here except you and Edith—not that you aren't both lovely enough to knock a man's eyes out! But propriety is certainly your middle name, and I'm sure it's Edith's too! Come now, eat your honey, and then put on your *lei,* and afterward we'll go over to the ranch house together and thank Penny Royal for both."

It took both time and tact to persuade her. She remained resentful and suspicious all day. But in spite of her wariness, she neither saw nor heard anything that could offend her, and finally her resentment subsided and her suspicions were stilled. She tried to accept Crispin Wood's adroit courtesies on their face value, and resolutely refrained from attributing any special significance to the constant attentions which Francis showered on Edith. Meanwhile, she came to think more and more gratefully and warmly of Guy Grenville.

Nearly a week passed before a second disturbing episode occurred. The day had been a delightful one. In the morning they had all motored over to the veiled but vivid valley known as Waimea Canyon, and Eunice freely admitted that nothing she had so far seen in the Islands appeared so beautiful to her. Clouds were drifting lightly across it as they approached; mists rose ethereally from its depths; all the landscape seemed mantled with mystery. Then a rainbow flashed suddenly across it and it was flooded with iridescence. Its towering walls of deep red rock, its rich and brilliant verdure shone with reflected radiance. It had become a dwelling place of light.

They lingered indefinitely beside the brim of the canyon, watching its changing colors and its mounting mists. Eunice especially was reluctant to leave; she was sure the rest of the expedition would prove an anticlimax; but she had been happily surprised in this respect too. They descended by an obscure road sheltered with overhanging hills to the secluded beach of Lawai, smooth and serene of aspect, but treacherous as to undertow, from which wide green lawns swept back toward luxuriant trees. Here, half hidden by the florid shrubbery, they found a small frame house of vague protective coloring where, Crispin told them, Good Queen Emma used to seek—and find—tranquillity and respite and—who knew? —perhaps a little romance, too. Then leaving this remote retreat, they mounted the winding precipitous hill again and swung out along the open coast, coming upon a promontory formed of dark volcanic rock, where a few frugal fishermen stood patiently swinging out their lines near a blow-hole on the stony beach from which a jet of water leaped with geyser-like force, its spray spreading like smoke over the water.

Eunice watched this "Spouting Horn" with fascinated eyes. There is always a spellbound sensation in observing a phenomenon which never exactly duplicates its own astounding tour de force! And when at last she turned reluctantly away from it, she realized how insidiously the "infinite variety" of Kauai's charm was taking hold of her. Each hour was bringing its own new revelation—the illuminated canyon, the sand, the sea, the shore. Yet it was not until she finally went among the fields of cane that she touched the innermost spirit of Kauai.

It was Crispin who suggested that they should bring their outing to an end by a walk through these fields, and Eunice's assent was enthusiastic. She had already regarded them with attention from afar. Guy Grenville's remark that any sort of a planter should learn all he could about products alien to his own had aroused her interest. She felt certain her grandmother would have felt the same way; and she resolved to increase her own slender store of knowledge, in order to pass it on to the valiant little owner of Evergreen. In the beginning the readiness of her response to Crispin's suggestion had been based mainly on this desire; but it swiftly became less detached. The cane closed in upon her with a sound that was like the rustle of silk, rising rich and ripe about her on every side. For, following Crispin's lead, she was making no mere progress along a bordered highway; she was penetrating into the deep heart of a vast plantation, on narrow trails which wound for miles and miles of lofty waving stalks. The fragrant forests which these formed were sweet with scent. They were in themselves beautiful, with the sort of secret beauty which does not reveal itself to the superficial gaze; and they possessed symbolic beauty also, for they testified to Hawaii's proud place in the world's great marts. The fluid which flowed so freely in these fragrant forests was more than potential food for millions upon millions; it was the very life blood of the Islands themselves. She knew that if its course should cease, their strength would end with its passing. The consciousness of this was brought home to her in the cane fields as it had been nowhere else. She went on and on, penetrating to their depths, smelling their scent, listening to their sounds, sharing their solitude.

It was a poignant experience. When the first rapture of it had passed, the sense of its significance still lingered. Eunice was so absorbed that she was startled when she felt Crispin touch her lightly on the arm and heard him speak solicitously.

"I really think we better turn back. We've come a long way. It'll be dark before we know it."

"Will it? I'd lost all track of time. This was wonderful, Crispin! Are we separated from the others?"

"I think we've gone a little farther than they have. I haven't seen or heard them for a while. Of course, it's impossible to keep more than two abreast, at the most, on these trails, and they branch out in all directions. But don't worry. Guy knows them almost as well as I do. So he'll look after Ruth. And I heard Edith saying she was tired already, that she didn't want to walk very far."

"There isn't any reason why I *should* worry, is there?"

"Of course not. I'm sure we'll find all the others waiting for us at the ranch house when we get there ourselves."

But they did not. Ruth and Guy were there, already dressed for dinner; but nothing had been seen or heard of Edith and Francis. Like most planters, Crispin dined early, and though life was so informal during the daytime, he liked to invest the evening with a certain amount of ceremony. The long table in the dining room was already decorated with sprays of rainbow shower, scattered on every side of a silver basket, which was filled with palm flowers and alamanda; and six young Hawaiian girls, who often came in to sing while dinner was being served, were waiting on the paved terrace, dressed in white, with small round bouquets of red roses placed over their hearts and wreaths encircling their flowing hair.

They were still clustered there, whispering and giggling a little, when Eunice returned from the guest cottage after dressing herself. Crispin was already in the drawing room manipulating the shaker which held the *okolakao* cocktails. He filled a glass and held it out to her with a smile.

"Aloha nui! You need this, after your long walk!"

She accepted it from him mechanically and turned toward Guy with troubled eyes.

"What do you suppose has become of Edith and Francis?"

"I told you there was nothing to worry about," cut in Crispin.

"Penny knows, Eunice. He'd tell you if there were," Guy said reassuringly.

"Don't people get lost in the sugar cane sometimes?" She asked persistently.

"Yes. When they go wandering about in long lanes that are unfamiliar to them. But not when they stay on the fringes of it, in plain sight of the open fields."

"They may have changed their minds. They may have decided to go farther in, after all."

"Edith never changes her mind. When she says she doesn't want to do a thing, she doesn't do it. And she didn't want to take a long walk today."

"Then what *can* have happened?"

"I can't imagine," said Crispin dryly.

The irony of his voice was unmistakable. Eunice recoiled from it as if he had struck her. Suddenly she felt that she could not stay where she was another instant, that she must escape from the humiliation that overwhelmed her. She set down her untasted cocktail with a shaking hand and started blindly back toward the guest cottage. But though she walked so unseeingly, her sensitivity to sound was magnified. Guy was saying something in an undertone to Crispin Wood, and while his words were hushed, she heard every syllable.

"Wouldn't it be better to let her believe that he *is* lost?"

"I don't see why. I think the sooner she learns to face facts, the freer she'll feel. And the happier, incidentally."

She put her hands over her ears so that she would not hear any more. Still holding them there, she stumbled into her room and sat down on the edge of the sleigh bed, shaking with such sobs that she could hardly keep her balance. Again she lost all track of time. She heard the little Japanese maid at the door, stealthily setting down a tray and shuffling off again, without speaking. She knew then that her own absence had been accepted, that she was not expected for dinner, that she would be left unmolested. The knowledge gave her a sense of respite, but it brought with it no lasting solace. She tried to ask herself the same question that Guy had put to Crispin, and to find an answer for it. Would she rather believe that Francis was lost than that he was false? She did not know, she could not decide. But other questions came crowding in upon her. When he returned, could she believe what he told her? Could she *pretend* to believe what he told her? Would it be better if she did so pretend, or if she forced herself to face facts? How could the latter course possibly make for happiness? She was sure of only one thing: it was not freedom she wanted, but bondage. In trustful submission she had been almost delirious with joy. It was only with doubting revolt that misery had come. If she shook off the chains which bound her to Francis, she knew that supreme wretchedness would be the result.

She was still sitting on the edge of the bed when he came in at midnight and told her that he had been lost. He said he was amazed that Crispin Wood had not sent out a search party. He added that it was incomprehensible to him that she and Ruth should have shown so little consideration of Edith. If they had not gone streaking off, with Crispin and Guy, he and Edith would not have become bewildered in the branching lanes. Now Edith was prostrated with exhaustion and shock, and it was all their fault. It was quite possible that she might have a severe illness. There was a dangerous chill in the night air. As far as that went, he felt ill himself. And he was certainly exhausted.

He did not even say good night when he lay down beside her. Eunice remained staring out into the darkness, rigid with cold and fear.

Chapter 7

IT WAS still very early, according to Mainland standards, when Eunice quietly crossed the flagstones leading from the guest cottage to the ranch house and entered the gun room. But Crispin Wood was already there, sitting at the table in the recessed window overlooking the fields and scowling slightly at the cards spread out before him. He rose with a pleased change of expression as Eunice approached.

"Do come over here and help me," he said invitingly. "I've dealt myself six hands and haven't been able to do a thing with any one of them, in spite of some very expert cheating."

"I'm afraid I wouldn't be of much assistance. I always overlook all my chances, at Canfield."

"Well, so long as you don't overlook them in more important matters— What about playing checkers with me then?"

"Checkers?" she repeated. She had always thought of checkers as a child's game. It seemed to her fantastic that a man of Crispin Wood's sophistication should consider playing it.

"Why, yes. There's nothing like a nice quiet game of checkers to refresh a tired planter in the middle of the forenoon."

"The middle of the forenoon!" Eunice exclaimed, involuntarily echoing his words a second time.

"Why, yes," he said again. "Don't forget I've been up since four-thirty—it's the regular rising hour around here. Not that I ever enforce it on my guests, like some of my neighbors. One of them even surreptitiously sets the clock ahead an hour when he goes to bed, so that he can get them up at three-thirty. He shuts off all the electricity by nine o'clock at night, too. They have to be in bed then."

"Is he crazy?"

"No, just Scotch. As a matter of fact, he's a rather agreeable fellow. You'll meet him tonight. He's coming here to a *poi* supper."

"A *poi* supper?"

"Yes. Own cousin—or perhaps I should say blood brother!—to a *luau*. The only real difference between a *luau* and a *poi* supper is that you eat the former under the trees and the latter on the lanai. You know what a *luau* is, don't you?"

"Vaguely. But, Crispin, I came to tell you——"

"A *luau* is our traditional Hawaiian feast," Crispin went on, as if she had not started to say anything. He had a way of interrupting when the trend of conversation was not wholly to his liking, but he did it so affably that he never sounded rude. "We cook pig and fish and chicken and breadfruit outdoors in an underground stone oven called an *imu*. Then we eat them with *poi*, which is a sort of gray paste made out of taro, and several other specialties of ours that *malahinis* don't usually care for much. But they enjoy the dancing and singing that go with them, and the generally festive atmosphere. I thought it was high time you saw a celebration of that sort. So I've invited in about fifty people."

"It's very kind of you," Eunice said, interrupting in her turn. At best she did not do it as gracefully as he did; and this time she spoke with considerable determination. "But I came over on purpose to tell you that I'm afraid we ought to go away tonight. You see, I didn't know anything about this plan of yours for a *poi* supper. You've been more than hospitable, but we don't want to wear out our welcome. And we really ought not to postpone our departure for Japan any longer. I've been looking up sailing schedules and I find there's a boat leaving Honolulu for Yokohama tomorrow."

"No doubt. But there's no boat leaving Lihue for Honolulu. They don't run every night. Didn't you know? Only three times a week. There won't be another now until Monday. So I'm afraid you'll have to reconcile yourself to staying with me that much longer at least."

"There isn't a boat until Monday?"

"No. Does that upset you very much?"

"Yes, Crispin, it does."

He had gone on shuffling and dealing his cards while he talked to her. Now he laid them down and rose.

"You've been a reluctant guest from the very beginning," he said slowly. "Am I such an inadequate host, Eunice?"

"You're a wonderful host. You know that. But it's true I didn't think it was best to come here. And I don't think it's best to stay. I hope you'll forgive me for saying so. I don't mean to be rude and I know you have meant to be kind."

He smiled, rather wryly, and shrugged his shoulders.

"You're a very naïve young lady. And a very guileless one. It's part of your charm, of course. But for your own sake I wish you were a little more secretive and artful."

"For my own sake?"

"Yes. You'll be so terribly hurt unless you build up some sort of defensive armor, unless you learn to fight back with the same sort of weapons with which you're attacked."

She turned away without answering, hoping that he would not notice her brimming eyes and quivering lips. The hope was entirely vain.

"I'm afraid I couldn't convince you that my advice is disinterested. But the wisest course you could possibly pursue at this moment would be to start a mad flirtation with me."

"I—I couldn't."

"Well, if I don't fill the bill, start one with Guy."

"Guy! He wouldn't think of such a thing!"

"Evidently you don't know much about men's thoughts. But at that, I'm not surprised that Guy seems safer to you than I do. That's why I suggested him. It really doesn't matter much with whom you have this mad flirtation—as far as you're concerned, I mean. The whole point is that you shouldn't fail to have it with someone, right away."

"I've just told you, Crispin—I couldn't."

"Why couldn't you, my dear?"

In spite of her preoccupation and distress, Eunice was touched by the tenderness of his tone. It moved her to speak with increasing candor.

"I—it never would occur to me to start a mad flirtation with anyone. I never did, even—even before I was married. I'm not that kind of girl. I just don't know how. And now that I am married, it would be impossible. Not only because I'd feel it was wrong. I would, of course. But besides that, I'm—I'm desperately in love with my husband."

"I know you are, Eunice. And so does he. If he weren't so sure of you, he wouldn't impose on you."

"*He* hasn't imposed on me. That is, he didn't, until——"

"Until the first unattached alluring young female crossed your joint path! You must have been married several weeks, hadn't you, by then? If he strays away that soon, on so little provocation, what do you suppose is going to happen by the time you've been married several years? Unless you take preventive steps of some sort?"

"I—I don't know."

"Well, I do. And I can't imagine anything more conducive to disaster than what you're proposing to do next. I'm not sure that you can drag Francis away from Edith, considering how far things seem to have gone already. But whether you can or not, he'll resent the effort. And if you do, your success will rankle. Why don't you just let him get tired of her? It won't take long. And meanwhile you could have a very interesting time yourself, if you'd only try to achieve a more receptive attitude."

"It's no use, Crispin, you and I don't look at all this the same way. I don't feel that two wrongs ever make a right."

"I didn't say they did. And I'm not suggesting that you should do anything 'wrong.' Don't be so terribly intense and earnest about it all, Eunice! I'm only suggesting that you should heed the good old Biblical injunction that when you go as a sheep among wolves you must be not only as harmless as a dove but also as wise as a serpent. Now please don't turn on me and remind me that the devil can quote scripture to his purpose."

"I won't. But anything would be wrong for me, if I thought it were, Crispin."

He shrugged his shoulders again, and this time his smile was a little wrier than before.

"Well, have it your own way—or as nearly your own way as you can get it. Heaven knows I don't want to hinder you —quite the contrary. By the by, I don't think Edith will give you much trouble today. When she came in whining about being ill and exhausted and all that, I told her to remain in bed, by all means, until she felt fully recovered. And I sent Suki in to stay with her. Just to be on hand if she needed anything, you know. Suki won't stir from her side until I give the word. And Edith won't be up again until she's allowed time for a convincing restoration to health."

He grinned maliciously. "It's too bad she should miss the *poi* supper," he remarked. "She always seems to enjoy celebrations of that sort. But it can't be helped. It never would do to let her get overtired again— Are you sure you won't change your mind and play checkers with me after all? Well, that's fine— I feel as if I were making some slight progress in your good graces at last!"

They were still playing when Guy drifted into the room an hour later, and at that point Crispin suggested that Eunice had better see if Ruth would not join them for a game of bridge. The forenoon passed quickly and pleasantly. Eunice's mind reverted every now and then, when she was dummy, to what Crispin had said to her. She was by no means prepared to act upon his advice. At the same time, she could not wholly dismiss it from her thoughts. Moreover, in the absence of even the most indirect reference to the scene which had taken place the evening before, she began to feel less self-conscious, both about her flight and the cause of it; and when Francis finally put in an appearance, there was no strain, either obvious or hidden, in the atmosphere. After lunch, when Crispin said he must oversee some of the preparations for the *poi* supper, Francis took his host's place at the bridge table; and when he and Eunice went back to the guest cottage to dress for the evening, he took advantage of the opportunity for easy apology which this interlude offered.

"I'm afraid I was terribly disagreeable last night, darling. I'd had a nerve-racking experience and I was all worn out."

"I know you were. I'm sorry too, if I seemed unsympathetic."

He stole a glance at her, but for once there was an inscrutable expression on her candid countenance. He tried another line of approach.

"Then I'm forgiven?"

"There isn't anything to forgive, is there? Except that you sounded cross, which didn't seem like you. But I suppose everyone is cross sometimes, even you. I'd be expecting too much if I didn't make allowances for that."

She had taken a green chiffon dress from the wardrobe and was considering it carefully. She did not appear to notice that Francis had put his arm around her.

"Let's kiss and make up, if that's the case, darling."

"We mustn't be late for the *poi* supper, Francis. Well, there! If you insist."

"There" had been the merest brushing of her lips against his cheek. The green dress, which looked easy enough to get into, was apparently giving her some difficulty; and as soon as the last snap was fastened, she opened the door and hurried away from the guest cottage, Francis following behind her.

As they approached the ranch house, they found that preparations for the *poi* supper had already begun. The musicians were arriving, the men wearing white suits and wide belts, after the Spanish fashion; the women dressed in *holokus,* so vivid as to coloring and so elaborate as to design that Eunice thought the missionaries who introduced the Mother Hubbard from which these graceful garments had been adapted would have had difficulty in recognizing the models for which they themselves were responsible. A few brief informal introductions took place; then singing and dancing commenced at once, with interpolations of the hula between spirited ballads; and presently a musical procession led the way through scented thickets to the *imu,* where flickering lanterns were held high in the darkness against the moment when the roast should be lifted out of the ground with all due ceremony.

Encircling a mound of dark earth, somewhat gruesomely suggestive of a child's grave, stood a group of men with lifted shovels in their hands. For a few minutes after the musicians and guests had assembled, there was a silence that seemed doubly tense after the sensuous song that had preceded it. Then a dismal chant, shrill and syncopated, suddenly smote the stillness. The shovelers began to scoop back the earth from the *imu* with frenzied haste. The sinister mound vanished completely; steaming vapor and pungent odors were wafted upwards. There was a clattering sound as the shovels struck the heated stones with which the victuals had been stuffed before they were buried; then, violently, these stones were hurled out of the ground. Finally, with all the pomp of a sacred rite, the fish wrapped in *ti* leaves, the succulent breadfruit, the sizzling pig and the smoking chicken were raised from the earth and borne in triumph to the festooned lanai.

This had been lighted by dozens of lanterns and decorated

with bunches of breadfruit which hung suspended from the ceiling. Under these had been laid a table shaped like a double "T," set for fifty and adorned with ferns laid flat upon a snowy cloth. Large bowls of *poi* and saucers filled with onions and tomatoes sliced together already stood by every plate. These were piled high with the contents of the *imu*, and the feast began, to the strumming of guitars and a special performance of the hula.

It was danced by a striking girl whose black hair, contrary to custom, was worn smooth and high, and whose scarlet *holoku* revealed every line and movement of her graceful body. The muscles of her beautiful back rippled under her sleek skin; her breasts, beautiful too, rose and fell in a succession of soft sighs which came more and more quickly. Her tapering hips swayed slowly at first; but soon they began to swing back and forth to a tempo of increasing speed which eventually assumed pulsing rapidity. Crispin, glancing at Eunice, saw that she was flushed, and that her eyes were downcast as if she wished to escape the implications of the dance by looking away from it.

"That's one of the very primitive hulas, known as 'Round the Island,'" he said. "The girl who's dancing it does it superbly, better than anyone else I know. You needn't be afraid to watch her—in fact, I want you to meet her. She's a distant relative of mine."

"I'm not afraid. But I am a little startled. Doesn't the dance seem rather suggestive to you?"

"Suggestive of what? Of vital rapture? Of the source of life itself? Do these shock you, Eunice?"

"No—but I don't like to think of them in connection with a dance—or a public demonstration of any kind. They're too sacred."

"The hula was sacred in its original conception, my dear. And it wasn't Hawaiians who debased it and commercialized it. It was Americans. Sometimes it symbolized a royal rite and sometimes spontaneous emotion. Of course there are various sorts of emotion—joy and sorrow and triumph and despair, for instance. The next hula will interpret quite a different sort from that you've just seen. Perhaps you'll like this one better."

While he was speaking a small group, matriarchal of aspect, presented itself on the lanai. It was led by a majestic looking woman who was dressed in a thin crisp *holoku* cut with a characteristic flowing train, and who wore a single *lei* of ginger blossoms which fell low over her matronly bosom. She established herself with composure and dignity in a large chair, and from this vantage point directed the selection of dances which her granddaughters performed, accompanying them, as they rendered these, with a pleasant humming and an emphatic tapping. The elder girl, who played the ukulele, was rather conventionally attired in a stiff fiber skirt and an orange satin blouse; but the younger, who was only a child, had apparently just stripped *ti* leaves from a tree and woven these into a costume. The fresh green rustled delightfully as she danced and fell gracefully away from her slim brown knees and small crossed feet when she sat down to rest.

"This is Sally's first program. Her dances are very simple," her grandmother said in modest disparagement. But her eyes were bright with pride as they rested on the child. Sally slipped into the rhythm of dance so swiftly and so naturally that she seemed to personify the melody of motion. Her pliant wrists twinkled, her flexible ankles flashed, her lithe little form seemed to sparkle. At one moment she was a figure of undulating languor; at the next the embodiment of lissome vivacity. The elements of earth and air, fire and water, with which her simple life was intermingled, the sweet flowers which were her constant companions, the friendly creatures with whom she played—all these she interpreted, becoming, in turn, the incarnation of each.

Crispin had watched Eunice quite as closely as she had watched the dance. He saw that her expression had changed completely, that this time it revealed unalloyed admiration. But he waited until the performers had withdrawn, amidst general and hearty applause, before he spoke to her.

"What did you think of that interpretation?"

"I thought it was beautiful beyond belief."

"You didn't feel it was the embodiment of a sin then?"

"No. It was just as you said, more like the embodiment of a sacrament. Between the two dances I'm completely dazed."

"It doesn't matter whether you're dazed or not. But you are supposed to be spellbound. Let's dance ourselves, while the spell's still upon you."

She rose readily enough. She had danced with Crispin many times now; the idea did not disturb her as it had at first; and numerous other couples were circling over the paved terrace and the springy grass beyond it. There was great variety and independence in their manner, but all were acting with a sort of joyous abandon, as if this dance were entirely different from those that took place between four walls, in the artificial atmosphere of a ballroom. As Crispin had said, it was a spontaneous expression of emotion, and his own share in it was natural and gracious. Eunice caught the contagion of it herself.

"If you'd only follow my advice and stay on here with us, you'd absorb our spirit before you knew it," Crispin remarked when they paused at last. He seldom spoke while he was dancing and Eunice had ceased to attempt perfunctory remarks when she was with him. She was a little breathless now, partly from exertion and partly from excitement. But Crispin, who had glided over the grass with his usual lack of effort, seemed even more composed than earlier in the evening. "You're learning fast," he went on. "You don't know it yet, but you are. You're rather warm and weary though, just now. The Kona weather still holds—it's very seldom we have a night like this. Come and sit down for a few minutes while I tell you what I'll show you if you don't run away."

Again Eunice raised no objection. They sauntered over to the edge of the knoll and ensconced themselves under a tree which veiled the moonlight without concealing it.

"Perhaps you really ought to go to Kona first," he continued musingly. "You had your mind made up to that. Well —you'd love to see the harbor there, with the waves rolling up to the very edge of the green lawns, and the little sampans, bobbing up and down beside the breakwater. You'd love to go sailing in a sampan yourself. I'd take you out in one, and the sea would be blue and choppy, and perhaps we'd see a shark following after us. There are some sharks around Kona. But you'd be safe with me."

"Tell me more," said Eunice eagerly.

"I'll tell you all you'll listen to. Of course, while you're on the Big Island, you ought to see Halemaumau—the House of Everlasting Fire. Its outer basin is as smooth as an agate bowl. But when you look down into its pit, you see a loam-like surface with scarlet lines running all across it, dotted with blazing points. And suddenly flaming fountains spring up from that network. All sorts of strange shapes appear on the lava. And sometimes even Pele herself, gorgeous courtesan that she is."

"Pele herself?"

"Yes—Halemaumau is her shrine, you know. She sits on a scarlet throne with scarlet lace foaming around her feet and holds court. Often she speaks. Would you like to hear her?"

"I—I'm not sure."

"Well, I am. Of course you want to hear Pele and to see her too. I'll arrange for both! But much as I want you to do that, I'd like even more to have you go to Molokai."

"The place where the lepers live!"

"You wouldn't see the place where the lepers live, my dear, except from a high cliff overlooking their tiny settlement. No—what you'd see would be the deep declivities high in the hills, which used to serve as the measuring troughs for sandalwood, and the spotted antelope ranging freely through the forests. The antelope are own cousins to the sacred deer of Nara. They've thriven and multiplied ever since they were sent here from Japan as a present to King Kamehameha, and they furnish royal sport to this day. But if I'm not mistaken, you'd rather go through the 'paddocks' to see them peacefully grazing, and joyously leaping from one ravine to another, than to track them down and kill them."

"Of course I would. I've never even been able to hunt foxes—it's one of the many reasons why I don't fit in Middleburg."

"Well, you'd fit in Molokai."

"I'm not sure. I'm not sure I fit anywhere, Crispin, except in Vermont. But I want to hear more about the sandalwood too.— You spoke of measuring troughs?"

"Yes. They date back to the days when sandalwood was the chief commodity for export. When the natives were put to hewing down trees in the forest, they were shown such hollows, and told that these must be filled before a day's work would be counted as complete and rewarded as such. Super-cargoes, coming up from the coast to represent the captains of the sailing vessels, bartered with the native chieftains on the basis of the live and fragrant 'boatloads' which they could see heaped up before them. Laborers and traders and kings—meeting together on these high hills, clustering about concavities dug out of the red earth, understanding each other because of the testimony of their own eyes as to what constituted fair weight and a good bargain—that's a glorious story which has never yet been fully told!"

"Why don't you tell it yourself—the way you've told it to me?"

"Oh, I'm not a storyteller! But someday I must capture an author—or rather an authoress—does anyone still say authoress? Well, I shall, at all events! A very young and charming authoress, if such exists, who will be my guest at Molokai while she writes the story of our sweet sandalwood."

"I know an authoress who could do it, if she would. Her name is Honor Bright."

"Oh, yes—I've heard of Honor Bright. I imagine that ten years ago she'd have been an answer to my every prayer. But didn't she marry into America's Royal Family? Isn't she the embodiment of conjugal bliss now, instead of the shining light of literary circles and the glamour girl of her time? I don't want an encumbering husband tagging along after my young and charming authoress. I'm rather fed up, just now, as a matter of fact, with encumbering husbands."

"I thought you started out to tell me about the sights I hadn't seen yet, not to talk about husbands."

"So I did. As a matter of fact, there's still plenty to show you on Kauai. You haven't even seen the Haena Cave yet— you know, the one Guy told you about the night we all met."

"The Hyena Cave?" said Eunice doubtfully. "I really don't think I want to see that, Crispin. Now the sampans and the sandalwood—those do tempt me a lot. But hyenas don't appeal to me at all."

He threw back his head and laughed. "Do you know you're very amusing, Eunice? I keep discovering new attractions in you all the time. I said Haena, not hyena."

"They sound just alike to me—and I might say the same thing about you, Crispin, that you've said about me— But do you realize how little I actually know about you? Nothing except that you are a great magnet and a great power! Within an hour after I had met Francis I had met his family, too; I knew all about his background, I'd heard a large part of his life history——"

"My life history is longer than his and my family smaller. We'll have to discuss those some other time— I'm acting like a very bad host and making enemies of my other guests in monopolizing you like this. Come—we'll go back to the lanai—now. But tomorrow we'll explore the Haena Cave."

She went to sleep with the thrilled thought of this exploration uppermost in her mind. She had remembered—while Crispin went on talking—Guy's original remark about it: That nymphs were said to swim in it, and Crispin's significant retort that nymphs were known to swim in it. Naturally she did not believe anything so fantastic, any more than she believed the stories about Pele. At the same time, her anticipation of visiting the cave was shot through with suspense and excitement. Francis found her provokingly detached when he tried to talk with her after their return to the guest cottage in the wee small hours.

"That was a pretty swell party, wasn't it?"

"Yes, it was. I enjoyed every minute of it."

"You looked as if you were, every time I saw you. Not that I could see you all the time."

"Did you try?"

"Not too hard— Did you take a little stroll or something?"

"Yes. It's very refreshing, isn't it, after dancing? I remember you told me so, the night we met Crispin and Guy at Waikiki, and I asked you what had become of you and Edith when I left our table. You took quite a long walk, as I remember it. Or did you sit on the sand? Or what?"

"You're not taking a nasty crack at me, are you, Eunice?"

"Of course not. Why should I?"

"Not reason at all. Speaking of Edith, it's a shame she had to miss the *poi* supper."

"It certainly is. I hope she'll be better in the morning. Crispin spoke of going to the Haena Cave. What do you suppose I thought he called it? Hyena! He made no end of fun of my mistake!"

"Do you yourself admit you're not infallible?"

"Yes, indeed! Did I ever say I was? But we won't argue about it at this hour in the morning! Is that actually the sun coming up? I don't believe Crispin will go to bed at all."

"You seem to have Crispin a good deal on your mind."

"Well, you said yourself he was irresistible. That gave me the idea in the first place. Not that I'm convinced yet. But I'm beginning to wonder if you mightn't be right about that, just as you are about so many other things. Good night, dear —good morning, rather!"

In spite of her excitement, she slept soundly when she finally did fall asleep; and for the first time she found the next morning that Francis had waked before her and had left the room so silently that she had not heard him go. Now that Suki was nursing Edith, one of the ranch house servants brought Eunice her tray when she rang for it, and there was slightly more delay than when the ubiquitous little maid had been completely at her service. She dozed off again while she waited for the tray, and when it finally came, she demolished her appetizing breakfast with zest. Then she bathed and dressed in a leisurely fashion. She had forgotten to wind her watch the night before, but this did not give her any concern. One of the great charms of life on the plantation was its freedom from a set schedule. But she was amazed to hear the tall clock in the hall chiming two as she sauntered into the gun room at last. This meant that luncheon was over, and that Crispin, according to the custom of the country, had probably gone to his own quarters for a siesta. Like playing checkers, this was a habit he had which seemed to her out of harmony with his active life and virile personality; in spite of the fact that he rose before dawn and remained unwearied until midnight, Eunice could not visualize him as an addict to naps. The idea was always slightly irritating to her, and now, as she sat down at the card table, aimlessly deciding to try her own luck at solitaire, the afternoon seemed as empty as the deserted room.

The chimes of the hall clock had signaled another hour and she had put away her cards with distaste and was wondering what to do with herself next, when she heard the welcome sound of footsteps on the flagstones. A moment later, Guy came into the room, carrying his pipe in one hand and a folded copy of *Punch* in the other.

"Cheerio," he said pleasantly, pulling up a chair and sitting down beside her. "I hope you had a good sleep? You certainly needed it, after last night's merry-go-round! But let me congratulate you. You were the life of the party."

"Don't be absurd, Guy."

"But you were. Everyone was talking about how lovely you looked and how beautifully you danced and how enchanting you were generally."

"I don't believe it. You're making it all up to please me and give me the self-assurance you think I need. By the way, where is 'everybody' now?"

"Why the dinner guests have all gone, of course. And Edith is still convalescing under Suki's watchful care. Ruth has a sick headache today."

"A sick headache?"

"Well, we'd call it that in England, especially in the case of a young lady. I believe, however, that in the States you'd call it a hangover."

"Ruth has a hangover!"

"Yes, she passed out completely, early in the game—to continue the resort to your colloquialisms. She was basely persuaded to drink more than one cocktail, and unfortunately these were not all of the same variety. This might have been disastrous in itself, but the *poi* supper added the final touch. The poor girl couldn't bring herself to wrapping that gray taro paste around her fingers and then pouring it down her throat. The mere sight of it turned her sick and the smothered smell of the fish and pork capped the climax. I thought perhaps a little fresh air would do her good, so I got her away from the table and propelled her toward the garage. A station wagon seemed to be the only available car at the moment——"

"The only available car?"

"Well all the others were previously occupied. But I managed to get her into that and took her for a nice long ride. She didn't appear to be conscious of anything I said to her from the beginning to the end of it. She kept swinging back and forth until I was afraid she would pitch out face foremost, and saying very crossly, 'It may seem like that to you, Mr. Grenville, but it doesn't to me.' I haven't the vaguest idea what she meant by 'that.' "

"I think it's simply disgusting. Ruth of all persons! What happened after the ride in the station wagon was over?"

"Perhaps I should blush to tell you, but I carried her to her room and deposited her on her bed. I took off her shoes and wondered whether I should 'loosen her clothes' as the Victorian novelists used to say. But I decided they were probably loose enough anyway. So then I left her to her chaste slumbers. Francis told me that he was wakened this morning by the sounds of the sad aftermath."

"Where is *he?*"

"He said something about going for a ride after lunch. I don't know whether he did or not. I confess I succumbed to slumber myself, at that time. Crispin didn't get his siesta though, or his lunch either, for that matter. He was called out, this morning, by some trouble at the sugar mill, and hasn't been back. It's nothing serious, I'm sure. But it has upset his day."

"It's upset mine, too. He promised to take me to the Haena Cave."

"I know the way there. I'd be delighted to take you, if you'd accept me as a substitute."

Eunice was conscious of an acute pang of disappointment. It was true that the more she saw of Guy, the more she liked him; but there was nothing about him which suggested either magic or mystery. Decidedly, he did not represent the ideal escort to the cave which had become so portentous to her. She hesitated, but she had no sound reason to decline his invitation. Time was hanging heavy on her hands; besides, she did not want to hurt his feelings. She answered before her reluctance had become too obvious.

"You're always thoughtful, aren't you? Thank you—I'd like to go very much. When shall we start?"

"Right away, if you like. It won't take me but a minute to get a car, and I won't have to resort to a station wagon this time. But we can't walk—it's too far."

Without any increase of enthusiasm, Eunice suffered herself to be helped into a motor and driven over the beautiful road on the west side of the island, through a large grove of *kukuis,* and along the Beach of Hanalei, where the sun streamed down on the hard bare sand. At the end of this road, she obediently alighted and stumbled along over a little scrubby path which seemed to be leading straight into the side of a mountain. This path was abruptly swallowed up in the immensity of a yawning aperture that opened suddenly and swellingly before the startled girl. Above her, a dark projecting rock jutted heavily over a vast grotto which was flooded by a strange emerald light which seemed to rise, as if by magic, from a deep and shining pool. Dim canals, branching back of this pool, disappeared into the distance; and as Eunice stood transfixed, straining her eyes to follow their course, a soft sibilant sound smote the stillness. For a moment no sight followed. Then out of the darkness a form emerged, white in the green translucency, and moved, gleaming, through the smooth water of a canal toward the pool itself. Eunice caught her breath and shivered as she saw it.

"Is that really a nymph?" she whispered. "The sprite of the

green grotto?" For a moment she almost believed that it was. She needed only Guy's confirmation of her credulity.

"At least it must be the embodiment of Kauai's enchantment," he answered. He spoke as if he too had come under a mystic spell. But somehow his words lacked conviction. He had linked his arm through Eunice's, and now he pressed her hand, gently and reassuringly. But the damage was done. She strained away from him.

"It's no more a nymph than I am," she said tersely. "It's a girl. And she isn't alone, either."

It was true. A second form was following the first, but through some subtle difference in its shape and progress, its outline was far dimmer than the first figure's had been. It seemed vaguely larger and vaguely darker, but even that was scarcely discernible. When the "sprite" emerged from the canal and clove quietly through the silent pool, her companion was overshadowed and then swallowed up in obscurity again. The strange light was focused, as if by magic, on the girl's slim body, and gave a gilded aspect to her hair, which streamed about after her as she swam. At last she drew herself lightly from the emerald lake and stood poised and perfect beside it. The cavern seemed suddenly suffused with fresh radiance.

"It's Edith," Eunice said hysterically. "It's Edith, and Francis is with her."

"Eunice, you must be beside yourself to say such a thing. You know that Edith is sick in bed, that Suki doesn't leave her for a second. It's some Hawaiian girl. No European swims like that, with her hair all around her in the water."

"Did you ever see a yellow-haired Hawaiian? I'm going to swim across the pool myself, under water. I'm going to surprise them before they get away."

Again she tried to shake herself free. Guy's restraining arm, unyielding now, was too strong for her. She was still struggling when the second form, so long submerged, also rose above the green water. All her strength went out of her as she stopped striving and watched it. The outline of it was less blurred than before; it was distinguishable as a man; but the man's face was hidden. His back had been toward the mouth of the cave as he swung himself up from the pool, and now that he stood looking at the girl beside him, his face was still averted. But there was an intensity about him which neither distance nor dimness obscured; Eunice felt that she could see him staring into the girl's illumined face. It needed no imagination to see him snatch at her when she turned away from him and swing her about by the shoulder. The next instant they were locked in a passionate embrace.

Guy was still holding fast to Eunice's arm. Now he put his free hand over her mouth just in time to stifle the scream that tore its way from her heart to her lips. He did not know how he was to get her out of the cave quietly and quickly before they themselves were seen and heard. But somehow, guided by blind instinct, he managed to do so, murmuring words of mingled encouragement and caution to her as they stumbled along, protecting her as they crouched down and crawled through the mouth of the cave, underneath the somber cowl of overhanging rocks. It was not until their groping feet had found the security of the scrubby pathway again that he straightened up and spoke to her.

"I want you to sit down for a minute and listen to me. If you try to run away from me I'll have to make you stay. Because it's important you should hear what I'm going to say."

Without waiting for a response, he seated himself on a stone, half hidden by overhanging bushes, and drew her down beside him.

"I want you to promise me you'll forget everything you saw—or thought you saw—in that cave," he said imperatively. "I'm not sure myself what I really did see and you can't be either. All sorts of optical illusions occur in such treacherous light. There's only one thing about today for you to remember: That Edith is laid up, in the guest cottage, and that Francis is out riding on the other side of the island."

"Do you take me for an utter fool?"

"No, I take you for a very great lady—a lady who shouldn't for an instant forget her own essential dignity and nobility. It's relatively unimportant whether other persons remember these qualities in themselves or not—provided they possess them in the first place, which is more or less debatable, in some instances. But not in yours."

"You expect me to stand by and watch another woman steal my husband without moving a muscle to prevent it?"

"I expect you to disregard the fact that another woman has *tried* to steal your husband—if it is a fact. But you don't know that it is. You don't know anything, for certain."

"I know that Francis is obsessed with Edith, that he's tired of me already, that he——"

"I say you don't know anything of the sort. Edith is a pretty little vampire who goes around looking for prey, I'll grant you that. But she doesn't always find it and she hardly ever holds it. Francis is far more likely to get tired of her than he is of you. And after all, what could you say, specifically, if you took the line of heavy and heated accusations? Merely that six of us went out walking in the sugar cane

99

and that two of us got lost! Don't you think that sounds a little thin?"

"You know they weren't lost! You know——"

"I don't know anything and neither do you. Please remember that, Eunice. You'll be so much happier if you do."

He was not cajoling her, as Crispin had cajoled her the morning before. He was pleading with her. But she was past caring now what form attempted persuasion took. It was all vain, it was all hateful.

"I've got to manage my life myself. I can't have outsiders interfering between me and my husband."

"But I thought that was exactly what you did fear!"

"I mean, I can't have you and Crispin interfering. I was referring to you and Crispin when I said outsiders. I wasn't referring to Edith."

"I'm sorry you think of me as an outsider. I hoped that by now you thought of me as a friend. So Crispin has 'interfered' also?"

"Yes. He talked and talked to me yesterday." Eunice went on swiftly, disregarding Guy's first remarks. "Not only about Francis and Edith. About other things too. Staying on the Islands, for instance. And I'd almost decided I would. But now my mind is made up differently. There's a boat leaving Linue tonight, and I'm going to take it."

"Alone?"

"Of course not. With Francis. When I get him away from the Islands, everything will be different. It was before."

"Don't blame the Islands, Eunice. Don't blame Francis either, if you can help it. And heaven grant you'll never blame yourself! Well—if you really mean what you say, if your mind is made up, we'd better go back to the plantation. Otherwise you'll miss the boat."

He held out his hand to help her rise, but this time he did not retain hers. The drive back to the plantation was a silent one, unrelieved by any sort of friendly conversation. As they drew up at the guest cottage, Guy was aghast to see that Eunice, instead of going directly to her own room, turned toward Edith's, where Suki knelt outside the threshold of the open door. The little maid's normally expressionless face assumed a look of warning and she put a small amber-colored finger against her full lips.

"Missy sleeping," she whispered. "Missy velly, velly tired. Sleeping all afternoon."

"What do you mean, all the afternoon?"

Suki appeared to consider an instant, without removing her warning finger.

"Suki give Missy her bloth, twelve o'clock, all same time

other Missy have her bleakfast. Houseboy bling both. Sick Missy asleep ever since."

As if there were nothing further to be said, Suki relapsed into silence, slumping down a little more on the mat outside the door as she did so. Eunice stood her ground.

"I don't believe you. I want to see her. I want to see her in bed."

With a mounting sense of disturbance, Guy saw that Eunice actually was looking into Edith's room, across Suki's crouching figure. Apparently what she saw there was incontestable. She stood still for a moment, without speaking, and then she went down the narrow lanai leading to her own room. Guy watched her until she disappeared. Afterward he started the engine of his car again and drove it to the garage. As he did so, he saw Francis dismounting in front of the stable. Francis hailed him agreeably, and giving his reins to a groom, walked across the strip of grass that separated him from his fellow guest, the puppies bounding out to meet him as he advanced.

"Hello, there! What have you been doing with yourself all afternoon?"

"I took Eunice to see the Haena Cave. It seems Crispin said something to her yesterday about going, and she was disappointed when she found he had been called away."

"Very decent of you. I'm sure she appreciated it— Do you happen to know where she is now?"

"I think she's in her own room."

"I reckon I better go and find her then. I haven't seen her all day. So long. Meet you for cocktails."

He disappeared in his turn, the puppies still tumbling around him. He certainly did not look guilty or even anxious, Guy reflected, watching him go. On the contrary, he looked the part of the contented and devoted bridegroom to perfection. Guy Grenville was possessed of a well-ordered mind and a calm disposition, but he was beginning to be disturbed himself, and he was considerably perplexed. He decided to seek out his host and see whether Crispin might save the situation, at least to the extent of postponing the Fieldings' departure again, even if he could do nothing in the way of clearing up menacing mysteries.

But Crispin, it appeared, had not yet returned to the plantation himself. He had telephoned early in the afternoon from the sugar mill to say how sorry he was that he was still detained; there had been trouble with both men and machinery. The houseboy who took the call had informed him that of his five guests, the three who were able to be up and around had all gone out. This seemed to satisfy him, for he had said that this being the case he would not hurry back. He would

101

see everything straight at the sugar mill before he came back to the ranch house.

Guy went into the gun room and sat down to smoke and wait. He did not busy his hands mechanically, with cards, as Eunice had done earlier in the day; but like her he listened to the chimes of the tall clock in the hall. He was not sure what time the inter-island boat left, but he thought this was about eight, and he considered Eunice quite capable of taking it, in her present mood, without so much as waiting to say good-by to her host. He rose and prowled restlessly about for a few moments, fingering the bowling balls and the *koa* cups, and taking two or three guns from the big rack. But the attention with which he regarded all these objects was superficial, and eventually he replaced them and went to stand beside the window where he could look out on the striped pineapple fields that had never failed to intrigue him before. This time he hardly saw them, partly because of his concern and partly because of the waning light, which faded rapidly. He had always vaguely missed the gloaming of his native land. But he had never felt the lack of it as poignantly as he did now——

When Crispin came into the room at last he had already dressed for dinner. Guy, usually far the more meticulous of the two, became keenly conscious of his own disheveled state when confronted with Crispin's immaculate white flannels. Apparently Crispin was immediately conscious of it also.

"You're not going native, are you, Guy? I've always thought of you as the personification of that legendary Englishman who invariably dresses 'to keep his own self-respect' even on a desert island! Not that I'm criticizing you—in fact, I've always thought the Briton in question must have had very little self-respect to start with, if he needed to bolster it up all the time— Where is everybody?"

It was the same question Eunice had asked. Guy began another categorical answer.

"I understand that poor Ruth hasn't yet recovered from her jag."

The corners of Crispin's mouth twitched. "If we're not careful, we'll have her looping all around the plantation the next time we have a party. To paraphrase an old saying, there's no fool like a chaste fool."

"—And that Edith is still asleep."

"Well, to paraphrase again, let sleeping bitches lie."

"—And that Eunice is packing."

"Packing!"

"Yes, she's definitely decided to take the night boat."

"What suddenly caused this definite decision?"

"I made a great mistake this afternoon. No doubt you'll find a maxim you can adapt to fit my case also."

"What did you do?"

"I took her to the Haena Cave. It seems you told her about it and she was disappointed when she found you wouldn't be able to take her."

"Well?"

"Well, when we reached there we found other visitors had preceded us. An undine of some sort came swimming out of one of the canals into the pool. I think Eunice would have easily been persuaded that this apparition really was a nymph if it hadn't been accompanied by a male escort. But eventually both bathers emerged from the water and took to a very intense kind of kissing. Of course we were a good way off and we never saw the man's face, but the undine certainly bore a general resemblance to Edith. Eunice leaped to the rather obvious conclusion."

"But Edith's in bed with Suki standing guard over her!"

"I pointed that out. It didn't do any good. She wouldn't believe her eyes when she came home and saw Edith in bed and Suki on the doormat."

"What's your opinion?"

"Only that you'll have to work fast if you want to keep Eunice from taking that night boat."

Crispin crossed the room and went out, stepping across the flagstones without either haste or hesitation. Then he knocked on the Fieldings' door. Since all the others stood wide open, Guy could not help overhearing him.

"Eunice, may I speak to you a minute? It's very urgent."

The answer that came from within was muffled. Eunice did not open the door, but eventually Francis did so. When he came out he spoke gravely to his host.

"I'm sorry that Eunice can't talk to you just now. She's in the last throes of packing. She says she asked Guy to tell you that we feel we must leave tonight. It's regrettable, but considering everything, perhaps it's best."

"What do you mean, considering everything?"

"I might mention a number of items. More specifically I mean that you gave Eunice a pretty severe shock today, if you'll pardon me for saying so."

"*I* gave her a pretty severe shock?"

"Yes. Do we really have to take it up in detail?"

"I haven't laid eyes on Eunice today."

"No. But apparently she laid eyes on you. Did you get your appointments mixed, or something? Because she understood that you invited her to go to the Haena Cave. And when you didn't turn up she went there without you. I'm sorry, Crispin, but there doesn't seem to be anything I can say. Eunice didn't want to come here in the first place and she has a terribly strong feeling about—well, about the sort of thing she saw this afternoon."

There's going to be murder done pretty soon—in a minute —right now—Guy was muttering to himself, he was unconsciously starting out across the flagstones. Then he was forcing himself to keep quiet and stand still. Francis had stopped talking, and in the pause that followed there was a poignancy which might indeed have meant murder. Guy waited for it to end, his self-control at the breaking point. But when the end came, it was not marked by the violence he had dreaded without being able to forestall it. It was marked by laughter. Crispin's laugh floated toward him, unrestrained and musical—Crispin's laugh and his final remark to Francis.

"It that's your story, stick to it," he was saying. At first his words brought infinite relief to Guy's troubled mind. But as Crispin went on, Guy felt anxiety pierce him again like a pain. "You make me laugh. I only hope you amuse Eunice half as much as you do me. I can afford to laugh at you— now and hereafter. In fact, I'll have the last laugh, as far as you're concerned. And don't forget that he who laughs last, laughs best."

PART IV
Halfway House

~~~~~~

Chapter 8

EUNICE AND FRANCIS stood side by side watching the dazzling shore line until it became dim.

The Royal Hawaiian Band, stationed upon the pier, was playing poignant music. The dock was packed with well-wishers who had arrived laden with *leis* for their departing friends, and who had lingered to watch the ship glide out to sea; as it slid away, they stood with upturned faces and outstretched hands, shouting final greetings and catching at multicolored paper streamers. From the topmost deck copper-skinned beach boys were diving into the churned water surrounding the ship. As it steamed slowly out toward Diamond Head, an escort of smart speedboats, buoyantly cleaving through the blue water, cut fanciful figures in the sea as a skater cuts them in the ice. The hair of their youthful, white-clad occupants, perching gaily if precariously above their swinging sterns, was swept backward by the breeze. Along the shore, mirrors were being twisted and turned, lowered and raised in the sun as a final salute; they flashed with the brilliance of jewels. Overhead airplanes swept by in faultless formation. Beyond the green hills sloping away in the distance rainbows arched in irisdescent splendor.

A great contentment, an untroubled peace, possessed Eunice's heart. Nothing could have persuaded her, during those first blissful days at Waikiki, that she would ever leave the Islands willingly; now she was glad to go. Francis had convinced her that his own attraction to Edith had been nothing more than a passing fancy, if indeed anything so ephemeral could be called a fancy at all, and that Crispin's indifferent manner, on the other hand, had cloaked the desire for a serious intrigue. But in spite of the relief which accompanied this reassurance, the return to Honolulu had been an anticlimax, after the original ecstatic arrival; the interval before the departure of the next boat bound for the Orient compara-

105

tively tame. She and Francis had driven around Oahu again, lunching at Coopers' Ranch, where they were invited to select from the multitudinous array there a hibiscus which should henceforth bear Eunice's name; but the most beautiful blooms all seemed to be named already; the striped, coral-colored flower which she finally chose did not appeal to her much. Neither did the strange fish, which all seemed to be staring at her, swimming about in the aquarium, or the feather cloaks in the Biship Museum, which caused her a pang because of all the little birds which had been sacrificed in order to fabricate them. She felt more and more as if she were living up to Edith's taunt of "doing the usual tourist things" as she went on with her sight-seeing. There was no warmth to it, and no wonder in it.

But now it was past. Hawaii lay behind her. The spell of Kona weather was over. Ahead was the vast Pacific and a brisk breeze was blowing. She had tossed her last *lei* on the water, less because she believed the ancient legend that if it floated back to shore the wish she made on parting with it would come true, than because she was sincerely glad of an excuse to make it disappear. When the Hawaiian flowers and the Hawaiian coast had vanished there would be nothing left to remind her of Hawaii itself. There were no lanais on the boat she and Francis had taken this time. It was a comfortable but unpretentious steamer, one of a merchant fleet that encircled the globe, stopping at many ports and carrying freight as well as passengers. There was not even anything suggestive of a bridal suite about the reservation they had secured. It was just a cabin, like any other cabin.

The breeze cut across her face, making it feel clean and cool. She glanced lovingly at Francis and saw that his face looked fresher too, that there was a ruddy glow beneath his tan, and that his eyes were clear and eager.

"When we get to Japan," she said, "let's do some mountain climbing, shall we? We've had so much swimming here, I'd like a change."

He nodded, agreeably, without answering, but Eunice did not miss a worded response. Their arms were linked together, and she was sure that once again their hearts and their minds would be linked in the same way, that they had left disharmony and disunion behind them. She did not say "forever," even to herself; she was not thinking in terms of eternity. As long as the immediate future was secure again, she could stay serene——

"Isn't this *wonderful?* I'm just *thrilled* that we're going to have another voyage together! It was so dull at the ranch after you two left that Ruth and I decided we simply couldn't *stand* it another minute. So we took the next boat after you

106

did, from Lihue, ourselves. We got in just this morning, and *have* I had a day! You can't imagine what a time I had getting a stateroom. Those stupid steamboat people insisted there wasn't a *thing*. But of course in the end they gave me the cutest little cabin—they always do! Ruth and I are all installed there now and we're going to be cozy as can be. We couldn't come out before because we were so busy getting settled, and we were just *breathless* after the terrible rush at the last minute. But it didn't matter, because of course we've seen all those silly performances they go through when you sail dozens of times already. Francis, you're looking simply grand. If Eunice wants to rest before dinner we can take a turn, can't we?"

Eunice had heard nothing, had seen nothing, until Edith was actually upon them—no approaching footsteps, no hailing voice. Now, swinging around to confront the interloper, she was still so incredulous that she did not instantly feel the full impact of her own anger and dismay. When it did come, its onrush was the more terrific because it was tardy. As she answered, she had to struggle to keep from shrieking.

"I don't want to rest before dinner," she said vehemently. "I'm not at all tired. Francis and I were just going to take a turn ourselves."

As their arms were linked, she succeeded in drawing him away, though she did not do so without difficulty. Francis seemed bent on welcoming Edith and lingering beside her, exchanging bright badinage with her; but finally he yielded to the pressure of Eunice's insistent fingers. There was no more talk of "taking a turn." She hastened from the deck to their cabin, without answering his jesting questions concerning her hurry; and once inside, she shut the door, and stood with her back to it, confronting him with unleashed rage.

"So you lied to me!"

"Lied to you, honey? About what? Why should I lie to you anyway?"

"You lied to me about Edith! Everything you told me about her and Crispin was false! If it had been true, she'd have been glad to get rid of us, she'd have welcomed the chance to be alone with him on the ranch!"

"Eunice, you must try to see things straight or you'll get into serious trouble. I told you I felt sure Crispin was bent on having a serious affair with Edith. I never said she was bent on having a serious affair with him."

"If it was Crispin who was in the cave with her, she certainly didn't seem very averse to it."

"You don't know that Edith was in the cave. You have the evidence of your own eyes that she was sick in bed that afternoon. You may have seen another girl friend of Crispin's

107

who looked something like Edith, at a distance. But suppose she was in the cave. Any girl can have a moment of aberration, I reckon, especially during that far-famed Kona weather, under the effect of island magic. That doesn't mean she'd stand for anything, indefinitely. Probably Crispin made himself so obnoxious after we were gone that she was driven to escaping from him."

"On the boat you were taking!"

"There isn't any other Orient-bound boat sailing this week, Eunice. You know that perfectly well. And there isn't any reason why Edith shouldn't go to the Orient, is there? After all, there are about a hundred other people on this boat who had the same idea."

"I believe you knew she was taking it! I believe you planned to meet her on it!"

"I give you my word of honor, I hadn't the slightest idea she meant to take this boat. You heard what she said: She didn't make up her mind, herself, to take it until yesterday. You and I haven't been separated an instant since then. If she'd written me or wired me or telephoned me, you couldn't have helped learning about it."

"She meant to take it all the time!"

"If she meant to take it, all the time, don't you suppose she'd have made sure of a good cabin, and so on? Edith likes luxury and she's got plenty of money. She wouldn't run the risk of being cramped and crowded just to give the effect of a last minute coup. If you'll think the matter over quietly, instead of raging and ranting so, you'll realize that wouldn't be in character."

He took a silver case Eunice had given him from his pocket, lighted a cigarette, and began blowing rings in the air.

"I might add," he went on pleasantly, "that it isn't in character for you to stand in front of a door, as if you were trying to keep me from walking out of it. Or to accuse me of telling lies and making assignations. What a way for a loving bride to act toward a devoted husband! Do lie down for a little while before dinner. You must be terribly overtired, to stage a scene like this. You'll feel better when you've had a little rest. Meanwhile I'll go and apologize to Edith for our rather curt reception of her. The poor girl must be wondering why on earth you dragged me off without even saying hello to her. It wouldn't be a bad idea to ask her and Ruth to sit at our table. I'll speak to the head steward about it. So long, honey. Don't try to do much unpacking now. I'll help you with it at bedtime."

She could not keep him from going; she knew it would be useless to try. But she stood looking after him, smarting with shame and resentment, her lulled suspicions roused again, her soothed feelings outraged afresh. From that moment onward, she remained watchful, alert and mistrustful. There was no more lounging as there had been on the previous voyage. She took innumerable "turns" in the course of the next few weeks, but they invariably seemed to lead back again to the place whence she had started—a place where Edith was always present.

After a few days, Eunice became grimly reconciled to the fact that Edith was inescapable on the steamer; but she looked forward to their arrival in Yokohama as to a day of deliverance. Edith had chattered volubly about the itinerary they would "all four have such fun taking together"—Kamakura, Tokyo, Nara, Kyoto, Kobe—and with newborn craftiness, Eunice had acquiesced to every arrangement proposed, but secretly she had been plotting with the purser; at the last moment she intended to say she had changed her mind, that she wanted to push straight on to Shanghai; she had made sure that her stateroom was available to that point.

Unfortunately she had neglected to make sure Francis would consent to occupy it to that point.

She should have been forewarned by the ease with which he had persuaded her to go to Kauai against her will. But she was not. At the back of her mind lay the conviction that since it was Hale money which was paying for the trip, Francis would hesitate to divert this to channels of which she expressed disapproval. After all, they had been visitors at Crispin's ranch, so that was different. At least she thought it was. Francis, to her intense chagrin, had another viewpoint and held to it.

"You reserved the cabin straight through to Shanghai? Without consulting me?"

"I thought you'd be glad to be guided by my wishes."

"I thought you'd be glad to be guided by mine. Especially as I've made no secret of them. I've always wanted to see Japan. It's the only country I really did want to see. You've kept talking about it yourself, too, about the mountain climbing and so on. You never said a word to indicate that the itinerary Edith outlined wasn't agreeable to you. She's had so much experience in traveling, I thought you were delighted to follow her advice."

"Well, I wasn't. I've had considerable travel experience myself. But I didn't want to start an argument with her. I thought it would be simpler to withdraw quietly at the last moment."

"If that's what you really want to do, Eunice, there's nothing to stop you."

She stared him, appalled. His manner was perfectly civil,

his voice as agreeable as ever. Only by implication was he uttering a threat. But the threat was there.

"You mean you'd let me go on to Shanghai by myself."

"Certainly, if that's what you're bent on doing. I can catch up with you in China."

"Of course you can't if Japan is eliminated from my schedule. That would mean I'd always be two weeks farther ahead than I originally planned."

"In that case it would really be futile for me to try to catch up with you, wouldn't it? I don't think I'd care for a vain pursuit, Eunice. I never have, you know. I always like a reasonable amount of assured reward."

"What will you do then, if I go on to Shanghai?"

"What you advised yourself, just now. I won't try to catch up with you. I'll go home. I've told you how I feel about that."

"Francis, you know I didn't advise anything of the sort. You know——"

"I know that I'm having all sorts of difficulty about following you, Eunice. And I don't want to start an argument either. If you prefer to proceed to Shanghai, I shan't try to stop you, as I intimated before. But I suggest that you be broadminded too, about letting me wander around, footloose and free—in Japan and elsewhere. Neither of us better make any binding plans for the future."

They never referred to the conversation again. Eunice went to the purser and told him she had changed her mind, wincing at the scarcely concealed scorn which she saw on his face when she did so. Francis was irreproachable in his manner toward her throughout their sojourn in Japan, which included no mountain climbing and followed closely to the lines Edith had suggested. Having won his point, he did not betray the slightest inclination to gloat over his victory. Indeed, his attitude toward Edith was so increasingly impersonal that Eunice began to feel the issue had been merely one of principle. Her suspicions were lulled and she asked herself, reproachfully, if her distrust had been unreasonable and insulting from the beginning. This self-searching took a doubly significant turn when she heard Francis give unresponsive rejoinders to several fresh suggestions from Edith, and the more urgent she was, the more evasive his attitude became. Once, when she spoke with slighting mockery to Eunice, he rebuked her so curtly that his bride could hardly believe her own ears. Later on when they were alone, he referred to the episode, and jestingly as he spoke, Eunice was quick to catch the real import of his words.

"Even if she was born in Vermont, Mrs. Francis Fielding of

Retreat, King George County, Virginia, is a very important personage," he said, pinching her ear. "No one except her husband is supposed to forget it for a minute."

His mood was so merry that Eunice ventured a retort to which, a few weeks earlier, she could not possibly have given tongue.

"And what about him? Is he supposed to forget it as long as he likes?"

"Yes, that's one of his prerogatives. Not that he's expected to abuse it. Do you think he does? Isn't my love-making respectful enough, honey? Don't you think I know how to treat my betters?"

As usual, he had contrived to swing the subject away from its original point. But it was impossible to take offense at the way he did it, or to reproach him and preach to him while he was so engaging. Eunice did not even try.

When the question of their next move came up, Francis made it clear that he was ready to go wherever she wished; the decision to push on to the Philippines was a mutual one. They saw what they could of Shanghai and Hongkong while the ship was in port, but they did not wait over to take another. When they reached Manila, they were both so enchanted with the city that they were also delighted with their decision. The fact that Edith and Ruth had made a similar one caused no friction between them. They accepted it in a matter of fact manner, without undue misgiving on one side or undue exultation on the other.

Between them they engaged a couple of *calesas* and went bobbing around in these small two-wheeled carriages. It was Ruth, quite as often as Edith, to whom Francis called gaily to accompany him, and in either instance her cousin always came close behind with Eunice. Oftenest, however, it was he and Eunice that led the little procession; and on the one occasion when Edith tried to alter this order, Francis looked at her with a cool stare far more cutting than his rebuke had been.

But Edith had a way of disregarding such episodes as if they never had happened. A few moments after they occurred, she was hanging on Francis's arm again and looking archly up into his eyes. If sometimes he shook her off, if sometimes he did not return her melting glances, she did not seem to notice that either. She begged him to buy her a costume of pineapple cloth and printed silk, such as the Filipinas wore, made with wide outstanding sleeves and a long trained skirt pinned up over a lace petticoat. When he bought two costumes exact alike, in gray and green, one for her and one for Ruth, and a much finer creation in purple and peach for Eunice, with the laciest of bodices and the most finely pleated of neckpieces, Edith received hers with shrieks of delight which entirely drowned out Eunice's quiet exclamation of pleasure. To cap the climax, he bought some flat sandals of dried grass and a gauze shirt for himself, and letting the shirt tails hang outside his white trousers, after the native custom, insisted that they should go for their afternoon ride "all dressed up." So off they went, after Eunice's first hesitation had been hushed, through the Walled City and across the ancient moat, down the Escolta and around the Luneta, their merriment increasing every minute.

In the evening they always danced. It was easy to make up a party of six, for here they had made use of their letters of introduction, and extra men were always available. Sometimes they went to the Polo Club, where the natural setting was like the *mise en scène* of a comic opera, or to the Army and Navy Club, where the orchestra played old-fashioned waltzes with the wistful touch that befits the "Beautiful Blue Danube." But oftenest they stayed at the Manila Hotel, where the pillared ballroom opened without windows or doors on the starlit ocean. Usually the first pale strip of dawn had begun to show like a ribbon between the sea and the sky before they went to bed. The urge to dance was in the air; old and young, rich and poor, foreign and native, were swayed by its spirit. Eunice and Francis, Edith and Ruth, were only following a pace that hundreds of others set. They could not tear themselves away from a scene that was still blithe, still crowded, at three o'clock in the morning.

But it was early evening which Eunice loved the best. That was the time when the sun splashed into the sea in a riot of red, and the lights came out in Cavite, across the bay, and on the vessels of the Asiatic Fleet anchored in the harbor. She looked at them intently as she sat listening to the Constabulary Band playing near the Rizal Monument; every night, as she watched them, a more poignant sense of the city's charm crept through her veins, entrancing her.

"Do you suppose there are such scarlet sunsets anywhere in the world as there are here?" she asked Francis one evening. They were alone, for Edith and Ruth had gone out to Stotsenburg for tea with some young officers; so they had idled along, knowing that dinner and dancing would be late. "The light spreads so—almost as if it would take in the whole world," she went on, when Francis followed the sweep of her hand without answering. "I'd like to follow it and see where it stops, wouldn't you?"

"I reckon so, sometime. But not tonight. I've felt tired all the afternoon. And my eyes hurt dreadfully. In fact, I was just on the point of asking you whether you'd mind if we didn't go out tonight. I'd rather tumble into bed than do anything else."

"Of course I don't mind if we don't go out. We've been going out far too much—it's no wonder you're tired. Let's start back to the hotel right away! What I do mind is to see you feeling so badly. Don't you think I'd better send for a doctor?"

"Nonsense! Of course not! I'm not ill—only damned tired. You're right, we have been rather overdoing the dance act. We might cut it out for a few nights."

It had never occurred to her that Francis might be ill, and she allowed herself to be easily persuaded that he was not. With more difficulty, she refrained from "fussing" over him. He tossed and turned for some time before he went to sleep, and his slumbers were troubled all night. Without being very clear in her mind as to what would help, she felt vaguely as if she ought to be sponging him off with cool water or at least bathing his brow; but lacking encouragement as well as experience, she did not try to do so. In the morning he was slightly nauseated. He turned away from his breakfast tray with distaste, and an hour later he was suddenly sick to his stomach. But he made light of it in the face of Eunice's distress.

"You ought to be doing this instead of me. Isn't it usually the first signal that a son and heir is on the way?"

"I believe so— Are you disappointed, Francis, because there isn't? I've been wondering for a long time, but you never said anything, and I didn't like to ask you."

"Why not? I'd have told you that I wasn't exactly disappointed, but that I was surprised. I took it for granted that you'd have a baby right away. It's a well-established tradition in the family that a bride and groom always celebrate their first anniversary by having a christening party at Retreat. I'm afraid we're going to break the precedent."

"I'm terribly sorry, Francis——"

"Why, honey, I'm not blaming you! I know you haven't been taking 'precautions'—that's the phrase, isn't it?—and certainly you've never 'resisted my advances.' But the women the Fieldings have married have been a fruitful lot so far. Only their light-o'-loves have been barren. Things don't always work out so conveniently."

She wanted to pursue the subject, but she could see that Francis was drowsy again. She sat watching him with troubled eyes, and her thoughts were troubled too, for more reasons than one. If he had taken it for granted that she would have a baby right away, she knew he felt thwarted because there were still no prospects of one; and unless there were soon, he would resent it. Here again they were at variance, for she

113

had secretly rejoiced that the complication of a child had not arisen; and though her conscience was clear enough, she was chagrined that Francis should have found her failing in any function he expected her to perform. For the first time she understood why primitive women prayed for pregnancy: it was not because of an irresistible maternal urge within themselves; it was because fecundity helped them to hold the favor of their lords and masters.

If she had a baby—*when* she had a baby—she hoped it would look like Francis. Her eyes rested on him with renewed admiration. Lying uncovered, except for a light sheet, his relaxed figure took on new lines of grace. His profile had a modeled look; she had never realized its full beauty before. But his pallor had a strange tinge to it. It was not only the absence of color which made this seem unnatural; its clarity was gone too. It was dull and cloudy. In its lack of freshness lay the only flaw she could find as she gazed at him, and presently it occurred to her that this change must be due to his illness. The next time he opened his eyes and looked at her, she asked him again, more anxiously than before, if he would not let her send for a doctor.

"Yes, if you want to," he answered absently, and closed his eyes once more.

She telephoned the office and the clerk assured her that he would send a physician right away. But it was more than an hour before the doctor appeared, and during the interval, Francis was sick again. This time he did not joke about his nausea; he lay limp and exhausted when the paroxysm was over, and Eunice could see little beads of perspiration on his temples. However, the breezy little doctor who eventually appeared did not seem to regard his condition as serious, much less alarming.

"Probably just a touch of dengue, Mrs. Fielding. Or possibly malaria. It's too soon to tell. Keep him quiet and see that he doesn't eat any solid foods."

"He doesn't want to eat any food at all."

"It's probably just as well. Is this your first experience with the tropics? Then you haven't had a chance to get acquainted with all our pleasant little pestilences. Fortunately most of them don't amount to much."

About noon, Edith telephoned. Her sprightly voice had an aggrieved note to it.

"I thought we decided we'd go out to Montalban today and that we'd arrange this morning what time we were to start. Have you forgotten about the picnic at the reservoir?"

"I'm afraid I did forget. Francis isn't very well, Edith."

"Then I'm sure he ought to have fresh air and exercise."

"The doctor says he ought to have absolute quiet."

Eunice hung up the receiver before Edith could argue with her any further. But the next morning she herself took the initiative in calling.

"Francis isn't any better, Edith. I think you ought to go ahead with your own plans and not consider us. He thinks so too."

"Do you mean he won't be able to sail on schedule for Singapore?"

"It's very doubtful. If he is, he'll have to be taken aboard the ship on a stretcher and stay in bed all the time he's on the boat. The doctor says he ought to transship right away for Java and get up into the mountains there, where it's cool. He's given me the address of a sanitarium which he says is very good."

"A *sanitarium!*"

"Well, it's a sort of combination of sanitarium and hotel. People who aren't sick can stay there too, if they've relatives and friends who are. Of course, if you'd like to come with us, we'd be glad to have you."

"To a sanitarium!"

"I suppose it won't be very exciting there. But that doesn't matter, of course, if it's the best place for Francis."

"Does Francis want to go there?"

"Francis doesn't care where he goes or what he does. He—he feels terribly ill, Edith."

"But what is the *matter* with him?"

"The doctor isn't sure yet. He says it's often hard to tell in the beginning, with tropical diseases. At first he thought it was dengue or malaria. Now he thinks it may be jaundice. He has a rather peculiar manner. He bursts in, fixes Francis with a strange stare and shouts, 'Sleep well? temperature? pulse? vomit?' "

"How awful—does he think the disease is catching?"

"I believe there's a difference of opinion whether dengue is or not. Malaria isn't, or jaundice. But of course you wouldn't want to take any chances."

"Well I should say *not!*"

The connection was cut before Eunice had a chance to say good-by. At lunchtime the room boy brought her a note on her tray:

"Dear Eunice:
  "Ruth and I have had the most marvelous invitation to go on an inter-island cruise with some perfectly delightful people we met night before last at the dance you didn't come to. It's a unique opportunity, and I really think we ought to take it, for we might never get another like it. We're leaving late this afternoon. Probably you'll

*still be here when we get back, if Francis is really as sick
as you think; but if you do get away first, give your
Java address to the room clerk, and I'll write you there.
We might be able to meet again in Ceylon.*

*"Give my love to Francis and tell him to buck up.
And look out for yourself. There's no reason why you
should get sick just because he has.*

"In great haste,
"Edith"

Eunice opened the envelope carefully, so that she would
not tear the paper when she did so, and tried to keep it from
crackling while she read it. Her hands were trembling when
she put it down, and she sat looking at the food in front of
her without even attempting to taste it. When Francis spoke
to her, she was startled.

"Is Edith clearing out?"

"Why, darling, when did you wake up? I thought you were
sound asleep! Is there anything I can do for you?"

"You might hand over that note."

"I'd—I'd rather not."

"Why? Was it 'personal and confidential?'"

"No-o. But I'm afraid it would hurt your feelings terribly."
The corners of Francis's mouth twitched.

"You overrate my sensitivity. I'm sure I'll be very much
amused. Come on, give it to me."

He stretched out his hand to take the note. Eunice could
see that his fingers had the same peculiar pallor that she had
noticed in his face. She could not summon an answering smile
to meet his. He still looked amused when he tore the note up.

"What sort of creature is it that leaves a sinking ship? I
don't seem to remember exactly."

"Francis, you shouldn't say such a thing!"

She tried to keep the relief from her own voice while she
reproved him. He continued to smile.

"You weren't really so silly as to think that Edith mat-
tered, were you, Eunice?"

"Darling, what else could I think?"

"Only that 'the flesh lusteth against the spirit and these
are contrary one to another so that ye cannot do the things
that ye would—' Should, if I may venture to correct St.
Paul. I thought it was New Englanders who were supposed to
know their Bibles! But Edith is right, you know, even if she
is lewd. There's no reason why you should get sick just because I have. You can shoot me off to a hospital and then
you'd be free to range around Manila by yourself. Probably
someone would invite you to take an inter-island cruise."

"Oh, Francis, how *can* you!"

She was kneeling beside the bed, laying her cheek against his hand and letting her tears fall freely. He reached over to lay his other hand on her hair, stroking it gently.

"Don't, honey. It's dangerous to care for any man the way you do. There isn't one on God's earth that's worth it. The only difference between men is that some of them admit their failings and some of them don't. I do. But it doesn't look as if I'd have an immediate chance to play the fool again. I wouldn't blame you if you looked on this damnable ailment, whatever it is, as a blessing in disguise."

"It'll be a blessing for me if it brings us closer together again. But it's terrible for you. If I could only do something to make it easier!"

With all her heart and soul she tried to do so. And in spite of her inexperience, she was not maladroit when it came to caring for an invalid. The breezy little doctor said there was no necessity of bringing in a nurse, as long as she felt equal to caring for her husband and he preferred her ministrations to an outsider's. She took temperatures and watched diets meticulously; she learned how to change the sheets on the bed while Francis was in it, and how to bathe and turn him with a minimum of discomfort to him. The absence of running hot water in their bathroom—it was brought to them only in small pitchers—and the paucity of service generally, complicated matters for her, but she managed. His initial symptoms persisted, but he did not seem to grow noticeably worse, and eventually the doctor told Eunice that he clearly had a case of jaundice, which was neither contagious nor dangerous, but which must run its ordinary course. The sailing for Singapore had once been postponed, but he saw no reason why it should be again. Reservations were so hard to get that they might find themselves caught in the rapidly mounting heat if they did not push along pretty soon. Mr. Fielding would be as well off on a boat as in a hotel; and he would be much better off when he got to Garoet, where the air was cool and fresh all the time, than he was in Manila, where it was only at sunset that a breeze sprang up. Besides, Mr. Fielding's expressed wish to be on his way was by no means negligible. It was necessary, as far as possible, to keep him cheerful. Anything which would serve to do this, or to actually raise his spirits, would be good medicine. Mrs. Fielding might use her own judgment in the matter.

It all sounded reasonable enough. Eunice was annoyed with herself because her acute anxiety persisted. Francis's increasing lassitude alarmed her, and the real wretchedness which accompanied his intermittent nausea wrung her heart.

She tried to believe that the sea would be beneficial and the mountains still more so, and she talked to Francis about the prospective change with forced gaiety. But she secretly fretted over the fatigue which traveling would involve before any real good could be accomplished, and when she saw how tired he was after the transfer to the ship, she felt that her worst fears were realized.

The first night at sea was stifling. Every time she rose, she found Francis's sheets and pillows drenched with perspiration. She spread them out, put her own on his bed, and lay down herself on the bare mattress. Later on, she took the towels from the bathroom and put these under him instead. The sheets and pillow slips would not dry out in the muggy room, and though she rang at intervals, hoping to secure fresh ones from the night watchman, there was no answer to her summons. In the morning, no steward appeared. She dressed hastily and told Francis she was going out to talk to the purser but that she would be gone only a moment. He nodded, without answering her aloud. His nausea had been worse than ever that morning, and now he lay exhausted, too miserable to care whether she spoke to him or not.

The purser's office was deserted when she reached it, so she went on to the dining room. The head steward, who had his back to the doorway, was arguing violently with another passenger and did not see her approach. She listened with an increasing sense of alarm to his exasperated words.

"It's not my fault that the crew has mutinied. You never know with these blasted Chinese! Go talk to the Captain if you want to—and if he'll see you. Half the people on this boat have tried to get up on the bridge already and they've been turned back with no mincing of words. If you take my advice, you'll hustle out and serve yourself. There's plenty of food in the galley. It won't hurt you to go and get it."

The angry passenger almost knocked her over as he turned, cursing, from his encounter with the steward. Eunice stood her own ground and spoke calmly.

"My husband is very ill. I don't mean that he's seasick, I mean he was ill before we came aboard, and that he's been getting worse all night. I've rung and rung and no one has answered my bell. I don't mind waiting on Mr. Fielding or myself, but I can't leave him for long. Someone will have to show me where supplies are—linen as well as food. And I want the doctor right away."

She transferred a ten-dollar bill from her hand to the steward's. His snarling manner underwent an abrupt transformation.

"Yes, Mrs. Fielding. Anything I can do, of course. But we're in the hell of a mess, if you'll excuse the expression. If we try to force the issue with these Chinese devils we may have murder on our hands. So far they're still at the harmless stage, just growling and insubordinate; but they can get their knifes out before you can say Jack Robinson. I'll send the stewardess to you, but I don't know how much use she'll be. She's the uppity sort, and of course she isn't supposed to carry trays to men. We don't have but one with us, this trip. The doctor's a queer bird too, long on hypos. I'm not saying anything against him though, mind you. He looks like a derelict but maybe he knows his own business."

Eunice was inclined to believe that the steward's unfavorable estimate of the ship's doctor was correct. He was not breezy and casual, like the one in Manila; on the other hand, he seemed to be moving about in a daze from which he came out only occasionally. When he did emerge, it was to denounce the diagnosis of the first physician in charge of the case.

"I don't see what that man in Manila meant by telling you your husband had jaundice. No one was ever as sick as he is with jaundice."

"Do you think he's sicker than he was the first time you saw him?"

"No question of it. He's a very ill man."

"And what do *you* think is the matter with him?"

"Malaria. His blood test makes that perfectly clear to my mind."

Eunice wished desperately that she did not feel so sure nothing was clear to the ship doctor's mind.

"Is there anything you can do to make him feel better?"

"I'm going to give him a hypo. That'll quiet him."

"But he's quiet anyway."

"It won't do him any harm to be quieter. And I'm going to put him on a different diet. He's not been having the right sort of food. He needs building up with meat and spinach."

"But how could he digest meat and spinach when he can't even retain a cup of coffee?"

"If you're going to argue with me, Mrs. Fielding, there's no use in my wasting time on the case. I've several other patients who need my attention and value my advice."

Eunice opened her lips and closed them again without speaking. When the doctor left the cabin, his air of defiance already fading and the dull look coming back into his eyes, she tried to move the position of the electric fan, so that a little air would reach Francis. But the atmosphere was still stifling; it was growing hotter every minute. The stewardess had come sullenly to the door half an hour earlier with a pitcher of lemonade. Now the ice in this was completely melted, and the water in the thermos bottle suspended above the washstand was lukewarm too. It would do no good to ring, to order more brought that was cold; the service on the ship was still in the skeleton stage. Two of the coolies had stabbed each other, and though otherwise no actual rioting had broken out, the ship's officers were alertly avoiding any action that would give rise to more violence. In Singapore there would be a time of reckoning; but it would still take thirty-six hours to reach the Straits Settlements.

As Eunice stood wondering whether she might risk leaving the cabin long enough to get cold water herself, before Francis missed her, she saw that he had already opened his eyes, that he was making a feeble gesture which beckoned her to him. The berth was so narrow that she could not follow her natural instinct of seating herself on it, close beside him; she drew up the straight-backed chair which was the only one the cabin contained.

"Eunice—you'll take me home, won't you?"

"Of course, darling. Of course we'll go home as soon as you like. We ought to have gone home from Japan. I know that's what you'd rather have done. You'd already told me you were longing for Retreat."

He shook his head slightly. At first she thought he meant that he had not wished to go home then after all, that she had been mistaken. Afterward she gathered there was another meaning to his words, though she still was not sure just what it was.

"And if we should have a son, you won't try to make him into a Vermonter, will you? That is, not entirely? You'll remember that he's half Virginian?"

"Of course I'll remember—as if you'd ever let me forget!"

Again Francis shook his head, this time with a faint smile. It was a long while since he had said so much, consecutively. But he went on speaking.

"You must cable to Guy. He'll be back by now. He'll be helpful to you. Much more than Crispin ever would be."

"Cable Guy?"

In the stress and strain through which she had passed, she had completely forgotten Guy Grenville, and the fact that he lived in Singapore. She brushed past the reference to Crispin entirely, but the reminder of Guy gave her a sudden sense of comfort and courage. Of course! Guy would know exactly what to do, and he would do it—quietly, kindly, expertly. Francis would begin to improve instantly once Guy had put him in the hands of the right doctor, in the right surroundings. And she herself would have someone to whom she could turn, someone in whom she could trust. She would not be utterly alone in her anxiety, twelve thousand miles from home. She rose quickly.

"I'm so glad you thought of Guy, darling. I'll send the cable right away."

"No. Wait a few minutes. Until I go to sleep the next time. There's something else I want to say to you."

"I love to listen. But I don't want you to tire yourself."

"It's never tired me to tell you that I love you. It doesn't now. You'll never know how much. I didn't know myself, until I'd lost you."

"Until you'd lost me! Why, darling, you haven't lost me! You couldn't if you tried! That's what marriage means. It isn't just a love affair that lasts a little while. It's 'for richer for poorer, for better for worse, in sickness and in health, to love and to cherish——' "

" 'Till death do us part.' That's the way it ends, isn't it, Eunice?"

Chapter 9

IN SPITE of her anxiety, Eunice had not visualized death as an actuality before. Now she could visualize nothing else.

She did not leave the stifling cabin again. She bribed the sulky stewardess as she had bribed the surly steward, and service of a sort was grudgingly given her in spite of the mutinous crew. The dazed doctor disappeared. In her desperation, she did not feel that it really made much difference.

Francis did not try to talk to her again, and she forced herself to refrain from giving tongue to her own anxious thoughts when he roused, intermittently, from the stupor into which he had sunk. She found that he liked to feel her hand in his, and that he was aware if she withdrew it, even when he seemed half asleep. She sat beside him, hour after hour, through the night as well as the day, waiting for the slight responsive pressure of his fingers against hers.

The boat was due to dock in Singapore at dawn. She was dressed before daylight, and when she had closed the last bag she sat down to wait as patiently as she could for Guy's arrival. A surprisingly prompt answer had come to the cable she had sent: "MEETING SHIP WITH DOCTORS AND AMBULANCE. EXCELLENT TREATMENT AVAILABLE HERE. CONFIDENT CURE CAN BE EFFECTED. KEEP YOUR COURAGE UP. GIVE MY BEST TO FRANCIS. DEVOTEDLY. GUY." The message had comforted her even though it had failed to cheer her, and every little while she extracted it from the bag where she kept it with her passport and travelers' checks and read it over again. She did so now as she waited.

The wait was much shorter than she had expected. The boat was still moving when steps in the corridor came to a stop at her door, and a murmur of voices preceded a gentle knock. She said "Come in" listlessly, without looking up and without rising from her chair by Francis's bed. Guy had touched her shoulder, reassuringly, before she was aware he was in the room.

"Cheerio, Eunice! Here we are! I brought Dr. Sterling along with me in the launch, and his assistant, Dr. Rowe, is at the wharf with the ambulance. Well, Francis, old man, this is rotten luck. But the worst of it is behind you now, I'm certain of that."

The doctor had begun his examination before Eunice had answered. He was an elderly, quiet Scotchman, the personification of kindliness and skill. Even in her surprise, Eunice noticed the swiftness and surety with which his fingers moved from Francis's yellow face to his emaciated body. She also noticed the gravity of the physician's benign and bearded countenance.

"We'll get this husband of yours up to the British Hospital straight away, Mrs. Fielding. I promise you he'll be well looked after there. But I expect you'd like to come along after us so that you can see for yourself that he's properly settled and hear the results of our diagnosis, before you go on to Government House."

"Government House?"

"My father and mother hope very much you'll come and stop with us there. I've brought you a chit from my mother."

Guy handed Eunice an envelope, bearing the seal of the lion and the unicorn. She looked at it in bewilderment.

"I don't know whether I ever mentioned that the Pater is Governor of the Straits Settlements. It's a Crown Colony, you know. As a matter of fact, I don't believe I did. The matter never seemed to come up."

"Guy, I'm overwhelmed with your kindness and your family's. But I had no idea— And I couldn't make a visit of that sort, feeling the way I do now."

"Of what sort?"

"In an official house. I couldn't play up to it. I'm worried and depressed. Colonial Governors live in a sort of royal state, don't they? I wouldn't fit in."

"You needn't see any more of the royal state than you choose, and you don't have to play up to anything. You'll have your own apartment and there'll be a motor waiting, night and day, to take you to the hospital whenever you wish to go."

"I—I'm so touched, Guy, I don't know what to say. But I can't. I can't visit anyone."

"Well, don't worry about it," he said still soothingly. "Mother thought it might be less lonely with us, that's all—that you might like the feeling there were friends all around you. But of course you can stop at the hospital if you'd prefer—at least until Francis is better. We won't take no for an answer after that— You can put Mrs. Fielding up at the hospital, can't you, Dr. Sterling?"

"I can enter her as a patient, too, Mr. Grenville. From the look of her I'd say she could do with a little care herself. You've had a tough trip, I can see that, Mrs. Fielding. But we hope Mr. Grenville is right, that the worst's all behind you now."

"You think it is, don't you?"

"I can tell you that better after we've had a check-up at the hospital. But that won't take any time at all. We'll be at the dock in a jiffy now, and then we'll whisk Mr. Fielding off in an ambulance while you come along with Mr. Grenville. Everything will be as right as rain, you'll see."

His cheerfulness was contagious; from the moment he came into the room he had inspired confidence, and before he left it, taking Francis with him on a stretcher, the gloom with which it had been permeated lightened perceptibly. Eunice herself stepped from the ship before the long-haired natives, with brightly colored sarongs tied around their waists, had finished helping the sailors to tie it up. She was quite unburdened by baggage; the second *syce* would see to all that, Guy informed her briefly; it would go through the customs without formalities and be taken from the dock in the lorry; later on she could decide what she wanted at the hospital and what could be taken directly to Government House to await her arrival there. Some of the terms he used were unfamiliar to her; but there was nothing baffling about his general meaning; and presently she gathered that a lorry was a truck, when she saw one marked "Government House" in large letters, standing on the pier, and that a *syce* was a chauffeur, when a white-clad Malayan, whose spotless uniform was enlivened by a tall red cap and a broad red sash, saluted respectfully at her approach and held open the door of a waiting limousine.

Left to herself, she would have gone through the city with unseeing eyes; but under Guy's gentle prompting, she began to look about her. Her first general impression of luxuriant green foliage and spacious cream-colored buildings, roofed in red or russet, was supplemented by intriguing details. Bullocks were plodding past, stolidly dragging their heavy carts among the automobiles; their gold-tipped horns were painted in contrasting colors, and their tassled-trimmed harnesses were bright with brass. At the crossroads the traffic officers

123

stood with long narrow pieces of wicker strapped to their shoulders; and Guy showed her how bullock drivers and rickshawmen and *syces* alike were directed by the sudden turning of these "wings." A Chinese wedding procession, glittering and noisy, crossed their path, and he explained the symbolism of its gay equipages and complicated arrangement. He also pointed out the people of different races in the teeming crowds, and told her how she could distinguish these from each other by their costumes and bearing, calling her attention to the long braids and high combs of the Singhalese, the folded turbans of the Hindus.

"Lady Singapore is hostess in the halfway house of the world," he told her. "The ships of every nation ride at anchor in her harbor, and the people of every nation walk in her streets. I don't need to tell you how glad I am you've given her a chance to welcome you among them—— Well, here we are, turning in at the hospital grounds already! I hope the ride didn't seem too long. The matron will take you along to your own room, and a sister will help you get settled. By the time you've had your breakfast, I'm sure Dr. Sterling will have his report ready for you and take you in to see Francis. I'll hang around a bit, in case you care to see me too. But I expect you won't, today, anyhow. Perhaps tomorrow you'd let my mother stop by——"

The hospital, set upon a hill overlooking the city and harbor, was built with long galleries open to the breeze, from which the wards and private rooms in turn led out. It was silent and orderly. An Eurasian nurse, functioning under the direction of a tall English sister, dressed in clear blue, took charge of Eunice, brought her tea and marmalade and toast, laid out clean clothes for her, led her to the place where a bath had been prepared. When she came back to her own quarters she found the sister waiting for her again.

"Your husband is asleep just now, none the worse for his transfer from the boat. It's important he should be kept as quiet as possible—no doubt you've been told that before. Dr. Sterling asked me to tell you that he wasn't quite ready to make his report yet and that he hoped you'd get a little rest while you waited for him. Why not try to go to sleep yourself? It would do you no end of good if you could. Then you'd be refreshed when Mr. Fielding wakes and asks for you."

Eunice did not demur. It was weeks since she had relaxed for even an hour, but now she sank gratefully into profound slumber. When she opened her eyes again, the light which filtered in through the blinds had changed in quality; the brilliance of morning had gone, to be succeeded by the lambency of evening. Disquieted for the first time, she reached for her bell pull. The tall English sister appeared instantly, a pleasant smile lighting her fine face.

"You slept straight through tiffin time," she said kindly. "But your nurse will bring you your tea straight away. Then Dr. Sterling will come in to see you, and later I will take you down to the men's wing so that you may go in to visit your husband. His condition is still the same. But you were completely exhausted. If you had not begun to rest when you did, I am sure we would not have needed to stretch a point in order to call you a patient."

The Eurasian approached for the second time with tea and toast and marmalade, and on this occasion they had been reinforced with soft boiled eggs, still in their shells, sliced bread and butter, and fruitcake. Eunice ate everything up, hungrily. She was just devouring the last crumb when Dr. Sterling put in a timely appearance.

"Now, then, I'm pleased to see you looking a little better than you did this morning," he said, sitting down beside her and speaking in the same kindly way as the nurse. "And if you'll stay in bed a good deal these next days, I'll be better pleased yet."

"But I want to stay with my husband, you know, Dr. Sterling. And I haven't seen him all day."

"Well, you'll be seeing him soon and you can stop in his room until nine o'clock, if you give me your word you won't talk to him except when he speaks to you, which won't be much, and that you won't go moving around disturbing him. If you could keep a bit of sewing in your hands, or a book to read, it would be a fine thing."

"I'll do anything you say, Dr. Sterling, if you'll only tell me about Francis first."

"I was coming to that. Of course you know he's in no immediate danger, or you'd have been called long ago. But I think you must make up your mind for an endurance test. That's why I don't want you to use up all your own reserves. You've gone fairly far along those lines already. Now you must follow the schedule I'll give you—so much sleep and so much exercise right away, so much diversion or relaxation or whatever you choose to call it later on. If you don't, you'll give out. You have no idea what the tropics can do to a young woman."

"I promise I'll follow your orders faithfully, if that will help Francis— What kind of endurance test do you mean?"

"I took the liberty of calling in another medical man, Mrs. Fielding, in order to verify my opinion before I talked with you. His diagnosis is the same as mine. We are agreed that your husband is the victim of a very rare tropical disease. I'm not astonished that its exact nature wasn't recognized in

Manila. It's a form of jaundice, so your doctor there wasn't mistaken, in a sense. But it bears something the same relation to ordinary jaundice that scarlet fever does to scarlatina."

"You mean it's more serious?"

"It's very much more serious. It has a thirty per cent mortality."

"That's high, isn't it?"

"It's very high. I know you're a brave woman, Mrs. Fielding. That's why I feel it's better you should hear the truth at once. You'd rather do that than grope around in the dark, wouldn't you? I thought so! Now I shall also tell you that you needn't be fearful for today or tomorrow or the day after that. If your husband's heart doesn't go back on him—and I don't see the least prospect of that—he can hold out a long time. But he'll have to fight overwhelming depression all along the way. That's one of the most complicated characteristics of this illness—the lack of desire to struggle as the siege goes on. And I don't know whether he can hold out long enough to resist starvation."

"Starvation?"

"Yes. That's where the fatal difficulty usually comes. He won't be able to take any nourishment except albumen water for days. Later on a little fruit juice. Nothing solid for weeks, no fats or stimulants of any kind for weeks after that. He's strong and young; that's in his favor; if he were flabby and elderly, he wouldn't have a chance. His greatest handicap is that he's so slightly built. Whether his own flesh will suffice to keep body and soul together, I can't say."

The doctor took her hand. "So you see it's a waiting game, Mrs. Fielding. I can't tell you how long the wait will be, or what its outcome will be. Only that you've got to face it. I know you can. Your husband depends on you. It didn't take me long to find that out. And I do too. I'm counting on you to help me see this through, to give him the will to live he hasn't got himself."

Francis depended on her. Dr. Sterling was counting on her. She could face it. She could see it through.

Eunice repeated the words over and over. At first she did so mechanically, as if they made a formula that was more or less meaningless. But gradually she came to put courage and conviction into them; and eventually she said them with fervor, as a woman exalted by faith might recite her rosary.

She did not rebel against the respite upon which Dr. Sterling insisted for herself. Before she had been in the hospital twenty-four hours, the white-clad night matron came to tell her that her husband did not seem so well and to suggest that she should put on a dressing gown and come at once to his room. She remained there until nine the next morning, when he had obviously rallied again. The episode reassured her rather than alarming her. Now she was confident that she would be called if any emergency arose; she ceased to worry lest Francis should need her and that she should not know it. She went to bed early every evening, took a long nap every afternoon, and walked back and forth around the galleries after tea. The rest of the time she sat silently in Francis's room, holding the book or the bit of sewing that had been recommended. Her grandmother had taught her to sew when she was a little girl, and though it was years since she had put on a thimble, she quickly recaptured both her skill and her interest. The needlework was soothing to her nerves and she took pride in the product of her fingers. This pride was redoubled after she found that Francis had noted what she was doing.

"I love to see you sew," he said unexpectedly one day.

He had not spoken for hours. She had assumed that he was still asleep. She spread her work out over her knees so that he could see it better.

"Do you really?" she asked demurely.

"Yes. It suits you. It's the sort of thing you ought to do regularly. What are you making?"

"Pajamas for you. That is, I never made any before, but I hope they'll turn out to be pajamas."

"Of course they will. Eunice, you're a treasure. Have I ever told you so before?"

"Something of the sort. But it didn't have any connection with sewing."

Another day, with equal unexpectedness, he asked her what she was reading. She flushed a little as she answered.

"There aren't many books here to choose between. This one is called *The Forest Lovers*."

"It sounds intriguing—and appropriate for us. We met in a forest, didn't we? And we were lovers right away."

She did not answer.

"Weren't we, honey?"

"Yes. Right away."

"Come here, Eunice."

She went over and stood by the bed, hoping that in the shuttered light the tears on her lashes would not show. They kept overflowing in spite of all her efforts at self-control; her voice trembled too; so often she was glad Dr. Sterling had told her not to talk much. She hoped it would not tremble now, or that if it did, Francis would not notice this.

"We're still lovers, aren't we? Not just a patient and his head nurse?"

"No, not that at all."

127

"You're not standing by like this because you're sorry for me, or because you think it's your duty, or anything of that sort? There, darling, you don't need to say anything more. I know now— Why don't you read aloud to me a little while? If it wouldn't bore you to start at the beginning of the book again?"

After that she read to him for hours on end. He suggested newspapers, and while those available did not supply them with much news, they were the source of considerable merriment. The first one they secured devoted its front-page spread to an article on "The Flora and Fauna of Singapore in the Year 1904." Another contained several blank columns under the bold type caption of "LATEST NEWS!" In an inconspicuous section, Eunice discovered several attacks on a speech Herbert Hoover had made about the international rubber situation. Some of these attacks were in editorial form and others in the form of letters, signed with bristling pseudonyms; all were pugnacious and bitter. But when Francis expressed a desire to see a copy of the speech itself, none could be found in the city, though Guy helped Eunice to instigate a diligent search, not only in the newspaper office, but also at Government House and the International Bank. He made a rather rueful confession in confessing his final failure.

"I asked an aide of my father's," he said—"one I've always regarded as a fountainhead of information!—to cooperate in the search. He was very eager to be helpful, but he was puzzled. 'Who is this man Herbert Hoover anyway?' he said. 'I seem to have heard of him, but I don't place him at all.'"

"Britannia still rules the waves but the Burns Detective Agency can give the British Secret Service cards and spades," observed Francis.

They all laughed together. Guy was occasionally admitted to Francis's room now for brief visits, for it had been discovered that he always took the initiative in leaving before he had tired the invalid and that his pleasant ways and optimistic outlook had a salutary effect.

"I reckon we'll have to fall back on romance, instead of rubber," Francis continued drolly. "But we've about exhausted the hospital's supply. Is there a bookshop in town?"

"Yes, of a sort. Shall I buy you *One Hundred Years of Singapore?*"

"No—I'm going to write a mighty tome with that title myself, based on my own experiences. Why don't you take Eunice along with you and see if you can't make a better selection between you."

Docile as she had been about following a schedule within

128

its galleries, Eunice had remained adamant on the point of leaving the hospital. Now, reluctantly, she consented to go out long enough to buy books. She was back inside of an hour, and stacked her purchases up between a pair of bookends, which she had bought at the same time, where Francis could look at them from his bed. He teased her about the lengthy list of titles. It was a long time since he had teased her about anything.

"Are we spending the summer in Singapore, Eunice? It looks to me as if you'd laid in enough light literature to last for months."

"I can read to you just as well in Garoet as in Singapore."

"Oh, yes—Garoet. That was where we were headed, wasn't it, when we left Manila before beginning my hundred years in Singapore?"

"I know it seems as if you'd been in bed forever. But it isn't so long, really. We've only been here three weeks."

"That's so. Well, in about three weeks more we'll begin to make plans for leaving, you wait and see."

"Francis, you must be feeling better, ever so much better, to talk that way."

"Of course I'm feeling better— Tell me what you saw when you were out today."

"Nothing much. I was out to buy books, not to see sights. I smelled more than I saw. Guy said one of the worst smells came from a rubber factory. I didn't identify any of the others. But I never was in a place where there were as many smells as there are in Singapore, all different and all bad."

Francis laughed again. "Well next time you go out, hold your nose and look around, so you can tell me what you've seen. You might even stop in at the rubber factory and find out if they have a copy of Herbert Hoover's speech there."

She saw that he was really interested, and the next afternoon, when Guy suggested that they should "take a turn," she raised no objections. She came back carrying an armful of orchids and brimming over with contagious enthusiasm about everything she had seen and done.

"Just look at the length of those stems, darling! The orchids stand as high as my head! I picked them in a garden, out in the suburbs, where Guy took me to tea with some friends of his. But we saw the loveliest sight of all as we were coming back to the hospital: a crescent moon, not tipped at all, but lying straight across the sky which was still all pink and fluffy looking. Everything was very quiet all around us when suddenly Guy touched my arm and said, 'Look!' And what do you think I saw? A man dressed in a white robe and a white turban sinking down to his knees on the grassy slope between the big cream-colored buildings.

After he had knelt he bowed very deeply and reverently there times. He was saluting the crescent moon!"

"We saluted a moon ourselves once, didn't we—a full moon shining over a swamp? You told me a story then too. I love your stories, Eunice. Go on!"

She did go on, until the sister came to say that it was bedtime, that Mrs. Fielding must go back to her own room. Francis pleaded for a reprieve.

"Let her stay just a little longer, Sister. And you send me up something to eat. I'm hungry."

Eunice and the sister exchanged glances. There was a world of meaning in the simple statement. For a long time Francis had swallowed his albumen water with infinite difficulty, he had seldom retained it for long, and his retching had been terrible to see. Eunice had watched him growing thinner and thinner, thinking as she watched what the doctor had said about starvation. That was why her eyes had overflowed so often, why her voice had trembled so. Now, at last, the hideous nausea was under control. Francis was hungry. That meant he was going to get well.

But it did not mean that it was safe for him to eat. The knowledge that he must continue to lie in his bed, combating terrible emptiness, terrible weakness, was deeply distressing to Eunice. Only the implication of his hunger assuaged her anxiety. And when Dr. Sterling asked her to give up her own room, she knew that the improvement was a substantial one. The other reasons the physician gave for his request were only incidental, as far as she was concerned.

"We really need the space, Mrs. Fielding. There's a great deal of illness in Singapore just now—not that this is unusual. But we stretched a point, as you know, to take you in at all. If His Excellency hadn't intervened—and now it appears Lady Grenville is becoming quite impatient to welcome you as a guest."

Lady Grenville had been to the hospital several times and Eunice had been drawn to her from the first. She was not overawed by the Englishwoman's imposing presence, as a girl herself less reserved might have been. Instead, she admired Lady Grenville's dignity and discerned its underlying dependability. When she discovered genuine kind heartedness as well, which she was not long in doing, she ceased to evade suggestions for a visit, and eventually she consulted Francis about the matter.

"Of course I think you ought to go. As far as that's concerned, you should have gone long ago. But you'll come back to read to me once in a while, won't you? During the intervals between the times when Guy is taking you out on the town? I wouldn't know how to get on without my head nurse."

He held out his arms. He still could not raise himself on his pillow, but his hands no longer lay, inert and limp, at his side. She leaned over him so that it would be easy for him to embrace her. She could feel his heart beating against hers, and the pulse of it was steady and strong. She knew that she had won, even before he told her so.

"Eunice, you've saved my life. I don't know what it's worth to you. But it's yours, darling. It's all yours. I want you to know that before you leave me, before you go to Government House."

Chapter 10

THOUGH EUNICE felt as if they were worlds apart, it actually took only about ten minutes to go from the British Hospital to Government Hill.

As the limousine, driven by the red-capped, red-sashed *syce*, turned into the imposing gateway, she caught a glimpse of tennis courts and golf links beyond spacious green lawns. Then the car came to a standstill at the entrance of an immense pillared building, dazzlingly white, which reminded her of her own childhood conception of the celestial mansions which her grandmother told her about. Several barefooted servants, dressed much like the *syce*, came forward to meet her and she found herself in a spacious white entrance hall, marble-floored, with a noble white marble staircase rising to the upper story. Here she was met by a prim young woman who introduced herself as Lady Grenville's secretary and took her to her room. The clanging of a gong, proclaiming that tiffin time was only half an hour distant, resounded just as she saw her last piece of baggage carefully deposited in a convenient place. But as she had nothing to do in the interval, she employed it by gazing at her new surroundings.

The room was about as large as the ground floor of a fairsized bungalow, and as high as a two-storied house—whitepillared, white-walled, green-shuttered, with dark, polished furniture. In the center of it stood the most enormous bed she had ever beheld. A door at one end opened into a bathroom of corresponding proportions; at the other end was an alcove sitting room containing a chaise longue drawn up beside a table on which were placed a shaded lamp, a big bowl of gardenias, and a number of books and magazines. A desk generously equipped with thick engraved stationery stood near this and in addition to the stationery, there was a printed pamphlet with instructions for guests.

"Mess Dress is always worn at dinner when His Excellency and Lady Grenville are present"—she read—
"Guests who may be without Mess Dress, should wear tail coats unless otherwise notified. . . .

"Guests are particularly requested not to give any tips to the servants in Government House. There is a servants' fund in charge of the aide-de-camp and contributions should be handed to the aide-de-camp.

"Guests are most particularly requested on leaving Government House to write their addresses in the book in the hall—and also to sign their names in the Visitors' Book which is kept in the porch room."

She had difficulty in focusing her thoughts as she read. She did not care what she wore or whom she tipped or where she signed her name. She cared only about Francis, who was lying desperately ill in the hospital; she wondered how she could be expected to follow a long list of printed rules at such a time, and she hoped her hosts would not be too severe if she did not succceed in doing so. But she could not dwell on the hope for long. She realized it was time to go to the upstairs "veranda" and there await the ringing of the second gong and the appearance of His Excellency and Lady Grenville. Two aides-de-camp, two private secretaries and several house guests besides herself were already assembled by the time she had traversed the corridor into the spacious upper hall, past the ballroom with its glittering chandeliers and its full-length portraits of the King and Queen of England; and after a few minutes' wait, the door of a suite on the left opened, her host and hostess appeared, and she was formally presented to them, quite as if she had never seen either of them before, though her acquaintance with Lady Grenville had by this time reached the stage of great mutual cordiality. Then a procession formed to descend to the dining room, and she took her place gratefully between Guy and a young aide-de-camp who had come several times to the hospital bringing chits and gifts from Government House.

The service was formal, the menu elaborate, and the decorations profuse. A Malayan footman stood behind every chair, and the multitudinous courses succeeded each other so quickly that Eunice found herself clinging to her knife and fork lest her plate should be snatched away from her when she laid these down. The red fish which the aide-de-camp told her was called *ekam merah* was very good; she liked it better than the curry of lamb and rice, hotly seasoned in itself and further surmounted with chutney, which was the next offering; and she did not like her pudding of cold molded tapioca, served with coconut milk and coconut sugar, at all. Guy saw her struggling to swallow it and quietly motioned to a servant to remove her plate.

"No outsider likes *Gula Malacca* at first," he said with his usual pleasant smile. "And this isn't one of those endurance tests Dr. Sterling likes to talk about. There'll be some fruit in a minute—mangosteens and so on. Or would you like something else?"

"Oh, no. I don't see how I could swallow another mouthful before dinnertime."

"Of course you can. There'll be lemon squash and tea, with all the usual trimmings, on the veranda at four. We meet there after our siestas and before we begin our sports. Would it interest you to see a polo game this afternoon? My mother would like to take you to one, unless you want to go back to the hospital."

"But I do. You know you promised."

"I did indeed. You'll find the car that's assigned to you waiting, whenever you're ready to start. But don't forget that our good friend the medical man hasn't released you from your promise to lie down every day after tiffin."

She had never found a pledge so hard to keep. She could hardly wait to share her first impressions of Government House with Francis. But what was more exciting still, she found him eagerly waiting to hear them, propped up on pillows for the first time, and proudly proclaiming that he had been feasting too, on a strip of cold dry toast and a sliver of chicken.

"I'm to have a meal every two hours. Not 'nourishment' any longer, a meal. That's progress, you know. So you didn't like the curry? I think I would— I'd like almost anything I could get my teeth into, when it came to that— What time do you have to be back for dinner?"

"At eight-fifteen. That is, dinner is at eight-fifteen. I have to be dressed and out on the veranda at eight. And then I have to be presented to Sir Geoffrey and Lady Grenville all over again. Twice a day, no matter how long I stay there, before lunch—tiffin I mean—and before dinner. The aide-de-camp explained it all to me. And he told me that when we played bridge after dinner, we must all be prepared to stop immediately, the instant His Excellency gave the signal. He said the Governor had a maxim that you could start a rubber at five minutes before eleven, but that you must never start one at five minutes past—if you did it would turn out to be the kind that went on and on through the night. He says this sometimes makes it hard for the guests who aren't playing at His Excellency's table, because those extra ten minutes can represent quite a lot of money to them. Not that he put it just that way. But that was what he meant— He's very nice."

"Maybe he could figure out something to keep you busy after five minutes of eleven. Though I imagine Guy's thought that all out."

"Well, they both spoke—separately, I mean—of taking a late ride to cool off before going to bed. They say the moonlight makes the sand in the coconut groves along the East Drive look just like snow and fairly floods the jungle that closes in beyond the Mandai Road."

"Give me my clothes this minute. I'm hearing too much about this Singapore moonlight. I want to take you out to look at it myself. Not that I think rides of that kind have a very cooling effect———"

"I keep thinking 'If Francis were only with me at Government House, it would be like living in a fairy tale.' "

"Do you think you could find room for me in that cunning little bed you've been telling me about?"

"You know I could find room for you any where and any time."

She did not trust herself to tell him how much she missed him, how large and lonely her splendid quarters seemed when she closed the door behind her after the last health to the King had been drunk and the last strains of music had died away, when the guests had dispersed and Their Excellencies had retired and the huge house was hushed for the night.

During the day, her pleasure in the pageantry of her surroundings buoyed her up. To be sure, she sometimes felt a trifle chilled or a trifle alien. She recognized the fact that Lady Grenville was an important and preoccupied personage; still it seemed strange to her that she never saw her hostess except at mealtimes, unless a special appointment to do so was made in writing. She knew that entertaining on a vast scale could not be smoothly and suitably carried forward without ceremonial attention; but she was oppressed by the dispatch of the seating plan, in the form of a folder, when she was dressing for dinner. The luxury of living, to which she was accustomed among the Middleburg millionaires, was characterized by a certain amount of heartiness and informality which was wholly lacking here; and personally she had always preferred the supreme simplicity of life in Hamstead with her grandmother to anything else. Moreover, she did not understand the local problems, centering on races, and the local politics, centering on rubber, around which the more serious conversations at Government House turned; the underlying reasons for building the great naval base, the sight of which she was proudly taken out to see, were mysterious to her, and sporting terms, as expressed by the British, incomprehensible. So was a large part of what passed for humor. There were moments when her powers of adaptability were taxed to the utmost, and only her deep sense of gratitude and her sincere efforts to achieve adequacy in strange surroundings upheld her. But after all, these moments were in the minority. On the whole, she enjoyed the exotic qualities of the setting in which she was so surprisingly playing a part.

However, she was beginning to notice that Francis received her accounts of her experiences with less enthusiasm than he had at first. He was growing restive, despite the fact that he was no longer confined completely to his bed, that every morning and afternoon he was taken in a wheeled chair to a veranda at the end of the men's wing, and that here he played cards and chess for a couple of hours at a time with other convalescents, and compared symptoms and adventures with them. Many of the men were stranded ship's officers: There was a Norwegian freight skipper with neuritis; two first mates, one a red-headed Welshman with dysentery, the other a Dutchman with malaria; a British ship's doctor with penumonia; and a chief engineer with a hint of Cockney on his tongue who enjoyed the distinction of having been "dead" for half an hour before a pulmotor saved his life. The landlubbers included a British civil engineer whose pretty Russian wife came and talked to him all day long; his Australian pal; a rich Borneo planter; a New Zealander, rubber-crazy; and—the only American except Francis—a man from a tourist agency who explained the difficulties of separating ladies who had been bosom friends halfway around the world and would be sworn enemies for the rest of the trip. There was only one disagreeable man there who would never speak to any of the others; he sulked in a corner and scowled; but all the others had marvelous tales to tell.

The red-headed mate was perhaps the most eloquent of all. He almost wept with emotion over the beauties of the Welsh tongue, and it was with difficulty that his companions prevented him from reading it to them out of his newspapers. He gave marvelous descriptions of his native land, where—according to him—the science of healing with herbs was still successfully practiced, and where congregations sang with beautiful deep harmony in little Welsh chapels. Shifting from this type of discourse, he might refer to the

135

time he bawled out the second engineer, or tell about the Malay who ran amuck on a boat entering Singapore and killed her captain and wounded her mate before he was overcome. Between yarns, the mate was always trying to get something which the doctor had forbidden him to eat from a stupid hospital room-boy, and, his efforts rewarded, would enjoy his choice morsel to the full. A few hours later, however, the men would hear him complaining of frightful pains, and evening would find him eating dinner curtailed by a sister who would not be convinced that his upset was due to a sudden chill.

The Norwegian skipper was not as talkative as the Welsh mate, but he was a good storyteller too. He especially enjoyed describing his experiences in the mine fields during the World War. The Dutchman, when not engaged in killing mosquitoes—his favorite pastime—was also an excellent storyteller.

The days passed, and the men talked on. They discussed the sad case of a lonely sailor dying downstairs, and the tragedy of the skipper, useless and jobless for a year to come, going home a passenger on his own boat. They marveled at the miraculous treatment which was slowly curing a boy who had been brought to the hospital to die of tuberculosis of the spine. They mourned for the man in the room next to Francis, whose case was perhaps the saddest of all. He and his wife had been taken sick in a hotel; his wife had died in the room with him, and he had then been moved to the hospital, bringing a picture of her to put at his bedside during the hours which he was sure would be his last. And still, unwillingly, he lived on——

Eunice had hoped that the masculine companionship which Francis was now enjoying and the liberation, both mental and physical, which this represented, would be cheering to him. It was true that the stories he heard diverted him while he was listening to them, and that he often repeated them to her, with relish, afterward. But on the whole he was less patient under progress than he had been under starvation and pain.

"I want to walk around. I'm sick of all these chairs and couches."

"A week ago you said you'd be satisfied if you could only get out of your own room."

"Well, that was a week ago. I never said I'd be satisfied with the same thing forever. And I'm starving to death. I'm so hollow that you could store furniture inside of me."

"You're having fish and poultry and fruit and vegetables and bread and jam now, aren't you?"

"Yes—all without an atom of gravy or butter! Did you

ever see a Southerner who ate his food without 'drippings'?"

"I've seen this Southerner when he really was starving to death. Now that he's coming back to life again, I'm not worrying because his bread isn't buttered."

"Well, I may be alive but I can tell you I'm kicking too. I don't see why that so and so of a doctor has to be so damned cautious about everything. I suppose it's because he's Scotch."

"It may possibly be because he likes his patients to get well."

"I want a julep," Francis went on, disregarding her comment. He clasped his hands behind his head and looked out beyond the gallery as if he were trying to see a mint bed. "A julep in a silver goblet that you can't see for the frost on it, unless you dig that off with your fingernails. I want two or three of them. And then I want some terrapin, served in a bowl and eaten with a spoon, so that I won't lose any of the cream or the sherry. Next I want a platter of fried chicken with corn fritters heaped all around it, and a whole ham with cloves sticking out of it, that I can cut myself in thick red slices. I want garden greens and rice and yams and beaten biscuit and pear preserves and pickled peaches. I want strawberry shortcake and coffee and brandy—the coffee in a big cup and the brandy in a big glass. I'd like to drink them out in the garden. That's getting prettier every day now."

"Tell me about it," urged Eunice. She really did not care much about the garden, as she had no gift for making flowers grow. But she knew Francis wanted to talk about it. "You know everything had been frozen when I was there in November, except some chrysanthemums and some cosmos. It must be beautiful in the springtime."

"It is. It's the loveliest garden I've ever seen. It's laid out like a checkerboard, in a succession of walks that separate it into squares. The walks are boarded with fruit and shrubbery and trees—mostly fruit trees. The squares have vegetables and strawberries in them. I'd get the garden greens and the berries for the shortcake out of those. There's a different taste to them when you pick them fresh."

"Yes, that's what grandma says too."

"There are three long walks that run north and south from the rail fence that separates the garden and the apple orchard," Francis continued, warming to his subject. "The middle walk is graveled with river pebbles. When Bina and Bella and I were children we used to pick up the pink and blue pebbles out of the walk. We liked the big ones for playthings, and the little ones we just ran through our fingers, like this."

He held up his thin white hands, and Eunice could almost see the pink and blue pebbles pouring across them. Retreat seemed closer than Government House at this moment.

"The other two long walks are made of grass. The cross-

137

walks cut across these. That's how the garden is divided into squares. The crosswalks are grassy too, except the first one bordering the house yard. That has banksia rose vines trained on a high frame along the first part of it. Then farther on come a crepe myrtle, a 'fire bush,' a monthly honeysuckle, a lilac tree and finally, close against the smokehouse, a shrub that father brought in from the woods. It has pretty light green leaves and little cup-shaped white flowers. It's a wild shrub. None of us know what its name really is."

"Couldn't you invent one?"

"Bina did. She's great on inventing things, you know. She called it the 'chalice flower.' It's her favorite, except for the pink mallow she brought up herself from the marshes. Mother's favorite is the arborvitae, though. Which one do you think you'd like best?"

"I don't think I know what either one of them looks like, darling. I can't remember that I've ever seen a pink marsh mallow or an arborvitae tree either."

"You can't!"

"No— I'm afraid I shan't be much good as a gardener."

"But women are always good gardeners! I never saw one that wasn't. My mother can make anything grow. She has what we call 'green thumbs.' My grandmother did too. *Her* grandmother designed the garden, but she developed it. They were both artists when it came to horticulture."

Francis spoke with the same pride about the flair for gardening with which all the Fielding women were gifted and in the same tone of voice as when he had spoken of the large number of children they had all had. It was evident that he considered the fruitfulness of the land under their care as being favorably comparable to their own fruitfulness. A sense of her own inadequacy, greater than she had ever experienced at Government House, swept over Eunice.

"I'll learn how to take care of the garden, Francis."

"You've had to learn a good many things since you met me, haven't you?"

"Yes. But you can't say I haven't tried."

"I didn't say it. What makes you so touchy?— The May cherry tree must be in blossom now, right back of Bina's chalice flowers, shading them. It throws its shade in every direction, and the cherries on it are so dark that they look almost purple in the shadow, and so sweet that we children could find them by their smell, in the grass, after they'd dropped off the branches from sheer ripeness. If I were home, I'd eat two or three handfuls of them while I drank my coffee and my brandy. If I did that I might be able to hold out without anything else until suppertime and then I'd have——"

"Francis, my mouth is beginning to water too. I don't think I can bear to hear what you'd have for supper."

"All right. I won't tell you if you're not interested. But that's what I lie here thinking about while the gnawing feeling gets worse and worse. What I'd have for dinner and supper and breakfast, too, if I were only at Retreat. And what I'd be doing if I weren't rotting away in this damned bed. How I'd strike out on the river in a boat and how I'd get on a good horse and ride over the plantation. The shad's running in the Potomac now, and the dogwood and Judas trees are out and the corn's coming up. It's great to go boating and riding at this time of year. And speaking of good horses, I'd go over to Warrenton for the Gold Cup and spend the week end at Todd Hollow with the Taliaferros—those cousins of mine your father bought Tivoli from. They live on an old mill site they've fixed up—mighty pretty it is too. There's a lot of land, with little stone buildings scattered over it— Don't you love all the stone down Middleburg way, Eunice? I do. There's nothing like it in King George— Well, one of these stone buildings was a barrel house once, and one was the miller's home, and another was the owner's, originally. Now the Taliaferros use them all, for themselves and their kin. They'd put me up in the barrel house, and we'd have lunch in the garden, with the old millstones in it, overlooking the stream. Then in the afternoon we'd go to the races. We'd lean over the paddock rail and size up the entries, and then we'd go to the bookies to place our bets, and tear up and down seeing who was giving the best odds. Blanche and Virgin would be there too, playing their hunches and nipping away at their 'consecrated lye.' They'd keep on hanging around the stables, but the Taliaferros and I would amble up the hill and watch the steeplechase from the lawn at Broadview. Bella and Bina would be there with their dates, giving them the time of their lives, and getting them to spend money like drunken sailors —babies like that are an easy mark for the chaps that peddle corsages and hot dogs and Coca-Colas. Millie Stone would be there too, still looking like an Oriental princess in spite of her tweeds, and Free would be flashing that famous smile of his all over the place. I reckon they'd speak to me now, and of course everyone else always has. It's a grand crowd. We'd hang around and have a few drinks and swap a few smutty stories. But all the time we could be looking out over the countryside for miles around, and it would have a soft sheen to it, the grass and the sky too. They wouldn't be hard and hot the way they are here."

"Darling, I know you're terribly homesick for Virginia. The minute Dr. Sterling thinks——"

"Yes, and the racing will be all over then until next year!

If I were in Todd Hollow this week end, instead of in the British Hospital at Singapore, I'd go from one cocktail party to another, after the races were over, and then I'd go to the North Wales Club for the dinner dance. I'd be more or less high by that time, but I'd keep right on toasting the winners, just like everyone else. Gosh, how I'd like to be there! I haven't had enough money to go to the Gold Cup in three years, and this year I could have gone. The last time I did go I sold an ancestral snuffbox to make it. It was worth a dozen of them, but the supply had run out, so I couldn't do that again. There wasn't anything else Mother would let me get rid of. She said no one used snuff any more, but that girls would go right on wanting to wear jewelry till the end of time, and if they didn't have anything but cameos and hair bracelets left, they'd have to make the best of them. I suppose girls do like jewelry. I remember some of the dames at the North Wales Club had on quite a lot of it—not cameos or hair bracelets either! Didn't you ever go to the Gold Cup, Eunice? Don't you remember what it's all like?"

"I went once. That must have been one of the years you couldn't make it. But I was disappointed in it."

"Disappointed!"

"Yes. I like to ride, but I—I don't know much about racing, Francis. That's another thing you'll have to teach me, if I can learn. But I'm always so afraid a jockey may get hurt, going over the hurdles, that I can't bear to look at the jumps. One jockey did get hurt the very first time I went to a race. He was taken off the track in an ambulance with a screaming siren, and the sound of it haunted me for hours. The horse had to be shot. I've never forgotten it."

Francis looked at her curiously, without answering. She went on, feeling increasingly apologetic as she did so.

"And some of the house parties are so terribly wild. Of course I know it must be different at your cousins'. But I went to one where there were ten unmarried couples—the girls sleeping in twos and threes and the men in single rooms—and the chaperon relegated to the third floor. My roommate roused me when she finally came in about five in the morning to say she was simply exhausted, because she'd spent most of the night taking off her bouffant dress and putting it on again. She'd kept hearing footsteps on the stairs, and she couldn't tell whether it was some other girl having a busy time like herself, or the chaperon tardily approaching to look the situation over. So she felt she had to be on the safe side, at least to the extent of having something on if she were caught in a young man's room. I can see that cerise taffeta still, and hear it rustle. That's something else I've never forgotten. It's easy to imagine the complications caused by the hoops."

Francis put back his head and laughed. "That's the best story you've told me in a long time. You've been getting rather geographical. Have you got any more like it up your sleeve?"

"No. Not that sort. But I heard something yesterday in Jahore that I thought might amuse you."

The merry look on Francis's face had already begun to fade. "So you went to Jahore yesterday," he said indifferently. "Was it a pleasant trip?"

"Very. The Sultan showed us his gardens. Then he invited us into his palace for tea. It was served by men wearing batik sarongs, and we had native rice cakes and meat sandwiches flavored with curry. They were very good."

"So you're getting to like curry after all? Who were 'we' by the way—you and Guy?"

"Yes. You've no idea how kind he's been to me, Francis."

"I reckon I have— Did the Sultan show you his harem by any chance? I'm sure that would have been a good deal more intriguing than his garden!"

"No, we weren't invited to do that and Guy said we would be allowed to. It seems strange, for one of the Sultan's wives is an English woman. Guy used to know her rather well, too."

"But not as well as the Sultan does, I suppose— How many wives does he have?"

"I believe there are four. They're obliged to become Mohammedans, if they weren't already, and to marry according to Moslem law. And if the Sultan wishes to divorce one of them, he only needs to shout 'Talak!' the first time she displeases him."

"I take it that means get out. Well, I always thought Mohammedanism had a great deal to commend it. Just feature the advantages of having four wives at once! Even if one were having a baby, and another were indisposed, and another were in a bad temper, that still wouldn't exhaust the agreeable available supply! And then they could all be replaced, if they weren't on the whole satisfactory, just by bellowing 'Talak!' I should think that would tend to keep the average of excellence mighty high. I'm glad you went to Jahore after all, Eunice. I'm sure it'll make you more appreciative of the advantages in your own matrimonial position."

"I do appreciate them," she answered, speaking with the shyness she had not yet contrived to overcome in the face of his badinage. There was almost a touch of humility in it, as if she were still dazzled by the splendor he had promised her, and had never grieved because it had been touched by tarnish or dimmed by separation. "The story I started to tell you was about the Sultan's harem, as it happens," she went on. "It seems that all the women in it, from the Sultana down, put their slippers outside their bedrooms at night. This is not so that the shoes will be polished, as it would be in an English house. It is to show their lord and master that they hope he will come in. Even a woman at whom he has shouted 'Talak!' puts out her slippers as a sign that she is longing for a reconciliation. That is, if he has only said it once. If he has said it three times, she knows that she has lost his favor forever, that she must withdraw from his presence. It must be very sad for her."

"Perhaps she's glad of the chance to withdraw."

"I don't believe so. Why should she be?"

"All sorts of reasons. She might find someone she liked better herself. Well, as I said, I'm mighty glad you went to Jahore. Where are you going next?"

"I think we're going out to dine on the sand at Sea View, and dance in the pavilion there."

" 'We' being you and Guy again?"

"Yes. Two young British officers and their wives are going too. The Governor and Lady Grenville are dining with the Bishop—he and the Attorney General are the only persons with whom they do go out to dine. And since they're going to be away, Guy thought——"

"I should say he had a very good idea."

Eunice had thought so herself. Now that the special privileges accorded her while Francis was dangerously ill had been abrogated, she was not supposed to remain at the hospital after regular visiting hours, and the unrelieved formality of the evenings at Government House had begun to pall on her; she was growing restive herself. The outing Guy had proposed would take them to a famous resort of which she had heard a good deal but which she had not yet seen; and she had formed a great liking for the young British officers and their wives who were to make up the party. This was especially true in the case of the elder of the two men, Colonel Durant, who had been her partner at the dinner given in honor of the Royal Sussex Regiment prior to its departure for England. Colonel Durant was a devotee of the polo field where she frequently watched him play, and a warrior of some renown, as she had heard from various sources, and as she could see for herself from the number of orders and decorations which he wore. With this background of achievement, she had expected that his conversation would be akin to those on politics and sports which alternately baffled and irritated her. But to her surprise and delight, after the first preliminaries, he began to talk to her about poetry; by slow degrees she discovered that he was a writer as well as a reader of this, and that he had developed his gift during three years which he had spent in a Turkish prison at the time of the World War. His story, told with much modesty and self-deprecation, fascinated her: Fearful lest he should lose all sense of decency, reason and hope, he had set himself the task of producing a certain fixed amount of verse every day. He had previously written nothing; but writing seemed the only possible means of mental escape from horrible surroundings, where physical escape was of course impossible. He had persevered; and among the results of his perseverance were some very beautiful poems. Encouraged by the sincerity of the interest she displayed, he had given a slim volume of these to Eunice. She kept it on a table by her bed, gratefully dipping into it during those intervals in the endless nights when loneliness and longing kept her tense and wakeful.

She discussed poetry in general, now, as she sat on the veranda of Government House. Captain and Mrs. Rowland were a little late; she and Guy and Colonel and Mrs. Durant sipped "million-dollar" cocktails while they waited for the others. Such drinks were not usually served there; but tonight Guy had ordered them, remembering how intrigued Eunice had been by them when she had first tasted them one afternoon at the Raffles Hotel, where he had taken her to call on some American acquaintances who were passing through the city. The "million-dollar" cocktails were reminiscent of Clover Clubs, as to taste, but they were much more potent, and they were served in champagne glasses. Privately, Eunice thought one of these quite enough for anyone to drink during the course of an evening. When Guy suggested a second round before they started for Sea View, she tried not to make her objection too serious.

"After all, you're going to drive, Guy. And I suppose there'll be something else with dinner."

"Something else! Well, I should jolly well hope so! Whatever you think, one cocktail doesn't make an evening. This is a party, Eunice."

It was certainly all very festive. When Captain and Mrs. Rowland appeared, they were breathless with apologies, and the drive to the beach was at top speed to make up for lost time. Most of the tables scattered over the sand, within sound of the surf, were already occupied when they reached their destination; but theirs stood apart, in the best possible place, and adorned with the most lavish decorations. In the center of it, a wreath of orchids encircled a miniature fountain playing over multicolored lights; and beside it, silver buckets containing bottles plunged in ice formed a glittering array. By the time they had finished their soup and fish and had begun their roast partridge, Eunice was already bewildered by the number of beverages that had been served. The second round of cocktails had been skipped at Government House in deference to her wishes, but it had made its appearance here instead. Sherry, Chablis and Pommard had followed each other in swift succession. There was champagne with the *soufflé surprise*; there were "rainbow liqueurs" afterward. She herself steadfastly refused everything until the champagne was served, when she consented to sip a little; Mrs. Durant and Mrs. Rowland followed her lead out of either inclination or courtesy—she could not be sure which —and were equally abstemious. Guy and the two officers, on the other hand, quietly quaffed everything that was offered them. She dreaded to have the music begin, feeling sure that none of the three would be steady either in his mind or on his feet when it was time to go to the pavilion.

Her fears were entirely groundless. Guy was as sober as she was herself when he rose and asked her for the first dance. His usual courtliness of manner was unchanged; so was the strange fresh youthfulness which she had noticed about him from the first. But as she glanced up at him, she thought she could visualize how he would look when he was older. His father and mother bore the mysterious resemblance to each other which so often characterizes married couples who have lived long and contentedly together. Both had crisp curly gray hair, merry eyes above solemn mouths, ruddy skin, firmly knit figures and a dignified bearing. In a quarter of a century, their son's flaxen hair would be crisp and white, his fair complexion florid, his slenderness expansive. But age would only add to his distinction; there was an indestructible quality to this. How silly she had been to think for a moment that anything so trivial as a few extra glasses of wind could impair Guy's reserve!

An unwelcome question forced itself into the forefront of her mind. Would the years deal with Francis as kindly as they would with Guy? Would any breach of complete temperance leave him so unscathed? Over and over again she had seen "gentlemen of the old school" in the South who had become derelicts by the time they were middle-aged. They could not "hold their liquor"; they could not pay their gambling debts or shake off their colored concubines. Would the struggle for life Francis had made serve a salutary purpose, causing him to shun anything that might lead to dissolution and disease? If it would, all her anxiety would be rewarded. But she was not at all sure that Francis had ever been frightened. For the most part, except when he was in a state of semiconsciousness or extreme suffering, he had been debonair even on the threshold of death. Now he was rapidly reverting to his old ways and his old viewpoint, and there was even a touch of testiness about him that had never characterized him before. She supposed this was natural enough, after his long illness. She had often heard that convalescence was in some ways the most trying period, both for an invalid and for his family. Still, she could hardly believe that the man who had told her so short a time before that his life was all hers, to do with what she would, was the same who that very afternoon had looked at her with critical coolness and jested about the advantages of a harem.

"Are you enjoying yourself, Eunice?"

She came back to the present with a start, forcing herself to focus her wandering gaze on the emblem of the Prince of Wales glowing against the wall.

"Yes, of course. What makes you ask?"

"Well, I thought, a while ago, that you were worrying for fear we were drinking too much. Have you forgotten the old saying that 'Englishmen in the East have hollow legs?' It's a strangely true one— And since we've been dancing, I've thought you were worrying about something else. Were you?"

"Not worrying exactly, only thinking."

"I'd like to think that there were never any worries in your life, Eunice, that all your thoughts were happy ones."

The music stopped abruptly. There was no time for him to say anything more. The dances were carefully spaced, with five-minute intervals between each for rest and refreshment; they began and ended on the dot. Promptly at quarter before twelve the orchestra played "God Save the King" and the guests all stood at attention; then they dispersed without even lingering long enough to drink one more Scotch and soda. When Eunice went back to the festive table for the last time, she found that the little group to which she belonged was scattering.

"It's such a fine night my wife thinks we should take a little turn before we go home," Colonel Durant said as he shook hands. "How about it, Rowland?"

"I'm sorry. But I have seven-o'clock duty in the morning. We'll say good night, if the rest of you are going on. What are you doing, Grenville?"

"That's for Mrs. Fielding to decide, of course. I haven't any seven-o'clock duty and I don't know that she has. Would you care for 'a little turn,' Eunice? You haven't been out on the Mandia Road by moonlight yet, you know. And I don't suppose there'll be many more chances."

"I think I'd like to go. I think I'd like to see it."

She said good-by to the Rowlands, listened while Guy talked to Colonel Durant about keeping their cars close together, and

145

made no comment as he helped her into his roadster and put the motor into motion. It was he who spoke first again.

"I was right, wasn't I, when I said there wouldn't be many more chances? You'll be leaving before long now, won't you?"

"I suppose so. Francis is growing very restless. And Dr. Sterling seems to think that in another fortnight or so, if he would promise to be careful——"

"You're still planning to go to Garoet?"

"Dr. Sterling thinks that's as good a place as any. And I can stay with Francis while he's in the sanitarium."

"It won't be easy for you, Eunice."

"I don't mind that. I've never wanted life to be easy."

"What have you wanted it to be?"

She hesitated. "Before I met Francis, I think I just wanted it to be pleasant and peaceful. But since then I've wanted a great deal more than that."

"We all want more than that, sooner or later, Eunice."

There seemed to be no answer she could make. They were passing through the groves now, where the moonlight looked like snow under the coconut trees. But though she had wanted so long to see it, she hardly saw it at all.

"Do you know how much I'll miss you when you've gone, I wonder?"

"Yes. Yes, I think I do, Guy."

"If you should ever come back, I'll be waiting for you."

"You told me once that Lady Singapore was hostess in the halfway house of the world, Guy. Do people ever come back to a halfway house? Don't they either go forever forward, or else retrace their steps for good and all?"

"Perhaps they do. God knows. I don't. Which do you believe you're going to do, Eunice?"

"God knows. I don't," she repeated after him. "But I think we're saying good-by to each other tonight, Guy, in every way that counts, no matter how often we meet after this— or how seldom."

The long corridor leading to the guest rooms in Government House was very still and only one light burned at the rear. Eunice could hardly see her own door, much less her visiting card in the slot on the panel. She stumbled over the shoes that had been neatly placed outside. Aghast because she had made so much noise at two o'clock in the morning, she opened the door with every precaution of slowness to keep it from creaking. As she stepped inside, she was surprised to see that not only the small lamp by her bed was burning, but also the larger one that stood by the chaise longue in her alcove sitting room. Mystified, she crept forward across the

146

vast expanse of floor. Then she stopped short, her bewilderment changing to fright. A man, holding a book in his hand and clad in a gorgeous dressing gown, was stretched out at full length on the lounge. She had scarcely stifled a scream when she saw that the man was Francis.

He closed his book, rose, and came toward her before she had recovered from the shock he had given her. Indeed, he spoke to her with a slight tinge of satire before she had found her own voice.

"Aren't you out rather late, Mrs. Fielding?"

"Francis! How on earth did you get here? What are you doing?"

"I came in a car that was parked outside the hospital and which I—borrowed. It was surprisingly simple. If I had known how easy it would be to make my escape, I should have done it long ago. I might have had more difficulty getting into Government House if the doorman hadn't recognized me. He'd brought me fruit and flowers several times. So I didn't need to explain that I was your husband and he accepted my statement that I wanted to see you quite simply. He even saw to it that I got the rather gaudy garments I have on. Naturally I couldn't stop to pack my bags when I made my getaway. I'll tell you details later, but by and large, that answers your first question. As to the second one, you've seen for yourself what I was doing. I was reading to while away the time until you came in—a very dull, moral book of verse, inscribed to you in flowery terms. Have you been collecting poets along the side, Eunice? Wasn't one cavalier enough for you?"

"You must go back to the hospital instantly," she said, disregarding his question. "You've taken an awful chance, one that might kill you."

"Nothing on earth would induce me to go back to the hospital. And I haven't taken as much of a chance as you imagine. I've been 'feeling my feet' in the dead of night, when no one would see or hear me doing it, for some time now. I've also been sampling tidbits from my companions' trays, on the sly. Nearly all the men on diets do that when they get together on the veranda. Some of them suffer for it and some of them get away with it. I got away with it, I'm thankful to say. I would have died if I'd gone on eating nothing but that cursed pap any longer."

"What do you suppose the Grenvilles will think of you, taking advantage of their hospitality like this?"

"I don't give a damn what they think, and I don't propose to take advantage of their hospitality long. There's a Dutch motorboat, the *Indropoera*, stopping here tomorrow night on her maiden voyage between Java and Rotterdam.

147

We'll take her and go straight through to Marseilles. Then it's a simple matter to get across the Atlantic. We'll be back at Retreat while there's still something left of the summer. I've had enough of seeing the world. I want to go home and that's what I intend to do. Is that all perfectly clear?"

"It's clear, but I don't think it's wise."

"Have you forgotten the traditional folly of the Fieldings? Now supposing you answer a few questions yourself, for a change. What were you doing out at this ungodly hour?"

"I told you I was going to Sea View for dinner. I went for a little ride after that."

"Oh—the far-famed moonlight along the Mandai Road. Didn't I tell you that when you went to look at moonlight I wanted to go with you myself?"

"Yes. But——"

"There aren't any buts. God knows that Guy Grenville is about as harmless as they come, and no doubt this new poet of yours is too, though you don't seem disposed to talk about him. But you're my wife, not my widow. I think Guy's under a slight misapprehension on that score. Perhaps the wish was father to the thought."

"Francis, how can you be so ungrateful and so unfair?"

"I'm not ungrateful, but I think Guy has acted the part of the perfect gentle knight without interruption about long enough. And I think you're rather unfair yourself. You talked with a good deal of feeling about having room for me any where, any time, and you told me a very touching story about the Malayan meaning of shoes placed outside a wife's door. But now that I'm actually here, you don't seem so glad to see me."

"Oh, Francis, I am glad! But I know how rash you are to act like this, I know how far from strong you must be."

"I'm strong enough to make you realize that you're still married to me. I think you need a reminder. And I don't believe you'll ever forget it again."

She had yearned infinitely for their reunion. But she had not dreamed that it would be like this, that Francis would take her without tenderness and possess her without compassion. He did not await the response which would have been so rapturous; he did not even want this now. What he wanted was mastery, recognized and enforced, as his marital right; and only through the subjection of a proud spirit and a sensitive being would his male supremacy, sapped through his illness, be restored in his own sight.

Dimly, Eunice was conscious of this; her understanding saved her from shame and enabled her to endure; her own loving kindness sustained her and gave her healing grace.

Afterward her memory was merciful; she forgot everything except the glory of being again beloved.

The child she conceived that night was born at Retreat on Christmas Day, while Bina and Bella were singing carols in the candlelight and the negroes were calling out "Christmas gift!" When her travail was over, Eunice took the boy from the colored midwife and named him Noel. She saw him both as God's gift to her and as her own triumphant answer to her husband's challenge.

PART V

The Mistress of Retreat

~~~~~~

Chapter 11

WHEN AUNT CYNTHIA, the colored midwife, sat before
the fire in the twilight, holding Noel on her knees and crooning to him, it seemed to Eunice that she cast a benignant spell
over the dusky room.

The bed where Eunice lay was in the shadow, its canopy
dim above its tall posts, the pattern of its quilt obscured.
The wardrobe where her clothes were kept, the lowboy
where her toilet articles were arrayed, were only undefined
shapes against the flowered wallpaper. The draperies were
drawn across the many-paned windows. There was no light
in the room except the reflection of the flames which flickered
first over the snowy folds of Aunt Cynthia's turban, then on
the pink face of the drowsy baby, and finally from the hearth-
stones to the broad waxed boards of the floor. But they did
not reach out far across the boards, and Aunt Cynthia did
not trouble with candles until later, when it was time to bring
Eunice her supper. She simply sat and sang. The flames also
made a soft sound which harmonized with her lullaby. Otherwise the room was very still. But it was permeated with gladness and warmth and the profound peace which fills a place
which is inviolable.

Eunice had always felt that Aunt Cynthia had strange
powers, but the first time she had seen the midwife she was
partly persuaded that these were evil rather than good. The
aged colored woman had appeared abruptly at Retreat, wearing a grotesque hat perched on top of her turban and hob-
nailed shoes that were far too large for her, and carrying a
covered basket and a long cane, neither of which had any
particular purpose. Eunice, who was conscientiously trying
to fathom the mysteries of horticulture, was in the garden
at the time of this visit, unheralded until Aunt Cynthia's own
clumping footsteps proclaimed its approach. She was a tall
spare woman, but she was bent with work and years, and the

loss of teeth, tardily replaced, had given a sunken look to her mouth and brought her sharp chin close to her nose. As she raised her stick by way of salutation, she was undeniably witchlike.

"Good ebenin', little missie," she said in a rich husky voice. "Ah reckon Ah ain't mistaken, is Ah? You am Marse Francie's beautiful young bride."

"I am Mrs. Francis Fielding," Eunice said.

"Sho' nuff, Miss Eunice," the crone went on, as cordially as if she had not been rebuked. "Blanche, she done tol' me Ah'd find you-all in de gyarden. Ah done come to see yo', caise Ah done heard somepin' else, somepin' mighty fine. Ah done heard you guine ter need Aunt Cynthia right by yo' side at Christmastime."

"I think you must be mistaken. I don't expect to be here at Christmastime. I expect to be at a hospital in Washington."

"Yo' spex to be at a hospital in Washington!" exclaimed Aunt Cynthia, with a dismay that revealed much more than injured personal pride. "Yo' cain't never! Yo' cain't be aimin' to let Marse Francie's baby be borned along with a whole passel o' po' white trash and took care o' by some triflin' white nuss that ain't never known what it was to look after quality's chillun and lub 'em! Don' do dat, Miss Eunice! I knows how ter do eberytin' dat's fitten fo' little new babies! Ah does it *right,* too! I brung mor'n half de babies in des county inter de world fo' mos' fifty years now! Ah dun help born ebery one o' Miss Alice's chillun, right here at Retreat, an' Ole Missus' chillun befo' dat! Don' stan' dere and say to me you ain' guine ter let me help yo' to born yours!"

"I didn't mean to hurt your feelings," Eunice said, a little less coldly. "I didn't know who you were, you see, when you first came up— I'm sure you must have taken wonderful care of my husband and all his brothers and sisters, Aunt Cynthia. But you see things are different now and——"

"Dey is different now!" exclaimed Aunt Cynthia, with mounting scorn. "How-all dey different? Yo' tryin' ter tell me, Miss Eunice, little new babies don' come from dese mudders jes' lak dese allus done? When you ain' never had one yo'self yet, nor seen one bornin' eider! Ah done had fifteen haid o' my own, an' Ah done los' count years ago o' all my udder babies. Ah spex nex' yo' guine ter tell me dey neber is inside dey mudders at all, dat young white women ain' got no wombs any mo'!"

"Aunt Cynthia, I don't think we better talk about babies. Just look at this crepe myrtle bush! Isn't it pretty?"

"Ah done come here to talk about Marse Francie's baby an' Ah'm guine ter do it," said Aunt Cynthia fiercely. "Ah know what de matter is! Yo'-all is a Yankee woman, yo'-all

151

is afraid ter hab yo' baby like quality. Yo'-all reckons in a hospital dem no count white nusses is guine ter gib you somepin' ter put you ter sleep so you won't know 'bout yo' baby comin' an' yo' can pretend it's 'different.' Yassam, an' how does yo' know while yo' sleepin' dey won' gib you anudder baby? Dey mouten gib yo' a girl, when Marse Francie eatin' his heart out fo' a little boy."

"I'm not afraid, Aunt Cynthia, but it's true I don't want to suffer unnecessarily and——"

"Yo' don' want to suffer unnecessarily! Yo' lissun ter me, Miss Eunice. Ah don' let mah ladies do no sufferin' dat ain' necessary, *no ma'am*. Ah gibs 'em a sheet tied ter de bedpost ter pull on *good,* an' Ah stays right by 'em an' lets dem press dey feet against mah pussun *hard*; an' den pretty soon, Ah puts dey precious baby right beside 'em in dey big bed, where dey can lub it all dey wants to. An don' carry it off ter no nussery where its own gran'mudder cain't look at it ceptin' tru glass an' its own daddy cain't gentle it in his arms. How-all Marse Francie guine ter see his wife an' chile effen dey way off in a hospital in Washington? How-all he guine ter be in an' out of dey room a dozen times a day, tellin' his wife he's fitten to bust with pride an' holdin' out his finger so as his little boy can clutch hold on it wid his tiny hand an' show how strong he am?"

Aunt Cynthia cast a triumphant glance at Eunice. Something told her she had scored at last. "Effen yo' reckons Ah'll let you suffer, more'n yo' can stand," she said, still scornfully, "effen you cain't trust me like mah udder ladies has allus done, yo'-all can talk ter ole Doctor Tayloe, up ter Barren Point, 'bouten me. I ain' got no objection yo' should hab Doctor Tayloe too, effen yo' wants him. He won' do yo' no harm while yo'se under mah care, an' he can gib yo' somepin' ter smell, if yo'-all has ter hab it, just as good as any Washington doctor. Yas *ma'am*— Ah wish yo' good ebenin', Miss Eunice. Ah'll be comin' back some udder day ter tell yo' what Ah'll be needin' when Ah comes ter Retreat 'round Christmastime."

Aunt Cynthia had shown characteristic shrewdness, not only in her hints about the inaccessibility for Francis of a Washington hospital, but also in her generous concession concerning Doctor Tayloe's merits as an adviser and lack of harmfulness as an accoucheur. Doctor Daingerfield, the saintly, scholarly rector of St. Peter's-at-the-Crossroads, where all the county families went to church, and Doctor Tayloe, the hard-pressed, kind-hearted physician of Barren Point, to whom all the county families turned no less trustfully for succor of another sort, were the two men who had made both the most favorable and the most profound impression on

Eunice since she had come to live at Retreat. She had been reared in the Congregational fold, and had always observed the forms of faith observed by her Puritan forefathers unquestioningly; but they had never stirred her deeply, and she had philosophically accepted her mother's somewhat spectacular "conversion" to Catholicism on the occasion of that lady's marriage to Patrick Hogan. Now, quite as philosophically, she had accepted her mother-in-law's dazed comment that none of the Fieldings had ever known a Congregationalist before, and that of course they had all taken it for granted that dear Eunice would go to St. Peter's-at-the-Crossroads with them. From the beginning, she had felt at home in the quaint little crossroads church with its square pews and its white woodwork; and in like measure, she had felt at home at Barren Point, where the Fielding and Tayloe and Daingerfield kin were prone to gather for a drink after divine service before scattering to their several homes for their copious Sunday dinner. But it had not occurred to her to consult Doctor Tayloe about the state of her health, any more than it had occurred to her to consult Doctor Daingerfield about the state of her soul. Having decided, belatedly, on the former course, as a result of Aunt Cynthia's goading, she had a twinge of discomfort lest the friendly physician's feelings might be hurt because she had not gone to him in the first place.

She need not have worried. He nodded with a somewhat quizzical smile when she asked him, rather haltingly, if she might "come to see him professionally"; but he made the counter suggestion that he should come to see her instead.

"My office hours are pretty irregular," he said ruefully, taking a long pull at his julep, as if he needed it. "They're bound to be, considering how much of the county I have to cover every day. My hayseeds and rivermen are scattered from one end of it to the other—not that my life's a circumstance to what it used to be when I made my rounds with a horse and buggy! But my office hours don't amount to much. I never get to church, either—not that I mind myself, but I know it's a cross to my old friend Roger Daingerfield, and I'd rather take a switching any day than hurt his feelings. I tried to explain to him once how it was—that people were just as apt to be taken sick at eleven o'clock on Sunday as any time on a weekday. He couldn't understand until his own wife was seized with premature labor pains on the Sabbath. Then he came whipping up to the Point as if the devil were after him 'Quick, quick, Beal,' he said, 'Vinnie's threatened with a miscarriage.' 'Sorry, Roger,' I said. 'I was just preparing to attend divine service at your church. I don't like to put it off when it's taken me so long to get around to it'—

153

I'm like your mother-in-law, Mrs. Fielding, it's hard for me to get around. Poor Roger was all in a sweat. 'But she's having a hemorrhage,' he said, wringing his hands. 'If you'll only come to her, Beal, I'll never say another word to you about going to church regularly.' And he never has, though he comes every Sunday straight from the pulpit to my eggnog and mint-julep parties."

"You took a rather mean advantage of him, didn't you?"

"Now, Mrs. Fielding, I wouldn't say that. But I can't argue with you about it at the moment. I've got to be off—sorry to leave before my guests, but after all I was here to welcome you, and that's more than I've been able to manage the last two Sundays. I've got two or three patients on my hands that are mighty sick, and they all live twenty or thirty miles apart —Yes, I'll be glad to drop in at Retreat one of these days. Nothing urgent, I suppose?"

She thought she could see a little twinkle in his eye, and she was still surer of this when eventually he did "drop in" at Retreat. She had made careful arrangements to receive him in complete privacy, which was difficult for her to achieve, and she had meticulously rehearsed everything she meant to say to him. Without being brusque he simplified the situation for her quickly.

"Of course I knew that you were going to have a baby," he said kindly, stroking his beard and jingling his watch chain. "No—you don't 'show it' yet, in the usual sense, but it's pretty hard to deceive an old doctor like me. So Aunt Cynthia came to see you— Well, of course she would! Quite a character, isn't she? And when she gets rid of her hat and her basket and her stick, she makes a very dignified appearance. She certainly has a gift— I've never seen a nurse who could touch her when it came to the care of a baby. As far as you're concerned, you'll have to decide for yourself. But you know even the old colored crones are all registered now, and are all required to take examinations. If you're asking my opinion, I think you'd get along famously. I'll stand by and try not to do you any harm myself, as Aunt Cynthia so tactfully put it. Now if you are going to give me a case, perhaps I'd better look you over. It won't take but a few minutes. There aren't so many formalities here as there are among the fashionable physicians of Washington."

As a matter of fact, it was all reassuringly simple. Eunice reorganized the plans for her confinement of her own satisfaction and amid widespread expressions of approval. Her mother-in-law, especially, babbled on for hours at a time.

"Honey chile, I sho'ly do give thanks you lost your way in the woods last November. You brought a blessin' the very first time you came to Retreat and I said so to all the children

154

before I went to bed that night. Mamie Love was so sleepy she could hardly listen—you remember she was ailin' at the time. But I couldn't leave my precious baby girl out when I was tellin' all the others the good news. 'Mamie Love,' I said, givin' a little shove to her shoulder, 'a beautiful young lady has come ridin' into Retreat on a beautiful black horse this evenin' and Blanche believes it's a 'token.' Blanche never makes a mistake about a token. Sometimes she sees a sort of sign wrong, but a real token is different. Now she says it's a token that your dear little chile is goin' to be born at Retreat on Christmas. I want you to come up to the attic with me, Eunice, and go through the deer-hide trunk where we always keep the baby clothes. It's a right pretty little trunk, too, studded with brass nails and it's got a girl's name on the top of it, done in brass nails too—Amanda. That was the name of one of Francis's great-aunts and she had the trunk for her honeymoon—she went to the 'Whites' and afterward north to Saratoga Springs. But by and by she brought the trunk back here and——"

"I'd like very much to see Great-Aunt Amanda's little deer-hide trunk and the old baby clothes whenever you want to show them to me, Mother Fielding."

"Well, now, we'll go up to the attic the first rainy day. I always like to go to the attic on a rainy day, the sound on the roof is so sweet. And now that the roof doesn't leak any more, of course that's lovely too. Maybe it's been wicked of me to hold back about those baby clothes until now. I do ask your forgiveness, I really do. But I didn't want you to take 'em to the hospital in Washington. There's a dress in that trunk that every Fielding baby, for five generations, has been put into as soon as it was washed, God love its heart, after it was born. The embroidery on that dress is six inches deep all around the hem, and it has the cutest little sleeves! I couldn't bear the thought that those northern nurses might ruin it—it's so fragile, it's fairly fallin' to pieces now. Then of course, there's the christenin' robe, all real lace, and linen shirts edged with tattin' and muslin bonnets and piqué capes and——"

"I think perhaps babies don't wear quite as many clothes as they used to, Mother Fielding."

"Well, perhaps, not up North, though you'd think they would, now wouldn't you, to keep out the bitter cold? Scalloped flannel petticoats and belly bands and bootees and knitted sacks— I'm afraid you haven't any of those left— I never did get around to puttin' camphor balls in that trunk and the last time I opened it up the moths flew right up in my face. But you won't have to make another thing, Eunice, if you don't want to, except the flannels, and I know you can't wait to begin sewing on little clothes. I'll show you how to feather stitch and turn French seams and punch the holes for eyelets——"

It had not occurred to Eunice that she was supposed to make little clothes, but that also she dutifully began to do, and soon to enjoy, in the same way that she had enjoyed her sewing in Singapore. It gave her a sense of tranquillity and creation, and this time the feeling was tinged with amusement, too; the garments she was making were so incredibly small that they were funny. She held them up for Francis to see when he came in after long hours in the open air with its freshness still on his face and the renewed vigor it was giving him revealed in every movement that he made.

" 'By baby bunting,' " she quoted. " 'Daddy's gone a-hunting.' Did you get a rabbit's skin to wrap the baby bunting in, darling? Just in case you didn't, I've been busy while you were gone. Look!"

Francis admired the baby clothes sincerely, and was pleased to find Eunice working on them. Aunt Cynthia too had nothing but praise for the prospective patient on the occasion of her second visit; and various county matrons began to drop in with blankets they had knitted which they bestowed upon Eunice, coupling their good advice with commendation. Eunice glowed with pleasure because she had won so much approval. It was not until Millie spoke to her on the subject, one day when she had gone to the Upper Garden, that she felt the slightest misgiving as to her course.

"I think you're crazy," Millie said tersely. "Haven't you any backbone at all, Eunice? It's bad enough for you to let all the Fielding family browbeat you without letting an old nigger witch do it too."

"Nobody has browbeaten me," Eunice retorted indignantly. "I didn't consult anyone when I changed my plans, not even Francis. I made up my own mind what I thought was best to do."

"Not even Francis?" repeated Millie mockingly. "But that was because you knew before hand what Francis preferred to have you do, didn't you? He probably sent that crazy old woman to you in the first place. It's unreasonable of him to expect you to have a baby at all, so soon after you're married, let alone expecting you to have it at Retreat in the dead of winter! I wouldn't dream of having a baby for five years more at least. Free doesn't want me to either. And when I do have one I'll go to the best specialist in the country."

"I'm glad I'm going to have a baby," Eunice said proudly.

Millie looked at her through slanting, half-shut eyes. "Maybe," she conceded. "Because if you hadn't started to pretty soon, Francis would have raised such an awful row."

Her eyes were still sufficiently open to see Eunice flush, and she went on, "It wouldn't surprise me at all if I heard he *had* begun to fuss because you didn't start right away, the minute you were married. You'd have had one by now if you'd done that; you might even have had a second one on the way before you were up and around. Don't look at me like that, Eunice. I know this breed of men around here. They brag about their 'stair-step' children just the same way they love to talk about themselves as trundlebed trash. I don't put anything past them. That's why I didn't marry one of them myself."

She stretched herself out luxuriantly on the long sofa where she was sitting, and Eunice watched her with a pang of envy. Millie never failed to produce a striking effect, no matter what she did or what she wore, and at the moment she was lounging with nothing on except a flame-colored Grecian robe and scarlet sandals to match. The bands of gold with which the dress was bordered divided the bodice into a deep V that met the golden girdle; together they served to accentuate both the soft swell of her breast and the extreme slimness of her waist. Her feet and ankles emerged, white and gleaming, from the divided draperies of her skirt. Confronted with such lovely litheness, Eunice felt doubly graceless and heavy.

"Has anyone at Retreat ever thanked you for all you've done there?" Millie asked mercilessly.

"Millie, why should anyone thank me? Why should I expect it?"

"Common gratitude, that's all. And I'm certain you did expect it—unless by the time you'd finished that exquisite expensive piece of restoration you'd learned not to expect gratitude from Francis Fielding or any of his tribe. But at least I'm sure you didn't think that little whelp, Peyton, would come back from college and say that you'd spoiled everything, that he couldn't recognize his own home any more, it was so gilded with Yankee dollars."

Eunice's flush faded, and her face grew very white. Peyton's first homecoming after her own return with Francis, and his unrebuked denunciation of her efforts to restore Retreat, had marked one of the bitterest occurrences of her married life. She could not think of it even now with calmness, especially as Peyton's attitude toward her had been one of continued contempt and dislike. But how Millie knew of the episode was a mystery.

"I think I'd better go home," Eunice remarked, rising. "You seem to be in an unusually bad mood today, Millie. I don't see why you and Francis ever bothered to bury the

157

hatchet, if you were both going to spend half your time digging it up again."

"Does Francis spend half his time digging it up too?"

"Well, not half. But I can't truthfully say he's much more complimentary about you and Free than you are about him and his family."

"He just talks that way. He doesn't mean half he says, any more than I do. You take us both too seriously, Eunice. Don't go. I promise not to be disagreeable any more. I was counting on you to stay for supper. Free is off somewhere seeing prominent citizens about running for Congress from this District, as soon as he's old enough. He wants to start laying the groundwork now. You can no more keep a Stone out of the Capitol than you can keep a Fielding out of— Oh, I honestly didn't mean to start again! No, I won't say it!"

Eunice was persuaded with difficulty. On the whole, she was thankful that the breach between Solomon's Garden and Retreat had been healed, at least superficially, by her marriage, and that normal relations existed again among the Fielding kinsfolk. But there were times when she found Millie exasperating, and this was one of them. It was only with the reminder from Millie that she might stumble or something if she started off alone in the dusk, and that it would be an awful waste, at this stage of the game, that she was persuaded to wait until Francis came to fetch her in the car. During the interval, in spite of her promise, Millie reverted to her denunciation of Aunt Cynthia.

"Why, she's a perfect hag! I wouldn't give her houseroom, not for a minute. And Doctor Tayloe is an old fogy. I'm sure he won't even wash his hands before he delivers you— if he gets there in time to do it at all. More likely he'll just leave you to the tender mercies of that midwife. Then you'll probably have eclampsia or puerperal fever or worse. You know my grandmother died in childbirth, right here on this place. People never tell you about cases like that, when they're talking about women like Cousin Alice, who have babies as easily as bitches have puppies. You couldn't kill them if you clubbed them on the head. They haven't brains enough to spill."

"Oh, Millie, you said you wouldn't start all over again! Please don't! I can't stand it!"

It was a long time since she had been so upset. Francis noticed it when he came for her. He had continued to treat Millie and Free with detached insolence, in spite of the patched-up peace, and he declined to come into the Great Hall now, giving lack of time as an excuse. His pretext was unconvincing in view of the unlimited and untroubled leisure which he enjoyed; but Eunice joined him without an argument. She herself was glad to leave, to escape from Millie and relax in the fresh coolness of the evening air. The smoothness with which Francis handled a car made driving with him a double pleasure, and the one they were in now had been one of her first gifts to him after their return from their wedding trip. She had delighted in finding excuses to make him presents, almost inventing anniversaries and other appropriate occasions; but as she looked back on this particular presentation, in the light of Millie's comments, it seemed to her that Blanche had been more excited about it than Francis himself. The car had scarcely been parked in the driveway for the first time when Blanche had run from the kitchen to her cabin, calling out to Uncle Nixon as she went.

"What you think, Uncle? All this past week we've been gettin' two aigs a day, and now Marse Francie, he got him a new car!"

Apparently Uncle Nixon had been excited too. Judging from the sounds that issued almost immediately from the cabin, he had reached at once for his banjo and had begun to sing. Later on, Blanche had led him tenderly out over the lawn, and he had felt every part of the new car, from its shining hood to its soft seats. Eunice had wondered then, as she stood watching them, why Francis did not ask him to get in and take the patient old blind man for a ride. But nothing of the sort had seemed to occur to Francis, and Eunice did not like to suggest it to him. She was afraid that he might turn on her with a flaunting question: Had she really given him the car? Or did she have a lien on it? He had talked that way about some of her other gifts——

"What's the matter, Eunice? What are you worrying about now?"

She came back to the present with a start, realizing that this moment contained a taunting question too. Did she really convey the impression that she was always worrying about something? As a matter of fact, she had been fairly free from worry for a long time.

"Did you ever hear why niggers never commit suicide, Eunice?"

"No—why don't they?" she asked in some bewilderment, trying to follow his train of thought.

"Virgin says, 'Hit's disaway: de white man he gits bothered en he go off en set down en worry en worry tell bimeby he kill hisse'f. De nigger he worry too. He go off en set down en worry en worry, but bimeby he go to sleep!"

She tried to laugh, not very successfully. "Millie has upset me a little," she admitted. "She thinks I'm very unwise to stay at Retreat for my confinement."

"I hope you told her you thought she was very unwise not to stay anywhere for her confinement?"

"No—I never think of things to say like that, Francis! I'm not half as clever as you are at repartee."

"You ought to be clever enough not to let a spoiled brat like Millie bulldoze you."

"She thinks you're rather a bulldozer yourself," Eunice said, with a faint smile at the similarity of the two accusations she had so recently heard, coming from such different quarters.

"Oh, she does? Well, if I were Free I wouldn't stop at bulldozing. I'd take a strap to her about once in so often. The whistling of the whip is the only kind of talk a girl like that will listen to sometimes. She's the type that inspired the old proverb about a woman and a dog and a walnut tree."

"I don't know it."

" 'The more they're beat, the better they be.' Free doesn't know how to handle her. She might develop into quite a person, married to someone who did. However, that's all beyond the point—except that if you're going to be silly enough to let Millie upset you, I reckon you better stop going to the Upper Garden."

"Now that Honor and Jerry are away and the Lower Garden is closed, there isn't any other place I can go to, that's near. I can't walk to the rectory or Barren Point, and you don't want me to ride or to drive myself."

"Why do you say *I* don't want you to? It isn't my fault, is it, that you can't ride or drive without running the risk of a miscarriage? As far as that goes, what's the matter with staying at Retreat? Especially now that it's all fixed up to suit you——"

They were turning in at the driveway as he spoke, and Eunice had a mental vision of this as she had first seen it, less than a year before, frozen into hard ruts and obscured by fallen leaves. Autumn was upon them again, but the driveway was wide and smooth and well graveled now, and every day the leaves were raked away from it. It curved gently up to the well-kept lawn, and beyond this rose the façade of the house, glistening with white paint. The shrubs around it were neatly trimmed; spruce shutters hung at the windows; at the rear there was a glimpse of the newly shingled cabin and the beautifully ordered garden. When she stepped inside, everything would be the same: soft rugs on waxed floors, walls hung with landscape paper, polished silver, burnished brass, rubbed mahogany; the evidences of all-pervading cleanliness and care——

"Doesn't it suit you too?" she asked, with a catch in her voice.

"Yes. It suits me—in a way," he said without enthusiasm. Then he added, "But don't you remember telling me yourself, the first time we met, that Tivoli had never been the same since you stepfather bought it? In spite of all he'd done to improve it? Retreat doesn't seem the same either."

"Retreat hasn't been sold! It's been kept!"

"Yes. That helps. But don't you remember *I* told *you* the first time we met that the spirit of old houses survives everything better than alien prosperity? Some of the spirit of Retreat has gone along with the bad road and the falling plaster and the rotten shingles."

"If you feel that way about it, it would have been better if I'd never tried to improve it!"

"Don't say that, honey." His voice softened, but Eunice still felt a lack of spontaneity. "Retreat was going to rack and ruin when you came. You've saved it from that. And you've done more. You've preserved it for posterity. My son will have a legacy my father couldn't give me. I know how much I owe you, Eunice. You mustn't imagine I don't, because I don't keep talking about it all the time. After all, debt is a mighty cheerless subject."

"Do you have to put it that way?"

"It's better than the way Peyton put it, isn't it? Perhaps we Fieldings don't know how to talk to our benefactors. I was afraid I didn't, very often, when I was sick in Singapore. But the trouble is, you rather heap your bounty on. And then you make it seem such a virtue! If you were only a little more casual about it all, it wouldn't get under my skin so. Then perhaps I'd behave myself better."

"Have you been misbehaving much lately?" she asked, with a lame effort toward lightness.

"Oh, only toward you! And you know all about that. You're so conscious of my shortcomings that they're beginning to get me down too. And apparently you haven't any at all. You do your duty as you see it about everything. Even when it comes to having your baby at Retreat. In your heart you'd much rather go to a hospital. But after you'd seen Aunt Cynthia, you decided it would be very noble to stay here and make the best of things, that they wouldn't be very bad at that. Now you've seen Millie, and she's convinced you that you're headed for the shambles and you want to back out and go to Washington after all, but that doesn't look quite so heroic. I don't see why you don't forget how it looks and go ahead. I shan't try to stop you—any more than I tried to stop you when you wanted to go to China."

"Francis, you're unjust again."

"Oh, for God's sake! You ought to have married a Yankee judge, not a southern planter."

He made no further effort to speak gently and reasonably. He was angry and his anger was never a mere flare-up. It endured. Bina joked about it. She said if there were any way of taking the lid off Francis, you would be able to see him boiling inside. But to Eunice his anger did not seem a matter of jest.

If they had only had a home of their own, Eunice reflected, such scenes would not have been so devastating. But there was no place that she could go to escape the aftermath of these. Bella and Bina had now both achieved beaux who arrived in flocks from Lexington, Staunton and Charlottesville to supplement the local supply. Eunice had never seen so many enamoured young men swarming through a house at all sorts of odd hours; they completely pre-empted the front and back parlors, and they were quite as likely to be there before breakfast as after midnight. Mamie Love's dolls and Mrs. Fielding's needlework were strewn impartially through the wide hall which served as a supplementary sitting room, and Purvis' school books, which he still approached with reluctance, and the butterflies, beetles, and other winged creatures which he loved to capture, were scattered all over the library. Upstairs the situation was no better. The elaborate bathrooms, made of Vermont marble, which Eunice had installed, had cut considerably into the bedroom space. Even with two persons in each chamber, there was only one guest room left, and Bella and Bina were already complaining that was not half enough to accommodate the collegians whose curricula afforded such ample leisure for week-end courting. As the necessity for a nursery began to loom large before them, their grievances grew greater and more vociferous. When Bina finally spoke about diapers in the drawing room as a drawback to dates, Eunice walked out of the house and disappeared beyond the orchard without saying a word to anyone. Francis found her, several hours later, in the ramshackle little lodge at the edge of the marshes.

"Why on earth did you stalk away like that?" he asked angrily. Eunice dreaded to see his anger aroused again. But this time she was angry too.

"I stalked away, as you call it, because I couldn't stand Bina's attitude another instant. She acts as if some moon calf from V. M. I. had more rights at Retreat than my baby."

"Well, why didn't you tell her that he hadn't, in no uncertain terms? And why did you come down here all by yourself?"

"I can't bear bickering. I think it's vulgar. And I came here all by myself to draw plans for remodeling the lodge.

I think the sooner you and I move out of Retreat the better."

Francis swung himself up on the pine table that stood in the center of the rickety floor and lighted a cigarette. He sat there dangling his legs over the edge and smoking for some moments before he answered. When he finally spoke, it was in his old winning way, the irritation entirely gone from his voice.

"I reckon I might ask Mother and the girls to come down here, if you'd like to have me—the boys wouldn't bother you so much if they were gone. This could be made into a mighty pretty little dower house and I know you wouldn't begrudge the money you'd spend on it. But I couldn't bring you here to live. When I spoke about using it for our honeymoon, I wasn't really more than half serious. And I never thought of it as a permanent proposition."

"Well, why shouldn't you think of it as a permanent proposition?"

"Because you're the mistress of Retreat now, Eunice. The lady of the manor doesn't live in a lodge. That's only suitable for the dowager."

"Now you *are* being prehistoric! As if I'd let you ask your mother to leave the house where she's lived ever since she was a bride! I never heard of anything so preposterous."

"Oh, yes, you have. I've been saying preposterous things to you ever since we met. You've rather liked some of them, too. But speaking of preposterous sayings—do you really have to keep talking about 'your' baby instead of 'our' baby? I have a claim of sorts on him too, you know, though I admit my share in his creation is small."

"I'm sorry, Francis. I won't do it again. I think I'm getting more disagreeable every day. I don't wonder you're tired with me all the time."

"I am tired with you occasionally, but I'm not now in the least. I'm tired with Bina, and I told her so after you left the house. I think the brat will behave from now on. And I don't think she'll talk about diapers in the drawing room again either."

He slid from his seat and put his arm around Eunice. "Let me have a look at those plans you've been drawing," he said persuasively. "You could have been a builder, if you'd been a man, do you know it, honey? You've got a smart lot of ideas." She handed the sketches to him and he studied them attentively for a few moments, his glance shifting from the bare shack itself to the penciled sheets he was holding; then he looked at her with a pleased smile. "These are mighty good," he said warmly. "I can see just how the lodge would look when you got through with it, and there was a big fire in the huge chimney piece and the table set for supper in

163

front of it and turkey-red curtains at the windows and a big lamp with a red shade. But it's like I said. I can't let you live here. If you don't want to hurt Mother's feelings, why don't you fix it up and let me offer it to the boys? They'd be tickled to death with it. And if we had the library to ourselves, and their bedroom for the baby, we wouldn't be so terribly crowded at Retreat after all."

"Why, Francis, that would be a wonderful solution! Do you really think the boys would like the lodge?"

"How could they help it? It would be a sort of—what's the French name for it?—a sort of *garconniere*—a special establishment for the young bachelors of the family where they could live by themselves and be independent hosts and develop a proprietary feeling. You'll have Petyon feeding out of your hand when he hears about this—not that Purvis won't be pleased too. It will give him all the space he needs to put his butterflies. And we could stick the girls' suitors down here to sleep—that wouldn't be a bad idea either, for various reasons."

"Do you—can you think of anything else I could do, Francis? Perhaps something that would please your sisters too?"

"Of course. Fix up the attic for them and the girls who come to visit them. Lord knows there's space enough there—Grandfather used it for his pupils' dormitory. If you divided it up and put in some closets and showers, we'd have undisputed possession of another chamber. And if you'd fix up the old schoolhouse as a recreation room—well, the front and back parlors would be vacated as if by magic."

"Why didn't you suggest any of this before?"

"You didn't ask me for suggestions, Eunice. You just went ahead making improvements—the same sort of improvements you'd have made in New England. You didn't stop to consider whether something else might work out better in Virginia, and you didn't want anyone to tell you what to do. You never actually said, 'This is being done with my money so I have a right to do it as I please.' But that's the way you felt, just as you did on our honeymoon. Isn't it?"

"I'm sorry, darling. Sorry and ashamed."

He put his arm around her again. "You needn't be, honey," he said. "You've done wonders. I've told you that before. But you've rushed your fences a little. Now just canter around the field for a while. You'll be a lot happier if you will. And so will all the rest of us."

Francis was right. They were all much happier after that. For the first time, Eunice began to bask in the glow of their gladness instead of shrinking under the weight of their indebtedness.

Peyton was the first to make an *amende honorable*. Eunice turned the sketches she had made for the lodge over to him, asking him to adapt them to his own preferences—possibly she had overlooked something he would have especially liked—a bar, or a bunkroom, for instance. He responded enthusiastically and began to come home from the University over every week end, instead of conspicuously absenting himself with flimsy excuses for a month at a time. His brother's predictions about an awakening sense of proprietary obligations and advantages had been promptly realized. He insisted on camping out at the lodge while it was still in a shacklike state, and he brought countless disheveled and delighted youths to stay there with him. In presenting these kindred spirits to Eunice, he never failed to pay her a tribute that warmed her heart.

"Fellows, this is my sister-in-law, Mrs. Francis Fielding—Cousin Eunice to all of you. She's promised me she'll be my hostess until I can find a girl just like her for myself. She knows that means a life sentence too, because the mold's broken— Could you get the beer, Eunice? Will you and Francie be over around ten?"

"Yes, I got the beer, but you mustn't ask me where. It's the dry kind you like. I hope there's plenty— Are you sure you want an old married couple like us butting in on your party when you're having such a good time by yourselves?"

"An old married couple!" — "Oh, come on, Cousin Eunice!" — "My dearest sister, you'll have the law after you, bootlegging like that. But we'll all come and get you out of jail——"

Gradually Eunice became more at ease with Peyton than she was with Bella and Bina. She enjoyed his camaraderie, and though she knew he did not take his college career as seriously as she had taken hers, the mere fact that he had managed to stay on at the University and that he had finally aroused Purvis to the point of making an effort to join him there, predisposed her in his favor. She could not suppress the feeling that the girls should be at good schools and that their male callers should be strictly supervised and limited. But she was conscious of their affection too, and she knew that Bina had gone out of her way to say she was sorry for her outbreak about the diapers.

"That moon calf from V. M. I. doesn't mean a thing on earth to me," Bina said airily. She had appropriated Eunice's designation and delighted in using it in and out of season. "I don't care so much for these military dates anyway. The buttons hurt— What's the matter, Eunice? I haven't said something else wrong, have I?"

"Bina, you shouldn't let these beaux of yours be so familiar. It gives me a queer feeling every time I see all you young people coming out in pairs from behind the cherokee rose hedge and the syringa bushes and the mimosa trees. I know that means some pretty intensive love-making. You should wait until you're engaged."

"But I am engaged, Eunice. I'm engaged to three of them right now. How can I tell which one I want to be engaged to marry unless I try to see how it seems?"

Eunice did not attempt to argue with her. Gradually she was learning that architectural improvements were not the only sort that must be attempted with tact. And her forebearance was rewarded. As the time of her confinement grew near, she found herself surrounded with loving solicitude on every side. It all meant much to her. But it was Francis's fostering care that meant the most. She had not counted on this, she had not realized that as the mother of his child she would seem far more beautiful to him than she had as a bride. She had been afraid that as she grew heavy and clumsy he would make her feel that he resented the loss of her grace. Instead, he told her repeatedly that she had never looked so lovely before, that there was a wonderful new light in her eyes and a wonderful new look in her face. She had feared that he might belittle the ordeal she was facing, speaking slightingly of her anguish and comparing her own lack of endurance to the courage of other women who had faced childbirth unflinchingly. Instead, he found something to praise, every day, in her conduct and bearing; and in the last desperate hours before Noel was born, he stayed by her side, encouraging her and supporting her until deliverance came.

"I declare ter Gawd, Miss Eunice, I neber did see no young husband so comfortin' ter his wife," Aunt Cynthia told her afterward. "Seems like yo' done draw on his strength fo' succor all de time. De wuss yo' pains was, de mo' he done help yo'. An' he sho' know how ter act like a gentleman at de bedside. My, my! Mostly I shoos 'em out ter de barn ter drink corn liquor till everytin's all over. But Marse Francie, he could nuss yo' hisself, effen he had ter. Ain't yo' glad now yo' done lak Aunt Cynthia tole yo', an' had yo' baby in yo' own bed, wid his own daddy dar when he come inter de world?"

"Yes—I am glad," Eunice whispered.

Her words were hardly more than a deep breath, but it was a breath drawn with relief and joy. After her labor she had sunk into abysmal slumber; now she had lost all sense of time and space; even her sufferings seemed remote, though she felt bruised and beaten. Only two realities remained in a shadowy sphere: She had brought a manchild into the world, and she had found fresh favor in her husband's sight.

Later on, she groped her way slowly back to other actualities and all of these were beautiful too: The brightness of the fire in the still room. The welcome warmth of the broth that was brought to her. The cleanliness and coolness of the linen sheets in which she lay. The healing skill of Aunt Cynthia's hands moving over her maimed body and making it whole again. The softness of her baby's hands, kneading her full breasts, and the sound of his lips as he drank thirstily from them. The light in Francis's eyes as he bent over to kiss the mother and son.

Both her readiness and her ability to nurse her child herself had gratified him immensely. He timed his frequent visits to her room so that he would be sure to find the baby with her, and then he sat down to watch the feeding, his infinite satisfaction richly revealed. Afterward he took Noel in his own arms and cuddled him while he talked to Eunice about the uneventful tenor of his life before he laid the baby down in the cradle and went quietly out again.

"It's been a wonderful day. I've never seen such weather at Christmastime."

"Everything is wonderful now, isn't it?"

"Yes, everything."

"Did many people drop in for dining day?"

"No, only the Tayloes and the Daingerfields. I said we'd have to skip that celebration on any sort of scale this year. I didn't want to run the risk of having you disturbed by a lot of noise."

"That was thoughtful of you, but I shouldn't have minded— Haven't you seen anyone else at all?"

"Hardly anyone— I met Millie when I was down by the marshes today. I went to see how the finishing touches on the lodge were getting along."

"Was Free with her?"

"No, he's bitten hard by this political bug. She might have known he'd never make a planter. He's away half the time. So Millie's ranging around by herself too. She certainly is a pert piece."

"I'm afraid she must be lonely."

"I hope she is. I wanted to tell her to get off our land, considering how long she'd stayed off it of her own accord. And what do you think she did? She asked me how soon she could come and see you."

"What did you say?"

"I told her not for a long while yet. I said you'd taken everything like a Trojan, but that you'd had a hard time, that Doctor Tayloe and Aunt Cynthia think the quieter you keep, the better. I said that even Mother hadn't seen you yet for more than a minute or two, and that I was keeping all the trundlebed trash at bay."

"Did Doctor Tayloe really say I couldn't see anyone for a long time, Francis?"

"Well, something of the sort. Perhaps not that exactly. But I'm selfish. I want you all to myself. You and our baby. You don't mind, do you, Eunice?"

"What do you think?"

"I don't believe you do. I hope you don't. You look so lovely, darling, lying there, with your long black braids and your big gray eyes and your wonderful white skin——"

"As lovely as I looked on the lanai?"

"As if that could compare to this! Why that was only pleasant! It might have happened to almost anyone. But this is perfect. And it couldn't have happened to anyone but us."

That was what Eunice herself thought, after Francis had kissed her again and had left her, and she lay listening to Aunt Cynthia crooning away in her rocker beside the fire.

Chapter 12

WHEN SHE first lived at Retreat, Eunice thought of time in terms of days. But soon she came to think of it in terms of seasons and eventually in terms of years.

She nursed Noel until he was ten months old, so her activities during the winter and summer following his birth were limited by his needs. Doctor Tayloe was most insistent that she should not get overheated or overtired, and Eunice found that the Fielding family needed no persuasion to agree that she should not undertake gardening, preserving or anything else that required much physical labor until after he was weaned. When Aunt Cynthia tearfully prepared to leave at the end of six weeks, she "trained in" a reliable young colored woman named Edna, who was a distant kinswoman of hers, as Noel's nurse. Edna was strong, willing and very plain. Aunt Cynthia explained carefully that she was "no box," and this, being interpreted, proved to mean that she was not careless in male company about her use of woods and haystacks. Edna herself put it differently.

"Ah aim ter stay right along side o' Marse Noel all de time," she said defiantly, when Eunice undertook to interview her about her dependability as a nurse. "Ah don' want none o' dem bull men foolin' around me. Ah isn't like Violet. Effen she gits into trouble, nobody guine to eben know who ter blame it on. Elisha an' Malachi ain't de only ones dat's runnin' after her. No, ma'am! De bery las' time she done go to de county seat, dey sat together on the stoop watchin' her start, and dey was singin' in a chorus 'Yah better stay home, yella girl. Nedda one ob us is aguine ter save yo' principles when yo' starts ter sob next month.' "

Eunice still shrank from such language and began to borrow trouble lest Noel should learn it at too tender an age; but Francis as well as Aunt Cynthia was insistent that Edna should be given a trial; and it was soon manifest that her trustworthiness had not been overrated. Her singled-hearted devotion to Noel was truly touching; and since it was characterized by an astonishing amount of intelligence, Eunice soon ceased to hesitate about leaving the baby in Edna's care for his naps and outings. She reveled in bathing him herself, before an open fire, and she could not be induced to turn him over to anyone else at night. Nevertheless, she soon had a certain amount of restricted leisure on her hands, and she devoted this with eager interest to organizing the scheme of life at Retreat more systematically, and continuing the work of restoration and improvement which was so well begun.

The household staff had already been somewhat augmented before the arrival of Edna, and gradually it grew larger still. Blanche was no longer expected to spread her well-meant but slatternly endeavors to every room; her work was confined to the modernized kitchen where she continued to regard the labor-saving devices with a certain amount of suspicion, and as far as she could without getting caught, did her cooking and cleaning as she had always done them. Virgin had taken more kindly to teaching and training; although he had been dazed when he heard Francis refer to him as the butler, in speaking to Mr. Hogan's chauffeur, he had now earned his right to such a designation and was immensely proud of it. Eunice had also taken several of Blanche's other children under her tutelage, not on the old payless basis about which Bina had talked so casually when the new mistress of Retreat had first come there, but with wages which made their eyes stick out and their mouths distend in wide grins. Violet, who was pert and pretty, did the chamber work and the mending and helped upon occasion in the dining room; Kate, who had blue eyes and who had "married out of her color" and afterward returned to live down her disgrace under her mother's wing, was the laundress; while on the grounds and in the gardens and outbuildings, Orrie, Elisha and Drew were variously occupied.

Eunice had never failed to consult Francis about her projects after the day that he had sought her out in the lodge, and she would have been only too glad to have him take the responsibility of the menservants, especially those who were employed outdoors, entirely off her hands. But he laughingly told her that she could get more work out of them in a day than he could in a week and left a large part of their supervision to her. She was a meticulous manager. Blanche was held accountable for every pound of sugar and every joint of meat that she used; Virgin could not lay a fork askew or fail to fill a glass that this was not noticed; Violet learned in short order that a missing button or a disarranged press would bring forth a prompt reprimand. If any of them failed to observe immaculate habits, both about their work and about their person, a rebuke was certain to ensue. Orrie, Elisha and Drew were all required to wear neat overalls while they were working about the grounds. When Blanche failed to change her turban, when Virgin appeared in the dining room with a frayed sleeve, when Violet "overlooked" a spot on her apron, Eunice warned them that the repetition of such an offense would mean their discharge. None of them had ever heard such a pronouncement uttered at Retreat. They "belonged" there. But they soon found out that Eunice meant what she said. Violet, who had permitted herself to doubt this, was relegated wageless to the cabin before she wholly realized what had happened to her. It took tears and time, aided by the intervention of "Miss Alice" in her behalf, to persuade Eunice to give her a second chance. She did not slip, visibly, again.

"Ah declare to Gawd," she told Edna in a grumbling undertone, "Ah spex Miss Eunice to undress me, one o' these days, to see effen mah shimmy am clean."

"She ain't got no need to trouble herself to undress yo', yo' frittermouth. She know widout lookin'. It's a gift she hab," Edna retorted in a superior tone of voice. Edna was inclined to put on airs. She alone in the staff had never been reproved, nor had there ever been a reason why she should be. But there had been one instance when Eunice herself had regretted a rebuke. She had reprimanded Elisha severely because he had a habit of coming into the house wearing a small shabby cap, so dingy that its original color was no longer discernible; she had told him sternly never to let her see him with it on again. The next morning, as he knelt on the hearthsone laying the fire, she saw that there was a bald spot, which had come to him prematurely, on top of his head, and she knew that with desperate pride he had been trying to conceal this from her. She was smitten to the heart, and longed to tell him that she repented of her ill-advised severity toward him; but Francis had warned her that she must never admit to the servants that she herself was at fault, so she could make only indirect atonement. She bought Elisha a set of neat white-duck caps, and told him she thought they were suited to the type of work he did. He understood her gesture and was grateful for it. The white caps set him apart from the other workers. He was enormously proud of them, in the same way that he was proud of the gold-rimmed glasses which he also wore.

The results which Eunice secured were amazing. She even succeeded in putting the fear of fire into the negroes, which her mother-in-law had assured her could never be done; unalarmed, they had often let the cabin stovepipe get red hot to the ceiling, menacing the safety of the big house as well as their own quarters; and their favorite threat, uttered half in jest and half in earnest when they were angry with each other, was that they would burn the place down. Eunice told them sternly that if they ever said such a thing again, she would be compelled to notify the police, and they believed her. But if she were the better organizer, Francis was an even sterner disciplinarian and none of the servants was deceived by his easygoing ways. They knew that he was more critical than he seemed, that he lacked Eunice's patience as a trainer, and that he could, on occasion, be ruthless in anger whereas she was always gentle at heart. They knew too that there was no surer way to fall from Marse Francis's good graces than to leave undone anything that Miss Eunice had mapped out for accomplishment. And they respected her. She was an exacting mistress, but she was a fair one. Francis, who did not always trouble to be fair, they adored.

When the house, the lodge and the cabin were all in perfect condition, and the garden and grounds had undergone as much improvement as it was possible to effect in one season, Eunice turned her attention to the outbuildings. The old barn had fascinated her from the moment she had caught the first glimpse of it, strolling out through the peach orchard with Francis in the early evening after their return from Singapore. It was a very large barn with a sloping gray roof, built beside the southern slant of a hill against which it leaned picturesquely. Its foundations, made of rose-red sandstone quarried on the place, formed an indentation which was solidly walled up at the back and sides, and arcaded through the middle with heavy, rough-hewn pillars of sandstone. The space thus formed was divided into stalls for the cattle.

"But isn't it too warm for them in summer?" Eunice had asked solicitously.

"They're never in it during the summer. They stay in the cowpen."

He pronounced the word as if it were spelt "cuppen." Eunice looked at him in bewilderment.

"C-o-w-p-e-n," he spelled, accenting each letter. "In the level barnyard at the top of the hill. Do you want to go there too?"

"Yes, presently— Francis, this end of the barn is for horses, isn't it? There seem to be about a dozen extra stalls, some of them boxstalls."

"Yes, there are plenty of stalls. But as you know, there are only two decrepit old horses. They belong to the same period as the carryall I came to fetch you in at Solomon's Garden, and various other old vehicles—an omnibus and two fathers'-top buggies—over here on the west side where it's walled off for a carriage house."

"We must get the barn repaired and brought up-to-date right away. When the stalls are sound and clean, we'll fill them with horses. A dozen would be just about the right number, wouldn't it? Because there are nine of us here, counting Noel—he'll be ready for a pony before we know it! and then we ought to have extra mounts for our visitors, or at least space for them to put their own horses."

"It would be mighty fine, of course— Are you interested in other kinds of stock too, Eunice—thoroughbred cattle and sheep and pigs?"

She was immensely interested in them. Indeed, she had always taken their presence in ample numbers for granted on a country place of any size. She had been deeply puzzled that very morning when she had heard Blanche say, "De calf am sold, Marse Francie. Yo' can employ yo'self wid all de milk yo' wants." *The* calf? Surely there should be twenty calves, to say the least, at Retreat! Encouraged, she said so at once. When the barn and the pens and the cribs had all been put in prime condition, there must be stock of every sort to fill them. And what about more chickens and some ducks and geese? She had already noticed the "gobblers"; the noisy creatures had thrust out their heads and made soft throaty sounds as she and Francis passed the turkey house. And the evening before, when he and she had been sitting before the parlor fire after everyone else had gone to bed, she had been startled by the sound of sharp, short strokes against the windowpane. Francis had teased her, telling her she was hearing ghosts again. Then he had led her outside, holding up a warning finger to show her that she must be very quiet, and had pointed to a rooster guinea and three guinea hens side by side on the casement windowsill, pecking at their own reflection revealed in the glass— So there were guinea hens at Retreat too, but Eunice wanted more of those. She liked them. They looked to her like little Quaker ladies, wrapped in shawls——

She did not stop with the renovation and replenishment of the barn: At the foot of the barnyard, under a pignut tree, she found a disused cider press. The lever was merely a long pole thrust through a large hole in the trunk of the tree; the press itself was roughly made and the trough below it was blackened with age; all were rotting from disuse. But beginning with that first autumn which she spent at Retreat, Eunice insisted that cider must be made again every year, and that barrels of vinegar must be stowed away in the old meat house to grow sharper and clearer as time went on. When she heard that herring had formerly been brought up from the river and salted away in kegs, she suggested that this custom should be revived too; and though she was subjected to considerable raillery, her suggestion was eventually followed.

"Wouldn't you like to start in making soap?" Francis inquired. "My grandmother used to make all her own soap, hard and soft both, after the War. Or would you prefer to begin butchering pigs? You might go out and have a look at the iron pots in the old kitchen. One of them was used for soap-making and the other for hog-scalding."

"I've been to see them already," Eunice retorted. "There's a third one, too, that she used for dyes, in case you've forgotten. She dyed the warp for rag carpets and the wool and cotton for the men's clothes and the knitting yarn for the children's sacks and gloves. Then in her leisure moments she made citron 'sweetmeats' and cut them out in the shape of loaves and fishes. She got that idea out of the Bible, of course. She used to read three chapters in the Bible and three chapters in Hall's *Meditations* every night before she 'retired.' She kept the Bible and the two volumes of the *Meditations* beside her workbasket on the little table with glass knobs that stood beside her bed. But she didn't 'retire' until she had stitched down the linen pleats of her husband's shirt bosoms by candlelight and heard her children's prayers and sung several hymns to them. I don't believe the evenings seemed long and lonely to her at Retreat."

"Do they seem long and lonely to you?"

"No—not now that I'm here. I had a few qualms beforehand—and Millie told me they'd be terrible."

Francis made a profane comment, as he was apt to do when Millie's name was mentioned. Then he asked if it were she who had told Eunice so much about his grandmother.

"No, that was Honor. She says your grandmother was a wonderful woman. She wants to write a story about her

173

sometime. She thinks her name was made to order for the heroine of romantic fiction. Sylvestra Cary—it is a lovely name!"

"I reckon she was wonderful—and lovely too. The Fielding men have usually married above them," Francis said, pinching Eunice's ear. "But you'll beat her yet, if you go on the way you've started. Did Honor tell you about the hog-killing too? She used to come over to watch that and I wouldn't put it past her to get that into a story."

"No, she didn't say anything about the hog-killing. You do that."

Eunice shrank from hearing this, but she had learned that Francis liked to talk about every feature of Retreat and she encouraged him to do so. They had been walking in the garden down the gravel walk while they had been discussing Sylvestra Cary, and now Eunice sat down on a rustic bench facing a big bed of yellow lilies, so that she could feast her eyes on their loveliness as a distraction while he told her of horrors to which she did not wish to listen.

"The hog-killing used to be a great event, even when I was a little boy," Francis said, sitting down beside her and plunging into his tale. "I can remember it very well. The hogs ranged through the woodland during the summer and early fall, collecting 'mass'——"

"Mass?"

"Anything they could find that was eatable—grass roots, for instance, or the nuts that had fallen from trees. Early every morning and evening they were called together so that Uncle Nixon could feed them corn. 'Mass' alone wasn't enough for them. All of us children used to love to hear the call that brought them scrambling down the hillside from every direction. It sounded something like 'Cho-hoge, choge, choge, choge!' "

"Didn't you hate to have them killed after you'd seen them running like that, free and joyful?"

"No— Children are naturally cruel little creatures! I used to count the days until the pigs were put in the pens to be fattened—that was about the first of November. Then the hog-killing itself came off sometimes in December—whenever it was cold enough. It was begun early in the morning, long before light, so that it could be finished in one day. The fire that was built under the big iron pot you saw made a glare all around it and lighted everything up."

"What was the pot used for?"

"To boil water for scalding off the hogs' hair— We children weren't supposed to get very close to the murderous scene, but we were allowed to look on from a distance. We could hear the pigs squealing and the men laughing, and we could see the slaughterers moving around in the eerie dawn lit by the firelight and plunging the stuck pigs into the great kettle of hot water. Several short, crotched poles were set up with one long pole laid across them, and after the hogs were killed they were hung up by their hind feet to this long pole to cool off and be thoroughly cleaned. At that stage we were allowed to come closer."

Eunice shivered a little. "And you didn't mind at all?"

"No— They weren't creatures any more then. They were bacon and we were proud of our bacon. Making it was a fine art, from the first feeding of the hogs to the final manipulations— After the slaughtering the 'chitterlings' were made. I don't believe you could stand hearing about that—you've done very well as it is. And the tails were roasted at the fire under the big kettle. I remember they always tasted of cinders. I ate them because I'd have been called a sissy if I didn't, but I never really liked them. The bladders were a great prize, though. They were given to us children to blow up for Christmas popguns. We'll have to see if we can't get one for Noel on his next birthday."

"Yes—if you used to be proud of your bacon here at Retreat, of course you ought to be again."

"You're not serious, are you, Lady Sylvestra Cary?"

"Of course. I can see the bacon we'll make, our own special brand. We'll have to find a name for it."

She was so absorbed in her work of reclamation that she hardly noticed the heat that first summer. She rose early and went to bed late, taking the first morning hours for her rounds of supervision and those in the late evening for accounts, correspondence, and consultation with Francis. She lay down after dinner only because she was told that insufficient rest, on her part, would react unfavorably on the baby; and she was finally persuaded to take what Blanche called a "vaporcation" late in the summer, because Doctor Tayloe warned her gravely that if she did not, Noel would have to be weaned before cool weather came.

"You're losing too much weight," he said, stroking his beard and jingling his watch chain. "Not that your baby's lost any—the way he's gone on gaining is amazing! And there's an old saying which I hope you won't mind my quoting, that 'the best cows are always thin.' But if you keep on getting thin, you may collapse one of these days, and that would be bad all around—almost as bad as changing Noel's milk in this heat. I want your second son to make the same grade as your first," he added, his kind eyes twinkling; and when Eunice protested that there was no prospect of a second son, he went on, "I'm just as glad that there isn't

175

—at the moment. But that doesn't alter the fact that you need a rest, and that I can see you're not going to take it at Retreat. What's this I hear about turning the old quarters into a guest house, and remodeling the old office for Francis? Isn't there going to be anything left unimproved?"

"The family is all more or less incorrigible, especially the head of the house," Francis said whimsically, coming into the room at that moment. "She couldn't improve the people to any appreciable degree, so she's taking it out on the place. And doing a mighty fine job. Don't you think so, Doctor?"

"Yes. But I'd like to see her lay off it for a while. Couldn't you get her away for a month or so? To see her grandmother, for instance? I should think the old lady would be pining for a look at this great-grandson of hers! And with the dog days crowding in on us, Vermont is a sight better place than Virginia for a nursing mother."

Eunice opened her mouth to protest, but Francis was too quick for her. "You're right, of course, Doctor Tayloe," he said. "I ought to have thought of it of my own accord. We'll get started right away. I'd like to go to Vermont myself —as long as I can go in August instead of November, the way I did before. Was I ever cold! But at this time of year, if we bundle up well and keep all the fires going, we ought not to freeze our noses. What was it I heard about the Hamstead climate, Eunice? That it was all right except that sleighing was apt to be poor between the Fourth of July and Labor Day?"

It had never occurred to Eunice that Francis would be receptive to the idea of going to Vermont. Indeed, she had not once suggested that he should leave Retreat since their return from Singapore; and his few short absences, to "take in" races and horse shows, had been without her and on his own initiative. She was pleased beyond measure at his attitude now; and the trip north, which they made by motor, with Edna installed on the back seat beside the baby's traveling crib and the baggage stowed away at the rear of the car, was a source of real delight to her. They took it unhurriedly, choosing the routes that offered most in the way of scenery and spending the nights at the restored inns which had begun to dot the elm-shaded countryside; and when they arrived at Evergreen, refreshed already, they found that Mrs. Hale had prepared a royal welcome for them, and that she was fairly quivering with suppressed excitement over their visit.

"Well now, I know how hard it is for a young couple to leave their own home," she told them. "But I was beginning to wonder whether I'd see this young man of yours before he got into long pants. I want to have a real good look at him." She took the unprotesting baby into her wiry little arms

176

and regarded him with an intentness which he appeared to return. "I don't rightly know which one of you he favors," she went on at length. "He looks to me some soberer than you do, Francis. I guess he takes after Eunice, that way. But he's got your coloring. I'm real glad he has. I like to see a boy look like his father."

"Just so long as he doesn't act like him, Grandma?" Francis inquired.

"Go on with you! I don't want to hear anything about your actions," Mrs. Hale retorted, giving him a little push. "I hope is isn't going to be so you can't find anything to pass the time while you're in Hamstead," she added irrelevantly. "The fishing isn't bad out at Silver Pond—so our neighbor, Paul Manning, says, and he ought to know. He'd rather fish than thresh any day. He told me he'd admire to have you go out to the Pond with him whenever you felt like it. Sometimes he camps out there, over the Sabbath, in a tent. I always go to the First Congregational Church myself. But you can do just as you've a mind to."

"The old lady wants to get me out of the way so she can talk to you," Francis told Eunice that night. But though she denied this, her protests were rather feeble. She knew that her grandmother was not primarily a prying woman; but neither was she blind to the fact that the old lady was inquisitive in characteristic Yankee fashion; and she was partially prepared for the questions which Mrs. Hale did indeed put to her as soon as Francis had obligingly betaken himself to Silver Pond with Paul Manning.

"You're looking kind of peaked, Eunice. I hope it's like you said, that you're just a mite run down after nursing the baby so long, and that you haven't got any complaint."

"No, I haven't got any complaint."

Eunice was faintly amused at her grandmother's choice of a word. She knew that complaint was colloquially used to designate an ailment, and Mrs. Hale, despite her excellent education, had always inclined toward local dialect. But the old lady was well aware that her granddaughter might misinterpret her expression; in fact, she was offering her the chance to do so, if she chose to take it.

"Well, I'm real relieved," she said in a voice of unmistakable sincerity. "Of course that husband of yours has a way with him. I've said that from the beginning. And I wasn't set against your marrying him, like that scatterbrained mother of yours— Have you taken the baby to Tivoli yet?"

"No, not yet. We've been waiting for cooler weather."

"M-m-m. Your mother hasn't been to visit you either?"

"Just for the day now and then. She was so scornful about everything and everybody that I wanted to get the place in

177

running order before I asked her to stay there. I have, almost, now. I'll write her as soon as I get back— Patrick has sneaked over by himself once or twice, in addition to coming with Mamma. He's tremendously taken with Retreat, and he thinks the sun rises and sets on the baby's head. He and Francis get along like a house afire too."

"That flannel-mouthed mick!" Mrs. Hale said contemptuously. She was obviously piqued because the rich Irishman her daughter-in-law had so inappropriately married had seen her great-grandson and his ancestral home before she had; but she also drew evident consolation from the fact that it was to Evergreen, and not to Tivoli, that the baby had been taken for his first journey. She did not dwell on that phase of the situation long, however. She reverted, still suspiciously, to the subject from which she had no intention of being sidetracked.

"I was real disappointed because you didn't get to India," she said. "You know I was set on it."

"Yes, I know. But I wrote you, Grandma, how it was: By the time Francis could leave Singapore, we were way behind our schedule. It was too late in the season then to go to India. And it seemed best to get home as quickly as we could, when he had been so sick and everything. Besides, I was going to have the baby and——"

"You couldn't have known you were going to have the baby when you left Singapore," Mrs. Hale said scornfully. "Do you suppose I can't still count on my fingers? I know Francis was sick and all that, but I still feel as if there was something I didn't know. You had a nice trip, didn't you?"

"Yes, Grandma, a beautiful trip."

"And that young scalawag behaved himself? He didn't ever go gallivanting around? Or come home under the influence of liquor? Or quote Scriptures to teach you it was ordained that a woman's husband should rule over her?"

"Francis never gets drunk, Grandma. He knows how to hold his liquor, and he really doesn't care whether he ever has any or not, except for the sociability of it. You ought to know by looking at him that he wouldn't be given to quoting Scriptures, either. I can't remember that he ever did it but once and that time he wasn't referring to any sort of rule."

"You're only half answering me, Eunice. A man hasn't actually got to speak a piece out of the Bible to act according to the passages that suit him. If Francis hasn't done that, along with some things that the Scriptures forbid with harsh words, I miss my guess."

"You always were a good guesser, Grandma. Since you're bound to have me admit it, I'll tell you that Francis does dominate me. He couldn't have got me in the first place or held me the way he has if he didn't. But he doesn't do it the way you imagine."

"I didn't suppose he'd beat you, Eunice," Mrs. Hale said tartly.

"Well, he might have," Eunice retorted, to her grandmother's horror. "That is—he said once when he was talking about someone we know, who's very willful, that if he were her husband, he'd take a strap to her every so often, that sometimes it was the only way to talk to a girl like that. But I'm not like that. I'm not perverse. I'm enraptured. The first time I ever saw Francis he promised me splendor. He's given it to me. Do you suppose I resent being 'ruled' by a man who can do that? Well, I don't! I adore it! I adore *him*. What difference does it make if he has some shortcomings? I didn't know there was so much glory in the whole world as I've found in his arms!"

Her voice rang with defiance and with triumph. Her grandmother looked at her through eyes that had suddenly grown misty and then turned away. The splendor with which Eunice had been invested shone in her face and the light of it was dazzling. The old woman whose own lover had died half a century before, in India, without ever giving her fulfillment, could not bear to look at it.

It was several days before Mrs. Hale questioned Eunice a second time. She had come as close to being cowed by Eunice's rejoinder as was possible for a woman of such intrepid spirit, and she had been greatly taken aback by the use of words which she did not currently include in conversation. But she had great resilience. Eventually she created another opportunity of seeing Eunice by herself, and opened attack on the subject which, next to that of her granddaughter's happiness, was nearest to her heart.

"I judge from all I hear that you've been improving your husband's property considerably," she began with due caution.

"It's the family property. It belongs to all that branch of the Fieldings. Of course I have an interest in it myself now, and so has Noel."

"Well, I wasn't thinking so much about that part. What I had on my mind was the amount of money you must be putting into it."

Eunice did not answer.

"It's costly, to make repairs," Mrs. Hale persisted. "If you so much as do a little painting and papering, the price creeps up on you. When it comes to plumbing and heating and lighting, you run into tall money before you know it. And you're doing more than that, Eunice."

"Well, it's my own tall money I'm running into."

"Yes, it is your own. But that doesn't mean you've got any call to squander it."

"Grandma, you advised me yourself to put money into Retreat."

"I advised you to keep it from going to rack and ruin. I never advised you to turn a shack into a *garconear*, if that's what you call it, or to fix up a stable for twelve hourses, or to pay out wages to four hired girls and four hired men all at once. I know you've got a good income, Eunice, but I don't see how you can keep up the pace you've set without cutting into your capital."

"When I get everything in good running order, I won't have to keep on making such a heavy outlay. It's only this first year or two."

"Then you have cut into your capital?"

"A little, Grandma. I haven't disposed of any stock. But I've borrowed money with some of it as collateral."

Mrs. Hale gave an exclamation of dismay.

"I felt it in my bones, Eunice Hale. Same as if someone had told me, I knew that was what you had done. Your father would turn in his grave if he knew it."

"Then I'm glad he doesn't. But it isn't a crime to borrow money, Grandma."

"It's worse than a crime; it's an act of folly," Mrs. Hale said crisply. "Tell me how much you borrowed, right this minute. I want you should pay it back. I've got plenty put by; I can take over the loan myself. Then we'll have it right in the family where it won't cause talk or trouble either —a Hale, cutting into capital! That's where the Spencer shift-lessness comes in!"

"After all, Grandma, the Spencers have shown a good deal of business sense."

"A good deal of business sense!" snorted Mrs. Hale. "All they did was to buy a barren-looking piece of land that was being sold for taxes! And come to find out it was simply riddled through with rock! If there ever was a family that prospered through good luck instead of good management, it's the Spencers. Think of all that timberland they bought just before the War when it looked as if fuel was going to be scarce, and they thought they'd need wood to burn. The coal strike petered out and they started making maple sugar as a by-product!"

"They made money too, Grandma, don't forget that."

"I'm not forgetting anything. I'm mindful that a fool and his money are soon parted, too, in case you've forgotten it. Here you are borrowing right and left to make up for cutting into your capital, and as far as I know, you haven't so much

180

as been over to Spencerville to see what shape your property's in for almost two years."

"I'm going, Grandma, before I start back to Virginia. But I've been waiting for Francis to get through with all these little fishing trips that you so kindly arranged. I think it would intrigue him to see the sidewalks and the railway station and the workmen's cottages all made out of marble, in such a little village. It's unique."

Mrs. Hale snorted again. "If it's unique, it's worth hanging onto. And to my way of thinking, the quarries matter a sight more than the sidewalks. You ought to spend part of every year in Vermont, Eunice, looking after your interests here, instead of staying in Virginia all the time and spending so much money that you have to——"

"Grandma, if you say anything more about cutting into my capital, I'm likely to say something very rude and disrespectful in return. Please don't keep tempting me so."

Grandma Hale pressed her lips firmly together. Finally she rose, and going over to the parlor window, looked out at her trees, as she was prone to do in all moments of strain and stress.

"I presume you haven't got a cent laid by for Noel's college education," she said at last. "And here he is going on a year old. I must begin planting more pines right away."

Chapter 13

THE GARDEN was at the height of its autumnal glory when Francis and Eunice returned to Retreat, and with a spontaneity she had never shown before, Eunice succumbed to its spell.

It was not only the flowers which were so beautiful—the late lilies, the vivid dahlias, the roses which were even more luxuriant and lovely than they had been in June. The fruit trees that grew here and there along the crosswalks and beyond the borders in the orchard proper were laden with rich fruit. The quinces hung in golden balls from the heavy limbs, weighing these down to the ground. Blanche baked them and served them every night for supper; and during the day, she stood over steaming kettles breathing in the pungent scent that rose from them and pouring their contents, toward the end of the afternoon, into the tall jars destined to hold preserves and marmalade, and the tall glasses set out in readiness to hold jelly. Mrs. Fielding confessed that putting up fruit was one of those things to which she had never got around; but she now sat in the kitchen vaguely helping Eunice who

181

had resolutely taken the situation in hand, since the time had come that she could wean Noel whenever it seemed best. She knew a good deal about preserving already, because she had helped her grandmother with it, from time to time, as a girl in Hamstead. But never, in that frugal New England kitchen, had she beheld such prodigality of supply.

Along the western side of the garden, beyond the fence, was a line of apple trees, pippins and "Jeanettes" and English cheese apples. Some of these went into jelly too, and some into cider; still others were converted into deep pies and sweet sauces; but for the most part they were eaten fresh, and a large dish of openwork "milk glass" always stood heaped high with them on the sideboard. Eunice loved to pick one out as she passed through the dining room and sink her teeth far into the firm white pulp that lay below the rosy rind. But most of all, she delighted in the products of the grape arbors. There were two of these arbors, both heavily laden like the fruit trees: The "long grape bower" stood at the eastern end of the gravel walk, covered with "Isabellas"; the purplish bunches of these were never wholly symmetrical in form, but they were as sweet as if sugar and sunlight had been imprisoned together inside their swollen skins. The "little bower" stood at the western end of the third crosswalk, and this was overhung with Clinton grapes, in beautiful full blue bunches. The Clinton grapes were tart, not unlike the wild grapes that grew in the woods; they were not so tempting to taste as the Isabellas; but the little bower itself was an enchanting place, airily built of narrow, whitewashed laths with a narrow bench running the length of it on either side. Eunice loved to sit in it on warm, still afternoons with Noel crowing in his carriage by her side, and a bit of needlework in her hands. But she did not accomplish much sewing at such times. While she was not playing with her baby, she was watching the garden walk for the approach of Francis, coming home to her after the hours that he had spent here and there on the plantation.

Many of the grapes went into Blanche's steaming kettle too, for jelly and for wine, and Eunice suggested spicing some of them also, to eat with venison later on in the fall. Her spiced grapes were a great success, and so was some conserve that she made out of tomatoes, drawing freely on the abundant harvest of these to concoct another delicacy that was new to Retreat. The unexpected skill that she showed in the kitchen, now that she was free to go there, won a slightly grudging approval from Blanche, but a chorus of praise from everyone else.

"Next year, when you aren't so preoccupied with this young man," Francis said, taking the expectant baby from her

182

and tossing him in the air, "you can begin with the figs and go straight through the season—and the garden. It'll take you quite a while to strip the 'Currant Walk,' but I haven't a doubt you can do it. Then there are all the cherry trees awaiting your attack—'black hearts,' 'red hearts,' 'skin and bone——' "

"I haven't the vaguest idea what you're talking about, Francis. Look out— You tossed him too high that time!"

"I never! Did I, Noel? There, you see— Why 'red hearts' and 'black hearts' and 'skin and bone'—at least the ones I was referring to then—are just different varieties of cherries. There's still another kind, called morellos, that I think is the best of all. I remember once when the morellos were ripe and I went out to pick them I found a partridge's nest against the roots of the tree. There were fifteen eggs in it."

"I hope you didn't rob it."

"I'll probably surprise you by telling you that I didn't. You're always watching guardedly for a cruel strain, aren't you, Eunice? No—none of us disturbed the proud parents or the nest or so much as climbed the tree until the baby birds were hatched. Did you ever see a young partridge, Eunice? I suppose not— Sometimes they start running away with a bit of shell still on their backs. And if you look into the nest after they've gone, you see that the shells are 'pipped' around the large end of the egg, so that when it was ready, the baby bird could raise that end as though it were a basket lid and walk out. Bella and Bina used to pick up shells of that sort and use them for their dolls. Probably Mamie Love still does. You might ask her. I heard her talking to one of her doll babies just the other day and she said, "Did you take that egg out of the nest or didn't you? Answer me now before I whups you *good!*' There are always lots of partridges in and around the garden. We'll watch them together, next spring, and teach Noel to look out for them too. It's amazing how young children can care for things like that."

"If you divert me, hunting for partridges, maybe I won't stick to my preserving. We only got as far as the currants when you were sidetracked."

"Oh, but I won't let you get sidetracked! Not a chance, now that I know what a famous cook you are! The cherries will be coming along too, and damsons in the sun, and raspberries in the shade, and two batches of strawberries, one late and one early——"

"Do Honor and Millie put up preserves?" Eunice inquired. She did not know exactly what prompted her to ask the question. But the answer to it filled her with a sort of righteous pride.

"Put up preserves? Is that meant to be a joke, Eunice? No

183

one gets much past Honor and she can turn her own hand to almost anything. She's capable and she works hard— The amount of writing she accomplishes is amazing. But when she's through with that for the day, she wants to sit still in a garden and enjoy it. If it looks pretty and is peaceful, that's all she asks; it doesn't matter a tinker's damn whether it's productive or not. As for Millie, the little slut never did anything useful in her life."

"Francis, I wish you wouldn't always use such awful words when you speak about Millie."

"It's the only way I've got of showing how I hate her— I have to admit she's a good shot, as good as any in the country. I've seen her up at four in the morning, going hard all day and coming home at night with a bigger bag than any man in the field. And she can train a dog so that it's staunch to point and gun. But she could no more keep house or run a place the way you do, honey, than she could fly to heaven on two wings."

"Do you really think I'm a good housekeeper?"

"Do I really think you ever slept with me? Ask me something harder next time, darling! Why you're the best housekeeper, and aside from that, the best all-around manager, in King George County. Of course, you haven't got as fine a house to keep or as splendid a place to manage as Millie has, if she'd only do it. But considering what I gave you to come and go on——"

"Someday this will be a finer place than Solomon's Garden ever was. You wait and see."

He glanced at her with amused admiration. So she desired to excel in ways where Millie had failed, to surpass the lovely little sophisticate who had so often teased and taunted her! Not the passion for improvement alone, but a spirit of rivalry was spurring her on and on to more ambitious undertakings. Well, he would not be sorry himself to see Retreat outshine Solomon's Garden. Far from it. If that was the way the wind blew, he would do everything he could to fan it further.— He could almost see the peacocks strutting across the lawns again, their feathers gleaming like jewels, their tails spread out like iridescent fans. He could almost hear the voices of archers floating toward him from the clump of catalpa trees which served as a windbreak for the target at which they were aiming with their beautiful bows made out of orange wood, and their arrows tipped with silver that shone in the sun.

But aloud all he said was, "Well don't forget to build a rabbit warren, while you're about it. This young man will dote on the little brown bunnies. When I was a youngster, I liked the rabbit warren better than anything else at Solomon's Garden."

In spite of her loss of weight and the exhaustion which was beginning, intermittently, to overwhelm her when she worked too long, Eunice had kept remarkably well ever since Noel's birth. Now when she began to wean him, her temperature suddenly flared up and she ached all over. For a day or two she kept on her feet, fighting off fatigue and pain; then, rebelliously, she suffered herself to be put to bed.

But she could not sleep. She was drowsy, but her splitting head and her aching breasts gave her no real rest. After two wretched nights, when she had kept Francis awake with her tossing and turning, thereby adding immeasurably to her own disquietude, she decided to move into the guest room until she was well. Noel had already been sent to the nursery at Doctor Tayloe's insistence. He was doubly difficult to manage when he could not see his mother; with both small sturdy fists he beat away the cup of milk which Edna coaxingly offered him; only hunger and separation would bring him to terms. Since Eunice had reluctantly recognized this, he was not a factor in her decision. She forced herself to lie perfectly still in spite of her discomfort until Francis had at last gone to sleep; then she slipped quietly from his side.

She had never slept in the guest room since the first night she had spent at Retreat, and so much had happened since then that the fright she had received there had been crowded completely out of her mind. Now, as she climbed into the high bed, she suddenly recalled it, and the memory vaguely disturbed her. But she was too wretched to worry. She lay down slantwise, thankful that she had the bed to herself, and that her restlessness would interfere with no one's slumber but her own. It was strange to think that separation from Francis could possibly be a relief——

Relaxed at last, she dozed lightly. But she felt cold, though the night was a mild one. She must be having chills as well as fever now, she thought, reaching half-consciously for the extra quilt folded across the foot of the bed; then she shrieked aloud. With the same half-forgotten movement that she had seen before, a dim figure had again detached itself from the post against which it was leaning, and with its white draperies fluttering in an icy zephyr, had disappeared into the darkness.

Her scream caused general commotion. It waked Noel, who immediately began to whimper and then to cry. It waked Edna, who in spite of her intelligence, was not immune to the prevalent superstitions of her race; and it waked Francis, who was anything but pleased to be roused from the first sound sleep he had had in several nights.

"Oh, for God's sake! What do you mean by creeping off here anyway? You weren't bothering me where you were— you only thought so. But you certainly have bothered me now. Come back to the bed you belong in. You're feverish and you're probably delirious. Good grief, listen to that kid howl— You'll have to nurse him now, if anyone is to get a particle of sleep the rest of the night. You're trying to wean him too fast— If you'd gone about it more gradually, it wouldn't have upset either of you so much."

"I've done what Doctor Tayloe told me to, Francis."

"He didn't tell you to leave a warm bed in the middle of the night and get into a cold one, did he? No wonder you've had chills and hallucinations. Anyway, you're going to do what I tell you now. In the morning you can thrash it out with Doctor Tayloe if you want to. Meantime, lie down again and take this bad boy and behave yourself."

When the doctor arrived, to Eunice's chagrin, he was inclined to back Francis up. "I think perhaps we have erred in trying to hurry things along," he said. "You're so drained of strength after the splendid way you've supplied this young man all these months, that I was afraid you couldn't hold out much longer. But it would have been better to risk a breakdown than to have you running a fever. The old bromide that you have to let nature take its course still contains a good deal of truth. Stay in bed, Mrs. Fielding, and make Edna keep Noel in the nursery. He'll gradually get used to not having you around all the time. That will be helpful in itself, and the oftener he sees that shining silver cup of his, the better he'll come to like it. But feed him yourself if he gets too obstreperous and you get too uncomfortable. A few weeks more or less won't really make much difference at this stage. It isn't as if there were another baby on the way, or as you especially needed your vitality for anything else at the moment."

Eunice could not help wishing that Doctor Tayloe, like Francis and her mother-in-law, would not keep referring to the arrival of another baby in the near future as a matter of course. She loved Noel deeply; but she felt she would enjoy him more, during the next year or so, if he were not crowded out of his cradle by a little brother or sister. Moreover, she had not forgotten her labor pains as speedily as Aunt Cynthia had assured her she would; and she was therefore also disposed to accept with a grain of salt the midwife's statement that "the nex' time eberytin' would be over befo' she knew it." Neither was she eager to map out her life indefinitely on a schedule which would fit in with two-, three-, and four-hour feedings. Now that everything was running so smoothly and in such beautiful order at Retreat, she wanted to entertain more and to go about more herself. Francis continued to make short pleasure trips without her; but so far, she had not even been to Tivoli——

She was unresigned as she lay in bed, and for the first time vaguely resentful of the role she was called upon to play. She was proud that she had proved a good housekeeper and an efficient organizer, prouder still that she had produced a sturdy son and that she had been strong enough herself to attend to his every need. But such pride was not enough to fill her life. She had not visualized herself merely as a manager and a mother; she had visualized herself also as a gracious and accomplished hostess, an outstanding influence in county life.

Eventually she said something of the sort to Francis. He did not sit with her as often, nowadays, as he had at the time of her confinement. He was indefinitely occupied about the plantation, though he gave her no very clear idea of what he was doing; so she had to wait for a chance to talk with him expansively and confidentially. She was again chagrined to find that he was not in sympathy with her scheme; he was completely satisfied with the current of life as it ran.

"We must have that long-delayed christening as soon as you're up and around. I thought perhaps we could plan it for our second anniversary as long as we couldn't for our first. I hope we can still squeeze the kid into the ancestral christening robe. Mother's heart'll be broken if we can't. And I think we should have an old-fashioned dance for the girls at Christmas, too. We've rather lost sight of the fact that they also have a right to 'entertain.' I imagine we'll be having a couple of weddings here before long, and I suppose Peyton will be bringing home a bride himself one of these days. Then we'll want to do something for her. I should think all that would take care of as many parties as you'd want to give, for the present, especially if you're so run down."

"I meant something more general in the way of company, something more——"

"Something more like what Millie goes in for? Oh, for God's sake leave that smart set she's so stuck on to her! I wouldn't give most of her own gang houseroom, and the political crowd Free is playing up to now isn't any better. While you're trying to outdo her, don't make Retreat into a roadhouse. We want our own family and our own friends here of course, and the better impression you make on them, the more pleased I'll be. But I don't want the latchstring out for every upstart who's taken a notion to move into Virginia these last few years."

"Our parties would be much more dignified and distinguished than Millie's. Hers would suffer in comparison."

"I doubt it. Not many people are worrying about being dignified and distinguished these days. What they like is a drunken racket. I don't want anything of the sort at Retreat. Put it out of your mind."

She made an honest, though slightly aggrieved, attempt to do so, and found that her active thoughts, thwarted in one direction, were turning more and more to the mystery of the apparition in the guest room. Nobody had spoken of the subject again. But one rainy day, when Mamie Love had brought her dollhouse into Eunice's room and was playing on the floor with it, Eunice brought it up of her own accord.

"Mamie Love—you're getting to be a big girl now. Haven't you ever thought you'd like a room of your own?"

Mamie Love was still sleeping beside Mrs. Fielding in a big four-poster, an arrangement which was eminently satisfactory to her mother, who never yet had called her youngest daughter anything but baby. Eunice was taking a shot in the dark through her assumption that possibly the arrangement was less satisfactory to the child herself. Mamie Love cast down her eyes, pushed a pigtail primly back over one shoulder, and moved a toy piano from one corner of the dollhouse drawing room to another.

"Do you mean would I like to sleep up in the attic, the way Bella and Bina do?" she asked cautiously.

"No—I didn't suppose you'd want to go so far from your mother at first. I thought maybe you would like the guest room, the one with the spool furniture in it. That's so suitable for a little girl. The rosebud paper in there is pretty too."

Mamie Love dallied with no staid preliminaries before she answered this time. "I wouldn't sleep in that room for anything," she said decidedly. "It's ha'nted."

"How absurd! What makes you think it's haunted?"

"Don't you think so yourself, Eunice?"

Eunice was considerably startled. As Francis had pointed out on the occasion of her first visit, the family slept on the other side of the house. It was only since her own marriage that the west wing had been regularly occupied. She knew that Mamie Love could not possibly have heard the disturbance she had made in the guest room herself, on either occasion that it had occurred; and she did not see how the child could have learned about the second episode afterward, unless Edna had been prattling. She knitted her brows with displeasure.

"If I believed it was haunted, Mamie Love, do you think I would suggest that you should sleep there?"

"Well, we put company to sleep there. Most company isn't bothered by ha'nts. They don't know about them and they go to sleep without watching for them. The ha'nts come into the room while they're sleeping. Except that you weren't sleeping when you saw the ha'nt the first time, were you, Eunice? You were different from other company, though. You belonged, from the beginning."

The child's tone was so fond that Eunice was touched. But she was not diverted.

"You haven't answered my question yet, Mamie Love. Do you think I'd suggest you should sleep in that room if I thought it was haunted?"

"I reckon maybe you think little girls aren't bothered by ha'nts any more than company is. But I'd die of fright if I saw a ha'nt, all in its angel clothes——"

"I'll tell you a secret, Mamie Love, if you'll promise you won't breathe it to a soul."

"Cross my heart and hope to die."

"I do believe that room is haunted. But Francis swears it isn't. So I thought I would ask some other member of the family to sleep in it. Just as a test. I chose you because I thought maybe you'd help me."

Mamie Love swelled with importance.

"What do you want me to do, Eunice? To help, I mean?"

"I want you to help me shove the press that stands against the south wall to one side. There isn't any door in that wall. But when the ha'nt, as you call it, disappears, it goes through there. I want to find out if there's any sort of an opening hidden behind that press. I tried to see before, and I couldn't."

"But, Eunice, you're sick abed, you oughtn't to get up."

"It'll only take a minute. I'll go right back to bed again. Francis and Purvis are down by the blinds shooting ducks and everyone else except you and me is taking a nap." It was on the tip of her tongue to add, "No one will ever know I got up." She was already suffering from slight twinges of conscience because she had secured the little girl's connivance, and she did not wish to add implied deception to her other peccadilloes. Without giving Mamie Love time to change her mind, she slipped out of bed, thrust her feet into slippers, wrapped a dressing gown around herself and stole stealthily into the guest room with Mamie Love on tiptoe behind her.

The press which stood against the south wall was empty, so it was not heavy. Between them the moved it without difficulty. Behind the place where it stood the wallpaper presented an apparently smooth surface. But Eunice ran her hand over it, pressing her fingers down hard as she did so. Then she cried out excitedly:

"Look, Mamie Love, the paper's cracking! And the crack is in the shape of a little door!"

Mamie Love stared at it, her jaw dropping slightly. But she pointed out a difficulty.

"How can we open it, Eunice, even if it is a door? It hasn't any knob and it's stuck tight."

"I'm going to slit the crack open. Run quick, and get the big nail file off my dresser."

Mamie Love darted willingly away to return in a second with an old-fashioned nail file. Breathlessly she helped Eunice insert this in the crack. With the file as a lever and four eager hands pulling, the door gave way, puffing little whiffs of dust into the girls' faces as it did so. In the aperture made by its opening they saw a short flight of low steps, and beyond this a small square room. The low ceiling slanted to the top of tiny, four-paned windows which had been concealed with clapboards on the outside. The paper, covered with delicate traceries, was so faded that the pattern was scarcely discernible. The muslin curtains were brown and weighted with the dust of many years. On the small tester bed the crocheted canopy and counterpane were mottled with yellow spots.

"Oh, Eunice, I'm frightened! How did this room get here?"

"It's always been here, Mamie Love. But it's so small, it was easy to hide it. I never even noticed that this guest room was shallower than the other rooms on this floor—or if I did, it never occurred to me to wonder what had become of the extra space. Of course the new papering was all done while I was gone on my honeymoon. But your mother must know the room's here, and Francis—probably all the family but you and me! And there must be some reason why they don't talk about it!"

She was so excited that she completely forgot how ill she felt. She forgot to feel aggrieved because she had been excluded from some cherished secret. She forgot to be frightened. But Mamie Love, shivering beside her, began to wail.

"I don't like this room, Eunice. It makes me feel queer. Let's go back and shut the door and never tell anyone we've been here."

"It makes me feel queer too, but I love it. See, it even has a little humpbacked horsehair trunk in it, just as a haunted room ought to have! I'm going to stay here and see what's in the trunk. But of course you can run away, if you want to be a little 'fraid cat."

"I'm not a little 'fraid cat, Eunice, but ha'nts can hurt you if you trouble 'em. Oh! Don't do that!"

Eunice had already flung up the lid of the trunk. A strange scent, like a perfume given forth by flowers long dried and dead, rose from its depths and floated through the musty room. Eunice could feel it in her face as she had felt the puffs of dusty air when she had opened the door. But she did not draw back. She bent over, trying to distinguish in the dim light the shapes of objects lying in the canvas tray, edged with pasteboard flowers, that lay before her. They seemed to be packets of some sort, but when she tried to lift them, the yellow ribbon which bound them together snapped in her hands, pulverized, too, and the separate pieces fell back in the tray. As she tried to reach for them a second time, she felt a hand descend heavily on her shoulder.

Mamie Love's wail had already risen to an outcry. Now Eunice cried out too. The terror with which she was smitten was so alien to normal fear that for a moment she was both blinded and paralyzed by it. It was not until she had been pulled bodily away from the trunk and had heard its lid thud heavily down again that she recognized that the force which caused this came from Francis.

She had seen him angry many times before and she had come to dread his anger. But never had she known it to be unleashed in the way it was now. He spoke to her scathingly, accusing her of stealth and prying, and of having lured a child into furtiveness with her. Then he turned to Mamie Love and shook her until her teeth chattered. Eunice knew that if he had happened to have a whip in his hand he would have used it. The effect he had on the little girl was devastating. She cowered before him, begging him between her sobs not to hurt her.

"Pl-ease, don't, Francie! I didn't mean to, honest I didn't! Oh—*Oh—don't!*"

"I'm going to take you out behind the garden house and switch you till you won't be able to sit down for a week. Don't try to pull away from me like that, you little sneak. If you do, I'll switch you twice as long and twice as hard. The way Yankee overseers used to whip bad niggers."

"Oh, Francie, don't—don't—don't—don't!"

"Francis, take your hands off that child. Don't you dare to hurt her."

"Don't you dare to interfere between me and my sister, you meddling outsider. Leave me alone, I tell you."

"Francis, Mamie Love didn't want to come here, she didn't want to stay. It was all my fault. I'll take all the blame. But how could I guess you were hiding something you were ashamed of?"

"Who said I was ashamed?"

"If you weren't, you wouldn't be so angry. It there weren't

a secret and a scandal connected with this room, you'd have never had it walled up. Unless you want to have them both shouted out loud, you better take your hands off that child."

"Are you threatening me?"

"You threatened her, didn't you? And you've spoken to me as no man living has a right to speak to any woman. Maybe your noble ancestors could talk to their poor shrinking wives like that. But I'm not poor and I'm not shrinking. You'll apologize to me for what you've said and done or you'll find out that I'm not a wife either in any way that'll really matter to you."

"So you're defying me too?"

"Yes. I'm defying you too. And if there's the slightest doubt in your mind that I mean everything I say, you're welcome to test it out— Come here, Mamie Love."

"I—I dassent."

"Yes, you do, too. Francis isn't going to shake you any more. He isn't going to switch you either. He was just fooling. Eunice is terribly sorry she let you get frightened like this. But no one is going to hurt you. Please stop crying and come here and let me wipe off your face and blow your nose."

Timorously, Mamie Love made a slight movement. Francis's fingers, which had been digging into her shoulders, were lax again. She slipped from under them without mishap and ran to Eunice. She felt her sister-in-law's arms close reassuringly around her. Then these too went lax.

Eunice had fallen to the floor in a dead faint.

Chapter 14

EUNICE WAS ill for so long that it was not until almost Christmastime that it was definitely decided the long-delayed dance could take place at Retreat.

Even a fortnight beforehand, Doctor Tayloe still shook his head and looked preternaturally grave when anyone spoke of it. The coaxing of Bella and Bina, who were aided and abetted by their mother, had not the slightest effect upon him. But when Eunice herself made a point of it, and he saw that she would be genuinely disappointed if she did not carry this, he finally weakened and consented to discuss the matter.

"You've had a bad breakdown, my dear young lady. I warned you before you gave out, and you wouldn't listen to me. Now you won't listen to me when I tell you that you shouldn't overdo again."

"Yes, I will, Doctor Tayloe. I will listen to you. But I'm not doing reconstruction work any more. It's all done. And I'm not nursing a baby any more. He's all weaned. Besides, I've been shut up for so long with nothing new to think about that planning a dance would give me a fresh interest. I'd enjoy it, truly I would. I wouldn't do any work. I'd just direct."

"Yes. I know something about the way you direct. From six o'clock in the morning until ten o'clock at night," the doctor said dryly.

"When we were rebuilding the barn! But that's all finished and stocked now. Have you been out to see our horses and cows, Doctor Tayloe? They're beautiful— Why you wouldn't compare building a barn with giving a party, would you?"

"I might, if you were doing it. You put a good deal of yourself into whatever you do, Mrs. Fielding."

"Couldn't you call me Eunice, Doctor Tayloe, the way everyone else does?"

He gave her one of his shrewd glances, but continued to sit fingering his watchchain. "I'd be mighty pleased to and you know it. But I can't take a bribe to make me wink at foolhardiness."

"Doctor Tayloe, I want to tell you something that perhaps I shouldn't. I—Francis and I had a bad quarrel the day I fainted away. It was partly my fault and partly his. I guess that's the way with most quarrels, isn't it? But we've never had a good chance to make up again—that is, not really. And I think if we could both get into the Christmas spirit together— Do you see what I mean? This is something he's wanted to do for a long time too."

"I see. Well, I suppose I have to say yes. But mind there are no fainting spells and no quarrels either, along about New Year's——"

"I promise there won't be— I'll start making up a list right away. Only I'm not sure I know whom I ought to invite and whom I ought to leave out."

"That does give you away for a Yankee sure enough. If you'd lived here all your life you'd know by instinct. You ask all the kinsfolk, of course—the 'kissing cousins' and the cousins both. Then for a big party like this, you ask some of the 'ain't cousins' too. But on no account any of the poor white trash."

"I can't tell the difference yet, Doctor Tayloe, in some cases, between the 'ain't cousins' and the poor white trash."

"Well, Francis will help you out on that and on everything else as far as the invitations are concerned. And I suppose you'll be calling on Willie Jones to play for you?"

"Willie Jones?"

"Yes, he's a famous fiddler. He's a Baptist, and most Baptists hereabout believe that the surest way to open wide the gates of hell is by dancing up to them—especially if you cross your feet when you're doing it. But Willie Jones has decided to take a chance on it. He loves to play his fiddle, and the only way he gets to do it much, except by himself, is to play for dances. I asked him about his eternal salvation once, and he looked at me in a droll sort of way and said he might be going to hell when he died, sure nuff, but he'd made up his mind he was going to have some fun while he was living."

"Is Willie Jones a gentleman of color?"

"No, he's a tenant farmer at Merridale, a plantation up Fredericksburg way. He lives in a little bunch of a house clinging to a big outside chimney, with a slanting black roof that lengthens into a porch extending across the breadth of the building. There are two fair-sized rooms on the ground floor, and two tiny ones lighted by dormer windows upstairs. It's very typical of an average overseer's domain, except that Willie keeps it neater than most. He's a bachelor and lives all by himself except for his fiddle. You'll hear him playing before you get on the porch. But he'll stop and make you welcome whenever you go there. You'll like him. He's quite a character."

"How does it happen I never heard of Merridale before?"

"Oh, it's gone out of the Fendal family, that used to own it. Some Yankees live there now, I don't even know who. And it's way back from the road, like all our houses around here—You wouldn't see it unless you set out on purpose. You might take a look at it though, when you go to hunt up Willie. It' worth seeing, if it hasn't been spoiled."

"Then you are willing I should ask Francis to drive me up to Willie's domain so that I can ask him about coming to play for my dance?"

"I reckon so, I reckon so."

The floor plan of Retreat lent itself capitally to a dance. The wide entrance hall alone could care for thirty couple comfortably; and when the French doors between the front and back parlors had been folded open and the furnitur moved against the wall, there was plenty of space for many more dancers, besides the "lookers-on" who would sit around the fringes or stay in the library. Eunice had never known cleaning and rearrangement to be so lightheartedly undertaken as it was now. It was even suggested to her, from several quarters, that the old block dry-rubbing brush should be brought out of its hiding place and used to polish th floor.

"What is the dry-rubbing brush?" she asked her mother

in-law. "Everyone seems to think it's needed before a dance. I never even heard of it before."

"No, honey chile, I never got 'round to havin' it used after I was married. It's got put away somewheres, if it hasn't been lost. Maybe Blanche is hidin' it out in the cabin. In slavery day the floors were waxed every mornin'——one of the house-boys would sprinkle wax on the floor and then two of the others would take turns runnin' the dry-rubbing brush over it. After the War, though, nobody bothered to run it except befo' a dance. But of co'se no one would think of havin' a dance without runnin' the dry-rubbing brush around any mo'n they'd think of havin' it without a fiddler."

A year earlier Eunice might have pointed out that since the floors were now regularly treated with liquid wax there was really no need of resorting to ante-bellum methods to produce a creditable effect for a dance. But she had learned some wisdom by experience. She praised Purvis when she saw him taking turns with Virgin in pushing the heavy block around, and encouraged Peyton to do the same thing when he came home for the holidays. She also urged them both out to gather large bunches of laurel and holly for corner clusters, and set Bella and Bina to making wreaths, for which they really had great aptitude. She hesitated about getting what her grandmother called "boughten" flowers to mingle with these for fear of spoiling the natural effect; but when her stepfather, upon hearing about the prospective dance, sent her enough poinsettas to fill a fair-sized green-house, she achieved a gorgeous showing with them. Though unguarded flames caused her a certain amount of trepidation, she could not resist the temptation of putting tall red can-dles amid the masses of scarlet bloom. When the open fires had been kindled too, no other lights were needed in the glowing rooms; and a great Christmas tree, placed at the south end of the entrance hall, gave the final touch of brilliance to a scene that was sparkling already.

At the last moment, however, an unexpected disturbance undermined Eunice's satisfaction in the effect she had achieved and threatened to jeopardize the smoothness of service at the party. She had already gone downstairs to take a last look around before the festivities began when unmis-takable sounds of altercation caused her to lift her party dress high above her ankles and dash hurriedly across the strip of frozen ground separating the cabin from the big house. As she opened the door of Blanche's habitation, she was amazed to behold Uncle Nixon, whom she had always thought the most harmless and gentle of the old retainers, vigorously belaboring Kate, who was bellowing lustily while the rest of the family stood on the sidelines, obviously enjoying the fray.

She gave an indignant exclamation which was not even heard until she raised her own voice to a scream. Then the onlookers turned to stare at her without so much as moving from their vantage point. Uncle Nixon and Kate continued their tussle as if oblivious of an intruder's presence. Eunice was obliged to hurl herself bodily between them in order to separate them.

"Shame on you!" she cried wrathfully. "Fighting among yourselves at Christmastime! Neglecting your work when I need you most! Stop screaming like that, Kate! You'll wake the dead! What do you mean by acting like this, Uncle Nixon?"

"She called me a Raybab!" panted Uncle Nixon, still hitting out into space with his aged arms, to which fury had given new strength. "What's mo', Miss Eunice, she done tole me yo' done said Ah was a Raybab. Ah cain't help what no Yankee woman calls me. But no nigger gal can call me a Raybab, withoutten Ah gits eben with her. Ah done hit Kate wid de tongs, an' she done smack me wid de shubble. After dat we got ter fightin'.'"

"After that you got to fighting! Uncle Nixon, I'm amazed at you! You're drunk, crazy drunk! That's what's the matter with you!"

There was nothing feigned about her astonishment. It was quite true that the thought had crossed her mind more than once that Uncle Nixon might have an Arab strain in him; it was not an unusual legacy, and his features were aquiline, his skin a clear brown; but as far as she could remember, she had never given tongue to the surmise, for she knew how touchy the negroes were on the subject of any admixture of blood. Aunt Cynthia frequently boasted that hers was "pure," and all Kate's own troubles had come about because she had married, as a "brightskin," a man darker than herself. It was inconceivable to Eunice that Kate should have sought to make trouble on this particular score, either because of what she had divined herself, or because of what, with the uncanny intuition of her race, she had picked from her mistress's mind. It was equally inconceivable how Uncle Nixon could have lost himself in liquor. Hampered as he was with blindness, he could hardly hunt for it unless someone had placed it so close to him that he could smell it. Eunice knew that it would be useless to try to track down the culprit until after Christmas week was over; none of the darkies would return to normal for at least that length of time. But she intended to mete out justice untempered by mercy at the earliest possible moment.

Meanwhile, the general atmosphere in the cabin was becoming increasingly unbearable. None of the house servants had so far stirred. Uncle Nixon, far from being downcast by his mistress's rebuke, had collapsed into a seat, shaking all over with enjoyment.

"Yassum, Miss Eunice, Ah knows Ah is drunk"—he tittered. Then he burst into uproarious song in which the others joined as a chorus:

> " 'Christmas comes but once a year
> An' every nigger mus' have his sheer
> Of apple cider an' 'simmon beer. Ha! ha! ha!' "

Eunice turned on her heel and walked out of the cabin, slamming the door behind her. Then she crossed over to the big house even more quickly than she had left it and ran up the stairs. She did not so much as glance at the twinkling tree and the candles flickering among the poinsettias as she hurried along. She went straight to her own room and breathlessly appealed to her husband.

"Francis, you'll have to come and help me out."

He was standing in front of his dresser, still in his shirtsleeves, putting a final touch to his tie. His back was toward her, but his mere reflection in the mirror seemed to emanate vitality and elegance. He reached unhurriedly for his coat, his immaculate linen gleaming as he moved.

"What's the matter?"

"All the negroes, from Uncle Nixon down, are dazed or drunk or something. And there's a fight going on in the cabin."

"Which you weren't able to stop?"

"No, I tried, but I couldn't do a thing."

"Really, Eunice, I'd rather not interfere. The last time I tried to handle a situation in my own way you had hysterics. I don't want to bring on another attack when you're just beginning to get back your health."

"Oh, Francis, don't let's quarrel now! If we've got to do it, let's do it tomorrow—or tonight—after our guests are gone! But they'll be coming any minute. You wouldn't want Millie to get here and have no one at the door to meet her."

"I don't give a damn whether there's anyone at the door to meet Millie or not. It might do her good if she had to turn a few knobs herself instead of having a liveried ape like Barrel Boxen bowing and scraping to her with every turn she makes. But since you're so distressed, I'll go over to the cabin and see what I can do—provided you'll promise not to find fault with my methods afterward."

"I'll promise anything you like, if you'll only hurry."

Francis tightened the buckled strap at the back of his vest

and shook his well-cut coat down over his sloping shoulders. "You better repowder your nose and do your hair over before you come down yourself," he said condescendingly. "You look all hot and bothered—not at all like the cool and collected mistress of Retreat that everyone is counting on seeing. I'll get Mother and the girls on the job and tell them to hold the fort. Bella and Bina are sure to be ready."

Still without haste he left the room, closing the door quietly behind him. Eunice watched him go with a lump in her throat and blurred eyes. All the pleasure, all the triumph of the celebration for which she had planned with such care and such pride had been wiped away. When her vision cleared so that she could see in her looking glass, her hair seemed to be perfectly smooth; but she unbraided it and plaited it again, putting in each separate pin securely; then, following a sudden inexplicable impulse, she surmounted the collected coils with a huge tortoise-shell comb. She had never used any make-up, but now something also impelled her to take the lipstick from a compact that was among her Christmas gifts and apply it hesitatingly to her lips. The result was remarkably becoming. Having gone so far, it seemed natural to go further. She opened another Christmas package and took the glass stopper out of the fanciful bottle of French perfume. The scent was rich and heady, strangely unlike the fresh lavender water she always used. She put a little behind her ears, then more rashly sprinkled it lightly over her black-velvet dress. But this no longer suited her either. It was too straight and simple, too subdued in tone. She took it off and threw it down on her bed. Then she went to the big press where she kept her clothes and opened the doors wide.

She had stopped in New York for two days on her way south from Hamstead and had replenished the wardrobe which until then had received comparatively little attention from the time she had bought her trousseau. Now she was fully stocked again, and most of the dresses she had never worn. She had hesitated to buy the one which she finally selected, but at this moment she was glad she had. It seemed suited not only to the season but also to the spirit which amazingly possessed her. It was made in the Spanish style, of crimson satin with wide hoops and a revealing bodice, and it was finished with a fichu and frills of black lace, caught up with red roses. It called, unmistakably, for long earrings, a glittering necklace, and a painted fan as accessories. Eunice rummaged through her disused belongings until she had found all of these. Then, without giving herself time to repent of her own daring, she went to the head of the stairs.

The party was already in full swing. Willie Jones was standing beside the Christmas tree plucking at his violin strings;

198

long flourish gave notice that he was ready to strike up a tune. Then he plunged into a lively strain:

> " *'Did you ever see the devil*
> *Come a-trotting on the level——' "*

he sang as he fiddled, breaking in on his own refrain. "Partners for the first dance!" he called out, and the next instant the hall was swarming with rollicking couples. Most of them fell into position more or less harmoniously for an old fashioned square dance; but a few merely sped past, bent on some more distant destination. Eunice could see the "moon calf from V. M. I." carrying a small guitar which he was pretending to play as he "chasseed" around; unperturbed because Willie Jones was singing a different ditty, he was singing himself:

> " *'I wish I had a needle*
> *As fine as I could sew,*
> *I'd sew Miss Bina to my side*
> *And down the river we'd go——' "*

Bina was shaking her head protestingly. But she was laughing at the same time, and she was making no effort to break away from her beau. Bella, disregarding both the quadrille and her sister's antics, was dancing cheek to cheek with her own suitor. Peyton had brought a girl from Charlottesville home for the holidays, but she was very decorous, outwardly at least; when the quadrille broke up, she was almost the first to disengage herself and fall sedately into the march of the "promenaders." Purvis and his first flame were nowhere to be seen; he was still young enough to be self-conscious, and Eunice thought it probable that he and his youthful ladylove would spend the greater part of the evening in front of the library fire looking through a microscope at the various winged creatures he had captured. Francis, on the other hand, was very much in evidence. He was standing at the foot of the stairway with a glass of eggnog in his hand, talking to Honor Bright. His attitude was one of admiring attention; but Eunice knew that he was not wholly absorbed. Seldom as his glance strayed from the celebrity at his side, he was watching like a hawk for any flaw in the demeanor of the servants who had begun to circulate among the guests with the first break in the dancing. Virgin walked slowly and heavily, instead of with the light dancing step he usually affected; he had a hangdog look, and he did not lift his eyes from the laden tray of fruitcake and poundcake which he was carrying. Violet and Kate, charged with beaten biscuit interlayed with ham, seemed even more subdued. The secret smile had faded from Violet's pretty provocative face, and Kate, usually so aggressive, looked like a scared rabbit; they moved along as warily as a cat picking its way over rough ground strewn with rubbish. Their uniforms were impeccable, but Eunice had a feeling there were tear stains on their cheeks. This might be imagination, though they both used paint, powder and face cream, and the customary brilliance of their make-up had certainly undergone some sort of eclipse. She wondered exactly what Francis had said to them, or done to them. She could not help remembering how readily he referred to whips.

She felt no inclination to go downstairs and join in the merrymaking herself. She was thoroughly upset. The outrageous scene in the cabin, the humiliation of her enforced appeal to Francis, the fact that her mother-in-law had received their guests without her—she might have taken any one of these episodes by itself as a pinprick, but all together they were piercing stabs. She was sorry she had coiffed her hair with a comb and put on a shimmering dress and gorgeous jewelry. It was all so pointless. She did not care about making a dazzling impression. She only wanted to please Francis. And it was a long time since Francis had looked at her with eyes lighted by love—not once since he had found her in the hidden room and she had defied him.

"Why, Frank! Is that a Goya portrait at the top of the stairs? It isn't—it can't be—a live lady! Not even Eunice could look so beautiful as that!"

It was Honor Bright, with the sixth sense peculiar to experienced journalists, who had felt her presence and looked up to see her. There was nothing to do now but come down. Eunice unfurled her fan and waved her handkerchief in an effort to respond to Honor's kindly compliment; but she was still without inner exultation as she descended the broad stairway. Francis was watching her with the same unsparing gaze that he had turned on the servants; she could not bring herself to believe that he shared Honor's candid admiration.

"I hoped you'd get here in time for the Virginia Reel," he said whimsically. "I was beginning to be afraid you'd fainted away again."

"Did you faint away?" Honor inquired, her kindliness touched with immediate concern.

"Oh, that was several months ago! Eunice decided to go ghost hunting, Honor. The results were disastrous."

"They shouldn't have been," Honor said quietly. "Every well-regulated house in Virginia has its ghost. We take them for granted, just like the windowpanes. Didn't you know that, Eunice?"

"Yes, I'd heard so. But there are lots of things, Honor, that I don't seem to take for granted as easily as if I had been born a Virginian. I'm afraid I'll always be branded as a Yankee."

"Branded? If you must take up such terms, why don't you say hallmarked, Eunice? There's something so sterling about you—and just now something so superb, too, if you don't mind my saying so!"

The intermission was over. Willie Jones was plucking at his strings again, and the "moon calf," still strumming at his guitar, had come back into the hall with Bina so close to his side that she did not look as if a needle were necessary to keep her there. Honor's charming husband, Jerry Stone, and his distant cousin, Freeman, who was also his son-in-law, were coming down the hall with Millie between them. They were a striking trio. Millie had on one of her Oriental dresses, a beautiful embroidered brocade. But as she approached Eunice, the harmonious colors seemed to fade from it and for the first time, as they stood side by side, Eunice was the more vivid figure of the two. Millie was instantly aware of this and instantly resentful of it.

"Come on, Frank," she said impudently. "You haven't asked me to dance with you once this evening."

"And I don't intend to, either," he answered. "Dance with your own husband if you can persuade him to ask you. As far as I'm concerned, I've been enjoying myself very much, so far, with your mother. Now I have a feeling I'm going to enjoy myself very much with my wife."

Chapter 15

FOR A long time the Christmas dance was a solitary land-mark in the uneventful life at Retreat.

"It wasn't always as quiet as this in King George, honey chile," Mrs. Fielding said to Eunice. She vaguely felt that she ought to defend the country's desuetude to her daughter-in-law, and in her scatterbrained way, she began to gather various items which would point to past animation. "Nowadays young folks get into motor cars, and go streakin' off in all directions, every chance they have. But they used to stay right in their own lovely homes and have the best times! There were surprise parties and picnics, and lots of euchre and whist of co'se. And then the tournaments There was never anything to equal the King George tournaments! They were held in the big field just back of the country seat, and we drove up there in our buggies, and sat in them while we watched the ridin'. It was mighty hot, for the tournaments were always held in the summertime, and there wasn't much shade—just scrub pines on the hills around the field. But we didn't mind that. We were all a-twitter even before the herald came out and played the bugle that was the signal for the knights to come ridin' into the field—the charge, it was called. The only bugle we had was one that had been all through the War Between the States and then stowed away in our attic, behind Aunt Amanda's trunk; it wasn't right powerful, and one year the bugler couldn't get a single sound out of it. He blew and blew until we thought his cheeks would burst, they bulged so; and still nothing happened until a little gray mouse came scurrying out of the big end of the horn."

Eunice burst out laughing. Her mother-in-law, far from being gratified by her merriment, looked aggrieved.

"Our tournaments weren't anything to mock, Eunice. The idea behind them was just as noble as when knighthood was in flower. Our knights all wore the colors of their sweethearts, as sashes, tied in true lovers' knots. They devised the rest of their costumes in all sorts of ways. I remember once Francis's father wore a pair of white riding breeches, and khaki leggin's laced up the side with baby blue ribbons. At the last moment he stole a white ostrich plume from his sister Fonnie's hat. Fonnie never did get around to puttin' her things away. And then he found Hilary Fielding's brown velvet smokin' jacket. He carried everything off wonderfully. I couldn't keep my eyes off him."

"No, I shouldn't think you could have," Eunice answered, managing, this time, to keep her merriment within bounds. "What was the tournament like itself?"

"The knights rode with long lances that shone in the sun. They had to put these lances through three loops, ridin' at top speed. The winner was the one who rode the fastest and pierced the most loops. His sweetheart was always crowned Queen of Love and Beauty at the tournament ball in the town hall that same night. I was Queen of Love and Beauty fourteen times."

Mrs. Fielding simpered and sighed reminiscently. Eunice rose to the occasion.

"I'm sure you must have looked lovely, Mother Fielding, wearing a crown. Was it made of flowers?"

"Yes, red roses. It was heavy but it was handsome. Of co'se the flowers wilted a little befo' the end of the evenin'; but they were lovely at first. The Queen was crowned when the coronation address was made, and the orator nearly always recited poetry at the end of it. There was one poem I've never forgotten. May I recite it to you?"

"I'd love to have you, Mother Fielding."

Mrs. Fielding rose, smoothed out her skirt and struck an attitude.

" 'The gorgeous pageantry of days gone by,' " she declaimed—
" 'The tilt, the tournament, the vaulted hall,
Fades in the glory on the spirit's eye,
And fancy's bright and gay creation—all
Sink into dust, when Reason's searching glance
Unmasks this age of knighthood and romance—' "

"That is romantic, Mother Fielding. I know you responded to it beautifully too. I didn't mean to make fun of your tournaments—it was only that your description of the little mouse was so amusing. I'd have loved to see a tournament myself. Why aren't they held any more?"

"Nothin's the same, honey chile, since cyars came in. We did have one tournament, with cyars, but it didn't seem so chivalrous and we gave the idea up. Our horses meant everything to us— You know the first race track in this country was right down at Mt. Airy, and all our beaux used to do their co'rtin' on horseback. Girls didn't have 'dates' in those days and go streakin' off with one young man. They sat in the parlor or on the po'ch with all their suitors gathered in a circle, and the more a girl had around her at the same time, the bigger belle she was. There were always half a dozen mounts around the hitchin' posts at every house where there was a pretty girl in her teens, and if it was a house where there were half a dozen daughters, you'd think a company of cavalry had been called out, most any evenin'."

"I'm sure you were the biggest belle of all, Mother Fielding. I'm sure even Bina couldn't hold a candle to you."

Mrs. Fielding was so mollified by Eunice's compliments that she was encouraged to go on talking about the past pleasures of the countryside in all their different phases. Eunice was terribly tired of her rambling, and early in the New Year she suggested to Francis that they might take Noel to make the long planned visit at Tivoli, which her illness had inevitably postponed. Francis agreed, readily enough, and on the whole their stay in Middleburg was a success. Noel was toddling now and talking a little. He was, as his great-grandmother had said, a somewhat sober child; and the unmasked favoritism which he showed his father did not particularly prejudice his other relatives in his favor. But he was sturdy and sweet tempered, and he was not long in winning his way into the hearts of the household at Tivoli. Besides, he had no monopoly on his partiality. Francis was a welcome figure everywhere. He had brought his finest mounts with him, and he was at once invited to join the Middleburg Hunt as a guest. He rode regularly, and he went with equal regularity to hunt breakfasts, hunt balls, and the numerous other typical festivities which the countryside afforded. His excellent connections, through the Taliaferros and other kinsfolk, and his own personality, which had never seemed more pleasing, alike contributed to his immense popularity; both Mr. and Mrs. Hogan basked in the reflected glory of these advantages. From the beginning, Patrick Hogan had got on famously with his stepson-in-law; now Mrs. Hogan was beginning to admit reluctantly that she did not dislike him either.

Eunice listened, with outward appreciation and some inner reservations, to the tardy praise heaped upon her husband by her mother. If she had been in a more buoyant mood, she might have gloated over it. She had looked forward with a hunger which she had never been capable in her girlhood to the pleasant worldliness, the luxury of living and carefree companionship which Middleburg afforded; and now she was debarred from most of the pursuits enjoyed by the hard-riding, hard-drinking, free-spending crowd into which she had been flung back after months of sickness, solitude and responsibility. To be sure, she went to bridge parties and cocktail parties, luncheons and dinners. But these might have taken place anywhere; they did not represent the sort of diversion she craved. And she could have no other, because she was pregnant again.

She conscientiously tried to be glad that she was going to have another child, but she did not succeed. Weary months of isolation and inactivity seemed to stretch out ahead of her. Her confinement would come in late September or early October, when the heat would still be intense. All summer she would be graceless and heavy; all winter she would be restricted by a nursing schedule; at the end of these she might have another breakdown. She could not foresee freedom of any sort for a long time.

Neither her mother nor her stepfather was especially helpful to her at this juncture. Mrs. Hogan had greeted Eunice exuberantly. She had just read in the paper that Lord Grenville, formerly Governor of the Straits Settlements, had been appointed British Ambassador to the United States. She seized upon this item as assuring her of an entree which she had long eagerly coveted and which she had never dared hope to achieve. But when she spoke to Eunice on the subject, she found her daughter strangely unresponsive.

"Why that's the very man who went out of his way to be so good to you in Singapore! I'm sure he and his wife will expect you to drop in at the Embassy in Washington whenever you feel like it and bring your family with you."

"I doubt it, Mamma."

"Why in the world should you doubt it?"

"Well, in the first place, the British are hospitable, but they don't like to have their hospitality taken for granted. And in the second place they like to have it appreciated. I'm afraid the Grenvilles may feel we didn't appreciate theirs. Our departure from Government House was rather abrupt."

"Abrupt? Why should it have been abrupt?"

"Francis was in a hurry to get home, Mamma. And— there were other factors. I can't talk to you about it. But I'm sure he wouldn't accept an invitation to the British Embassy, even if he had one. And I don't feel sure he'll ever have one."

"I can't believe that Francis would be abrupt. I must say he has very nice manners. But even if he and the Grenvilles don't get on, you and I could go to the Embassy without him."

"No, we couldn't, Mamma. I'm sorry, but there isn't a single thing we can do about it."

Eunice herself had suffered from a certain amount of heartburning when she read of Lord Grenville's appointment, and she had dwelt with a wistfulness she could not wholly suppress on all that the loss of Guy's friendship increasingly represented to her. She had often thought of this before, in her more desolate moments at Retreat, but never with as many cogent and conflicting reasons as she did now. Mrs. Hogan, however, had no way of divining all this. It seemed to her that her daughter was more unreasonable and more unco-operative than ever, as far as she was concerned. She argued, then sulked, and finally took refuge in chilly silence.

Aside from the social climbing in which she was so petulantly engaged, Mrs. Hogan's principal preoccupation at the moment was with her bathroom, which she was occupied in redecorating. The walls were completely lined with mirrors, against which climbing pink roses of a mammoth variety had been painted in oils. Spurred on to further ingenuity by the startling effect of these, Mrs. Hogan next extended her floral scheme to take in the fixtures also, and full-blown roses, in ever increasing profusion, appeared on the porcelain. Then she began on the accessories. Bath salts, soap, powder, and perfume, scented with rose, were easy enough to secure. But to find them in just the right shade of pink, and to provide receptacles for them shaped like full-blown roses, was considerably more difficult. She actually took a special trip to New York in order to achieve these ends; but she did not even suggest that her daughter, whose lack of enthusiasm for the bathroom she had not failed to sense, should go with her.

Patrick tired hard to be kind, especially during his wife's

absence. But his lusty viewpoint on the subject of an increasing family, was not in harmony with Eunice's own feelings.

"The more the merrier, the more the merrier," he roared, when the news of Eunice's prospects was broken to him. "Even if you did get off at a slow start, my girl, I'm taking my oath you'll show all of them your heels before you get through! October, you're after saying? And Noel not two till come Christmas! Not so bad!— Not so bad!— But speed it up a little the next time! My dear mother, God rest her soul, had a saying that a grown woman who hadn't a baby either in her arms or under her apron didn't know the full meaning of life. Faith she must have known it well, for right often it was she had the two at once. My brother Tim and me were just ten months apart, and then for good measure, the twin girls came along the next year! And never did I see my mother when she was lacking a laugh any more than a baby. 'Tis a woman like that her son sets store by, Eunice, as I pray the Blessed Virgin you'll find out for yourself; and 'tis a woman like that her husband clings to, whether or no he has a roving eye and an itching foot. Yes, my mother was right—it's the hearty young wife with her man in her bed and her babe at her breast who gets the most out of life."

Eunice's devotion to her stepfather cracked under this sort of talk. She considered it coarse and crude and did not hesitate to say so. Patrick's Irish temper flared, and he told her she could keep a civil tongue in her head or get out of his house. It was Francis, with his gift for pouring oil on troubled waters, who brought about peace. But Eunice's gratitude to him was grudging. She was displeased by Patrick's general attitude, but she was grieved over Francis's. He had given her no cause for complaint, as her grandmother would say. He had ceased to harbor the grievance he had cherished all the fall, since her appeal to him at Christmastime. He was consistently courteous to her in the presence of her parents and their friends, and in his intimate moments alone with her he was still loverlike and beguiling. But he did not give her the feeling that she was indispensable to his happiness or that he was concerned over her condition. She began to believe that his passion was impersonal, that only his innate virility and his irresistible charm had saved them from a second estrangement. She would have preferred, a thousand times, that her second child should have been conceived as her first one had been than that this should happen.

His name had not yet been linked with that of any particular person, at least to her knowledge, and she knew that amidst the set in which she was now moving such news traveled fast. But she lived in hourly dread that it might be; she could not believe that the affair with Edith, which time had not blotted from her memory, would prove an isolated instance of faithlessness. He saw a good deal of Flora Treadway, whom he had met at Solomon's Garden the evening he had brought Eunice back, here, after their first encounter in the woods. Eunice could still see Flora as she had looked that evening, wearing emerald green satin and blowing smoke through a long jade holder, as she regarded Francis with detached insolence. She was not detached any longer, or insolent either; she was very chummy with him, and she referred to him in horsey but admiring terms. She seldom seemed to wear emerald satin, or its equivalent, in Middleburg; indeed, Eunice had hardly ever seen her when she was not in a riding habit. She had left her ancestral abode in Upperville, and lived in a rambling, low-lying house which she had built herself on the top of a hill, alone except for her servants and her dogs, of which she usually had a dozen or so at her heels. She did not go in for lovemaking, but her living room was always overrun with men who dropped in to play bridge or talk over the latest sporting events while they drank her excellent liquor. Francis found his way into this charmed circle very early in the course of his visit to Eunice's parents and soon he was regularly to be found lounging in one of the great leather chairs encircling the fire burning beneath the mantel where Flora's silver trophies were arrayed and her blue ribbons dangled down. No one intimated that he or any other man found his way to the more private parts of Flora's house, however, and Eunice had no special misgivings on that score. But leaving Flora out of the picture, the fact remained that the locality was overrun with smart and sophisticated women of all ages, married and single, very few of whom were averse to a more or less serious affair with an outstandingly attractive young man; and Francis was obviously deriving so much satisfaction from his fox hunting and steeplechasing, his late dancing and later suppers, that she could not help wondering whether he were not experiencing some added pleasures which were less apparent to the casual observer.

If she could have accompanied Francis on his outings and shared in his diversions, Eunice would have enjoyed the pleasant countryside itself, so different in character from King George. But the contrast was not enough for her now. She did not care whether she saw sprawling holly-grown fences or neat stone walls, a "checkerboard" garden or great terraces of box, a flat riverbed or misty mountains; the air of ordered prosperity which surrounded her now was no more pleasing to her than the atmosphere of rugged wilderness in the Northern Neck.

As the weeks went on, a great longing for her own home

and its habits of living began to overwhelm her. She tried to tell herself that nothing could be more unpleasant than Vermont in March, that the worst of the winter would not be over in Hamstead when the spring flowers were already blooming at Retreat, and that she and Francis and Noel would probably all catch bad colds if they went north at such a treacherous season. It was no use. She heard sleigh bells ringing in her sleep and tasted maple sugar in her dreams. She thought incessantly of the broad valley with the gracious hills sloping down to it on either side of the river, and the snow-covered mountains rising, beyond them, to the frosty starlit skies. She saw her grandmother's pines, clustering sturdily row upon row around the cozy white clapboarded house, and the lilac bushes in the front yard and the white paneling in the best parlor. Most of all she yearned for the old lady's vigorous and wholesome presence, her sharp tongue and shrewd mind and kindly heart. One evening when Francis and her mother and stepfather had all gone to the North Wales Club and she had stayed behind alone, she felt she could not stand the echoing stateliness of Tivoli's great octagonal rooms any longer. She sat up for Francis, and when he came home, she told him she wanted to start for Evergreen at once.

He raised no serious objections to her wish. Indeed, his response suggested that while the whims of a pregnant woman were sometimes rather meaningless, it was, on the whole, best to indulge them. He would enjoy a "sugaring off" himself, he said; what he had heard about these, when they had been in Hamstead the summer before, had made him feel they must be rather intriguing. What was it she called the last of the sap that was gathered? Oh, yes, the "frog run." Well he thought he would like to be in Vermont for a "frog run" sometime. Perhaps next year he could. He had made so many engagements just now that he did not see how he could break away. He could hunt with the Orange Pack two weeks longer. Yes, it was true that he had originally disapproved this extension of the hunting season into the fox breeding period, but he had changed his mind about that; he did not think it did much harm after all. Besides, he had all his arrangements made for taking part in the point to point races, and the Gold Cup would be coming along too before they knew it—he never intended to miss the Gold Cup again. On top of all this, there was that Gymkhana for the Red Cross—he would be riding in pairs at this benefit. And he had half promised that he would go in with some other men on a project they had for bringing the Red Fox Tavern back to life again—he thought she would be very helpful, by and by, about that, when they got to the point where they could actually undertake restoration and redecorating.

But all this need not prevent her from going away. The following morning, if she chose. Or rather that same morning. Was it actually four o'clock? Hadn't they best be going to bed? She mustn't forget that it wasn't good for her to get too tired——

She wavered, wondering whether she could stand separation from him, convinced that it would do no good, this time, to urge him to come with her, concerned as to what might happen during her absence. But her longing for Evergreen was like a clear call. She could not resist it.

"I'm sorry you feel you can't break away. But since you're so much engaged, and so far ahead, you won't miss me if I leave you, will you?"

"Not any more than you'll miss me, I hope—— Do you feel very strongly about taking Noel? It'll be mighty cold for him up there just now."

"Oh, I couldn't bear to leave Noel!"

"But you can bear to leave me— Well, I suppose I must make the best of it. How long are you planning to part me from my wife and child, relentless woman?"

"I think if I could stay there just a week I'd be satisfied— I believe I know now how you felt about Retreat when you were sick in Singapore——"

"Well, so long as you're learning— A week, then? I can depend on that?"

"I didn't mean that literally. Why don't we say that when you're ready to leave Middleburg you'll wire me? Then I'll meet you at Retreat as soon after that as I can get there."

"I'd say you'd driven a mighty shrewd bargain. Still the Yankee, aren't you, Eunice? I suppose I'll have to say yes— Now what about a little sleep?"

He had contrived to put the burden of his own choice on her, as he always did. But she was too exultant to nurse a grievance. Even the long dull railroad journey, with its numerous changes, bad connections and slow trains did not dampen her spirits. She reached Evergreen exhausted, but triumphant; and the exhaustion evaporated as if by magic in the crisp air which she drank in with deep breaths. The snow was still firm and dry. She could walk on it without difficulty. She found the sled which she herself had used as a child and took Noel out on it. She built him a snowman and taught him how to throw snowballs. He too throve in his changed surroundings. His appetite was prodigious, his energy inexhaustible. His cheeks grew red as apples, his laughter rose in a shout and ended in a gurgle. His great-grandmother regarded him with immense satisfaction and remarked that she would have to "eat the words" designating him as a sober child. But she herself grew sober at the mere suggestion that any time the telegram from Francis might come, and that her house would be empty again.

"It would be a real good thing, Eunice, for you and Noel to stay on till cool weather. Just look how that pindling child has picked up! And you don't look like the same girl yourself as you did when you came— You could have your new baby right here at Evergreen. I'd just as lieve you should as not."

"Grandma, I couldn't make all that trouble for you."

"You know just as well as I do, Eunice Hale, that it wouldn't be a mite of trouble to me— I haven't any complaint, but it's lonely here sometimes. It livens things up for me to have a family living here again. Besides, I want you should use the house for anything you've a mind to. I want you should get into the way of it. It'll be yours someday."

"Oh, Grandma, please don't talk about that!"

"We've got to talk about it sometime, Eunice. I'm still spry, but I'm not so spry as I was. There's no use denying it. Not but what I make out all right— Did you notice that new blue spruce I bought me, the one out to the back of the house?"

"Yes, Grandma. It's a beautiful tree. Where did you get it?"

"I bought it at a nursery up to Fryeburg, Maine. I set it out myself and kept the expense down that way. Not that I aim to make a practice of buying trees. I stick pretty close to seedlings. But Jane Manning and I, we were to Fryeburg for a missionary meeting and I saw this tree out in a field. It set out with a lot of others similar to it, but somehow it seemed different. I kind of took a fancy to it. I brought it right home with me in the back of the Ford."

Mrs. Hale went to the window and looked out over her pines, according to her habit. But when her glance fell on the blue spruce, her eyes continued to rest on it, and they were lighted with more than mere pride. Eunice knew that the old lady had a special place in her heart for the purchase which represented such a rare departure from her usual frugality, even before her grandmother went on speaking.

"If I'm spared," she said. "I'll see that blue spruce the handsomest tree in Hamstead— Now we've talked about that long enough. I want you should tell me something about the way you've been spending *your* money—I presume you've gone on spending it?"

"Yes, Grandma, but after this next year——"

"After this next year fiddlesticks. That's what you said last year. You'll find something else to spend it on, after this next year. You mark my words, you'll have more and more expense all the time— What does that good-looking scalawag you married *do* with himself all the time? Does he shuck corn once in a while or is he always off shooting ducks?"

"He has lots of friends, Grandma. They make all sorts of demands on his time."

"What kind of demands?"

"Well, they like to have him fish and hunt and ride with them."

"I guess I ought to have asked you what kind of friends he had, instead of what kind of demands they made on him. It doesn't sound to me as if he was going with the substantial citizens in the community. What sort of terms is he on with the doctor and the minister and the banker?"

"Grandma, Doctor Tayloe brought Francis and all his brothers and sisters into the world and still treats them as if they were under ten. He wouldn't dream of fraternizing with them. Besides, he's too busy to fraternize with anybody. He rides all over the county taking care of hayseeds and rivermen, as he says, and never takes time off except to have a mint-julep party every Sunday. His wife makes wonderful mint juleps. Of course in the wintertime she serves eggnog instead. That's very good too."

"Do respectable people go to these gatherings?"

"Oh, yes! Everyone goes straight from church. And Doctor Daingerfield, the Rector, is always there. He and Doctor Tayloe are great friends. He's a nice vague old gentleman, nearly seventy years old. He's a great scholar and a great saint, but he's very frail. He hardly ever steps beyond the churchyard at St. Peter's-at-the-Crossroads. He doesn't have many parties because he's too poor, and when he does have one, there isn't much to eat and drink. His guests take turns in giving classical readings, or they play charades unless they play croquet. *His* wife raises daffodils and performs on the harp."

"The *harp?*"

"Yes— And the banker, Mr. Tate, is poor white trash, so of course nobody invites him to any parties and it wouldn't do him any good to give one, because no one would come. Besides, he refused to accept Francis's notes before we were married, and Francis hasn't ever forgotten that."

"I presume he's forgotten they weren't worth the paper they were written on though. I know the type—we have 'em even in Hamstead— Well, is he a joiner? Does he belong to the Masons? Is he a church member?"

"I believe he was confirmed when he was about fourteen. It's 'done' about that time, just like putting on long trousers and starting to slick back your hair. He goes to church every now and then to please his mother and Doctor Daingerfield,

and he was really very interested in having the baby christened. Nothing but the very best champagne would do— I
don't think he's a Mason. If he is, he's never mentioned it.
But his grandfather did belong to the Order of the Cincinnati,
so I suppose he could too, if he wanted to."

"What part of the farm work does he take over himself?"

"Why he rides around the plantation and supervises it.
He——"

Grandma Hale interrupted with one of her characteristic
snorts.

"His brothers and sisters are all able-bodied, aren't they?
Can't any one of them turn a hand to earning a little money?"

"Well, Peyton wants to be a doctor. I'm very glad he does.
He's going to stay on at the University. And Purvis is going
there next year. He's interested in natural history. But none
of that will cost me anything. Jerry Stone had insisted on
giving them their education, just as he planned to do before
I came on the scene."

"Land sakes, didn't any of them ever hear of such a thing
as working their way through college?"

"Vaguely, the way they've heard of headhunting. But
Grandma, you shouldn't blame them. You're always 'provid-
ing for college educations' yourself!"

"For my own flesh and blood I am."

"Well, flesh and blood stretches farther in Virginia than it
does in Vermont— And I don't believe the two older girls
are going to be an expense to me much longer. I think they're
probably going to be married before long."

"To good providers?"

"I hope so, Grandma. Let's just make up our minds that
they are."

It was easy enough to say, at Evergreen. But when she
was back at Retreat, Eunice found it somewhat harder to
"hold the good thought." Her mother-in-law met her with
the joyous announcement that Bella and Bina had both been
invited to spend Easter Week at the University, which they had
been pining to do for a long while. They were on their way
to Charlottesville that very moment—she was sure Eunice
would not mind that they had taken her car!—and she was
missing them so she felt as if her heart was going to break
right in two. But they had all been having the loveliest time
together before that. They had gone to Richmond and
stayed with Cousin Kitty Cary, whom they had hardly seen for
years, and Cousin Kitty had known all the best places to pick
out clothes for Bella and Bina——

"I remember when I was invited to Easter Week myself,"
Mrs. Fielding interrupted herself to say dreamily. "I had a

blue grosgrain silk with velvet bows on it and some old lace around the neck and a white tarletan over flame-color. The underskirt to the tarletan was only sateen, but it did look like silk under the sheer white. The blue was made out of a bedspread. Girls used to wear real flowers in their hair then, and I had some flame-colored geraniums to match my underskirt, and the prettiest fuchsia bells! I was the belle of the ball in spite of my makeshifts, but of co'se I'm mighty happy that Bella and Bina could have everything they wanted without tearing the beds to pieces— My white tarletan was the curtains, did I tell you that, Eunice?"

"But wasn't it very expensive to buy complete outfits for Bella and Bina, all at once?"

"Now I tell you, honey chile, I just made up my mind I wasn't goin' to worry about expense when we were all havin' such a lovely time at Cousin Kitty Cary's. You and Francis must take Noel and make her a nice long visit yo'selves one of these days. She's pinin' to have you."

"But how did you pay for the clothes, Mother Fielding? Where did you get the money?"

"Eunice, dearie, I didn't get any money. I just charged everything. I never did get around to havin' charge accounts at any of the Richmond stores myself, but when I mentioned your name, and said you-all were Mr. Patrick Hogan's stepdaughter——"

"You had all those clothes for Bella and Bina charged to *me?*"

"Why, honey chile, you don't *mind*, do you? I thought you'd be so pleased to know they were goin' to have such a nice time goin' to all those dances and suppers and breakfasts down at the University, and of co'se if they were goin', you'd want to be proud of the way they looked beside other girls that don't begin to be as sweet and pretty as they are. You've said over and over again you'd like to send them off to some school, and Easter Week is so much more important than learnin' a lot of things out of books that they won't ever need to know when they're married and livin' with nice young men in darlin' little homes of their own."

Eunice did not attempt to argue the point. But when the statements for the "outfits" came in, she looked them over gravely. Apparently these had been very complete, and she had not allowed for such an expenditure. She would be obliged to meet the bills by slow degrees, a little on account or a few at a time, and she had never done such a thing in her life. By the fifteenth of the month, evey penny she owed had always been paid; but she could not possibly manage to do so this time. Her gravity was the greater because she was beginning to doubt whether all her disbursements at Retreat had been wholly wise. During her absence, the negroes had grown slack. There were weeds in the garden and there was dust in the house. She was constantly finding tools that had not been put away, stalls that had not been cleaned, gaps in the fences that had not been mended. She spoke to Francis about these various evidences of neglect, trying to do so pleasantly and at the same time firmly.

"When I put everything in good order here, darling, I took it for granted that it would be kept so. I'm a little discouraged because it hasn't been."

"I'm afraid you took too much for granted. Not many niggers die of overwork, any more than they die of worry. Especially when no one is standing over them. You and I have both been gone for several months."

"Yes, but now that we're back, I hope there'll be an improvement. I hope you'll undertake to see that there is. Because you handle them so much better than I do, dear. I've never felt the same toward any of them. Except Edna, since Christmas, and they know that I don't. Besides, everything is such an effort for me just now. I'm beginning to mind the heat already. And Noel uses up a lot of my strength. He bounds all over me, and if I let him out of my sight for a minute, he runs away. I can't manage much more than taking care of him, even with Edna's help, on top of the housekeeping. The linen is all mixed up, and a lot of china is broken, and there isn't a single room that doesn't need a good scrubbing. Please take over all the outside supervision, Francis."

"All right. But you'll have to give me a free hand, as I've said before."

"Do you mean about management or about money?"

"I mean about both. I can't get the sort of results you want if I do any pennypinching. Perfection comes high, Eunice. You know that yourself."

"If we could cut down just a little, until I get caught up with the investments I've made here——"

"We can cut down as much as you like. But then you mustn't have hysterics every time you see a loose hinge or an uncurried horse."

"Do you think I'm hysterical, Francis?"

"I think you're inclined to make mountains out of molehills. You always have."

"Would it help at all if I specified a certain sum that I could afford to put into the place every month and asked you to keep within it?"

"A sort of schoolboy's allowance? No, I don't think that would help, Eunice."

214

"What would?"

"I don't know. I reckon we better just drift along."

Nothing could have seemed to her more unwise. But because she herself did not know what to suggest that might be helpful, and because she felt so unequal to any sort of exertion, she followed the course of least resistance.

In May, Bina announced that she wanted a June wedding. Without a qualm, she had thrown over the "moon calf from V. M. I." in favor of a personable young gentleman named Jenifer Dymoke, whom she had met at the University during Easter Week. His people were not "kin" to the Fieldings, but they were socially secure besides being well-to-do; Eunice did not need to be told that Francis would wish to put his best foot foremost when he gave his sister in marriage, and that it was right and reasonable that he should. She did not dare to borrow any more money on her marble stock; but she sold some bonds, paid off the indebtedness incurred for the Easter outfits and offered to furnish the funds for the trousseau. As a matter of precaution, she went to Richmond with her mother-in-law and sisters-in-law while this was being bought. But even so, she did not succeed in keeping them within bounds. Bella was to be maid of honor, and Mamie Love a flower girl; they needed dresses too. So of course did the mother of the bride; she had set her heart on a "rainbow effect"—pink for Bella, blue for Mamie Love, and lavender for herself. The feeling of plenty about them, after so many lean years, had gone to their heads; Eunice, who was responsible for having given it to them, could not successfully suppress it again.

The wedding took place on a perfect summer day, in the long hall. This was beautifully banked with roses of every sort —hundred-leaf and blush cluster, damask and English hedge. Above these towered branches of "smoke," the sweet scent of its oval green leaves mingling with the perfume of the flowers, the feathery masses of its dusty pink bloom soft above the brilliance below them. The bride was a vision of loveliness as she came down the stairway on her oldest brother's arm, clouded in real lace, and followed by her "rainbow"; and the ceremony, with the attendant festivities which followed, was completely in harmony with the charm of the setting and the nobility of its tradition. Mrs. Fielding, who had beamed with bliss up to the last moment, sobbed audibly while the services were going on, which Eunice discovered was in the best tradition also. She revived, while the wedding toasts were being drunk and the wedding cake cut, but when the bridal pair had made their hilarious departure, she collapsed again. Eunice sat beside her, holding her hand and supplying her with dry handkerchiefs for the greater part of the night, listening with amusement which she tried to keep from scorn as her mother-in-law rambled on.

"I can't go to sleep, Eunice, for thinking of my dear little girl. Wasn't she just the sweetest bride you ever did see, honey chile? But she's just a child herself, and I can't bear to think— You know I never did get around to telling her any of the facts of life and here she is gone off alone with that Dymoke boy——"

"She's married to him, Mother Fielding. She wanted to marry him. She was simply crazy to. I don't think you need to worry about her."

"Oh, Eunice, dearie, you don't know what a mother feels like when she sees her poor innocent little girl start off like that. It comes over her all of a sudden that she ought to have warned her. And I never said a word. I was so busy with her pretty clothes and the wedding cake and all——"

"If you're feeling so badly, Mother Fielding, you better start telling Mamie Love about the facts of life tomorrow morning. You ought to have plenty of time before she gets married. I'm afraid it's too late for Bella already, from some things I've seen and heard."

"Now you're mockin' me, Eunice, and that isn't kindly of you. What's come over you, honey chile? You didn't used to mock any of us when you first came here. You were just so lovin' and givin' it was like Jesus' Mercy."

Eunice had never aspired to "Jesus' Mercy," but she was genuinely concerned lest Mrs. Fielding's accusation might be just, lest she might really be commencing to lack loving kindness toward her husband's family. In the succeeding weeks she redoubled her efforts to be gentle and generous; and in the main she had reason to feel she was successful. Retreat had settled down to a state of summer desuetude, and it was not hard to accept each uneventful day as it came with the agreeable indolence of which she had such abundant example. Eventually Bella departed to make Cousin Kitty Cary another visit, and Purvis and Peyton went together to stay with the Taliaferros at Todd Hollow. With the family reduced to four, the tranquillity of the big house became all-encompassing. Therefore Eunice was mildly astonished to notice signs of restiveness among the negroes again. When she asked Francis what it meant, he shrugged his shoulders.

"We're getting near camp meeting time. Last year you and I were in Vermont when it came off, and the year before we just missed it because of our prolonged honeymoon."

"What happens at a camp meeting?"

"Why it's a sort of 'revival,' where the niggers 'get religion.' Some of them call it 'getting happy' and I reckon maybe that's a better expression. There's a good deal of another kind of getting too. We always have a new crop of babies the next spring."

"I think it's disgusting," Eunice said hotly, "to talk about 'getting religion' and—and the other kind in the same breath."

"Well, you asked me. Camp meetings are another form of local life you'll have to learn to take as a matter of course. While they're going on, all the time isn't spent in 'getting,' though. Quite a little of it goes into drinking bootleg liquor and fighting. I shouldn't be surprised if the fighting struck pretty close to home this year. There's bad blood between Elisha and Drew. I saw something sticking out of Elisha's pocket the other day, and when I investigated, I found it was a bag of black pepper that he had bought to throw in Drew's eyes, in case their next argument grew too heated. Of course I took it away from him. But that's no sign he won't get some more."

"But can't you put a stop to all of it?"

"No, Eunice, I can't. There's no use trying. And there's nothing you can do about it either."

She knew that this was true, and she endeavored to dismiss the whole matter from her mind. But the thought of the camp meeting made her nervous, more nervous than she had ever been before in her life. Every fresh sign of intractability among the negroes troubled her; every unaccustomed noise startled her. She found herself, during the peaceful evenings, watching and listening. She could not rest in the arbor where she had formerly found such peace. The nearness of Francis was no longer a solace and a mainstay.

They were sitting alone in the twilight when the sound for which she had been subconsciously waiting suddenly smote the air. She had never heard a sound just like it before. But it made her think, at first, of the noise hogs made when they fought each other. Then it seemed to her as if women were screaming raucously in the distance; before they died away, the screams echoed as if in reverberation through the woods. Eunice half rose, with a stifled cry on her own lips. Francis put out a restraining hand.

"Sit still, Eunice. There's nothing you can do. I've told you that all along."

"But what's happening?"

He hesitated. "I don't know. But if you're not afraid to stay here alone in the house with Mother and Mamie Love, I'll go and see."

"What do you *think* is happening?"

"Eunice, you're very persistent in asking about things that it hurts you to hear. I'm afraid that some men have come home from the camp meeting drunk and that they're carrying off girls against their will."

"You mean rape?"

"Something of the sort. Yes— For God's sake sit still, Eunice. I'll telephone the police at the county seat. Then I'll start out for the woods myself, if it will make you feel any easier."

"There's someone here, trying to get in. There's someone fumbling at the back door now. Don't leave me, Francis, I can't stand anything else."

Francis freed himself from Eunice's clinging hands and strode hurriedly into the hall, switching on extra lights as he went. Then he unbolted the heavy door and flung it open. In the embrasure stood Blanche, wringing her hands and wailing.

"Oh, Marse Francie, come quick! For Gawd sake come! Dey is killin' my boy Orrie."

"What do you mean, they? Who's trying to kill him? Where is he?"

"He am in de plum bushes, Marse Francie. Kate an' me done hide him dar. But dey's guine ter find him yet, dey's fo' sho'. Dey's huntin' for a gun ter finish him off."

"Eunice, call the police for me. Come on, Blanche. I'll go back to the cabin with you. If you won't tell me who 'they' are I'll have to find out for myself."

With hands shaking so that she could hardly pick up the receiver, Eunice called the operator, asked her to notify the police that there was trouble at Retreat, and, if possible, reach Doctor Tayloe as well. Then she turned swiftly from the telephone and started toward the cabin herself. She was confronted with Uncle Nixon, swaying unseeingly toward her. He was unmistakably drunk again, and he had a knife in his hand, which Kate, who came pelting after him, was trying to wrest from him. Both of them had been cut before Eunice, snatching at it herself, could get it from them; blood streamed over their clothes and hers, drenching and staining them. She rushed on to the cabin, shuddering at the slimy feeling of her hands and the clinging dampness of her dress.

She found Francis standing between Elisha and Drew, holding each of them firmly by the wrist as he shook their story out of them. They had come back "drunk ugly" from the meeting, they were confessing; "spoiling" for a fight and ready to find fault with everything. The absence of hot bread from the table had been enough to start them growling, and soon their growls had turned to curses over this insignificant trifle. Orrie had stayed home from the camp meeting so that Elisha and Drew could go; he had done their work as well as his own, feeding and watering the animals besides weeding the garden. He was feeling inordinately self-righteous, and now he stood up for his mother and the girls, who had shared his seclusion at Retreat. How were they to be making biscuit all the time with the pile of work there was nowadays at the big house? His question was provocative; it was just such a signal that Elisha had been waiting for. He leaped upon Orrie, knocked him down, and bumped him back and forth until he was unconscious; then he had kicked him where he lay and turned upon Drew. But Drew had grievances of his own against Orrie. He had told these excitedly, warding Elisha off as he did so, and finally they had joined forces. Together they had gone off to get a gun. It was while they were gone that Blanche and Kate had hidden Orrie in the plum bushes. And when the boys had come back, bringing a gun and an unloaded revolver between them, Uncle Nixon had managed to get the gun away "by the smell." It was Marse Francie's arrival that had made it impossible for them to pursue the blind man or to search for Orrie and "finish him off." But they would do so yet.

"The police are on their way. I'm going to hand you both over to them. You can stay in the lockup until after the camp meeting. Then you'd better start looking for jobs. You're through here."

"Oh, Marse Francie, don't say that! Don't send us away from Retreat!"

"Shut up, you damned scoundrels! Blanche, get Uncle Nixon onto his bed. Kate, help Violet drag Orrie out of the plum bushes. When Doctor Tayloe gets here we'll find out whether he's been killed already. If he has, you'll all hang for it."

"Before Gawd, Marse Francie——"

"Shut up and go to hell. If Orrie isn't dead, we'll send him to a hospital. That'll keep him out of mischief till his thick skull heals. And you can pay his bills out of the money Miss Eunice has given you, instead of spending it on vaseline to grease your dirty wool."

He wrenched their wrists again without relaxing his hold on them. Then, with curiously contradictory gentleness, he spoke to Eunice.

"You get back to the house, honey, and have a bath. Then go to bed and try to keep calm. Nothing else can possibly happen on top of all this. But I'll be with you as soon as I can. And I'll bring Doctor Tayloe in to have a look at you, too, when we've found out what's happened to poor Orrie."

"Poor Orrie" proved to have been the drunkest of the lot. But he also proved to have concussion of the brain and various bodily injuries from blows. After Doctor Tayloe had established these various facts, with very little of his customary kindliness, and had stanched the blood that still flowed from Uncle Nixon and from Kate, he in turn went over to the big house, walked wearily up the broad stairway and knocked at Eunice's door.

"May I come in? Francis asked me to make sure you were all right before I started back to Barren Point."

His answer was a low moan. He went quickly into the room and crossed to the bed.

Eunice's second son was born prematurely, before morning. He lived only three hours.

Chapter 16

It was after the death of the baby that Eunice lost track of time at Retreat, except in terms of years.

There was the year that Purvis went to the University and the year Bella was married, and the year Mamie Love, looking very smug and satisfied, was confirmed. These coincided with the years that Doctor Daingerfield had a slight stroke and Honor Bright wrote another best seller and Freeman Stone was elected to Congress. This constituted the neighborhood news.

The same years were marked by development on Noel's part which was steady, though it was never startling. Eunice taught him his prayers and his letters, and he had his first lessons in horsemanship, like every boy on the place from time immemorial, through riding the horses to be watered at the old trough beyond the big barn. He was not a charming child, or a precocious one. But he was happy, healthy and good humored, tractable as far as his mother was concerned, and so lost in admiration for his father that he was almost pathetically eager to anticipate Francis's every wish. He was never impudent, and he never flew into rages; his Grandmother Fielding, in comparing him to her own sons and brothers, gave his conduct a high tribute. But she did not begin to show the affection for him that she lavished on Ada, Amy and Alicia, the three spoiled little girls that Bina brought home for indefinite visits at Retreat. Jenifer Dymoke had not proved a particularly good provider after all; and since Peyton's medical studies kept him away most of the time, and Purvis had always preferred to stay at the big house, it seemed logical—at least to everyone except Eunice—to offer the *garconniere* to the young couple for their "vacations."

"You know, honey chile," Mrs. Fielding told Eunice, "we've

always opened our arms wide to all our daughters-in-law and sons-in-law at Retreat. You found that out yourself, didn't you? I'm mighty pleased that Jenifer is contented to stay here so much. Lots of young men wouldn't settle down the way he has. Now if darling Bella's husband could only do it too——"

Bella had not married as early as Bina. For some time she had continued to "play the field," as Francis expressed it. Then her irresponsible choice had fallen on a midshipman she had met in Annapolis during June Week, which had supplanted Easter Week at the University as a glamorous occasion in her mind. The midshipman, whose name was Ned Norris, came from Indiana and he had no visible means of support; but Bella had been undeterred by any mercenary considerations. She had made a "real love-match," as her mother said, and she was even more beautiful as a bride than Bina had been, though considerable strain and stress had preceded the wedding. When everything was in readiness for it, and the date drawing near, an extraordinary mimeographed missive had suddenly been circulated throughout the astonished county. It bore the letterhead of Ned's ship, and was inclusively addressed to "My friends and relatives and those of the family of my fiancee, Rosa Belle Fielding." Though the composition bore unmistakable signs of haste, the body of the letter was divided into four parts, neatly enumerated. The first section announced that due to circumstances beyond control the prospective bridegroom would be forced to postpone his wedding since his leave of absence had been canceled and that therefore it was impossible for him to leave his ship. The second section apologized for the form the announcement took, explaining that the mimeograph being the only means available to "notify everyone as soon as possible," Ned had used it so that everyone should be "inconvenienced as little as possible," and that he was sending copies direct to his own relatives and friends and entrusting his fiancee with the task of notifying hers. The third section apologized at some length for the postponement itself and the fourth announced that Ned hoped it might be possible for him to set another in the near future.

Bella's first reaction to this had been one of violent rage. She received a sheaf of the circulars enclosed in a hastily scribbled note, which in spite of its passionate protestations of love and loyalty, did nothing to appease her. The postponement of a wedding at the bridegroom's instigation constituted an affront that no girl in the Fielding family had ever been called upon to endure, though several, Bina among them, had made last minute changes in matrimonial plans themselves. Ned's own helplessness in a situation which he

221

was powerless to control or alter did not seem an extenuating circumstance to Bella. Only Eunice's reasonable reminder that the circular letter had already been dispatched direct to the unfortunate midshipman's own friends and relatives, and that therefore his side of the story would inevitably leak out, prevented Bella from proclaiming that she had discovered some hitherto unrevealed perfidy in the young man and had withdrawn from her engagement before her life could be wrecked. Her anger descended on Eunice also, when the paragraph which precluded her from taking any such steps had been pointed out; and still raging, she permitted the circulars to be mailed, and then waited, like a young tigress at bay, ready to spring upon anyone who mocked or misinterpreted these. Her mother meanwhile collapsed completely and remained secluded in her room; her brothers assumed a belligerent attitude not unlike her own, and her sisters, while voicing their heartfelt sympathy, both managed to convey the impression that nothing of this sort could ever happen to them.

Millie was the first visitor to appear at Retreat after the circulars had been sent out, and Eunice, who was carefully watching the entrance in a conscientious effort to ward off intrusion upon the scene until conditions were quieter, met her at the door.

"Did you ever hear of anything so funny in your whole life?" Millie asked as she came up the steps. "Really, Eunice, I've scarcely stopped laughing since I got that letter. It's a scream. Did you count the number of times the baffled bridegroom used the words possible and impossible? And did you ever hear of another man who carefully enumerated the reasons why he couldn't marry a girl?"

"I don't suppose the poor boy had time to put much polish on his literary style. He had to get out his letter in a hurry. And he must have been so upset anyway, that he couldn't think very clearly. I'm terribly sorry for him. This must be an awful blow to him."

"I'll bet it's a worse blow to Bella. How's she taking it?"

"She's disappointed, of course. A change of plan is always upsetting. But after all, she's a reasonable human being. She knows that some circumstances are beyond control."

"Eunice, I never believed you'd lie so. I'll bet Bella is foaming at the mouth and tearing tulle to pieces at this moment. And I'll bet Cousin Alice is having hysterics and that Francis has his gun out."

"Perhaps you'd better postpone your visit, Millie, if that's the way you've sized the situation up. Of course I'm delighted to see you. I'd like to have you take tea with me in the garden. But if you think Francis might come out to meet you with a gun——"

"Well, I'll risk it. I'd rather like to see Francis with a gun. You've made this the loveliest place, do you know it, Eunice? Free says that people talk to him about it wherever he goes. And Honor thinks you're the eighth wonder of the world."

"I don't know anyone whose good opinion I'd rather have than Honor's. I'm sure she understands conditions thoroughly, that she'll help to smooth them out in the eyes of the county. Not that anyone with a grain of sense is likely to misunderstand them, of course. But I'm glad Honor and Jerry are home just now."

Honor did help to smooth conditions out, and the prevailing tensity was fortunately of brief duration. The wedding took place only a few weeks behind schedule, and in order to compensate as far as possible for the ordeal through which Bella had passed, Eunice encouraged her to arrange it on a defiantly elaborate scale. The county was more than silenced; it was overawed by the "arch of steel," the cake cut with a sword, and all the other glittering paraphernalia of Naval pomp and circumstance. A tragedy had been turned into a triumph. Bella was more than beautiful; she was exultant.

Her husband's first land duty took him to Guantanamo, which Bella adored, though she found the cost of living in Cuba so high that she kept cabling home—at Eunice's expense—for more funds. The periods of his sea duty she spent as a matter of course at Retreat; and her children, to whom she tactfully gave the family names of Hilary and Charlotte, were both born there. Sometime after their birth, Doctor Tayloe spoke with visible embarrassment to Eunice about his bill.

"I do hate to mention the subject," he said, jingling his watchchain, "but you know what most of my practice brings in. My old hayseeds give me potatoes—sweet and Irish—and turnips and cabbage, when I've cured their children of colic and seen their wives through everything from cancer to consumption. My rivermen bring me fish and oysters for the same sort of service. Of course, in a way, that's equal to money. But it doesn't go far, and I'm hounded all the time by the thought that I might lose Barren Point, the way the Fendals lost Merridale."

"Of course you won't lose Barren Point, Doctor Tayloe. As if I'd let you! You know I'd sign a note anytime——"

"Haven't you signed a good many notes already, Eunice, since you came here?"

"I've signed a few—but my credit's still good, and I'm not too short of cash. How much does Bella owe you, Doctor

Tayloe? Is it the usual fifty for each confinement, or were there some surplus expenditures? I'll make out a check right away."

In her turn she was ashamed to offer him so little. But in spite of her reassuring statement, her balance in the bank was not large enough to give her any leeway for unexpected demands upon it; and that very morning she had received an extremely disquieting letter from the manager of the Spencer Marble Works. Owing to the size of advance orders, he explained, the business had not suffered as much as most under the first shock of the depression; one of the governmental buildings in Washington, for which the contract had already been signed, had in particular been a godsend; but now offers were falling off in both size and number, and in order to underbid their competitors, the directors knew that they would have to do some strong slashing in prices. The manager hoped they would not be obliged to turn off any of their men, especially the skilled sculptors and designers, and those who like their fathers before them had spent a lifetime in the marble works. But at the moment, it looked as if nothing could prevent such a step——

Eunice dreaded to show this letter to Francis for several reasons. In the first place, she had long before discovered that though he felt flattered when she consulted him, it was best to be sure beforehand that she was ready to abide by his advice. In regard to everything pertaining to the negroes and the place, and to the adjustment of family differences, this was almost invariably excellent. No one but Francis, she knew, could have restored discipline and order after the frightful catastrophe of that distant camp meeting, or kept the general tenor of life at the big house smooth on the surface, in spite of the manifold cross-currents beneath it. But the subject of money was apt to become a bone of contention quickly. Both of them were hampered at the outset by the knowledge that it was wholly hers. Moreover, Eunice could not entirely escape the feeling that her largess had been ill-rewarded by lack of appreciation for all that it represented, by an ever-increasing tendency to take advantage of it, and by the failure to turn her investment to good account. With the cheapness and availability of labor, the climatic advantages of Retreat, and the understanding of its resources which came from lifelong and inherited association with these, Francis should have been able to make money, once his property had been put in order, instead of squandering more and more of it all the time. This, at least, was Eunice's view of the situation. She had never been able to wholly fathom her husband's. She thought that possibly, back of his irritability on the subject of money, lay a faint lurking shame for his indolence and irresponsibility. But she could not be sure, even of this.

The second reason she dreaded to speak to Francis on the subject of the marble works was because an admission of their present problems would also be an admission of their fallibility. She had always taken the stand that their prosperity, like that of her grandmother's farm, was so firmly founded that nothing could undermine it. She had never said, in so many words, that the combination of Yankee thrift and Yankee products was unconquerable while the South was the seat of slothful habits and slipshod methods, but she had inferred it more than once. Now, if she confessed that even marble had not been strong and solid enough to withstand the shock of the market crash which had come the year before, she would be laying herself open to retaliation which would be none the less bitter for her to bear because it would be so skillfully worded.

There was still a third reason why she was reluctant to seek her husband out. They did not quarrel any more with the frequency and violence that had marred their early married life. But one of the causes for this lay in the fact that each passing year saw the gulf that had opened up between them a little wider than it had been the year before. They quarreled less because they were no longer close to each other, because they had become withdrawn from each other, because they cared less— At least because Francis cared less. That, facing the issue unflinchingly, Eunice saw as the truth. At first her power over him had been twofold; her loveliness, no less than her wealth, had been a lure. But once his possession of her was assured, it became less provocative. He soon took it as a matter of course. If she could not continue to meet his need for money, would she have any hold over him at all, now that his urgency had changed to habitude? And could she bear to abandon her last claim?

It would be horribly hard— That also she forced herself to face. For Francis had told her the truth when he said she never would be able to get him out of her mind or her heart. All her thoughts were still centered on him. She still listened for his step and thrilled to his touch. During their long periods of separation she always missed him unutterably; and it never occurred to her that the time would come when he would accept her absence philosophically. But this was what had happened. Once when she came back to Retreat, she found that he had moved his belongings into the nursery which Noel was rapidly outgrowing as such. He had ousted Edna, dislodged her cot and Noel's crib and installed twin beds there. Since then he and Noel had occupied these, to the child's unfeigned delight and Francis's apparent satisfaction. She had been too proud to protest, too heart-hungry to retaliate by denying Francis when he still came to her, taking compliance for granted——

It was springtime again, and she had been sitting in the arbor when Doctor Tayloe sought her out. She was not too far from the house to see the bees swarming on the clapboards close to the eaves, to hear them busy in the walls and to smell the honey they were making. When she first came to Retreat, she had often seen this dripping down behind the fallen plaster; and though the plaster was now repaired, all attempts to dislodge the bees themselves had been futile; the carpenters had found crossbeams under the clapboards filled in with brick, and an effort to move these might have proved disastrous. So the soft steady roar of the muffled buzzing went on at the season when the bees were not dormant. It was a sound she had come to find soothing. But it did not soothe her now.

She had grown to love the garden too, more and more, as time went on, and though she had never achieved the same skill there that she revealed in the house, the garden at Retreat had gradually become one of the "show places" which journalists sought to exploit and tourists clamored to see. During the process of the "improvements" which she had carried forward so sweepingly, some of the humbler flowers had been banished from its borders, and when she went now into the adjacent pastures and saw the blue bottles and stars of Bethlehem still blooming bravely, she had moments of feeling as if they were like human beings who had been doomed to exile through no fault of their own and whose quiet courage was a reproach. Because this feeling was so strong, she had declined to permit further uprooting; hollyhocks had now spread themselves broadcast, pre-empting the lower square and two large frames above the gravel walk were thickly overhung with coral honeysuckle. The snowballs were untrimmed too; they were at their loveliest, just on the point of turning from jade green globules to snowy spheres; the syringa bushes were drooping under white drifts, and the mimosa was a mass of feathery green and golden pellets——

The soft sound of spading, not far from where she sat, cut across her reverie. She rose and went down the gravel walk to find Elisha bending over a bed of iris, apparently annihilating it. She gave an exclamation of dismay.

"What are you doing there, Elisha? Haven't I told you dozen times I don't want any more flowers disturbed or destroyed?"

The negro, who was squatting on his haunches, grinned up at her cheerfully. His white cap was perched at a jaunty angle. The sunlight, shining on his gold-rimmed glasses made them gleam, and his white teeth shone too. He had taken to wearing sideburns, which gave a ludicrous look to his flat face. " 'Deed Ah ain't disturbin' or destroyin' anythin', Miss Eunice," he said. "Ah's guine ter save dis po' flag. It's rootbound."

"Rootbound?"

He lifted a coil of roots twisted together like brown snakes and spread it out for inspection. "When de roots crowd in on each udder like dat, Miss Eunice," he said, with the air of a patient teacher clarifying something which should automatically be clear to the dullest pupil, "de po' plants gits choked. Ain't yo' wondered why yo' didn't habe no blooms on dis flag, ter speak ob, dis year? It was caise it was all rootbound. Ah's separatin' dese wicked roots an' spreadin' 'em out ober fo' beds 'stead ob one. Den dey won't crowd each udder no mo'. Nex' year yo'll habe all de pretty flowers yo' can use."

He returned to his work without further explanation, and Eunice had the feeling that presently he forgot she was there, as he continued to disentangle the clumps and clear the earth, putting carefully spaced plants in neat rows. The negroes had all repented with such unquestionable grief and sincerity for their disastrous wrongdoing at the time of the fateful camp meeting that Eunice herself had not been able to harden her heart against them, when they had been released from the hospital and the jail respectively, and had come back begging to be allowed to stay at Retreat, which was their only haven. She could see them still, as she had seen them from the window of her bedroom then. Aunt Cynthia had drawn her couch close to it so that she could get what little air was stirring that sultry September day; and looking down, aimlessly, as she did everything at the time, she saw Drew sitting on the back steps whittling one little stick after another, and Elisha standing beside him in an attitude of utter dejection; they were waiting for Francis to come home. When their master did appear, he was carrying a crop in his hand. He had been riding, as Eunice knew; but the two renegades did not seem to think of this, though it was such an everyday occurrence. They cringed as if they were waiting for the crop to fall on their bent shoulders. The blows which Francis dealt them that day did not come from a whip, however. He lashed out at them with his tongue instead. If they had not killed Orrie, he told them, that was no fault of theirs; Orrie had lived because his skull was so thick. But they had killed their master's baby as surely as if they had used a gun for that too. They had done murder and they deserved to hang for it. He would see that they did yet, if they ever came near the place again. Meanwhile he would have them put on the road. Miss Eunice had been at death's door for weeks. If she died, he would lead a posse and lynch them with his own hands.

The thought of lynching, like the thought of rape, was terrible to Eunice; the mere word unnerved her. When Francis had sent the negroes homeless away, when she had seen them shuffling down the driveway with hanging heads and limp arms, she had interceded for them.

"Nothing will bring the baby back to life now," she had said to Francis sadly. "After all, it isn't their fault I lost him. The most we can say is that it's the fault of a system or a social order. Perhaps it's my own fault because I couldn't accept the natural results of these. You tried to make me understand that I must and still I didn't. Let the boys come back. It's cruel to keep them away."

"If you feel like that about it, I'll take them back by and by. After they've found out jailbirds can't get jobs and that it hurts to go hungry. But I won't take them back yet."

She had winced. But she had been too weak to press the point. A whole year—another of those periods in the terms of which she now thought—had passed before Drew and Elisha, emaciated and defeated, were permitted to return to Retreat.

They had never fallen far from grace again, and the renewed deference with which they had treated her ever since had been proof positive of their good intentions. But she had remained withdrawn from them in spite of her leniency toward them. Tears came to her eyes when she saw the flowers they had never ceased to heap on her baby's grave. But this was less because she was touched at the tenderness of the tribute than because she was still tormented by the wanton wastefulness of the loss which they had precipitated.

She was close to crying now, as she moved slowly down the garden walk, leaving Elisha and his iris behind her. Had he unconsciously hit upon a phrase which fitted every thing and every one at Retreat, when he told her the flowers were "root-bound?" Was it not true of them all? She thought that it was, and there was fear mingled with the conviction, a dread for the future if she too should succumb to the prevalent inertia and stagnation. *If* she should succumb to it? Had she not succumbed to it long ago? Otherwise why should she hesitate to go at once to her husband, to tell him candidly how matters stood with her, and to ask for his help in a campaign of retrenchment and intensive effort? She made a firm resolve that she would hesitate no longer, that she would seek him out before the afternoon was over, brave his anger, accept its consequences, and whatever his attitude, chart a clearer and better course for herself from then on. She would not sit on in the garden as she so frequently did until the mimosa leaves had closed for the night in tight little curls, and the silvery slimness of the "ghost plants" had taken on an eerie sheen, and everything was engulfed in warm dusk lightened only by the fireflies flitting through it and the flashes of lightning that presage a storm.

She had no idea where to find him. He had disappeared after dinner, according to his habit, vaguely bent on "going over the plantation." She thought he might have returned to the house, but a search revealed that it had sunk into its usual state of post-prandial somnolence, and that Francis was nowhere to be seen. As she went out again, she saw Uncle Nixon emerge from the cabin door with his banjo in his hand and feel his way cautiously to his special easy chair. With her usual conscientious effort to avoid recoil, she spoke to him.

"How are you feeling today, Uncle Nixon?"

"Po'ly, Miss Eunice, po'ly. Ah dun got de misery agin fo' sho'. Ah dun cut mah hair, an' Ah sho'ly did hope Ah'd feel better when Ah did that. But dis time it didn't seem ter make no kinda difference."

Eunice knew the ritual connected with the hair which Uncle Nixon cut. He never burned it or threw it away, but placed it in a box on the mantelpiece, until he could bury it under running water. He was convinced that this helped him to ward off the misery, especially in his head. But apparently for once the device had failed.

"I'm sorry. But it ought to get better soon, in this beautiful spring weather."

"Ah dunno, Miss Eunice, Ah dunno. Ah's gittin' ter be a mighty ole man. Ah spex Ah ain't guine ter be much longer o' dis world."

"Nonsense! Why you're young enough to be Aunt Cynthia's son, almost, and just see how spry she is. I thought she was even livelier when Miss Bella's baby was born than she was when Master Noel came along seven years ago— You haven't heard anyone say where Master Francie went this afternoon, have you?"

"No'm, Ah ain't. Ah ain't heard nothin' about Marse Francie dis long while back. 'Ceptin' dat Kate, she say he spends a powerful lot ob time in de woods dese days. But Kate, she dunno what she's talkin' about, mo'en half de time. She's carryin' on caise her husband, he's threatenin' ter di-vorce her for desertion."

"But she did desert him!"

"Yassum. But now he wants ter keep all de chillun."

"I thought she left them with him anyway."

"Yassum. But not fo' good. She meant ter bring 'em all here, when she got 'round ter it. Now he say he'll set de police

229

on her, effen she tried to. An' she say, she cain't understand why he lay claim to all seben ob 'em, 'specially when ain't none ob 'em hissen."

Eunice turned away, torn, as she so often was, between vexation and amusement. Because of the general implications of indolence, it always disturbed her to find that the darkies had borrowed her mother-in-law's pet phrase; and the carefree unmorality, which had never been rebuked, was another source of concern to her. But at the moment she was not disposed to take Kate's latest involvement overseriously; she was too much absorbed in her own problems. She was already halfway down the walk when she answered Uncle Nixon.

"Well, I hope it all gets straightened out somehow— If Kate thinks Master Francie's in the woods, I believe I'll see if I can't find him. It's a nice day for a walk."

"Law's sakes, Miss Eunice, why don't you jes settle yo'self on der stoop and listen ter Uncle Nixon sing? Ah's aguine ter sing a mighty pretty song. Ah don' believe yo' habe eber heard."

He began to strum, and then lifted his voice. The plaintiveness and poignancy of his music had the same mystic charm for her that it had always held. Involuntarily, she paused to listen and then sat down again.

> *"Ole Marse callin' from de Golden Gate:*
> *Nigger, come along; doan you hyar me?'*
> *Ain' jes' ready, Marse. Wait a bit, wait;*
> *Ole Marse tryin' fur to scyar me.*

> *"Ole Marse shoutin' when de Sperits rise*
> *Why down yaunder in de gyarden:*
> *'Nigger ain't you honin' fur de blessed skies*
> *Boy, ain' you thirstin' fur de Jordan?'*

> *"Cyarn come yit awhile, Marse, dat's sho'*
> *Youse disrememberin' de season;*
> *Spring comes er steppin' pas' de cabin do';*
> *May's hyar, Marse, dat's de reason.*

> *"All de worl' er smilin' laka yaller gal*
> *Lit up fur Sunday go ter meetin',*
> *Jas'mine bloomin' by de cabin wall,*
> *Dis ain' de time o' year fur greetin'.*

> *"Holler fur me, Marse, long shuckin' corn,*
> *'Bout de time old Borus gittin' savage.*
> *Cyarn leave de gyarden dis shimmery morn,*
> *'Bleeged to finish settin' out mah cabbage."*

230

Eunice rose resolutely. "That is a lovely song, Uncle Nixon," she said, in a voice that shook a little. "I'd love to sit and listen to some more. But I can't. I've got to go and find Master Francie."

"Couldn't you'-all wait till he comed home fo' his supper?"

"No, not this time. I'm going out to meet him."

It was, on the face of it, a futile undertaking. The woods at Retreat covered acre upon acre, and she had not the faintest idea what direction Francis had taken, if indeed he had gone into them at all. Should she search back of the barn or down by the marshes or in the general direction of Solomon's Garden? Without any definite reason, she finally decided to do the last, choosing one of the "critter paths" with which she was vaguely familiar. The dogwood was most plentiful in that direction; and though it had now passed the full bloom of its beauty, there might still be a little left in the more sheltered places. She had always loved Honor Bright's description of it in one of her earliest poems—"Stars fallen from Heaven to light a dark forest." If she did not find Francis on the trail she had chosen, at least it would eventually lead her to Honor's home and she would rest for a while at the Lower Garden. There was a graciousness and a fortitude about Honor which never failed to uplift her.

The woods were strangely still. There was hardly the crackling of a twig as she went along, or the twittering of a bird; for the first time, Eunice forgot to listen for the sinister sound of rustling that came when a snake glided past. The fresh green of the trees had expanded in recent rains; the leaves made a canopy overhead and the trail was steeped in twilight. The starry dogwood was all gone. But blue lupine and pink laurel and rosy azaleas were blooming all about her, and the air was heavy with the scent of wild honeysuckle. No wonder Francis loved to walk in such a place, no wonder that he came there often. If only they could walk there together, perhaps they would come close to each other again again——

There were very few clearings in this part of the forest. For the most part the trees stood close together, straight and slender, shutting out the world. But Eunice was coming to a clearing now. She remembered it and its location, though she had only seen it a few times in all the years she had lived at Retreat. It was green, even greener than the trees; wild flowers grew among its grasses, and the forest closed in round it. It was a secret place. The trail did not pass through it, but skirted it to one side. It lay apart. Eunice had always felt that it was a sort of sanctuary, that it should not be lightly entered. But as she approached it now, she decided to go in and wait, hoping that by some miracle Francis might have chosen this direction too, that soon she might hear his steps in the woods. Besides, she was very tired. She had come farther and faster than she had realized. She would feel better for repose, and the refreshment that would come with it.

There was still no sound as she turned from the trail to the tiny path that led from it to the clearing. It was so overgrown that she almost missed it. But when she had found it, she went swiftly down it, joyful at the thought of the hidden beauty that lay before her. She parted the leaves and looked ahead.

In the midst of it Millie and Francis were embraced.

PART VI
Evergreen

~~~~~~

Chapter 17

ABIGAIL HALE would never have deigned to admit that she was lonely, and she was equally averse to recognizing the natural infirmities of age. But as a matter of sober fact, the prim little house at Evergreen seemed increasingly empty to her with the passage of years, and she was more and more confined to it. When she moved with her old alacrity rheumatism caught her sharply between her shoulders, her breath came quickly, and she felt a sudden pain in her heart. She found that she could no longer dart out to the clothesline in all sorts of weather without suffering for it, that she could not run up and down the stairs or scrub the floors; she could not bend over for hours on end, weeding her garden and planting her pines. Next she discovered that it was also necessary to shorten the hours she spent in the kitchen, if she were not to be utterly exhausted before her early bedtime. She had always eaten sparingly, but she prided herself that she knew how to set a good table, and no baker's bread or "boughten" preserves had ever found their way into her pantry. Now the kneading of dough and the boiling of fruit seemed to sap up the last ounce of her strength. She was faced with the alternatives of admitting "hired help" to her house or of patronizing the proprietor of the corner store.

After some reflection, she chose the former course. For years, a semicripple named Mem Mears, who lived on a small meadow farm halfway between Evergreen and Hamstead village, had done her chores. He had lost an arm in a mowing machine when he was a young man, but in spite of his handicap, he managed to do a great deal of work himself. Besides, Mrs. Hale owned good machinery, and he had no difficulty in getting extra men for plowing and haying and threshing, because she in turn was willing to supply them with the necessary equipment for their own planting and harvesting. Mem handled all these details for her and he was invaluable to her; but he collected his wages only at infrequent and irregular intervals, saying he preferred Mrs. Hale should keep his cash for him because then he would know it was safe and he would not be tempted to squander it. The neighbors said he would squeeze a penny until it screamed, however. He had substantial accounts at several savings banks, and his title to his own neat little farm was unencumbered. He never neglected it either, in spite of Mrs. Hale's well-known capacity for getting her money's worth out of anyone who worked for her.

Mem had been christened Remembrance, but almost everyone had forgotten his real name; Mem seemed to suit him. He was honest, industrious, slow and shrewd. His wife, Sue, was very much like him, except, as Mrs. Hale put it, that she was "some spryer." It was to Sue whom Mrs. Hale turned when she made her difficult choice, and Sue rose expertly to the occasion. She came to Evergreen three times a week, did the washing, scrubbing and baking, and returned, unflustered and unfatigued, to take up her interrupted occupations in her own little house. She still had so much spare time on her hands that she accepted regular orders for nut bread, gold and silver cake, and other delicacies in which she specialized. Both she and Mem were utterly devoted to Mrs. Hale; they never failed her, except when an act of God in the form of a spring freshet, which annually inundated the pasture land on which they lived, made the dirt road between their place and the main highway, which led to Evergreen, impassable.

On the days when Sue was not with her, Mrs. Hale was usually alone. She was respected rather than beloved in the village, which as a whole stood slightly in awe of her. She was a "bookish woman" as well as a smart woman; she knew more both about the classics and about current events than most of her neighbors. Though she was never condescending in her conversation with them, they felt that she was in a position to be, and the knowledge made them vaguely uneasy. Besides, she accomplished more, and she was in "More comfortable circumstances" than any of them were. One item of superiority would not have weighed them down. The combination of several seemed to have that effect.

She would have been the first to rejoice if she could have broken down the invisible barrier. Indeed, she made repeated efforts to do so, for her isolation troubled her and hurt her pride. But while everyone acknowledged that her work on the school board and in the Village Improvement Society was outstanding, the acknowledgment was made admiringly, not affectionately. In a community where the use of Christian names was almost universal unless nicknames were substituted for these, very few persons called Mrs. Hale Abigail, and none called her Abbie. She was a prominent personage.

The advent of Noel upon the scene of her seclusion had been the source of unmitigated joy to her. The little boy loved her wholeheartedly, and showed her that he did. She had not dared to hope, on the occasion of his first visit, that Eunice would bring him to Evergreen regularly or frequently; and when she found that he was to spend every summer with her, she hardly knew how to keep her happiness within decent bounds. Throughout the long winter evenings while she sat alone before her well swept hearthstone, with her knitting in her hands and her face turned to the window where she could see her pines, she counted the months and then the weeks and finally the days before he would be restored to her. When he left her again, she found herself listening for the rumbling of the little cart in which he gathered up dead leaves, for the cautious lifting of the cover on the stone cooky jar, for the tread of sturdy feet and the sound of a banging door and an eager voice calling out, "Grandma! Where are you?" It took her a long time to reconcile herself to the unwelcome silence which followed his departure.

Next to Noel's visits, she enjoyed the rarer and briefer ones which Francis paid her. He never stayed long at Evergreen and the timings of his arrivals and departures alike were unpredictable. Occasionally he accompanied his wife and child when they came North, which was usually just after the Fourth of July, or appeared to fetch them back to Virginia just after Labor Day. More often he simply arrived unheralded during the course of their visit, remained for two or three days during the course of which the atmosphere at Evergreen was greatly enlivened, and departed as casually as he had come. The neighbors liked him. They "dropped in" more often when he was there than at any other time of the year; the fishing excursions with Paul Manning, initiated when Francis had first come to Hamstead, had been repeated many times; and it was widely agreed that he was the "life of the party," whether the Legion or the Library was giving a benefit. He catered to Mrs. Hale, cajoled her and charmed her. She forgot to fret because she could not "pin him down to anything" as long as he was with her. It was only when he had gone blithely away and she and Eunice were alone, after Noel had been tucked into bed, that she questioned her granddaughter and reproved her for the way she was "letting things drift" at Retreat.

She was much more tried with Eunice than she was with Francis. She told herself that this was unjust, that Eunice's conduct, aside from her imprudent extravagance, had been

235

irreproachable, whereas there was no doubt in her mind that Francis had been guilty of indolence and philandering, to say the least. But she had expected nothing else from him, unless Eunice were strong enough to spur him into wholesome activities and restrain him from vagrant pastimes, and she was disappointed because her granddaughter had lacked either the "gumption" or the canniness, or both, to do this. If she herself had married the wild young missionary who had gone streaking off to India, instead of the stolid farmer who had plodded along year after year at Hamstead, she believed she could have done a better job.

Sometimes a sigh escaped her when she dwelt on this, though neither Mem nor Sue nor any of her infrequent callers ever heard her breathe one. This happened only when she was by herself, except for the lazy cat purring on the hearthstone. She kept the letters that came from Retreat in the drawer of the little table that stood near the window, and during the intervals of her knitting, she took these out and read them.

"Dere Grandma—" wrote Noel—

"I am well I hoap you are well. I have a new pony daddy is going to let me enter him in the Warrenton Show. His naim is Jolly do you think that is a nice naim. We have sum new pointer puppies two. I am lerning to ad and subtrack. Mother teeches me I can take six away from ten. Daddy says I will be all rite if I can put too and to twogether he does not teech me any thing but we have good times.

                                        "Love from
                                          "Noel———"

"Dear Abbie—" wrote Francis, who unlike her neighbors had called her that from the first.

"As you see by the above address, I'm in Middleburg again. The show season is almost over and it seemed too bad to miss the last of it, especially since Eunice can look after everything at Retreat all right without me at this season. I came over Friday so that I would be here in good time for the meet on Saturday. I did not bring a mount of my own with me, because Patrick keeps a grand one for me here all the time now and for short visits it seems better not to bother. Speaking of Patrick, he asked me to remember him to you. Really you and he ought to be friends, for once you got over the first hurdle you and he would get along famously. Your daughter-in-law didn't send you any message.

"I'm riding right along, in both pairs and singles, and

at last I am getting fairly good at steeplechasing, after deciding that I never would be. However, I think Noel is going to be a better horseman in the end than either Eunice or I. He's got great staying powers already. I believe he'll always be in at the kill. If you are willing, I shall ship his new pony along when he goes to Hamstead this summer. Eunice is talking about starting earlier than usual this year, possibly about the middle of June, but I want her to wait until the spring shows are all over because Noel is beginning to enjoy them so much and he can ride in two or three of them this year for the first time.

"Well, I must be getting down to breakfast, it's almost noon. I reckon you're starting dinner around now and I can almost smell the applesauce and hear the roast pork crackling in the oven. When you're saying grace, remember the black sheep which made off with your ewe lamb. He thanks his lucky stars every day that this brought him into the same fold with you.

"Love from the renegade,
"Francis of Fielding's Folly."

These were the two latest letters Mrs. Hale had received, but they were typical of many that had preceded them. Eunice's were longer and duller; she wrote regularly every Sunday, whether she had anything special to say or not. Mrs. Hale failed to take out her most recent letter when she removed the other two from the little drawer. It had bored her the first time she read it, and she saw no good reason for being bored all over again.

She was telling herself this with a little sniff, when the telephone rang. She had never liked the telephone, which seemed to her a nuisance when she was busy and an intrusion when she was resting. Often she pretended she did not hear it, and went straight on with what she was doing. She had done this several times already that day, and after a moment's indecision, it was what she did now. She could not imagine what anyone could want to say to her at that hour of the night, it being well on toward nine o'clock, and she decided that she did not care. Presently she put the letters back in the drawer and the unwilling cat outdoors. Then she folded away her knitting and read a chapter in the Bible before she started upstairs to bed. She did not use the electric lights for this purpose. She turned those off, and took one of the little candles from the table in the hall where she had always kept them ever since she came to Evergreen as a bride.

She had never changed her bedroom either. There were pillow shams on the bed, embroidered with the words—

237

The first line was on the left-hand sham and the second on the right-hand sham. The letters that made up these lines were large, worked in red cotton, and adorned with many curlicues. The shams themselves had scalloped edges which stood stiffly up against the headboard and overlaid the Marseilles spread. Mrs. Hale removed them, folded them neatly along the crease which ran down the middle of them, and laid them on the couch in the corner. Then she took off the Marseilles spread and folded this with the same care. Afterward she brushed and braided her hair and washed from the china bowl and pitcher that she still kept in the commode, in spite of the adjacent bathroom. Then she undressed, disposing her garments neatly over the back of the chair that she kept for that purpose and putting on a long-sleeved cotton nightgown, which buttoned down the front and was finished with a neat yoke, before the final underclothes were removed. At last she blew out her candle and knelt beside her bed to say her prayers.

She still said "Now I lay me" as she had when she was a little girl, though with the passing years she had been obliged to revise the list of persons whom she asked God to bless after she had besought the Lord to take her soul if she should die before she waked; so many of those for whom she had once prayed were already safe in His keeping. Noel and Francis and Eunice were the only ones for whom she was genuinely interested in praying now, and she did it in that order. Afterward, as a matter of duty, she asked the Almighty to remember the poor, the heathen, the wicked, the President of the United States, the minister of the First Congregational Church and all her neighbors. Then with relief she slipped into the Lord's Prayer:

> "Our Father who art in Heaven
> Hallowed be Thy name——"

There was no question about it, someone was pounding against the front door with the knocker. She tried to disregard this as she had disregarded the telephone, and to go on with her prayers:

> "Thy kingdom come, Thy will be done
> On earth as it is in Heaven——"

But someone was calling, too, in the intervals of knocking

with redoubled force. Involuntarily she pricked up her ears, half recognizing the voice.

"Grandma! Grandma! Can't you hear me? Let me in!"

She rose from her knees, forgetting how much it hurt her to do this hastily. The sharp pain that shot through her so often now stabbed between her shoulders and at her heart. She had to stop and steady herself against the bed before she reached for her wrapper and went, with enforced slowness, to the window. Before she reached it, she heard the pounding and the calling again.

"Grandma! Please come to the door! It's Eunice. Eunice and Noel."

Mrs. Hale raised the window and leaned cautiously out.

"Eunice! Eunice Hale, what are you doing down there? What do you mean, hollering to wake the dead at this hour of the night?"

"Oh, Grandma, I thought I'd never make you hear me! I'll explain everything afterward. But do come down and let us in first. We're so tired we'll drop where we stand if you make us stay out here another minute!"

Mrs. Hale groped for her matches, relighted her candle, and started down the stairs. Then she remembered the electricity. She set the candle down beside the others like it on the little table and switched on the light in the hall and the one by the front door. She pulled back the bolt and lifted the latch. As she did so, Eunice pushed Noel in front of her and stumbled inside after him, locking the door again herself before she put her arms around her grandmother's neck and hid her face on the old lady's shoulder.

"Don't unlock it again whoever comes, whatever happens," she whispered hysterically. "Francis may try to find me here, he may try to take Noel away. Don't let him. He's bad, through and through. I've left him, I've left him forever. I've come home to Evergreen to stay."

Chapter 18

THE FIRST thing to do was to find out how long it was since they had had anything to eat. The second was to get Noel to bed. Mrs. Hale did both before she tried to talk to her granddaughter.

Eunice could not remember when they had eaten lunch, or supper, or whatever it was. But Noel could. He had just learned to tell time, and he was very proud of this accomplishment.

"We stopped at a drugstore in Simsbury," he said. "Mother

239

tried to telephone you from there while I had two ice-cream sodas. There was a big clock outside. It was five minutes past three."

"Ice-cream sodas at five minutes past three! And here it is going on ten o'clock! Come out to the kitchen with me this minute, both of you. I'm going to heat you some milk and set out some bread and cold meat and pickles. I've got half a rhubarb pie in the icebox too."

The kitchen at Evergreen was a cozy place. It was conveniently arranged, but Mrs. Hale still cooked on a wood-burning stove and covered her tables with red- and white-checked cloths. She told Noel to wash at the sink while she got things ready; there was hard and soft soap both there. She said nothing at all to Eunice, who had sunk into the big rocking chair which stood in one corner, until, rather sharply, she told her granddaughter to stop her foolishness and drink up her milk.

"You come along with Grandma," Mrs. Hale said to Noel, after she had briefly watched Eunice's half-hearted efforts. Noel had needed no urging to eat. He had ravenously gulped down everything his great-grandmother set in front of him, and when he slipped obediently from his chair in response to her summons and wiped his mouth on his bib, he was still munching a cooky, half of which he continued to hold in his hand. But his eyes were heavy. He made no protest at being led off.

"I don't have to take a bath, do I?" he inquired drowsily, as he climbed the stairs at Mrs. Hale's side.

"Land sakes, no. You don't even have to brush your teeth, if you haven't a mind to. I want you should be tucked in quicker'n a cat can wink its eye."

"Don't I have to say my prayers either?"

"You can say 'Now I lay me' to yourself, after you've cuddled down. You don't need to say it out loud."

He was not too sleepy to put his arms around her and hug her heartily when she pulled the covers up over him. In fact, she was aware that he was clinging to her, as if he were vaguely frightened and troubled. She continued to sit beside him, smoothing back his hair and stroking his cheeks, after he had finally lain down.

"You're glad to see Grandma, aren't you, Noel?" she asked reassuringly. "You know you'll have a good time at Evergreen?"

"Ye-e-s. But I did want to enter Jolly in the pony show. I wanted to ride him there. I asked Mother about it and she said I couldn't this year after all. And Daddy had promised."

"Well, I presume you can ride him there some other time instead. And this summer you can ride him here."

"Are you sure, Grandma? Are you sure Daddy will send him to me? Jolly and my pointer puppy? I would have asked him, if I'd had a chance. But I didn't. Mother was in such a hurry. I don't know why she wanted to hurry so, but she did. I didn't see Daddy to say good-by to him before we came away."

Noel had never been a whimpering sort of child. It was one of the main reasons why Mrs. Hale set such store by him. But she could see his lips quivering now.

"I have a notion your father'll be along to see you pretty soon. Don't you fret. You go to sleep like a good boy while I tend to your mother. I want to sit with her for a spell too."

Eunice had not moved from the old rocker when her grandmother went back to the kitchen. and her cup of milk stood on the table beside her, still undrained. Mrs. Hale picked it up, carried it to the sink, and washed it with the rest of the dishes. She put the remains of the food back in the icebox. Then she went and sat down beside her granddaughter. She took Eunice's hand and patted it.

"You're all tuckered out," she said kindly. "Why don't you come straight to bed yourself? You can tell me whatever's on your mind in the morning."

"I am tired. I've driven almost right through from Retreat. Noel slept on the seat beside me, so I didn't stop, except for two or three hours, just before dawn. I was afraid Francis would get here first. I'm afraid he'll get here now before I can explain to you, if I don't do it right away."

"Well, I can't see that it would make a mite of difference if he did. I aim to see him myself, whether you want to see him or not. And I aim to have that poor little tyke see him. He's just about heartbroken because he didn't have time to say good-by to his father. Two wrongs don't ever make a right, Eunice. I don't say Francis hasn't been mean to you. I presume he has. But that isn't any reason why you should take it out on Noel."

"I didn't intend to take anything out on Noel. I only intended to get him away from Retreat as fast as I could."

"You intended to get away from Retreat yourself as fast as you could," Mrs. Hale said dryly. "And of course you wanted to bring Noel with you. I'm not blaming you for that. Leastwise not until I've heard the whole story. Your side of it and Francis's too."

"Francis won't tell you the truth! He'll kiss you and wheedle you, the way he always does. And you'll be like clay in his hands, just as you've always been—just as I've always been! It doesn't matter whom he's dealing with, if it's a woman. He convinces her because he bewitches her, whether she's eighty or eighteen."

241

"I guess there's something in what you say, Eunice. But I've a notion that maybe this time Francis will tell me the truth, as he sees it. You can tell me the truth as you see it before you go to bed, if it'll make you feel any easier. I only thought the rest would do you good."

"Francis has been unfaithful to me! Again!"

"What do you mean by again?"

"He was unfaithful to me before our honeymoon was half over!"

"Well, you forgave him then, didn't you? If you could do it once, I should think you could do it twice."

"Oh, Grandma, how can you say such a dreadful thing!"

"I wasn't aiming to say anything dreadful. I was just reasoning things out. And I was thinking of the way Francis would reason them out. I don't believe it ever entered his head you'd leave him, no matter how many times he was unfaithful to you. It's probably happened more than twice, when you get right down to it."

"I'm terribly afraid it has. I don't know, I don't want to know. But this was different. I had to leave him this time. I'll sue him for divorce, too, if he so much as sets his foot inside my room. I'll name a corespondent. The whole of King George County can rock with scandal for all I care! And it will. If you knew whom I found him with, in the woods——"

"I don't want to know, Eunice, unless I have to. I haven't a mind to go around prying into other people's affairs. And I don't want to see you make a fool of yourself just because some other young woman has. I want to see you show some sense and some gumption. You've got your child to consider and your home. I'm not going to have you causing talk while I'm here to prevent it."

"Grandma, I'm never going back to Retreat, never—never—never! I can't begin to tell you what it's done to me. It's filled me with fear and shame and grief! It's sucked up my strength and my fortune like a vampire! If I don't get away from its ghosts and its greediness and its scandals and its snakes I'll lose my reason! It's cost me one child's life already! I'm going to save the only child I have left before it's too late!"

Mrs. Hale rose resolutely. "You're beginning to talk like someone on the stage," she said shortly. "I wish I had a sleeping powder in the house. If I did I'd give it to you. But I haven't. I've never needed such a thing. I've always slept without rocking. So you'll have to get along without powders too. If I can just get you to bed, you'll be all right. I'm going to put a hot-water bottle to your feet, and warm you up some more milk, with brandy in it. You mark my words, you'll feel better in the morning."

She did not leave her granddaughter until Eunice was sleeping profoundly. Then she went to take a last look at Noel before she went back to bed herself. The little boy had not stirred since she left him, but by the light of her lifted candle she could see the stains of tears on his face, and he was clutching at a corner of the sheet which he had twisted into a wad as if he had drowsily searched for some toy which he missed, and sought to form a substitute for it. There was a lump in her throat when she turned away, and for once in her life she did not "sleep without rocking." She tossed and turned for a long time, and when she finally dropped off, she had one strange dream after another.

She seemed to be bending over a tub filled with water, bobbing for apples at a Halloween party. But she could not catch them because she was not young and spry any more. She had a sharp pain in her back, between her shoulders, and another, sharper still, in her heart. But she kept on trying, because a man was standing in the shadows behind her, and she wanted to show him that she had gumption, so that he would be proud of her. Although she could only see him dimly she knew what he looked like and she knew that she loved him. At last she straightened up and faced him. Then she cried out, because it was not the lost lover of her youth who was standing there. It was Francis Fielding.

Her own cry wakened her. When she opened her eyes, she cried out again, before she could stop herself. It was broad daylight, and Francis actually was beside her, holding her hand reassuringly and murmuring comforting words to her. When he saw that she recognized him, he leaned over and kissed her.

"Did I frighten you, Abbie?" he asked with a smile. "I'm mighty sorry— I've been sitting here quite a while. Sue let me in the back way. She's in the kitchen getting breakfast. I'm going to bring yours up on a tray."

Mrs. Hale bristled. "Stuff and nonsense!" she said indignantly. "I never ate my breakfast in bed in all my life, unless I was ailing. And I've never ailed much. Go downstairs this minute so's I can get into my clothes and come down myself."

"Please, Abbie— I want to talk to you. And this is the only place I can be sure we won't be interrupted or overheard."

"Francis Fielding, you needn't start trying to coax me. It won't do you any good, this time."

"I'm not going to try anything of the sort. I know it wouldn't do any good, this time. But I must talk to you. And

243

I thought it would be easier and pleasanter, for both of us, if we had something beneath the belt. Sue has the coffee pot on, and she's making fresh doughnuts. I haven't had anything to eat since I can remember. Please let me bring up a tray for both of us, Abbie."

"I think you and your wife have both lost your senses," Mrs. Hale grumbled. "When Eunice and Noel got here last night, she couldn't remember when she had had anything to eat either. But Noel could. He had had two ice-cream sodas at Simsbury at five minutes past three in the afternoon. It was going on ten when he told me so."

Francis rose and pushed back his chair. Then he went out of the room without answering. But Mrs. Hale had seen the expression on his face before he went, strained and wretched. She had never seen Francis look otherwise than fresh and gay in all the years she had known him, and though she knew he did not deserve her compassion, she could not help pitying him. But she did not permit herself to lie still, softening, while she awaited his return with the tray. She locked her door, washed her face and brushed her hair. Then she tidied the bed and put on a featherstitched sacque before she unlocked the door and lay back against the plumped-up pillows. She tried to greet Francis grimly when he came in with the tray. But in spite of herself, her features relaxed in a reluctant smile. It was set with all her best china and adorned with a small nosegay of Mayflowers.

"Why you look as fresh as a daisy, Abbie!" he said, setting the tray down with care on a small table and drawing this close to the bed. "But it's a shame to hide your figure under that sack. You've every reason to be proud of it and I reckon you are. I don't believe you weigh a pound more than you did when you were a girl. I've always said you were the prettiest old lady I ever saw. You have the softest, whitest hair and the snappiest, bluest eyes in the world. Generally you have the pinkest cheeks, too. They're not quite as pink as usual this morning. But I'm hoping you'll color up, under my compliments. If they don't do the trick, perhaps this coffee will."

He poured the coffee out expertly while he talked, and again Mrs. Hale felt her heart melting within her. Eunice had known what she was talking about when she said that no woman could steel herself against his blandishments. But Mrs. Hale tried to do so while she sipped from her cup and listened to Francis rambling agreeably on. He had been out to look at the blue spruce, he told her, while Sue finished frying the doughnuts. He had never seen the new growth when it was so fresh; it really was almost the color of a spring sky. And there was such a striking length to it! Every dark oough was tipped with four inches of bright bud, and the top looked as if a candle were arising from it. He could not discover that there were any dead limbs on the tree or scraggly ones, even close to the ground— As far as he could tell, all the pines were doing well too.

"Yes, they're thrifty. I aim to plant six thousand more this year. Maybe Noel can help me some. His grandfather wasn't any bigger than he is when he began."

"I think Noel would like to. I think he'd do it well, too. He's an orderly sort of youngster."

"Yes, he is."

It was not until the coffee and doughnuts had both been consumed that Francis said anything more serious than this. Then he set the table to one side and lighted a cigarette.

"What did Eunice say to you last night?" he inquired.

"Suppose you tell me your story before you start asking questions," suggested Mrs. Hale, trying to speak sharply.

"I've been playing the fool, that's all."

"Eunice didn't put it that way. She said you'd been committing adultery."

"Did she use those words?"

"No. Not exactly."

"Then I won't either. But I have been playing the fool. I'm very sorry. I'm even somewhat ashamed. I'm prepared to tell her so. I'll ask her forgiveness and promise to do better."

"She won't forgive you because she won't believe you. She won't listen to you because she won't see you, unless you break down her door. I wouldn't advise you to do that."

"I shan't do that. I'll just wait around until she will see me. When she does, she'll forgive me because I'll make her believe me."

"I presume you've made her believe you before this and forgive you before this. You can't do it now. You might just as well take my word for it."

"I'd take your word before I would anyone's in the world, except Eunice's. But you don't expect me to let her go without a struggle, do you, Abbie?"

"She's gone already, Francis. If you were set on keeping her, you ought to have done your struggling before she left Retreat. She swears she'll never go back there now. She means it."

"What did she say exactly about that?"

"My memory isn't what it used to be, Francis. But as near as I can recall she said the place filled her with fear and shame and grief. She said it suoked up her strength and her honey and then she went on about its ghosts and its snakes. Finally she said she had lost one child there and she didn't propose to lose another. There was more to it than that. But that's the gist of it."

"Well, if that's the gist of it, I reckon I can get along without hearing the rest. I reckon I've heard enough already."

He laid down his cigarette and walked over to the window. Mrs. Hale watched him intently. When he turned back again she saw that his face was even whiter and more drawn than when he had first come in.

"You say Eunice wouldn't believe a word I told her," he said slowly. "Probably you won't believe me either. But I'll tell you the truth just the same. I love Eunice. I love her dearly. And I admire her more than anyone I ever knew in my life. At first I just coveted her. She was beautiful and she was rich and I wanted her and her money for my own. When I got her I knew I was lucky, but I didn't know at first how lucky. I didn't find that out until I was at death's door and she stood there beside me. It was then I began to realize the sort of stuff she was made of. Meanwhile I'd failed her. I've kept on failing her, in one way or another, ever since. But she's been everything I'd hoped for and more in my wife. And she's never failed me. I didn't think she ever would."

"I guess you expected too much of her, Francis. She's just a human being, same as the rest of us. A human being can't stand but so much."

"She's stood a lot. But I didn't know she took it so hard. I didn't know how she felt about Retreat. If she deserts it, it'll disintegrate. She's rebuilt it, she's held it together. She's done more than that. She's saved its soul. She can't take salvation away from it now."

"I guess you ought to have told her all that, Francis, a while back, instead of telling it to me now. As far as she's concerned, Retreat can fall to pieces tomorrow. She won't lift a finger to save it again."

"I don't believe you. And I don't believe she'd try to take Noel away from me, not if I talked to her."

"She has taken him away from you, Francis. It's like I said. If you wanted to keep them, the time to do it was before they left. They've gone now. I don't know how they got such a head start on you, but they did."

"I was—out when Eunice decided to leave. When I came in, she was gone already. Then I tried to reach her at Tivoli first. I couldn't start North until I knew for certain she wasn't in Middleburg, or on her way there. And I tried to telephone you, but you didn't answer."

Mrs. Hale rather resented these repeated reminders that she had not answered her telephone. She tried not to let her own slight sense of guilt tinge her attitude.

"I wasn't asking any questions, Francis. I never was one

to pry into other people's affairs. All I said was, she and Noel are gone now."

"I'll get them back."

"Maybe. Someday. Not at the present time."

"If I took Noel away with me, wouldn't Eunice come after him?"

"No. She'd sue you for a divorce. She did say that and she used exactly those words."

"Sue me for a divorce!"

It was obvious, as Mrs. Hale had foreseen, that the thought of divorce had never once entered Francis's mind. She considered it probable that there never had been one in the Fielding family, that he recoiled from the thought on general principles, as she did herself, besides being cut to the quick at the idea that Eunice could contemplate legal separation from him. But she went steadily on, hardening her heart against him at last, as Eunice had hardened hers.

"Yes. A divorce on the grounds of adultery. She says she can name a corespondent. Maybe more than one. If she can, you better take my word for it that there isn't a court in the country that wouldn't give her complete custody of the child."

"So that I'd never see him?"

"Not unless she let you. And if you want to know my opinion, she wouldn't do that, not for a long while, anyway."

Francis had come back to her bedside while they had been talking. Now he rose a second time and walked over to the window again. Mrs. Hale sat up straighter in bed and continued to speak to him although his back was turned to her.

"I don't want you to get a wrong idea, Francis. I don't think she wants a divorce. Leastways she hasn't said she wanted it. All she said was she'd sue you for one if you tried to so much as set foot in her room. If you go away I kind of think she may quiet down. I think all she wants is that you shouldn't try to make her go back to Retreat, that you should leave her here in peace, and leave Noel here with her. I think he'll let him come to visit you once in a while, if you do that. I don't think she'll try to separate him from you altogether."

"You think she'll let him come to *visit* me once in a while! My only son! You think she won't try to separate him from me altogether! And do you think I'll let her bring up the heir of Retreat in Vermont, like a Yankee?"

Francis had wheeled around, his white face blazing. The old lady stiffened. "There's worse creatures in the world than Yankees and worse places than Vermont," she said sharply. "I guess Eunice has seen quite a lot of them both. All she wants to, for the present. Of course you'll do as you've a mind to, Francis. You're a grown man. But if you'll take my advice, you'll start straight back to Virginia, without so much as trying to see Eunice."

"She's my wife! I have a right to see her."

"Yes. I'm not stopping you. I'm only telling you what'll happen to you if you harp on that now."

"I suppose next you'll suggest I ought to go without seeing Noel!"

"No. I wouldn't go so far as to say that. I guess you better speak to Noel before you start back. He was fretting some last night before he went to sleep, about his pony and his puppy——"

"I'll send his pony to him. I meant to do that anyway. I wrote you I did. And I brought the puppy with me. It's down in the kitchen now. Sue has fed it. I was waiting for Noel to wake up to take it to him."

The anger had gone from his voice. It sounded tired now, as tired as his face looked. Again Mrs. Hale wished that she did not feel so sorry for him.

"Well, that was thoughtful of you, Francis. It was real thoughtful." The old lady paused, because she choked. Then she forced herself to go on. "I presume I ought to tell you," she said slowly, "that Noel was fretting about something else last night too. He was fretting because he hadn't had a chance to say good-by to you. There were tear stains on his cheeks after he went to sleep. I saw them because he hadn't washed his face. If you do go up to his room and take the puppy with you—well, it would be real nice. I don't think he'd take it so hard after you'd gone, if you did that. He'll take it hard enough anyway, because he sets such store by you. But maybe——"

Suddenly she found that she could not say anything more. She tried, and then she saw that the need for trying had passed. Francis had gone out. She was alone again. The room had never seemed so empty before.

Chapter 19

THE PONY and the puppy were both immensely popular at Hamstead. It was largely due to his generosity in sharing them with the neighbors' children that Noel was so firmly intrenched in their good graces when he started school in the fall.

He had never been to school before. His mother and his great-grandmother had taught him at home and he had been a willing pupil though he was not a brilliant one. Now he was ready for the third grade. He was younger than the other children in it, but he was large for his age, and mature. He was not at a disadvantage in any way.

Early every morning he helped Mem with the chores. He filled the woodbox and emptied the swill pail and fed the hens. At half past eight he left Evergreen and walked to the village. At eleven he left shool and walked home again. He did not ride his pony because none of the other boys had ponies, and he thought it might hurt their feelings if he rode Jolly to school. He had an early dinner and went back to school in the afternoon. Then he helped with the chores again. But these did not take very long. He also had time to play. Most of the boys and several of the girls living in the neighborhood usually came back to Evergreen with him, and they all took turns riding Jolly through the pine groves. They played croquet and they played ball too. When it rained, they went out to the barn and played hide-and-seek, or else they came into the house and played tiddlywinks and parcheesi, or built villages with stone blocks or modeled small objects with plasticine. Later on they built bridges with meccano and ran Noel's electric train over the rails which Grandma Hale let them lay down in the shed chamber, where no one slept. But that was not until after Christmas. Noel's father sent him the meccano for a birthday present and the electric train for a Christmas present.

"Daddy always said it wasn't fair that I should go without a birthday present just because I happened to be born on Christmas," Noel told his friends. "He always gives me two presents." Noel's friends were very much impressed. They were always impressed when Noel talked to them about his father, who was evidently a very remarkable father indeed. They were all eager to see him again, and they hoped he would come back to Hamstead soon, so that they could; it was quite a long time since he had been there. They understood that he was very busy on his plantation in Virginia so that it was hard for him to get away, but they hoped that later on he would be able to do so. They felt that they would have even better times at Evergreen if he were there, though they had such good times already.

Grandma Hale was very kind to them. They all called her Grandma now because it came naturally to them to say the same thing that Noel did, and she seemed to like it. She gave them red-cheeked apples and fat hermits and great foaming glasses of milk. At Christmastime she let them have a candy-pull too; and when Noel did not seem as happy over this as she had thought he would be, she told him he might have a birthday party as well as a Christmas party, on the same principle that his father gave him a birthday present as well as a Christmas present. She urged him to invite his friends

249

to return and roast popcorn in front of the fire, and afterward to make these into balls, stuck together with molasses. She added marshmallows to the popcorn and chestnuts to the marshmallows. It was a very nice party, but Noel still did not seem as happy as she had hoped he would be. She was troubled, because she could not think of anything more she could do to give him a Merry Christmas.

When he had asked her to let him decorate the blue spruce with electric globes he had bought out of his allowance, she had permitted him to do that. When he asked her to hang up her stocking beside his, she had done that. When he inquired why Mem and Sue did not come in calling out "Christmas gift" and why no one in the house sang carols and why there was no holly in the woods and no suckling pig on the table, she had tried to answer him in a way that would be both comforting and convincing. But she knew she had failed. She knew that he was homesick for Retreat and for his father, and that there was a point beyond which she could not go in helping him to forget them.

At last she had an inspiration. She beckoned to Noel with an air of great mystery and whispered in his ear. She asked him if he could keep a secret. When he solemnly assured her that he could, she unfolded her plan.

"You go to bed tonight like a good boy, same as usual. But after your mother's asleep, I'll come back and wake you up. We won't disturb your mother because she needs her rest. But you and I'll go down to the telephone together and I'll put through a call for you. I'd just as lief as not. Then if you're a mind to, you can talk to your father. You can wish him Merry Christmas and he'll wish you one. You can tell him how pretty the snow looks on the pines, and that you paid out your own money you earned doing chores to decorate the blue spruce and that you had your friends in for a candy-pull. He'll tell you what all your little cousins are doing at Retreat and what there was for dinner and——"

"Oh, Grandma, *honest?* Cross your heart and hope to die?"

"Yes, sir, honest. Cross my heart and hope to die."

"But you don't like to talk over the telephone. And maybe you've got other uses for your money——"

He was picking up colloquial phrases fast. It was one of the many ways he had which pleased Grandma Hale.

"I don't aim to do any talking after I've put the call in. I'll let you talk. And I haven't got any use in the world for the money I'm going to spend on this. I had it laid by, on purpose."

"Gee, Grandma, that's great! Boy, it'll be grand to hear Daddy's voice——"

Their plan worked out to perfection. The next day Noel's

face was radiant, and he whistled as he started out to do his chores. When he came in again, after he had dumped his load in the woodbox, he went over to his grandmother and hugged her. He did not say a word and neither did she. They shared their secret in satisfied silence. But the episode gave her so much food for thought that eventually she decided she would have a good talk with Eunice before Christmas came around again. She had really shown great forbearance in not attempting to have one earlier. In all the time Eunice had been at Evergreen, her grandmother had not once questioned her or advised her. But there were limits to such reticence and Mrs. Hale felt she had reached these after a year and a half.

"That child misses his father," she said one evening, without preamble. Noel had just gone to bed, and she and Eunice were sitting alone, before the fire. "I've a notion it would be a good plan for you to let him make a little visit at Retreat, seeing that he'll be having a vacation pretty soon. He could stay here for Christmas, if you're set on that. But he could spend New Year's in Virginia and still come back in good season to start the winter's term with his class."

"He's too young to travel alone yet. It's a long hard journey, with two changes. He'll have to wait until he's older."

"If you think he's too young to travel alone, I'd just as lief take him myself as not. I presume Francis and his family would make me welcome at Retreat. And I could stop off for a day in Washington. I've always wanted to see the Monument and the Congressional Library. I don't think Noel's too young to get some enjoyment out of them himself. He'd remember a trip like that, when he got older."

"You'd take him to Retreat!"

"I'm not in my dotage yet, Eunice," Mrs. Hale said acidly. "I guess I'm still capable of boarding a train and looking after a child. Anyway, I aim to have a try at it. If I'm not spared to get home, you can come and fetch Noel back here yourself."

Eunice was deeply displeased at the turn things had taken and she did not hesitate to say so. But there was, after all, very little she could to. She was only her grandmother's guest at Evergreen; she knew that if she proved too untractable the old lady would be quite capable of telling her that she had worn out her welcome. And it would not suit her at all to leave Hamstead, at least for the time being. It had been a refuge to her in more ways than one. Her grief and fury had slowly subsided in its quietude; and as she regained her emotional balance, her mental outlook and her general health had become greatly improved. She still kept both her heart and her mind closed to any consideration of Francis; but her anguish over his faithlessness had gradually grown less acute, as month after month passed by, and nothing occurred to reopen the wound he had inflicted but which time was slowly healing. Although she never took the initiative in mentioning him, she did not shrinkingly evade Noel's innocent questions about him any more, or her grandmother's more practical inquiries. She told the little boy it was necessary for her to remain in Vermont all the time for the present. Didn't he remember that when he was very small they had come there for just a few weeks every year, and that gradually these weeks had been lenghtened into months? Well, now a few months were not enough either, out of a whole year. She had a great deal to do at Evergreen, and Daddy had a great deal to do at Retreat. Grown-up people were busy, they could not always live where they pleased or do what they pleased; two of them could not always stay together. When Noel was grown up himself, he would understand. Meanwhile he must be a good boy and believe that his mother knew best. For instance, it was best that little boys should stay with their mothers, if their mothers and fathers could not stay together. But yes, of course, he could write to his father every week if he wanted to——

After long-continued vagueness, Eunice's answers to Mrs. Hale's questions finally became as practical as the queries themselves. No, she did not intend to do anything about a divorce, as long as Francis let her alone. And as long as her stepfather and her grandmother let her alone too, she added warningly. She had bitterly resented their interference, on religious and ethical grounds respectively, and had eventually told them both sharply that if they put so much pressure upon her, she might be driven to doing almost anything. The time might come when legal separation would seem advisable, to safeguard property and other interests; if it did, she would consider it. But no such problem was imminent. As a matter of fact she was getting her affairs into good shape again. She had not sent a penny to Retreat since she left it, and she was spending practically nothing herself now. At this rate it would not take her long to be solvent again, in spite of the aftereffects which the depression had had on the marble industry. When her debts were all paid, she would begin to think about how best to reinvest her surplus for Noel's benefit. But it would still be some time before there was any surplus——

Eunice's management of her money was making a good impression on her grandmother, and she knew it. She scrupulously paid her share of the modest expenses at Evergreen in cash; she put a dollar in the contribution box at church every Sunday morning; and when there was a good movie in Wallacetown, seven miles away, she took her grandmother and Noel to see it. Aside from this, as she pointed out herself, she was spending practically nothing. She bought no new clothes for herself, and for Noel only the warm woolens that he needed. She did not serve liquor to her infrequent visitors or choose expensive cuts of meat from the butcher. She did not keep a horse for herself, though riding would have been a welcome diversion to her, and she traded in her car for one of less expensive make which did not use so much gasoline. She went to Belford to the dentist, and once a month to a meeting of the Board of Directors of the Marble Works in Spencerville; but she did no gadding about whatsoever. All this was so pleasing to Mrs. Hale that the old lady was inclined to let sleeping dogs lie, as far as her granddaughter's more intimate affairs were concerned. If it had not been for Noel's restrained misery over his separation from his father that first Christmas, she would not have taken issue with Eunice about a trip South during the next winter holidays.

As it was, she carried her point triumphantly. She and Noel departed in a state of ill-concealed excitement and did not return to Hamstead until the third of January. The excitement in which they came back was even greater than that in which they had gone off. Noel almost never chattered; but he did not once stop talking to his mother from the time he entered the house, early in the afternoon, until she had finally got him to bed. His grandmother had taken him to New York as well as Washington and to Tivoli as well as Retreat, and Francis had been everywhere with them. It was true, Noel said, that Daddy was very busy on the plantation; Mother had been right about that; but he had taken time off to be with Noel and Grandma. Edna was working in Washington now, taking care of another little boy; they had been to see her and she had cried when she hugged him; but she had a nice place and good wages. Kate had gone back to her black husband in Warsaw; she had a new baby. Her husband was very pleased about that, and he had taken Orrie into business with him at his garage. Blanche and Violet were doing all the work in the house, and Drew and Orrie all the work outside, except what Daddy did himself; he had cut their wages, but he had promised them a bonus next year if the crops were good. Uncle Patrick had bought some of the horses; Noel had been to see them at Tivoli and they seemed happy there; he had given them sugar in their stalls. But none of the cows had been sold, or the pigs or the chickens. Daddy was getting lots of milk; he was selling some in Tappahannanock and Warsaw both and there had never been so much egg money. Daddy had been pleased to hear that

Noel fed the hens at Evergreen and that he was learning to milk himself. Daddy had sold a lot of hams and sweet cider and grape juice and preserves, and Blanche had a share in the money that came from the juice and the jam. Daddy was going to plant three big fields with tomatoes in the spring; a canning factory was going to buy all he could raise. Daddy was very well. He looked bigger than he used to and browner. He had taken Noel with him when he went hunting. He had shot two wild turkeys, and he told Noel that next year he would get him a gun of his own. Daddy had shown him how to shuck oysters, and it was great fun. They had been down on the marshes together, and up to the county seat. There were lots of things he and Daddy could do together that Ada and Amy and Alicia could not do with their father because they were girls——

"Noel, couldn't you save something to tell me tomorrow? I'd love to hear it then. But it's time you were asleep now."

Noel could not wait, however. He went on and on. Aunt Bina and Uncle Jenifer had been at Retreat for Christmas with Ada and Amy and Alicia but they were not at lodge all the time any more. They were living with Uncle Jenifer's family in Richmond. Aunt Bella and Hilary and Charlotte were not at Retreat at all. They had gone to California where Uncle Ned was. Uncle Peyton was planning to help Doctor Tayloe with his practice when he got through medical school; they would have a doctor right in the family. Uncle Purvis had won a prize at the University for something he had written about snakes; the prize was cash money, and he would be able to pay his own expenses with it that spring. Mamie Love had a boy friend. He lived in Fredericksburg and came down to see her on his motorcycle. Cousin Free and Cousin Millie were not at the Lower Garden; they lived in Washington because Cousin Free was in Congress now, but Noel had not seen them when he and Grandma and Daddy went there. The House of Representatives was not in session when they had gone to the Capitol, so they had not seen any Congressmen. But they had seen a real live ambassador: the British Ambassador. He had been very nice to them all and so had his son. It seemed strange at the Lower Garden without Cousin Free and Cousin Millie. Aunt Honor and Uncle Jerry were at the Upper Garden though. They had all been over there to dinner; Grandma liked Aunt Honor and Uncle Jerry a lot; she had invited them to come and visit at Evergreen. Aunt Honor thought she might, too, while she was writing her new story. Grandma had promised to take Noel back to Retreat during his spring holidays. Daddy said the shad would be running then, they could go out on the river together——

254

Eunice was in a state of turmoil when she finally silenced him and went downstairs again. Unconsciously he had given her a complete picture of the effect that her desertion had made on Retreat. It was not disintegrating, as she had pictured it; it was pitched to a point of productiveness which it had never reached before, even in the golden days "Before the War." And Francis was not degenerating either. He was "bigger and browner" than he had ever been before. He had even made his peace with the Grenvilles. He was working at last, and his son worshiped the very ground he trod on——

Her grandmother glanced up shrewdly as Eunice re-entered the sitting room, but she knitted on in silence. The clicking of her needles and the purring of her cat made the only sounds. It was not until she put her work away and found her place in the Bible that she spoke.

"I guess I'll go to bed in good season," she said. "I've had quite a trip. Now I'll rest up so's to be in good shape for the next one."

Eunice stiffened. "I understand you've made plans for going back to Retreat in the spring. I really think you might have consulted me, Grandma, before you did that."

"You don't say? Well, I dislike to differ with you, Eunice, but I think I'm still capable of making up my own mind what I want to do without help from anybody. I'm not in my dotage yet, even if you think I am. I don't feel called upon to spend all my time in Hamstead, or to keep that smart little tyke cooped up here, just because you've taken it into your head that's what you want to do. I enjoyed myself on that trip and so did Noel. I presume he's told you how we found things at Retreat. I was favorably surprised, I've got to admit it. Francis is doing real well. He's had to take out a heavy mortgage, but he'll pay it off. I'm not a mite worried about that. He didn't have any trouble getting the bank to take his note this time either. I had some talk with that Mr. Tate myself, the one you called poor white trash. He's a sensible man. He and Francis have got to be good friends."

"I guess it's a good thing I left Retreat, Grandma. I seemed to have accomplished more by leaving than I ever did by staying."

"I didn't look to have you say that quite so soon, Eunice, but I knew you'd say it someday. I don't want you should be bitter and I want you should see things straight. You've got to remember that if you hadn't ever gone to Retreat, it would have fallen to rack and ruin. If you hadn't ever married Francis, most likely he would have gone to pieces too. You put them both on their feet to start with. What's happening now never could have happened if it hadn't been for you. Don't talk about doing more good by leaving than you did

255

by staying and don't get to feeling that way either. If the time comes at last when you can face facts again and you're in earnest about doing good, you better start thinking about how much good you could do if you'd go back to your home and husband."

"Grandma, I've told you what I'd do if you started talking about that again."

"Don't you threaten me, Eunice Hale! Not with a divorce or anything else. I never thought I'd live to see the day when I'd agree with that Irishman your mother married. But he's right when he says you'd be committing a crime if you broke your marriage vows. You'd break them just as much as Francis has, if you divorced him. Didn't you make a solemn promise before God and man that for richer for poorer, for *better for worse*—Land sakes, Eunice, what's come over you? What are you crying about?"

Eunice fled to her own room. She needed its sanctuary. She could not speak of the memories evoked by her grandmother's reference: The stifling cabin on a ship manned by a mutinous crew; the indifferent stewardess and the dazed doctor; the recumbent figure outlined by a drenched sheet; her own quotation from her marriage vows and the response Francis had made to her, " 'Till death us do part.' That's the way it ends, isn't it?" It had not ended that way. There had been hideous moments during the last months when she had wildly wished that it had—not that she might have lost Francis at the end of her dreadful vigil in Singapore, but that she herself might have died after the birth of her second baby when her life was still relatively secure and serene, not rocked and tormented as it had later on become. Recently, since she had been quieter of spirit, these moments had been fewer and farther between. But the agony hitherto concentrated in them overflowed again now.

Her grandmother did not argue with her any more on the subject of her marriage, but eventually she did suggest that Eunice should "get around more." There were some fine families in Hamstead—the Marlowes, who had given a cabinet officer and two senators to the nation; the Nobles, whose outstanding member was a doctor who had become internationally famous; the Mannings and the Grays, whose prominence was more local, but who had always produced substantial citizens. It was high time Eunice should get better acquainted with these people at least, if she were going to remain indefinitely at Evergreen; then there were always the Elliots, the Austins, the Wells's and numerous others besides——

"I don't want you should make a similar mistake to the one I have," Mrs. Hale told Eunice. "I've sort of shut myself up with my pines. Not but what I've found them good company. Now that old age is creeping up on me, though, I could do with a few more friends. You've shut yourself up with a grievance. That's worse. It isn't natural and it isn't healthy. I'm going to pave the way so's you can take my place on the School Board and the Library Committee one of these days. But I've never thought meetings had much sugar and spice to them, taken just by themselves. I'd a sight rather be asked out once for supper than serve ten years on the Ladies' Aid. Well, of course you'll do as you're a mind to, Eunice. But I'd like to see you buy a few new clothes in Belford and ask Mary Manning over for a cup of tea with you now and again and go out to Silver Pond with a crowd over Fourth of July. I don't want to see you sit and sulk the rest of your life."

Eunice flared up again over the way in which this advice was tendered; but she knew it was good, and little by little she acted on it. She had not felt lonely at first. But her isolation during the week her grandmother and Noel had spent at Retreat had been trying to her and now she was beginning to crave companionship of her own age. She sensed that Hamstead was half curious and half critical about her separation from her husband, and she was self-conscious over this attitude; it prevented her from forming close friendships. But she began to "drop in" on her neighbors when she went out for her daily walk and she was pleased when she found they were not indisposed to visit her in return. She offered to entertain the Village Improvement Society, and received a warm response to her gesture; and when she went to Boston instead of Belford to do her indicated shopping, she invited Mary Manning to go with her, and they spent several days at the Ritz, taking in the shows as well as the shops before they went back to the country.

Though Mrs. Hale had not talked to her again about Retreat, Eunice knew, from the remarks Noel let drop, that the old lady had not abandoned her plan for returning South in the spring. Eunice did not protest against it this time, except in her own heart. But secretly, her resentment and her bitterness kept increasing. Coolness came between her and her grandmother, and Noel noticed that his mother did not answer any more when he talked to her about his father. He was troubled and puzzled again and he resolved to speak to his father concerning the matter when he returned to Retreat. He had a little calendar that he kept in his bureau drawer, on which he marked the days, and when the last one to be crossed off came and went, he was happier than he had been all winter. He could pack his own suitcase now. Mrs. Hale had taught him when they traveled together before, and he knew exactly what to put in it, after he had listened to a word of caution about the warmer weather he would find as he went farther South. It was not until the neatly packed suitcase was clutched firmly in his hand and they were all standing on the station platform together, waiting for the train to come in, that he was conscious of anything except joyful release in the prospect of leaving his mother. Then something in her face smote him.

"You won't be lonely at Evergreen all by yourself, will you, Mother?"

"No, I shan't be lonely, Noel. I shall be very busy."

It did not seem to him that his mother was very busy. It seemed to him as if she did not have enough to do, as if her days were for the most part idle and empty, in spite of the few friendships she was forming. They did not look to him full and rich as his father's did. But he supposed that she was busy in ways that he did not understand. She spent endless hours at her desk, doing sums. She took long walks alone over the snowy pastures. She went to Spencerville to meetings. Probably it was all very important.

"Well, if you shouldn't be as busy as you expect, after we're gone, you could come to Retreat too, couldn't you?"

Eunice avoided her grandmother's gaze. "Yes, Noel, I could, but I don't believe I shall. I don't believe it would be best."

"I think Daddy would be very pleased to have you. I'll give him your love, shan't I?"

"Look out, dear, the train's coming— Stand back on the platform. Good-by, Grandma. I hope you won't be troubled with rheumatism while you're gone. Good-by, Noel. Do just what Grandma tells you, like a good boy."

"Yes, Mother. Whatever Grandma and Daddy say."

Daddy did take him fishing. It was while they were out together in a big flat-bottomed boat that Noel spoke to his father about his mother. He had tried to do so before. But every time he tried, something happened in the pit of his stomach, and stopped him. This time he made up his mind to go on, no matter what happened.

"Daddy——"

"Yes, Noel. Don't talk now. Good fishermen keep quiet."

"But, Daddy, I have to. I have to talk to you about Mother."

Francis drew in his rod. "All right, Noel. If there's something important to say about your mother, of course you must talk to me."

"I just wondered— Couldn't you ask her to come back to Retreat, Daddy?"

"Yes, I could. But I don't think she wants me to. I'm afraid she would say no. So it wouldn't do any good, would it?"

"But, Daddy, why should she say no? She says she has to stay in Vermont because she is so busy. But she doesn't seem very busy to me."

"She is, though, Noel. If Mother tells you she is busy, you must believe her. Besides, she's happier in Vermont than she was in Virginia. That's another reason why she might say no, why she might not want to come back."

"She doesn't seem very happy to me either, Daddy. She cries a lot. She thinks I don't see her, but I do. I don't tell her that I do, because I know she'd rather I didn't see her."

"That's right, Noel. That's the right thing to do."

"And she doesn't talk much. She doesn't talk to Grandma, or me or Mem or Sue. Not to *anybody*. Ladies talk to someone, don't they, if they're happy?"

"Yes, Noel, generally. But some ladies talk more than others. Your mother doesn't ramble on when she hasn't anything to say. I think her silence is sweet, don't you? It's restful. It's rested me lots of times."

"May I tell her you said that, Daddy?"

"Yes, of course. And you might tell her too, that it would make me very happy if she would come back to Retreat. Just to spend Christmas. I suppose you won't be coming back again until Christmastime yourself. But if she would come with you then——"

"I'll tell her, Daddy, as soon as I get back to Evergreen. I don't believe she'll say no. I don't see how she could. Because Christmas is very special for us, isn't it, Daddy? It's Jesus' birthday and it's mine too. He let me share His birthday with Him. He doesn't do that for many children, does He? I've always been so glad he did it for me——"

The last thing that Noel told Francis before he left Retreat was that he would be sure to give the message to Mother the minute he got back to Evergreen. He thought about it on the train too. But he did not think about it all the time, as he had expected he would, because part of the time he was thinking about Grandma. She was very quiet instead of being chirpy and merry the way she usually was; and when he finally spoke to her about it, she said she had a little pain between her shoulders, and another, a little worse, in her heart. She said these pains did not amount to much. But she told him she would be glad to be back at Evergreen, settled in her own bed. There was nothing like your own bed when you were ailing.

"Are you ailing, Grandma? Is there anything I can do for you?"

"I'm not so spry as I used to be, that's all, Noel. I'm not

259

in my dotage, like your mother seems to think. But I guess I better not go gallivanting around any more. I guess I better stay in my own home."

"Won't you take me to Retreat next Christmas, Grandma?"

"Well, we'll see when the time comes. I don't like to promise, not at the present moment. But you're getting to be quite a big boy. If I can't take you next Christmas, maybe you should go by yourself. I shouldn't be a mite surprised."

Noel did not feel so hopeful. He had heard his mother say a great many times that she did not approve of children traveling alone. The queer feeling came back to the pit of his stomach at the thought that Grandma might not be able to take him to Retreat, and it seemed doubly important now to persuade his mother to do so. He resolved to lose no time about it, to speak to her the very first thing after he and she had Grandma comfortably settled in her own bed.

But he did not do it after all. Because when he and Grandma got back to Evergreen, they found that Mother had company. She had not been lonely while they were gone, because an old friend from Hawaii had come to see her. He had come the very day after they left, and he had been there ever since. That is, he was staying at the Hamstead Inn, but he was at Evergreen most of the time, just the same. He was a very jolly man, and he had cheered Mother up a great deal. Noel liked him. His name was Crispin Wood.

Chapter 20

MRS. HALE was not at all glad to see Crispin Wood, and she showed it. She spoke to him sharply and looked at him suspiciously. It had not occurred to her that Eunice would have company, especially male company, during her absence. Mrs. Hale had always taken company very seriously. Its imminent arrival meant scrubbing the cellar stairs and getting the Tuscan rose china off the top shelf in the pantry and baking three kinds of pie. She doubted whether Eunice had done any of these things. As far as that went, she doubted whether the present visitor would have cared whether she did or not. He seemed to be more interested in Eunice than he was in Evergreen. But that did not alter the principle.

"Who is this Crispin Wood?" she asked Eunice after she was settled in her own bed. She had been obliged to go to bed, even though there was company in the house, almost immediately after her arrival. She was so terribly tired, and suffering such acute pain, that she could not keep on her feet another minute.

"He's a very prominent planter from Hawaii. I wrote you about him when I was there."

"Is he the one you and Francis stayed with when you were on your honeymoon, instead of going on to India like I wanted you should?"

"Yes." Eunice flinched from her grandmother's question, but she answered it steadily enough just the same.

"Well, what's he doing in Hamstead? He hasn't got any business interests here, has he?"

"No. He came to see me."

"Did he ever come to see you while you were still at Retreat?"

"No. He wrote to me sometimes, but I never answered the letters—then."

"I presume that means you have answered some since you came here— Did you know he was coming to see you?"

"No. But I'm very glad he did. It was a pleasant surprise."

"It's a surprise to me too, but I can't say I'm any too well pleased. I hope you haven't forgotten that you're a married woman, Eunice."

"Can't a married woman have a caller in Hamstead?"

"Well, it causes talk. And as near as I can see, he's come early and stayed late. Have you had him to supper?"

"Yes, Grandma, every night. We've had some delightful evenings together, in front of the fire. We've read aloud to each other and talked about all sorts of things. We've taken walks in the afternoons too—mostly down the lane to the river. There seems so much more point in walking if you do it for fun, instead of doing it because you know you need exercise. It's a long time since I've been walking for fun."

A groan escaped Mrs. Hale as she turned over in bed. Eunice could not tell whether mental or physical pain was the cause of it. But when she went down to breakfast the next morning, she found that for the first time the old lady was not there before her; and when she went upstairs again and tapped on her grandmother's door, the voice in which she was told to come in had a strange sound.

"I'm ailing, Eunice. I guess I'll have to stay right where I am a while anyway."

"I'm very sorry, Grandma. I'll send for Doctor Noble right off. It's a relief to know he's home. I'll tell him to bring a nurse with him."

"You're going ahead a mite too fast, Eunice. I said I was ailing, and I said I thought I'd stay abed for a while. But I didn't say a word about sending for David Noble, let alone having a strange woman in the house. I guess I'll be all right when I get rested up. I've had quite a trip. Those Government buildings in Washington cover quite a considerable space, and I've dragged through every one of them with Noel. But I figure I can get along first rate with you and Sue to take care of me. I'd be much obliged if you'd bring me up a good strong cup of coffee and a couple of fishballs."

"Grandma, I believe you're playing possum."

"I haven't the least idea what you're talking about, Eunice."

Eunice brought up the coffee and the fishballs, and sat beside the old lady while she consumed these. Mrs. Hale seemed to have a good appetite, and she sat up very straight against her pillows. At first Eunice was inclined to think that her suspicions were justified, that Mrs. Hale was inventing her ailment in order to keep her granddaughter's hands too full for company. But her color was peculiar, and it was evident that she moved with difficulty. As she lay down again she closed her eyes.

"I believe I'll take a little nap," she said. "You get the old dinner gong that I used to ring for the hired men when they boarded here and set it beside my bed. Then I can make you hear me if I need anything. You stay where you can listen. And don't you go telephoning David Noble or entertaining company behind my back either."

"I won't telephone Doctor Noble, Grandma, unless you're not better by afternoon. I can't very well send Crispin Wood away when he comes, though. I've already invited him to dinner."

"Well, you can tell him that after this he'd better take his meals at the Inn until I'm up and around again. He's paying board there, isn't he? I should think he'd want to get his money's worth."

Eunice repeated this, without either editing or embellishment, to Crispin when he sauntered up from the village half an hour later. He laughed, without rancor.

"I'm sorry she's ill. And sorry she seems to have taken an instantaneous dislike to me. But I've waited a long time to come, Eunice. Now I'm going to stay."

"I *shall* have to keep the house quiet, if her heart really is bothering her. But we can take walks down on the meadow again as soon as I can persuade her to have a nurse."

"What about motoring over to Spencerville? You said something about a Directors' Meeting. And I've been wanting to see the marble works."

"I doubt if I can leave her for a whole day. I'll have to find out first, Crispin, how sick she really is. But if she won't let me send for David Noble——"

By evening, however, Mrs. Hale was perfectly willing that her granddaughter should send for the doctor. He looked very grave when he beckoned Eunice into the white-paneled parlor after examining his patient.

"She's in a very critical condition. Of course she may rally briefly. Or she may go off at any moment. Naturally it's folly to talk about not having a nurse. She must have one right away. But she needs you too. Put Sue in charge of Noel and the kitchen and stay with your grandmother all you can. I'm afraid you might be very sorry, later on, if you didn't."

"I have a visitor——"

"Yes. I heard. News travels fast in Hamstead. I'll explain the situation to him if you'd rather not do it yourself."

"I don't mind doing it myself."

She did not find it as easy as she had expected, however. Crispin was sympathetic, but immovable. He had not the least idea of leaving Hamstead, and he said so.

"I might be helpful to you, Eunice, if anything should happen. That's the way to refer to it, isn't it? I'll be glad to do anything you'll let me."

"I don't know exactly what there'll be to do. I don't know much about these things."

She shrank from the dreadful details with which she would soon be called upon to deal. She had evaded the thought of death in all its implications since the loss of her baby. Now she would not be able to avoid it any longer. Waves of resentment at the cruelty of the common lot swept over her, almost as strong as the waves of sorrow——

"I'm going to stay by, Eunice, until it's all over. Then I'm going to take you away from here. I'll comfort you, I'll make you forget."

"Take me away from here?"

"You knew I'd come to take you away, didn't you, Eunice? You knew all the time that I wouldn't go back to Hawaii without you? Don't look at me that way, Eunice. You know I love you, that I'd loved you for years."

She did know it and yet she had indeed looked at him with antipathy. Upstairs her grandmother lay dying, and he stood there talking to her about love and life. She shrank away from him.

"Don't touch me. Don't speak to me."

"I'm sorry, Eunice, if I've startled you, if I've spoken to you at the wrong time. I only want you to know that you can rely on me, I only want you to feel your happiness is precious to me."

"How can I be happy? How can you speak to me about happiness now?"

She left him, fleeing up the stairs. She was breathless when she reached her grandmother's room. But she forced herself to enter it quietly, and to seat herself in silence. Mrs.

Hale seemed to be sleeping, and Eunice knew that David had given her some sort of sedative. But after a few moments she opened her eyes and looked at Eunice appealingly.

"What is it, Grandma? Is there anything I can do for you?"

"Yes. You can listen to me. I want to talk to you."

"I'm listening. I'll listen as long as you like."

"I'm going to die, Eunice. And I can't die easy, with things the way they are now."

"What things, Grandma?" But she knew.

"The way matters stand between you and Francis. I blame myself considerable. I asked you, the first time you came here after you were married, whether you had any complaint against him. You told me you hadn't, but that question of mine put the idea in your head. I ought never to have asked it. I'm not a prying woman, generally speaking. I don't see why I didn't keep my mouth shut that time."

"Grandma, please don't blame yourself for that. Your question didn't put the idea into my head at all. I did have a complaint against Francis, even then, but I was too proud to admit it."

"You were too happy to admit it—'enraptured,' that was the word you used. You said it didn't matter if he had some shortcomings. You said he'd given you splendor, that you didn't know there was as much glory in all the world as you'd found in his arms."

"You have a wonderful memory, Grandma. But I wish you didn't feel you had to remind me of what I said then. Because the splendor's all gone now."

"You haven't lost it. You've just set it aside. You can find it again, in the same place and the same way you did before. I never expected to speak out so plainly, but I feel called to now. You and Francis ought to live like man and wife again. You ought to be in the family way too, every so often. It's a crime to bring up a child all alone, like Noel. If he had some young ones in the same house with him, he'd lose those sober ways of his— That's another thing I blame myself for. It was me suggested that you should spend part of every year in Vermont to get away from the heat and look after your marble interests. But I never dreamed when I said it you'd start staying away from your husband for months at a time, let alone leave him altogether. The Scriptures say it isn't good for man to live alone. Take a man like Francis, I don't know as it's possible. Women won't leave *him* alone."

"He won't leave them alone. You're making me say things that are very painful to me, Grandma. But Francis wasn't false to me because I—withdrew from him. I—I didn't. He was false because he hasn't got it in him to be faithful."

"And are you going to be false to him because you haven't got it in you to be forgiving?"

"I haven't been false to Francis, Grandma."

"Yes you have, too. There's more than one kind of falseness, and I've told you that before. You ought to have seen him when he came here after you left him, leastwise long enough to give him a chance to tell his side of the story. You don't know to this day what it was. You ought not to have threatened to divorce him if he so much as stepped inside your room. As long as he's your husband he's got a right in your room. You ought not to have separated him from the only living child he's got. It's bad for the child and it's bad for him. You ought not to have stopped having children. If you'd had three or four, instead of one, you couldn't have picked up bag and baggage and struck off without a word of warning. And you wouldn't be listening now to another man who's trying to make you false to Francis the same way he was to you, a man who wants you should live in sin with him."

"Grandma, don't say such a dreadful thing."

"Eunice, don't you do such a dreadful thing. There may be something the matter with my heart, but there's nothing the matter with my eyesight or my hearing either. I'm thankful I'm going to my death with all my faculties. I saw the way that man looked at you last night. I heard what he said to you this afternoon. He wants you should go back to Hawaii with him—another man's lawful wedded wife and the mother of his child! I'd like to know who'd be commiting adultery then, if you should do such a thing as that!"

"But, Grandma, you misunderstood. You couldn't have heard correctly, way off here. Of course Crispin didn't mean that he wanted me to go to Hawaii with him while—while I was still married to Francis. He only meant that if I were free——"

"Free! Free because I'd be dead! That's all! That man never said one word to you about marriage. I know because I was standing at the head of the stairs. I never eavesdropped before in my life, but I got out of bed and listened this time. I was bound and determined I hear what David Noble said to you and I heard considerable more than I'd bargained for. I heard every word Crispin Wood said, too."

"Then you ought to know that all he is trying to do is to comfort me and to help me."

"I don't know any such thing, Eunice Hale, and you don't either. If that was all he'd been trying to do, you'd have put your head down on his shoulder and let him do it. Instead of that you ran upstairs as fast as your legs could carry you. So last I had to be pretty spry to get back to bed before you got

265

here. You know what he's up to just as well as I do. You haven't let him make any improper advances yet, except with his tongue, but you've been turning the idea over in your mind, thinking that you might. You don't like living like a widow when you aren't one as well as you thought you would. You want to live with a man like his wife again. You're too proud to send for your own husband and tell him so and say you're willing to let bygones be bygones if he is, and that you hope the two of you can do better in the future than you've done in the past. Maybe you've forgotten, Eunice, that the Scriptures say pride cometh before a fall and a haughty spirit before destruction. If you go to this other man you'll fall and he'll destroy you. Not just because you'd be living in sin with him. That would be bad enough, however you look at it. But the worst would be that all the time the man you really loved and wanted was your own husband and you were too proud to say so."

Mrs. Hale hoisted herself up on her pillows and pointed an accusing finger at her granddaughter. "Don't you answer me back, Eunice Hale," she said sternly. "I know what I'm talking about and nothing you can say is going to make a mite of difference. I'm kind of tired now. I'm going to lie down and take a little nap before that strange woman David Noble is so set on sending in gets here to disturb me. I've had my say. But if you've got any respect at all for a dying woman's wishes, you'll go to the telephone the minute you get downstairs and call up Francis Fielding. You'll tell him I want to see him before I go. I hope I'll be spared until he gets here. He puts me in mind of a man I knew when I was young myself. Well, I've told you that before. I don't want to go repeating myself, as if I were in my dotage. But I would admire to have Francis sitting here by this bed, smiling at me. He certainly has got a way with him."

Chapter 21

THE CANDLELIGHT was soft in the paneled parlor.

Eunice had brought in the candlesticks from the little table in the hall where her grandmother had always kept them. Two of them stood on the mantel, two of them on the square piano, and two of them on the breakfront bookcase. There were none beside the coffin itself. This was not the custom of the countryside. But none were needed. Those which Eunice had placed so familiarly around the silent room cast their soft rays on the still face and form of the woman who lay at rest there, bringing added beauty to the features and the figure which were beautiful already.

Eunice had always felt that Francis was beguiling her grandmother when he told her that she was the loveliest old lady he had ever seen. Now she wondered if he had not truly beheld beauty to which her own eyes had hitherto been blinded. For Abigail Hale's beauty was unquestionable now. A triangle of fine lace rested lightly on her white hair, one point meeting her calm brow, the others folded across her throat, half veiling it from view; but where the line of it could still be seen, this was lovely. Her robe was brocaded satin, white, too, soft and full. Above it, her face rose like a cameo; over it, her hands lay like alabaster. But they had none of the hardness and coldness of carven stone. There was a bloom to them, and a light, as if celestial flowers and celestial radiance had come close to them.

Over the edge of the square piano, between the two candles, was a long spray of white lilies; the mantel and the bookcase were both banked with white roses. The air in the paneled parlor was sweet with their scent, but it was not heavy. The window where the star of Bethlehem hung, overlooking the pines, was open. Eunice went and stood beside it, looking out at the trees herself. Twilight was just beginning to fall; it was darker in the house than it was outdoors. She could still see the pines quite clearly.

Francis entered the room, paused a moment in the center of it, and then came over to Eunice and took her hand. "You've made everything very beautiful," he said.

"It's her beauty. I didn't create it."

"You've interpreted it. Interpretation is almost as important as creation."

"There was wonderful material. I didn't know death could be so beautiful. I'll never dread seeing it again. I know now that 'The end of birth is death, the end of death is life.' "

" 'And wherefore mournest thou?' That's the rest of the quotation, Eunice."

"I know. But I'm mourning because I'm bereft. I don't feel frightened any more, but I do feel lost. I don't know where to turn or what to do."

"Your grandmother hoped you'd turn to me. She hoped your heart would tell you what to do."

"Yes—I know," Eunice said again. "And it would be easy —now, tonight, Francis. It would be easy but it wouldn't be honest. I can't pretend, just because Grandma has died. I want your compassion, but I don't want anything else."

"I shan't offer you anything else, Eunice, unless you do. But I wish you'd accept that. And I wish you'd let me talk to you tonight. Because tomorrow night I shan't be here."

"Why not?"

"Your grandmother wanted to see me before she died and she wanted to be sure I'd stand by you until after the funeral. She knew it would be hard for you, in lots of ways. I promised her I would. I hope she understood. But toward the end I wasn't sure that she did. She didn't call me Francis the last time she spoke to me. She called me Ethan."

"I never knew before what his name was. Not that it matters— There's no reason, Francis, why you shouldn't stay on —after the funeral."

"Oh, yes, there is. There are several reasons. You've just told me the principal one yourself. I could tell you several others, if I thought they were important. I don't. But I do think it's important for me to tell you something else. Would you come out in the pines with me and let me talk to you?"

"I don't think I can talk tonight, Francis."

"I'm not asking you to talk. I only want to talk to you."

Eunice glanced toward the still figure at rest in the candlelight. "We can't talk in here. And I can't leave her like this— alone."

"She isn't alone. She's with that young lover of hers. They've met again. She's with St. Michael and all angels. St. Michael is blowing his trumpet and the angels are singing alleluias. She's on her way up the golden stairs to the gates of heaven in this glorious company. The dead aren't lonely, Eunice. Only the living."

"Are—are you lonely, Francis?"

"Of course. So are you. And poor little Noel is loneliest of all. The tears were dripping down on the kindling when he brought it in. I told him perhaps he'd better let Mem finish up for him tonight, and he said no, Grandma depended on him to bring in the wood and he was going to do it. Just because she was dead didn't make any difference when she depended on him— Come, dear, get a shawl or something. We'll go out while Noel does his chores. Then we'll be back when he needs us, later on."

She founds herself yielding to the pressure of his persuasive fingers, as she had so often done in the past. A scarlet cloak, which she had bought from the Canterbury Shakers, was hanging in the hall; it was suspended on one of the high hooks fastened to a board where in Revolutionary days the Hales had hung their saddles, bridles, whips, and other paraphernalia of riding and hunting. Francis lifted the cloak down and tried to wrap it around Eunice. She drew away.

"A *red* cloak? Oh, Francis, I couldn't, today!"

"Of course you could. St. Michael always wears red, doesn't he? And think of the Fra Angelico angels! That's the sort of company your grandmother's keeping now, as I reminded you. If she could see you, don't you think she'd enjoy having you dressed like the glorious company? I do, anyway. I love to see you in red. It's the perfect foil for your black hair and white skin. I've never forgotten how you looked in that Spanish dress at the Christmas party. I used to wish you'd wear more of that sort of clothes."

"Why didn't you tell me so? I'd have been pleased that you cared. I'd have been glad to do it."

"Well, you seemed so satisfied with your cool grays and greens that I didn't like to upset you. But I've told you now. So you know how much it would please me if you'd let me wrap this red cloak around you and come out with me."

She made no further resistance. He opened the door for her and put a steadying hand under her elbow as they crossed the strip of rough ground that lay between the house and the pines. There were a few stumps in the grove where trees had been felled or blown down. He indicated one of these as a seat for her, and then himself sat down at her feet.

"Won't you be cold, Francis, sitting on the ground?"

"No, the pine needles make a warm covering for it. And I shan't sit here long anyway. It'll only take me a few minutes to say what I must about Millie and me."

She had known this was coming, she had braced herself against it, yet now she felt she could not face it. She turned away from him, and her very voice was one of resistance and recoil.

"Do we have to talk about it at all, Francis?"

"Yes, I reckon we do. But I won't hurt you any more than I can help, or any longer than I can help— Can you remember the way Millie received us when we went back to Solomon's Garden together, the evening we met?"

"Do you think I could ever forget it?"

"Then how do you suppose I felt that night, insulted by my own kinswoman in the face of the girl who'd just promised to marry me? I swore to myself that I'd get even with Millie someday, that I'd taunt her and humble her as she'd taunted and humbled me."

"You know I loathe the very thought of Millie. But didn't she have a good reason for taunting and insulting you? You admitted the next morning that there had been an 'affair' of which she didn't approve, you said the girl had died."

"I was a fool to tell you half the truth. If I'd told you the whole truth I'd have had to use some pretty ugly words and I knew you'd shrink from them. You do still, Eunice. But I'll use them now. I didn't seduce an innocent young victim and abandon her to perish bearing my illegitimate child. I suppose you've been picturing something of the short all these years. But I had been helling around with the local harlot, and I hadn't made any particular effort to keep it quiet. I always get found out anyway, so I've never felt there was much use in trying to hush things up. I do better when I let them take their course and then smooth them out afterward. Usually I'm pretty good at that, as you know."

"Yes, I do know. But there comes a time, Francis, when no amount of smoothing out can repair the damage that's been done."

"I discovered that, of course. But I didn't discover it soon enough."

He touched her hand lightly but lovingly. There was a world of meaning in the fleeting caress.

"As a matter of fact, no amount of explaining would have done any good at the time I've been talking about either. The girl died under mighty suspicious circumstances. There was a verdict of suicide, but the truth is murder was probably done. Naturally everyone who'd ever been seen with her came under a cloud. I wasn't suspected of having killed her. But I was suspected of having horned in on another man who didn't know how rotten she was and who was insanely jealous. It was a bad business all around and a noisy one. Millie took the attitude that I'd disgraced the family—not because of what I'd done, but because the county rang of what I'd done. Her theory is that lewd living among the landed gentry should always be carried on in gilded secrecy."

His voice was very bitter. Eunice did not answer him. But she had not been able to escape the impact of the stark sincerity which was so alien to his intrinsic plausibility.

"So Millie called me the maverick of the family and turned her back on me and closed her home to me. Free upheld her in everything she did and said. Not that Free or any man in his royal family, except good old John, Jerry's elder brother, is in a position to do much stone-throwing. But that's beyond the point. The point is Millie and Free made an outcast of me, and my mother and sisters and brothers all suffered for it too. My mother took to chattering to hide her fright from herself. Bina left school because her classmates gossiped so, and Bella couldn't be induced to go because she knew she'd have the same sort of grueling. Purvis hid too; and Peyton's gambling and drinking were a form of bravado. Mamie Love was a sickly child; she needed special sorts of food. The reason she was laid up the first time you came to Retreat was because she wasn't getting it. I couldn't buy it for her. We were all beginning to go hungry, when it comes to that. We didn't have any cash and we couldn't get any credit; even the tradespeople and the banks knew that our own kinsfolk wouldn't stand by us in a pinch. We were disgraced every way, in the eyes of the county. Of course it was all my fault to start with. But I didn't reason that way about it then. I reasoned that it was Millie's fault. Can you see how I might have, even though you know I reasoned wrong?"

"I—yes, I can see that part, Francis. It doesn't seem altogether strange to me."

"Does it seem altogether strange that I hated her like hell, that I swore I'd get even with her someday?"

"No—but how could——"

"Eunice, I don't expect you to understand the rest. You're not a man; a man would understand. And you're what used to be called 'a pure woman.' I don't see why we ever stopped calling women that, when they deserved it. There isn't anything in the world they can be called that's more beautiful. Well, a pure woman can't understand the way the other kind feels and reasons and acts. So I can't make Millie comprehensible to you. I'll just have to tell you the bare facts and ask you to take them on faith. I never sought Millie out. When I used to tell you I hated her, that wasn't a blind, I wasn't lying to you. I know you must have been thinking all this time that I was, but I wasn't. I wasn't going straight from you to her all those years."

Darkness was closing down on the grove. The shadows under the trees were black. But on the horizon, a narrow strip of gold still showed. Eunice looked at it and drew a deep breath.

"I'm thankful for that, Francis. I'm grateful to you for making me listen while you told me."

"But Millie sought me out over and over again. The time came when she wanted me and she was willing to go to any lengths to get me. She was willing to wait and wait and wait. She was willing to listen when I told her I wouldn't take her as a gift, that she didn't tempt me any more than if she'd been a hairy, toothless old hag. That was what I did at first. She was willing to have me play with her desire the way a cat plays with a mouse, meeting her at dusk and pretending I was weakening, and then laughing and leaving her. That was what I did later on. The first time I laughed at her was that evening by the marshes, just after Noel was born. It was more than seven years after that when you found us together in the woods. Seven years is a long time for a woman to wait for the man she wants, Eunice."

Keeping her eyes steadily on the strip of gold rimming the horizon, Eunice tried to keep her voice steady too.

"That day in the woods—it's hard for me to say, Francis——"

"I know, darling. It's all hard, it's all hideous, for a woman like you. But you're trying to ask me, aren't you, if that was the first time I'd ever taken her? Yes, it was the first time, and the last time too. It would have been the last time even if you hadn't found us. That was the way I planned to heap the final humiliation on her— To cast her aside as soon as she thought she had won at last. To tell her again that I didn't want her, that she didn't mean a thing on earth to me as a woman, that she was only a channel of revenge."

He took a fold of Eunice's scarlet cloak between his fingers and ran them over it, as if he no longer ventured to take her hand, but as if the touch of her very garments was precious to him.

"It's a sordid story," he said in a low voice. "But anyway, I've told you the truth at last. It's bad enough to live in shame and sorrow without living with a secret like that too. A secret from your wife, whom you love. I'm not asking you to forgive me, I don't expect you to forgive me. But at least there are no secrets between us any more. That's something, isn't it?"

"Yes. That's something," Eunice said faintly.

She half rose, and sank down again, finding that her shaking knees would not support her. The darkness in the grove was complete. Francis himself had risen, as if there were now no more to be said. But instinctively aware of her trembling, he waited for her to make the next move. When she proved unable to do so, he spoke again, very gently.

"I know you can't help thinking hardly of me," he said. "But try to stop thinking hardly of Millie, if you can, Eunice. I've talked about her like a cad, but that was only because I had to, if you were to know the truth. There are some dark chapters in almost every woman's life—you're the bright shining exception! You never strayed around searching for wild passion flowers; you've gathered red roses in a walled garden. Millie hasn't been wise enough to confine herself to that. But she isn't bad through and through the way I am. She was horror-stricken when she found you'd left me and she's never once tried to see me alone since. She's never reviled me or reproached me for what I did to her either. She's been big enough not to be vengeful, the way I was; and she's tried to run straight and play fair again. She's making Free a good wife now—better than she ever did before this happened. And thank God Free doesn't know that it ever did happen. He's very fond of Millie. He has been, ever since he was a boy. And he's very proud of her; she's proving a great asset to him in Washington. Incidentally, she's made a great hit at the British Embassy. The Grenvilles all admire her immensely, and Free is pleased as punch at the added prestige their approval is giving him. She's his ideal of what his wife should be, just as you were—just as you are—my ideal. And now—now she's expecting a baby, Eunice. She' going to have a child at last. You know what that means—all it means. You wouldn't want the shadow of your hatred hovering over her while she's in travail, or afterward, when she and Free and the baby are alone in the firelight, the way you and I used to be with Noel."

"He's told me everything. I can't let him go without telling him about Crispin!"

The words hammered away in Eunice's head like a refrain as she and Francis and Noel ate their sad supper together. Noel did not try to talk. He choked over his milk and pushed it away. Eunice and Francis made a pitiful attempt at both eating and conversation. The house was full of food the neighbors had sent in. Row after row of pale pies stood in the kitchen, flanked with jars of pickle and preserves; there were also two or three meat loaves and some layer cakes. Eunice knew that these offerings were kindly meant; but she could not help wondering why expressions of sympathy, in the country, nearly always took the form of food, which seemed to her the last thing to which the bereaved would be likely to turn. She said so to Francis, who proved more understanding. It probably had its source, he said, in the need that had formerly existed to feed large numbers of relatives who came from a distance, and who were obliged to remain for several meals at least, owing to the difficulties of transportation. Such persons had to be fed, and the immediate family was in no condition either physically or emotionally to provide for this feeding. Under these circumstances, offerings such as those she had received were highly practical. New England, like the South, did not change its habits easily. What she was seeing now was a survival.

"It's surprising, the number of ways Vermont and Virginia are alike," he went on. "I wonder why we don't think of that more often, instead of dwelling all the time on the number of ways in which they differ. We'd understand each other so much better, if we only could. There's the same sentiment about background and tradition, the same stress on a family strain that's strong and stable, the same reverence for integrity. You and I will have to go into all that one of these days."

He's going to ask me to come back to him. He's beginning to think as if I were back already.

The hammering in Eunice's head went on and on. *He said he knew I'd never forgive him, but now that he's told me everything, now that he's rid of the burden of secrecy, he feels differently already. He's hopeful. If it weren't for Grandma, he'd be almost happy. He's shown me already how much he cares, in one way. But presently he'll show me in*

*other ways too, if he can. And I can't let him. I've got to tell
him everything.* Aloud she only said, "It would be interesting, if we could— Noel, darling, can't you eat anything at
all?"

"No, Mother, I can't. I'm not going to try any more. I
want to go in and see Grandma. I want to go all by myself."

"He isn't afraid in the least," Eunice said wonderingly to
Francis after Noel had left the room. "But I don't know if
it's good for a child— Do you think I ought to let him go in
there alone?"

She did not realize until after she spoke that she had asked
Francis's advice, that she had already begun to turn instinctively toward him again. He answered her in the same
natural way.

"Of course. Why shouldn't it be good for him? He knows
that after tonight he'll never see her again and he wants to
say good-by to her in his own way. He'll always remember
her as she is now, clothed in queenliness and peace. Surely
you wouldn't deprive him of a memory like that, Eunice!"

Left to herself, she would have joined Noel in the candle-
lighted parlor after a few moments, even if she could have
persuaded herself to let him go there alone. Now she saw
that Francis was right. She made a suggestion in her turn.

"If you should meet him outside the parlor, Francis, when
he leaves it—you do everything like that so well! You could
make it seem as if you just happened to be passing through
the hall. And you could go upstairs with him and stay with
him until he fell asleep. He hardly slept at all last night. He
cried and cried."

"I know. I'll do that, of course. But when I come down
I'll find you in the sitting room, shan't I? I hope so. Because
I want to talk to you about Retreat, if you'll let me."

*He wants to talk to me about Retreat. He wants to tell
me what he's done with it himself since I left there. He wants
to say he's trying to make it worthy to receive me again,
and that he hopes someday—after I've done everything I
need to here, after I'm rested, after I feel better—But I
can't. I believe he's told me the truth this time, but I couldn't
risk being hurt again. And he would hurt me again, just as
he's hurt me before. I've got to feel safe and at peace. I
can't stand any more insecurity. I've got to live my own
life. I can't let him absorb it again. We needn't be enemies
any more. We can write to each other. We can even see each
other sometimes. But——*

"Noel's gone to sleep, Eunice. I think he'll sleep straight
through the night now. Tomorrow'll be hard for him, of
course. I'm mighty glad Patrick is coming. Patrick will buck
him up no end."

"Yes. He loves Patrick dearly. But not as much as he loves you."

She had not heard Francis come back into the room. He sat down opposite her in the chair facing the hearth where her grandmother had always sat, and picked up the fire tongs. It seemed natural to her to see him sitting there. But the words which were so unwelcome to her still kept on hammering in her head. She tried to disregard them, to speak of something that had no connection with her.

"Francis, I've been thinking— Why don't you take Noel with you when you leave tomorrow—since you really feel you must leave tomorrow? If he could have a complete change, if he could be with you, it would help him to forget parts of what's happened here that it's better he should forget. He could stay with you at Retreat until it grew too warm there. Then you could send him back. He's grown so self-reliant, I think he could travel alone now."

"That's a wonderful suggestion, Eunice, as far as Noel and I are concerned. But it would leave you all alone in this desolate house."

"I think I'd like to be all alone, for a little while. Sue and Mem will stay with me whenever I need them. Or one of the neighbors. And Honor Bright has wired that she's coming to visit me, by and by. Besides—you've been very honest with me, Francis. I've got to be honest with you too. Crispin Wood is here."

There was a long and complete silence in the room. Finally Francis laid down the fire tongs and spoke very quietly.

"What do you mean by here, Eunice?"

"He's in Hamstead. He's been here for nearly two weeks. He came just after Grandma and Noel went to Retreat. Grandma found him here when she came back. After I sent for you, after it was clear she was dying, naturally he didn't come to the house any more. But he hasn't left town. And when everything's all over, when you've gone back to Retreat, he'll come back here."

"Against your wishes?"

"Yes—no—I was glad to see Crispin, Francis, when he came. He's always written to me off and on. You must have known that. I never hid the letters. In fact, I spoke to you about them, once or twice."

"Yes, I did know he wrote to you. But I didn't know you wrote to him."

"I didn't, at Retreat. But since I came here—once in a while, I have. Very impersonally. And he's told me, several times, that if he ever came to this part of the 'Mainland' he'd look me up. I didn't take it seriously at all. I was amazed when he actually did appear. But I was flattered, and pleased.

I never would have supposed I was the type a man like Crispin would remember so long. And I've been very lonely. I haven't any close friends here—almost none my own age. And Crispin seemed to supply everything that was missing. You know the effect he has."

"Yes, I know."

"Of course I didn't dream then, he didn't dream, that tragedy of any sort was approaching. Even when Grandma was first sick, I didn't believe it was serious. I thought it was partly put on, to keep me from seeing Crispin. I'll never forgive myself for that."

"She didn't like him?"

"No, not at all. And she was very suspicious of his motives."

"I suppose she had reason to be."

"Yes, Francis, she did."

It was out at last. Having said it, she drew a deep breath; and with one of those strange tricks which her memory so often played her, the thought of the night she had found Francis in her room at Government House flashed through her mind. There had been no reason, specifically, why he should have been jealous of Guy Grenville; he had admitted this himself, even in the midst of his resentment and rage, and since she had been living in retirement, he had actually become friendly with Guy, from whom she herself had never heard since their parting in Singapore. But his jealousy of his own prerogatives had carried him to violent lengths. Was he still jealous of these? And if he were, how would he react, now that there was every reason why he should be jealous of Crispin? A strange pain stabbed at her vitals, a pain compounded half of fear and half of hope; and in its wake came an overwhelming sense of resignation and of relief. If through no decision or volition of her own she were swept back into Francis's arms, the emptiness and aimlessness of her life would come to an end. Whatever the uncertainties of the future might be, the problems of the present would be solved. It was one thing to say she would never forgive Francis when she sat in distant judgment upon him; it would be quite another to persist against pardon if she were again encompassed by his love. It was one thing to weigh the advantages of life with Crispin during Francis's absence, when there seemed no chance that he would ever come close to her again; it would be quite another if he claimed her as his own, in the very presence of death. Among the many truths that he had driven home was the reminder that her grandmother had hoped she would turn to him in her hour of trouble, that her grandmother had said her own heart would tell her what to do, if she would only listen to it. She listened to it now, and it told her that the greatest tribute she could pay to the woman who lay at rest in the candlelight would be in the acknowledgment of her wisdom, through acquiescence.

She sat very still, waiting for Francis to move first, sure that it would be only a matter of moments before he asserted himself. And still he did not stir. The silence in the room which had seemed so friendly only a little while ago now became more and more fateful. Finally Francis rose slowly.

"I reckon there's nothing much I can say," he remarked. "I forfeited my right to say anything long ago. I don't mean just because of Millie and—and the others. I mean because I acted as if I took your love as a matter of course, and because I didn't return it in the ways that would have meant most to you. I did respect you and trust you and you knew that for I showed it; but I didn't show you the devotion that would have made you feel you were essential to my happiness. Perhaps men like me are always failures as husbands. We're all right as lovers, but we don't last long in that role. We neglect our opportunities if they're easy for us to enjoy; and if a woman's only thought of her husband is as a lover, she thinks she's lost him when he ceases to act like one. She'd know she hadn't if she'd thought of him as a companion too. But men like me don't make companions of their wives; they only make them legalized mistresses and the mothers of their children. It's a terrible mistake. After it's too late to do anything about it we realize that. At least I do."

Eunice gazed at him in bewilderment. She had not expected him to talk to her in this detached reasonable way. She had expected him to take her in his arms.

"Everybody makes some mistakes, I suppose," she said haltingly. But Francis did not respond to her overture. He shook his head.

"Crispin wouldn't ever make the same kind of mistakes that I have," he said. "He'd never forget that you want to feel a firm foundation underneath your feet, first of all. You'd still feel it there after he became your lover, after he'd put you on a pinnacle; he'd be your friend and your worshiper. You have a right to demand tribute like that—companionship and adoration and ardor, altogether. He'd give them to you. He'd make you a new Eve in his snakeless paradise."

She could not deny it. She knew that it was true.

"Besides," Francis went on, "I don't feel I have a right to say anything because this problem of yours is the kind you have to think out for yourself anyway. You're the only one who can decide what you want most out of life. Crispin could give you almost everything, I should suppose. But just the same, you need time and peace and quiet to think that over. I won't bother you by talking about Retreat just now. I'm not surprised you want to be alone for a while either. I'll take Noel with me when I go tomorrow. But don't be afraid. I'll send him back to you before the hot weather comes, wherever you are."

Chapter 22

WHEN EUNICE received Honor's wire about an intended visit, it did not occur to her that this was actually imminent. She knew how crowded Honor's schedule always was, and she visualized the suggestion as an indefinite one, dependent on many other conflicting engagements, and announced mainly for the purpose of bringing comfort and cheer to her. Therefore she was greatly astonished when Honor and Jerry both arrived in time for her grandmother's funeral. They secured accommodations at the Inn and left their belongings there; and after the funeral was over, Jerry took his leave at the same time as Mr. and Mrs. Hogan. But Honor lingered, helping Sue to put the house to rights, while Eunice went upstairs to lie down; and eventually she brought a tray, daintily set, and joined her in a cup of steaming tea and some spicy cinnamon toast.

"What makes you get up again at all this evening?" she asked, as she set the tray aside and lighted a companionable cigarette. "There isn't a thing you can do tonight, and you're simply exhausted—there's always a terrible letdown after strain and sorrow of this sort. I'm glad Francis took Noel away—it was the most sensible thing in the world to do. But I'd like to move over from the Inn, if I wouldn't be in the way. Jerry has had to go to New York on business— He's a slave to that paper he owns. I couldn't go with him because I'm too close to a deadline. It's simply fantastic how chronic that state seems to be! This would be an ideal place for me to get through the agony of the last few chapters on my new novel, if you'd let me stay. Of course I don't want to intrude——"

"Honor, you know you wouldn't be intruding. You know your presence would be a godsend. Are you pretending, or is there really another novel under way? What's it about this time?"

"I'll tell you tomorrow. But now I do wish you'd try to get some real rest. Don't worry about the flowers or the telegrams or anything. I have them all carefully listed. And the house is as neat as a pin."

"Are the funeral chairs gone?"

"Yes, every one of them. Don't think about them, Eunice. The parlor and the sitting room look just as they always have, homelike and friendly and pleasant. Tomorrow I'll have manuscript and reference material and all the tools of my trade strewn around. But I'll try not to be too untidy. I'll try not to make a nuisance of myself."

It was amazing how thoroughly the tools of Honor's trade effaced the look of emptiness in the sitting room. Actually she was not an untidy writer; but her supplies took up considerable space, and her typewriter made a companionable sound. She tapped away busily for hours on end, interrupting herself only to look back at something already set down on the neatly stacked sheets at her side, or to consult the scribbled notes, motley volumes, and other source material which was also arranged in neat piles all around her. She did not talk at all, and indeed she was so absorbed in what she was doing that Eunice thought she had forgotten she was not alone. But Eunice herself was gratefully aware of a second presence in the room. She was able to sit down composedly at her own desk and begin the task of acknowledging expressions of condolence. When Sue came to say dinner was ready, Honor shook her head, abstractedly, and murmured that she was not in the least hungry, that she was at a very crucial point, that she simply must finish that paragraph before she stopped to eat. It took several attempts to drag her away from her work before any of these was successful; she ate her dinner without losing her air of absorption; and it was not until late in the afternoon that she finally pushed back her typewriter, announcing that she had reached a good stopping place and that she was through for the day.

"Let's go for a walk, shall we, before supper? I need some fresh air and exercise after all that intensive effort!"

"Yes— I want to go to the cemetery to make sure everything is all right there and to put fresh water on the flowers. Do you mind going there with me?"

"Of course not. I'd be glad to go. But afterward I think it would be nice to go down the lane through the meadows to the river, don't you? Crispin says that's the walk you especially like. Then this evening I want to talk to you about my story. That is, if it wouldn't bore you."

"Bore me! I've been fascinated watching you work today, Honor. I never knew before how books came into being."

Honor laughed. "No two writers work alike. Books come into being differently—they're not uniform like babies! But they're just as painful to produce, and they take at least as long. Well, shall we be on our way?"

Eunice asked more questions about the book as they went along. What was its name? It had no name yet, Honor told her. She was hoping that Eunice would help her to choose one. But if she did, she must agree to keep this secret until Brooks and Bernstein, Honor's publishers, announced its forthcoming appearance. There was an old superstition among authors that it was bad luck to tell the name of a book before the official announcement. That was interesting, Eunice said, and meant it. Was this an historical novel on which Honor was working now, or had she finally been persuaded to do something modern? Her articles were modern enough for anyone, Honor said, laughing again; that was why she liked to stick to antiquity in her fiction, by way of contrast. So far she had never succeeded in prying herself loose from Virginia, its archives and its private papers formed such a treasure-trove. But someday she would like to write a story with a New England background; not to mention several on different phases of the far-flung American scene. She wanted to do one on Puerto Rico, for instance; there was a legend about a lady who dropped a fan on the Cathedral steps, and in so doing started a civil war. She had always meant to look further into that legend when she had time. And she would like to do a story on Hawaii, too. She was sure there were any number of legends to be uncovered there——

"On Hawaii? Really, Honor? Would you like to do one about sailing vessels and supercargoes and the traffic in sand alwood?"

"Would I? Why it would be an answer to an author's prayer! What made you ask me such a question?"

"Because, years ago, a—a friend of mine who lives in Hawaii suggested just such a story, Honor. And I said then that you were the ideal person to write it—the only person who could write it! But I've never thought of it again, until this minute."

"Was the friend who suggested it Crispin Wood, by any chance?"

"Yes, Honor, it was! And he's in Hamstead right now! You could talk to him about your story here!"

"Yes, I knew he was in Hamstead." Honor spoke a little dryly, just as David Noble had done in speaking of Crispin Wood a week earlier. "Jerry and I saw him at the Inn. Jerry knew him before—those Stones know everyone, Eunice! Well, I'd be glad to talk to him about the story, if I have a chance. Do you think he's planning to stay here long?"

"I don't think he has any definite plans for leaving. We can ask him to come over some evening."

"It won't be necessary to ask him, will it, Eunice?"

Again Honor's tone was very dry. It was not like Honor to speak in that way. Her voice, like everything else about her, was beautiful and gracious. Eunice, glancing at her now, as she moved lightly along the country road, was struck anew with Honor's loveliness. The tan tweeds she was wearing enhanced both the charm of her coloring and the ease of her carriage. Her face was fresh, her figure flexible. Her hair, wound about her head in bronze-colored braids, became her like a crown. To Eunice, she seemed the personification of feminine fulfillment and feminine perfection.

"Honor," she asked almost desperately, "were you ever troubled or puzzled or unhappy about anything? Did you ever in your life feel utterly defeated and utterly prostrated? You seem so successful and so serene—so *triumphant!* It doesn't seem possible that you were ever touched by any kind of tragedy."

"Doesn't it, my dear?" Honor asked.

The dryness had gone from her voice. It was very tender. She put her arm around Eunice.

"Didn't anyone ever tell you?" she said. "I didn't have a happy home or a happy girlhood. My own mother died when I was born. My stepmother hated me. I stayed as much as I could with my mother's parents, at the Lower Garden. They were aged and frail and poor. I got engaged on my sixteenth birthday to a man old enough to be my father. I did it partly out of pique and partly out of pity. The man's dead, he's been dead a long time. I mustn't talk to you about him. But I went through every kind of hell while I was married to him. I started writing partly because I needed money so much for my little girl—Millie—and myself, but also partly because it helped me to escape, mentally at least, from my husband. Then I fell in love with Jerry. And I wasn't free. Then after I was, he wasn't. I was in love with him for ten years before I could marry him."

"Oh, Honor, I'm sorry! I didn't know! That is, I knew so little that it didn't seem important. Please forgive me! I wouldn't have asked you such a question for the world if I had dreamed——"

"I'm glad you didn't dream, Eunice. I'm glad I seem so happy to you now that you couldn't think of me as otherwise. Because I am. I've found complete satisfaction in my work, after years of discouragement and defeat. I've found complete happiness with my husband, after years of misery and loneliness. Success and joy don't come of their own accord. You have to fight to get them, and afterward you have to fight to keep them. But they're worth it. They're worth all the slaving and sacrifice. You're utterly spent now, exhausted and crushed. You mustn't think about strife of any kind. But someday you'll take up the struggle again yourself. And you'll win out, too."

Eunice returned from her walk immeasurably refreshed and uplifted. She had loved Honor from the moment she met her; now she saw her as an unfailing source of solace and inspiration. She felt as if she could sit at her feet forever, if Honor would only stay with her. She felt as if she could listen to her indefinitely, if Honor would only go on talking. The homage she was eager to pay shone in her face. Honor, who had evoked hero worship many times before, knew how to deal with it. She did nothing to repulse Eunice. At the same time she did not open the way to further confidences or more revealing intimacies. Instead, when their evening meal was over and the house was steeped in quietness, she reverted to the subject of her book.

"Did you ever read my first best seller, Eunice? The one called *The Safe Room?* Not that there's any reason why you should have. I never expect my friends to read my books! But I had a special reason for asking."

"No, Honor, I never did. Of course I'm going to read it now. I'm going to read everything you've written— What was the special reason?"

"Well, the title of that book came from a discovery I made at the Lower Garden: When the house was first built, the daughters of the family slept in a room that led out of their parents', and had no other opening. It was supposed to be effectually guarded during a period that wasn't as prim and proper as most historians would like to have us believe—in fact, it was a period that was pretty wild! This theoretically 'safe room' proved anything but that to the three sisters whose story I found in some old documents—the story I rewrote myself, in fiction form. What I didn't find out at the time was that 'safe rooms' were quite general; Solomon's Garden furnished only one example of a curious custom, as I afterward discovered. Many of the oldest houses in Virginia were built with them. When I made this discovery, I decided to track down the history of all the others I could find. That's what a best seller does to you. It makes you want to repeat a success."

"Did you find as much interesting material as you expected, Honor?"

"I found a great deal. But where do you suppose I found the most arresting of all? At Retreat!"

"At Retreat!"

"Yes—Francis helped me to piece the story together himself. He came to me of his own accord a year ago last winter

282

and told me he'd be glad to have me write it—as fiction, of course. He said he'd made a great mistake in trying to hush it up. He acted as if he wished he could make amends. Perhaps you know why."

"I can't tell until I hear your story. But perhaps I do."

Eunice could not say anything more. Her voice seemed to sink into the silence as she spoke. The house was so still that it was uncanny. She wished she might hear some small familiar sound. Yet she knew that the least creaking, the least rustling, would startle her. Even Honor's voice startled her when Honor went on talking.

"He knew I'd been interested for some time in writing the story of Sylvestra Cary, whom his grandfather, the first Francis Fielding, married. You told him that yourself, didn't you? I remember speaking to you about it first."

"Yes, I told him that myself."

"You probably can give me points on Sylvestra. You must have learned a lot about her that I don't know myself. But how much do you know about Hilary Fielding, your Francis's great-grandfather—who was my great-uncle by the way? His sister Mildred married my grandfather, Hubert Brockenbrough."

"Well, I knew that. And I knew he kept peacocks, and that he believed Osage orangewood made the best bows. Not very much else, except that he had an enormous family like all the Fieldings, up to this generation."

"This generation isn't through having families yet, so you can't make the comparison, Eunice. Why part of it has just begun! By the way, have you heard the good news? That I'm to be a grandmother?"

"Yes. It doesn't seem possible. That you should be a grandmother, I mean! You don't look or act any older than I do."

Honor laughed. "Then you must be looking and acting older than you should," she said lightly. "But don't let me stray from my story. It centers around this large family of Hilary's that you just mentioned. Their pet was Melissa, the youngest daughter. Her sister Agnes, especially, simply doted on her. She was five years older than Melissa and looked a great deal like her—beautiful in a blonde angelic sort of way. Melissa's looks were very helpful to her—first, because she was apparently the personification of guilelessness and second, because of this resemblance to Agnes, who really was angelic. You see, Melissa fell in love with a young man whom her parents wouldn't accept as a suitor; and she succeeded in stealing out to see him, night after night, because her sister changed rooms with her. Agnes went to bed early in the room that led off her parents'—the 'safe room'—where Melissa, the youngest daughter, was supposed to be guarded, according to ancient custom. And when Melissa came in very late, she went to Agnes' room, on the other side of the house."

"Which side?"

"The east side. The guest rooms were on the west side, and Hilary Fielding and his wife Sophia and their daughter Melissa—supposedly—slept there. None of the others. Why?"

"Honor, I have a feeling you're going to tell me something I've wanted to know for a long time. Please go on!"

"Well, during the War Between the States, Sophia decided that she had better take her daughters away from Retreat, to stay with her own family, the Turbervilles, until hostilities were over. Of course her husband and all her sons had gone to the War; and though the Yankees hadn't actually threatened Retreat, it was in the very midst of the region where they did the most foraging for food. There was no telling when they might do more than that, for of course Fredericksburg was in the very thick of the fighting. Chatham was spared only because General Lee said he could not bear to shell the house where he had courted his wife, and Hickory Hill, where poor 'Runey' Lee had barely escaped with his life, had been overrun twice in one year. The Turbervilles lived in a much safer neighborhood. Sophia was a good organizer and she made all her preparations to transport her five daughters across Virginia, which wasn't an easy matter, or a quick journey, in those days. And at the last moment, when everything was in readiness, Melissa came down with a sudden fever and couldn't start."

"But Sophia started anyway? She decided that the safety of four daughters outweighed the sickness of one? She left Melissa behind in the care of her faithful slaves?"

"Yes. Yes, that is exactly what happened. But for a long time nobody knew what happened next. Because none of them ever saw Melissa alive again."

"She died in that room! I know she did! *The little room they walled up!* She was killed there—or she killed herself!"

"No. This time you're only partly right— Are you sure you want to go on talking about this, Eunice, tonight? That is, it doesn't frighten you, does it, when we're all alone here, and there's such a strange stillness in the house, and it's so soon after——"

"Of course it frightens me! I have creeping chills racing all over me! But if you stop now, Honor, I'll never forgive you. Tell me what part I did guess right, tell me what actually did happen."

"Sophia and the four daughters who went with her had hardly made good their escape when a company of Union soldiers did arrive at Retreat. What is more, they stayed. They were billeted there during a reconnoitering expedition. As fa as they could see, there was no one on the place but some old slaves. The slaves told the commanding officer that the gentlemen of the family were all with the Confederate Army and that the ladies were away visiting relatives. It sounded logical enough."

"But didn't the soldiers see Melissa?"

"Don't be so impatient, Eunice. Let me tell this story my own way. It seems that the captain and one of his lieutenants shared a large room on the second floor. The first night they were there they slept profoundly. They were exhausted by their day's march. But the second night, when he was less weary, the lieutenant was disturbed by soft, mysterious sounds and the feeling that someone had passed close to him. He lighted a candle, without waking the captain, and quietly searched the room. When he found no traces of intrusion, he decided he must have been dreaming, and went back to bed."

"He wasn't dreaming though, was he? He did see something, he did hear something!"

"Yes. That was what he decided afterward. The next night he wakened in time to catch a glimpse of a blurred white figure crossing the room at the foot of the bed and disappearing into space. He was convinced that he was not deluded this time. He roused the captain, told him what had happened, and suggested that they should take turns watching the rest of the night. He reasoned that the intruder must be the same one that he had heard the night before, and that if this were so, it would return again."

"Did the captain believe him?"

"More or less. They were always on the lookout for spies of one sort and another, you know. The captain thought this might be one. He volunteered to take the first watch. After the first hour, he roused the lieutenant and said that so far nothing had happened. He settled himself to sleep again, and the quiet darkness lulled the lieutenant too. But suddenly he was startled into alertness again. He strained his eyes through the darkness. Then he saw unmistakably a dim figure standing at the foot of the bed, with one hand resting on the post at his feet."

"Yes! That is what it does! And what did he do?"

"He cried out 'Who goes there?' and that roused the captain again. They both cried 'Halt!' and they both reached for their pistols. There was no answer from the figure. It moved swiftly away. So they fired simultaneously. Then they saw the form sink to the floor. They lighted their candles and sprang up. On the floor at their feet lay a lovely young girl, with blood pouring from her breast. One of them had killed her!"

"Honor—I—I know it's all true! I've seen her myself. It's her ghost that still haunts Retreat! Isn't it?"

"I don't know, Eunice, dear. I only know that's the story Francis told me—the story I'm trying to write. But there are still so many pieces to fit together. Of course the young officers were overcome with horror, of course they tried to get some explanation out of the slaves, to learn why this girl had stayed behind when her mother and sisters had gone to a place of safety. The only thing that was clear was her fatal presence, and the fact that when the company had taken possession of the house, she had hidden in her own room, putting a press in front of the one door leading into it. In the night, when she thought the officers were asleep, she had slipped out and so come to her death. They thought she went out to get food."

"And you don't think so, Honor?"

"Certainly she had to get food. The slaves must have prepared it for her. I shouldn't wonder if she went down cellar to eat it, for one of the doors there has a faded inscription on it reading: 'The Yankees came today' with a date, Jan. 13, 1864. I can't think who would have written it if she didn't. Francis showed it to me but it's almost effaced. I'm not surprised you never discovered it— There's another that reads: 'The Yankees came again,' the date to that's obliterated, but she probably wrote that too. Then there's an obliterated statement with a signature— Well, anyway, I don't think Melissa stayed down cellar long at a time. I think she probably went out to meet her lover every night too. I doubt if her fever was real in the first place. Do you think if it had been, Agnes, who adored her, would ever have left her? Agnes knew. She knew Melissa was snatching at her last chance for happiness —without guessing in what sense it would be her last."

"Is she- -buried at Retreat?"

"Yes—in the garden. The Union officers buried her with all honor and dignity. And finally they found her family; they offered to give themselves up, to take any consequences of their act. The family would not permit them to be punished. They would not permit Melissa's grave to be marked. Because you see, in time, they learned why she had stayed at Retreat instead of fleeing to safety. They felt her death had been in retribution for her sin. They wanted her shame buried with her."

"And still she goes out to meet her lover!"

"Haven't you ever heard, Eunice, that love can be stronger than death? Don't you believe it?"

"I don't know. I don't believe anything can be stronger than death—or I didn't before you began to talk to me. *Oh— Honor!*"

A bell was ringing, loudly, insistently, through the house. Eunice caught hold of Honor and clung to her, smothering a scream. The clanging of the bell rang out again. Honor detached herself quietly from Eunice's clinging hands.

"Don't be frightened," she said quietly. "There's someone at the front door, that's all. I know everyone in Hamstead uses the knocker, but there's an old-fashioned bell-pull, isn't there? It isn't late—not too late for a caller." She glanced up at the clock and then down at Eunice again. "Sue has been gone a long time," she said still quietly. "I'll go to the door. If that is your friend Crispin Wood, do you want to see him?"

Chapter 23

EUNICE DID not want to see Crispin Wood and she said so decidedly. She was still under the spell of Honor's story, and she shrank from a summons recalling her to the problems of the present when she longed to dwell on a mystic scene peopled by the past. Shaking her head and putting her finger to her lips, she indicated that she would creep quietly up the back stairs; and as soon as she was out of sight, Honor went alone to let Crispin in. An hour later, she tapped at the door of Eunice's bedroom and entered in response to a muffled answer.

"I've put the cat down cellar and turned out the lights," she said in a matter-of-fact way. "You were very sensible to go to bed. But I enjoyed Mr. Wood's call very much. We talked about that Hawaiian novel. I asked him if he didn't think *Sweet Sandalwood* might be a good name for it, and he said he did. He invited me to come and stay on his Molokai ranch while I wrote it. That really would be quite an inducement to me. I'm wondering whether Jerry could get away. Of course I couldn't leave until after this story about Retreat is finished—you haven't thought of a good name for it yet, have you, Eunice? And I've been thinking about Millie's baby, too— But considering that nowadays grandmothers are only allowed to look at babies through glass———"

She laughed and sat down on the edge of Eunice's bed. Eunice was beginning to listen eagerly for that frequent lovely laugh of Honor's.

"Incidentally, Mr. Wood suggested that it might be a good plan if you came with me," Honor continued. "Of course, he gave all the reasons for this but the real one. However, they sounded plausible enough. You do need a change and a rest, you do need to get out of this desolate house. There probably isn't a pleasanter place in the world than Hawaii.

287

I don't know whether the idea appeals to you or not, but at least you might think it over."

"Do you—if you were in my place, Honor, would you think it over?"

"No." said Honor abruptly. "If I were in your place, I'd go back to Francis so fast you wouldn't be able to see me for the dust. But then, I've never had a particle of pride when it came to a case like that. and I've always believed in snatching at all the happiness I could get, no matter what I had to pay for it. You're very different, Eunice. I don't know what came between you and Francis. I don't want to know. I've had my suspicions, and if they're correct, you couldn't possibly be blamed for leaving him. No matter how badly he's behaved though. he's behaving a great deal better now. I should think you could almost afford to take a chance on him, since he's tried to prove his penitence and succeeded fairly well. But if you don't think so——"

"I'm afraid. Honor."

"Well, it's all a matter of opinion. So if you decide you want to go to Hawaii, under chaperonage, I'll try to take you there. I certainly would get a lot out of the trip myself. I believe Jerry would enjoy it too. And from present indications, I should say that the only thing short of dynamite that would dislodge Crispin Wood from Hamstead would be a promise from you to join him under his own vine and fig tree."

The words were spoken as much in jest as in earnest. But as time went on, Eunice came to feel they were true. Crispin did not in any way molest her. But he prolonged his sojourn at the Hamstead Inn indefinitely. The suspicions which his stay there aroused were lulled to a very considerable degree by the lavish but tactful way in which he spent money; this was not without its effect, even in so puritanical a place as Hamstead. His manner of approach to the "natives" was tactful too. He was not pushing. or presumptuous, or condescending. but the friendly fashion in which he responded to the slightest display of cordiality was disarming. Nor did his conduct suggest anything scandalous. True. he was seen to saunter daily in the direction of Evergreen; but Sue Mears, painfully tight-mouthed by habit, stepped completely out of character when it came to a question of the "goings on" there. It was Honor Bright Mr. Wood saw mostly, she disclosed; him and her sat for hours, smoking cigarettes and talking about stories. Sometimes they had a drink, too. But land! She had never heard anyone talk so much. There seemed to be no end to what they had to say. And all about books, books, books! Either one of them might have been squint eyed or hair-lipped for all the interest they took in each other, as far as she could see. Eunice? Oh, Eunice was up in her own room most of the time. She seldom ever came down when Mr. Wood was there, and when she did, Mr. Wood and Honor Bright went straight on talking. Eunice said she had letters to write. Sakes, the amount of *writing* of one kind or another that was going on in that house was something. She had never seen the like of it. No, she hadn't heard them say anything about the will, but she presumed Eunice must be in comfortable circumstances. No, there wasn't anything going on to cause talk and nobody had breathed anything about a divorce. But she did hear tell that Noel would be back in July——

Hamstead was secretly somewhat thrilled to have a "real live authoress" lingering in its midst. Though Honor stuck to historical backgrounds in her novels, as she had said, her treatment of these was as "modern" as that of her articles. Consequently her books had always been purchased with some hesitation by the Library Committee and had been kept on a secret shelf, whence they were removed only upon request by adults But Honor herself, like Crispin, was very disarming. Hamstead began to believe that her books could not be so very wicked after all, since they were written by such a lovely lady; and she and that handsome husband of hers, who came regular as clockwork to spend the Sabbath with her, were certainly a picture together. Jerry Stone contributed in no small degree to the leniency with which Crispin and Honor were regarded. His prematurely white hair and the essential elegance which he never seemed to shed, no matter what he wore and did, invested him with great distinction, to Hamstead's way of thinking. Besides, the village was not unaware that he owned the largest newspaper in New York and the most important tobacco plants in the South; that he was on terms of intimacy with the current occupant of the White House and that a cousin of his had actually once been President; that his brother was the Senior Senator from Massachusetts and his stepson a rising young Congressman from Virginia. The aura which surrounded Honor Bright, who merely wrote books, was dim compared to the one with which Hamstead visualized her husband, who vicariously represented so much political power.

All three of Eunice's visitors were faintly amused at the importance their presence had assumed in the eyes of the neighborhood. She herself was grateful for it on several scores, but largely because it served as a screen for herself. She missed both her grandmother and Noel poignantly, and her feelings concerning Francis and Crispin were in a state of turmoil; at the same time, she was a prey to such mental and physical lassitude that initiative effort of any sort represented an ordeal for her. Like many persons outwardly self-controlled, her emotions were the more devastating because they were restrained; and now that they were not only intense but conflicting, her battle with them was exhausting. She longed for her grandmother, whom she had lost forever. She longed for her child, whom she felt she would be selfish to reclaim. She longed for her husband, whom she could not bring herself to trust. And she longed for Crispin, less as an individual than because he represented escape from all the realities which she had not the strength or the means to avoid alone, and glamour which was otherwise lacking in her humdrum life.

Part of this glamour was due to the element of secrecy which still surrounded him. She had never been able to persuade him to tell her whether his origin was Portuguese or Hawaiian or a mixture of the two. She did not know whether he had an immediate family, and if so, where they lived or what they did. She could only guess at the multitudinous sources of his power and prestige. Her feminine curiosity was piqued by so much mystery. But whenever she tried to satisfy this curiosity, Crispin adroitly directed the conversation into other channels.

"Crispin Wood sounds like an English name. Did your people come from England originally, Penny?"

"Do you think I *look* English?"

"No. Not in the least. But——"

"Don't let's talk about what I look like. Let me tell you what you look like. You look like the chaste Diana enshrined in a sylvan glade. You look like St. Clare of Assisi, cloistered and sacrificial. You look like Beata Beatrix, a vision beside the Arno. You look like Edith of the Swan-Neck, searching for Harold on the Saxon battlefield."

"Crispin, how could I? None of them looked anything alike."

"I think they did. I think they were all sisters under the skin. Or if they weren't, sometimes you look like one and sometimes like another. Except that you're much lovelier than any of them ever were."

"How can you be so absurd? I'm just a nice neat New Englander in her early thirties."

"A nice neat New Englander with eyes like stars and skin like snow and the most beautiful brow in the world."

As he spoke, he put out his finger and traced the outline of her face and throat. The touch was so light that it could hardly be called a caress. But Eunice flushed under it.

"I don't see how you learned all that classical illusion," she said, trying, at one and the same time, to hide her own con fusion and to delicately extract more information from him. "Did you specialize in that sort of thing at college?"

"In what sort of thing? Beautiful women? Every wise man specializes in beautiful women whether he ever goes to college or not. But not many men are fortunate enough to find a woman as beautiful as you are."

"Crispin, it's impossible to take you seriously."

"Well, don't. Just take me. That'll do for the present."

She felt that she should speak to him sternly when he talked to her in such a vein, but somehow she never did. His badinage gave her more pleasure than anything she had experienced in a long time. It filled a want of which she had hardly been conscious till he supplied it. She had kept trying to tell herself that she had everything that was really essential to her happiness—a promising child, a pleasant home, good health, and an adequate fortune. Sue had not been mistaken in supposing that Eunice was in "comfortable circumstances." Her grandmother had left a small trust fund for Noel which provided for his education and assured him of a modest income while he was getting a start in life. She had also left bequests to Remembrance and Susan Mears "in recognition of their able and faithful services"; to the First Congregational Church, the Public Library, the Village Improvement Society, the Hamstead Cemetery Association, and the American Board of Foreign Missions. There was a memorandum in connection with the last to the effect that she hoped the money would be used to spread the Gospel in India. Evergreen was Eunice's for life; after that it was to go to Noel, if he wanted it, which she hoped he would. If he did not, it was to be used as a home for the orphans of missionaries, and there was a provisional endowment with which to run it in case this happened. The income from the rest of her property went to Eunice, though she was effectually prevented from touching the principal; but this income was reduced by two further provisions: The mortgage which Francis Fielding had placed on his property entitled "Retreat" and located in King George County, Virginia, for the purpose of "keeping it from decline, and saving it for his son and heir, Noel Hale Fielding" was to be paid off, out of the estate, as soon as the just debts and funeral expenses had been met, and before any other division of the property had been made. And any "future issue" of Eunice Hale Fielding was safeguarded by the same sort of trust as had been established for Noel, "provided that said issue was also the issue of Francis Fielding."

Eunice had not been at all pleased with either the terms or the wording of the will. She resented the inference that she might not always be wise in her use of capital, and she considered the reference to issue both indelicate and insulting.

But it meant a great deal to realize that her financial problems were conclusively closed. Mrs. Hale had been a much wealthier woman than her granddaughter had supposed. The income Eunice was now assured, even after all the bequests were paid, was a substantial one in itself; taken in conjunction with the dividends from her marble stock, she could not begin to spend it, living as she did at present. Noel was independently provided for; the cost of upkeep at Evergreen was negligible; she required only the simplest of wardrobes and she did practically no entertaining. Of course she could spend large sums on charity, but as long as this was impersonal it made no vital appeal to her; it had the same lack of significance and warmth that was missing in her life as a whole. She felt that her future would be meaningless to her unless she could use it with prodigality for her own pleasure and with bounty for the happiness of those whom she loved.

But the number of those whom she loved seemed to have shrunk so. She had loved her grandmother, and her grandmother was dead. She had loved her husband, and he had been faithless. She had loved her husband's mother and brothers and sisters, and they had abused her generosity. She had loved Millie and Millie had been a false friend. To be sure, she loved Honor, but there was nothing on earth she could do for Honor; it was all the other way around. And now there seemed to be nothing she could do for Noel either. He had written her, begging to be allowed to stay on at Retreat, and she had consented, for it was all too plain that the letter was spontaneous, that it had not been inspired by Francis or even written with his knowledge. To whom could she turn, then, except to Crispin? He did not want or need her money. But he wanted something else she could give him, and he could give her so much in return——

At last she told him that she would go back to Hawaii with him when he went himself.

Though Sue had sized up the situation at Evergreen shrewdly enough as a whole, Eunice and Crispin were actually seeing a good deal more of each other than Sue suspected, or would admit to suspecting, even to herself. They often sat by the fire in the sitting room, talking and reading, long after she had returned to her own farm, and Honor had gone to bed. Moreover, Crispin had very naturally offered to drive Eunice's car for her, when she went here and there on business pertaining to the settlement of her grandmother's estate, or to Spencerville for directors' meetings; and this offer resulted in many hours of motoring over the Vermont hills and numerous tête-a-tête meals at small out of the way inns. Crispin had persuaded Eunice to resume her riding, and had bought a horse for himself. They had also resumed the pleasant cross country strolling which had been such a source of pleasure to them both when Crispin first came to Hamstead and which Mrs. Hale's fatal illness had interrupted; and it was during an interlude in one of these walks that Eunice finally spoke to Crispin about the future, as it affected them jointly.

The late reluctant spring of New England had at last shown signs of renascence. Along the river banks, the willows no longer stood stark and naked; they were covered with a light feathery coating of green, and they swayed backwards and forwards in a fitful breeze which blew from the South. The river itself, freed from the ice floes which had long choked its current, made the rushing sound that bespoke eager release. The sun shone reassuringly over the neighboring pastureland. Crispin, taking off his tweed coat, spread it out on the ground and waved a generous brown hand towards it.

"Won't you sit down? I think we could actually linger here for a few minutes without running the risk of catching pneumonia."

Eunice laughed. She had not laughed much, in a long time, and it was pleasing to herself, as well as to Crispin, to find that she could.

"It isn't much like Hawaii in May, is it, Crispin?"

"There's nothing like Hawaii in May," he said tersely. Then he added, "I'd like to prove that to you."

"I know. I think you've been very patient while I've been trying to make up my mind."

"I've been patient for nearly ten years. On top of ten years, a few weeks more or less don't matter."

"I simply can't believe that you've cared that much. I can't understand *why* you should care that much."

"Oh, I've had my moments of extraneous diversion. But I have been faithful to thee Cynara! in my fashion.' Not that I understand it myself. Of course you attracted me instantly. But I wouldn't have believed, either, that the attraction could be strong enough to withstand circumstance and separation. You seem cool enough and aloof enough to discourage any man. But appearances must be deceptive, to an unusual degree, in your case. Actually you burrowed your way under my skin, and curled up there, close to my heart."

The way in which he spoke was very winning. Eunice was conscious of unaccustomed warmth and unaccustomed pleasure as she listened. Suddenly she ceased to feel that she must be on her guard against Crispin, that she must always retreat when he advanced. She looked at him with an answering smile, and he was quick to grasp its significance. He picked up the looped ends of her belt, which were finished with

293

knotted fringe, and swung them rhythmically back and forth for a moment. Then he made a pretense of drawing her nearer to him with them.

"Please come home with me, Eunice," he said. "I promise you that you'll never be sorry. I'll go further than that. I promise you that you'll always be glad."

"I don't believe much in promises, any more."

"All right. Then let's not promise anything. Either of us. Let's just go."

"Do you really mean that? Would you be satisfied if I should just go—without promising anything?"

"Of course. You're right not to set too much store by promises. They're superfluous, however you look at them. If people don't want to keep them, they get broken. If people do want to keep them, what's the point in them anyway?"

Eunice laughed again. Crispin was certainly very cheering. But she wanted to make assurance doubly sure. She grew suddenly grave.

"You understand, don't you, Crispin, that I'm not certain I could ever bring myself to divorce Francis?"

"Of course. I shan't try to influence your decision about that in the least."

"You'd be content without—without marriage?"

"Absolutely. Nothing I've ever seen of marriage has led me to believe it was essential for happiness. If I'd thought so, I'd have married long ago. Naturally I'm very glad now that I didn't. Because, if I understand you as completely as I think I do, you might sometime feel that a second experiment with the holy estate of matrimony was worth while. In that case I'd like to qualify as a candidate for it myself."

He was still toying with the fringed ends of her belt. Now, instead of pretending to draw her closer to him, he made a show of pulling her to her feet.

"But till you do feel that way," he said, "why worry about it? We can talk about all that later on. You're trying to put the thought of death behind you. Why not put the thought of divorce behind you too?"

She had risen, impelled to movement by some deep inner urge, almost as much as by anything he had said or done. He put his arm around her shoulder.

"Look at those trees!" he said. "Can you remember what they were like a few weeks ago? And see what they're like now! They're comparable to the way you were feeling a few weeks ago and the way you're feeling now. Listen to the river! Can you remember how choked it was? Now the ice is all gone. It's flowing freely along towards the inevitable sea. There's a comparison for you there too. The cold is over and the winter. Forget them. Don't think of anything except the spring and the sunshine and all that they'll mean to us when we see them and share them in Hawaii!"

Chapter 24

IT WAS on this note that Eunice made her decision to leave Hamstead.

It was agreed that this decision should bind her to nothing, that she should go to Crispin Wood's ranch as his guest, the way she had done before. No, not the way she had done before, something within her said sharply; before she had been Francis's bride, and now she and Francis were separated past any hope of reunion; but aloud she confirmed Crispin's soothing statement. Honor and Jerry were both going with them. Honor had finished *The Tryst,* as the story with Retreat as its prototype had finally been named; now she was eager to begin her *Sweet Sandalwood.* The voyage would give her all the respite she needed; her energy was as boundless as her enthusiasm. Jerry, on the other hand, was frankly in favor of a vacation. He had not the slightest intention of being pursued by business burdens during his absence; he proposed to lounge and loaf from the time he left New York until he got back there again.

He was not quite as indolent as he had predicted, but his attitude was certainly one of untroubled leisure. Eunice had ample time to study it, for they decided on an expansive journey, beginning with a trip through the Canal which included brief stops at Havana and various South and Central American ports, and a stay in Hollywood sufficiently long for Honor to renew her contacts there. They had already been gone well over a month when they started on their last lap from San Francisco to Honolulu; and in the meantime Eunice had seen more of Jerry than in all the years she had known him. It was they who oftenest occupied the adjacent chairs on the sun deck, reserved for the entire party, for Honor was reading proof and revising her final copy of *The Tryst* and Crispin spent long hours on the tennis court and in the swimming pool. Sometimes Eunice and Jerry hardly spoke all day; at other times they engaged in desultory and impersonal conversation. Jerry made it clear that he enjoyed this, but he never attempted to bring a more personal note into their talks; when they were almost at their journey's end, Eunice did so herself.

"Jerry," she said without preamble, "what do you think of this trip anyway? My part in it, I mean. I'd like a disinterested male opinion. Honor has told me what she thinks and Crispin has told me what he thinks. But Honor's a woman and Crispin is biased. You're a man of the world. How does it look to you?"

"It looks to me as if you'd had a grand time," Jerry said promptly. "I think you got a tremendous kick buying out the town before we left New York. I never saw a woman get so many dresses in so short a time; and not one of them, as far as I can see, represents one of those costly mistakes you keep in your closet—to borrow a bit from *Vogue*—or is it *Harper's Bazaar*? I think you got a kick out of sitting at the captain's table in that high-colonnaded dining room on the ship we took going through the Canal, getting superservice and watching the arched ceiling roll back, on purpose so that you could see the stars overhead. I think you got a kick in Havana, too, and in Panama and San Salvador, when we were given the keys to the city, so to speak, and invited to go the limit by the Latin American officials as well as our own. It's bucked you up a lot. You look and act like a different woman than you did when you left Hamstead. But I don't know that the kick's going to last. I think you may get a sudden letdown, like after too much champagne."

"I don't ever drink too much champagne, Jerry."

"Of course not. I didn't mean that literally. I was trying to explain the principle. Excitement isn't your normal nourishment, the way it is some women's. At least it doesn't look that way to me. I may be mistaken though."

He took a pipe and a pouch from his pocket, filled the pipe with tobacco, and began to puff away contentedly. "Honor hasn't said much to me," he remarked eventually. "I gathered that whatever you'd discussed with her was more or less confidential and Honor's very scrupulous about confidences. And neither you nor Crispin has said anything. However, I gathered that this trip was a test. That's all right as far as it goes. It's a good idea. But I'm wondering how it can possibly be a fair test. Because I think you might like living with Crispin, for a little while. Just the same way you've liked this trip. But I don't see how you could like it indefinitely, any more than you'd like buying out Hattie Carnegie every day, or going endlessly to parties in one port after another. You didn't have enough finery or enough parties in Hamstead. This is the inevitable reaction. You didn't have enough stimulating masculine society either. Your attraction to Crispin is the answer to that. But I don't think it'll last much longer than the thrill you get out of the colored balloons and the fancy snappers at the captain's dinner."

"Why not?"

"You ought to know yourself, Eunice. But if you really want me to tell you, I'd say it would be because the thrill

296

wouldn't be real, in the first place; it would be just as artificial as the baubles I've just mentioned. And it would be pricked and stripped just about as fast."

He took his pipe out of his mouth and tapped it on the edge of his chair.

"If you want to get rid of Francis for good and all, I suppose in a way that's your own affair," he remarked. "Of course, I'm a Catholic, born and bred, myself. So if I started an argument with you we would never get anywhere. Though I don't know why we shouldn't, come to think of it. Catholics and Puritans are a good deal alike, when it comes to questions of basic decency. And that's the sort of question you're asking yourself. It isn't just a matter of dogma to say that a woman ought not to divorce her husband in order to marry another man. It's a matter of fundamental righteousness."

"But, Jerry, I'm not at all sure I shall divorce Francis. And if I do, it won't be in order to marry Crispin. It won't even be on account of—of anything Francis has done. I thought you understood that. It will be to achieve a form of separation that's practicable, in case I find I can't keep on drifting along, as I'm doing now."

"Yes, I understood that was your general viewpoint. But are you sure Crispin understands it too? And are you sure of *his* viewpoint?"

"Oh, yes! We had a very satisfactory talk on the subject. I explained to him exactly how I felt. And he said he wouldn't dream of urging me to marry him, under all the circumstances."

Jerry took his pipe out of his mouth and looked at Eunice searchingly. She returned his gaze with slight bewilderment, but no evasion. He shrugged his shoulders slightly.

"Well, I won't preach to you," he said, after a pause which seemed to indicate that there was something with which he was not wholly satisfied, but that he was not blaming Eunice for it. "No doubt your grandmother did that and no doubt your stepfather is still doing it. I can't help telling you though, since you've asked me, that I'm all against your tentative plan, on practical grounds. I think you'd better make up your mind to live with Francis or to live alone. I don't think there's any middle course for you. Besides, I believe someday you'll find you can forgive him after all; and it would be a bad break, for you as well as for him, if you found that out too late. You couldn't go back to Francis if you'd lived with another man first. Not that he wouldn't take you. Of course he would. But something inside of you would hold you back."

"I can't forgive Francis, Jerry. I've tried and I can't. What he's done is abhorrent to me."

"Well, I can understand that. He's got some pretty grave

faults. A priest would say he'd committed mortal sin, and I suppose he has. And mortal sin is appalling to a woman like you—a good deal more appalling, in a way, than it is to a priest, who sees such an awful lot of it and knows that bad as it is, it isn't beyond the realm of Divine forgiveness. If you can't stand the memory of Francis's mortal sin——"

"It's not just the memory of it, Jerry. It's the dread of it in the future."

"Why do you borrow all that trouble? Why don't you give him a chance? If you find that he doesn't deserve it, you could always leave him again. And when it comes to that, if you can't face the future with Francis, what makes you think you could face it with any man? At least any man that you'd want? You'd better do what I said, if you're afraid. You'd better face it alone."

Jerry put his pipe back in his pocket and rose. Apparently he had decided to go below decks. Then apparently he thought better of it.

"As I said, Honor has great gifts of reticence," he remarked. "So I suppose she never told you why I was expelled from school when I was a youngster? Or why I married her sister when I was engaged to her? Someday you might ask her. If she won't tell you, I will. I'll tell you now what she said to me when I hesitated to marry her because of all my past sins, though I adored her: 'I know you'll never fail me, either for your sake or my own. You'll never risk losing me again. You'll never risk betraying me or wounding me. You'll shield me and cherish me. You'll love me as you love your own soul all the days of your life. You've gone through fire and water to get me. You'll never let me go again."

Jerry's voice broke before he had finished. Eunice could see how deeply moved he was, though he had turned away from her and was looking with apparent absorption toward the bow. She was immeasurably moved by his confession, and she waited with deference, hoping that he would say something more.

"It wasn't such a bad way for a woman to reason," he said at last. "At all events I know Honor's sincere when she says she's glad she married me; and I do love her as I love my own soul. I commend her logic to you. Give it careful thought when you consider Francis again."

But Eunice still avoided serious consideration of Francis. Her talk with Jerry had given her added respect for Honor's husband, and she was aware that much of the wise advice he had offered her was based on his own bitter experience. But with a slight sense of shame, she wished that his advice had been more worldly and less lofty; and she could not help feeling that once she had spoken to him on the subject of her personal affairs, he should have considered this subject closed, unless she brought it up again of her own accord. Instead, he reopened it several times, each time indicating, tactfully but unmistakably, that he thought she was heading for trouble. Moreover, he had a way of joining Crispin and herself, which seemed to her less and less accidental as time went on. Agreeable as he made himself, she resented both his mental and his physical intrusion. However, as he had observed, she had extracted an enormous amount of pleasure from the trip so far, and she was determined to go on extracting pleasure from it without permitting her enjoyment to be clouded by disturbing thoughts.

At the moment, the present was enough for her. She was trying to shut away the past. She was resolutely disregarding the future. She was actually angry with herself when Crispin took them straight to Molokai. This was ostensibly so that Honor could get the background for her story at once and begin work on it with the least possible delay; but Eunice knew it was really in order that she herself might not be reminded of Kauai. She was angrier still when she found, after the first few days, that the place had no enchantment for her, that she was bored with it and disappointed in it.

She freely admitted that this was not Crispin's fault in any way. Again he was an utterly charming host; again the entertainment and the accommodations he offered his guests were unique, tasteful and luxurious. Honor was enthralled with the sandalwood troughs in the heart of the deep forest, and visualized at once the laborers and traders and kings meeting together in the high hills and clustering about the declivities dug in the red earth, of which Crispin had spoken so glowingly. She explored the island and closeted herself to scribble on alternate days. Meanwhile Jerry began to hunt antelope with zest. But Eunice was interested in neither sports nor exploration. She did some aimless reading and riding, but neither sufficed to fill her days. At last she turned to needlework which she had neglected for a long time. The conditions under which she did it were reminiscent of those which had prompted poor Ruth to produce her endless embroideries. As she herself stitched away, Eunice could not help thinking of Ruth and of her inadaptability. She wondered what had become of her. At last she asked Crispin, one day when he and she had ridden over to his little camp on the windward side of the island.

This camp was no more pretentious than the "little grass hack" which had become the topic of a popular theme song, but it formed an agreeable objective for a day's outing. Indeed, Crispin himself frequently spent the night there with two or three cronies when he was hunting antelope, and he had suggested that Jerry might sometime like to do this too. He referred to "roughing it" on these camping expeditions, but Eunice felt sure that he contrived to be very comfortable there. Her own acquaintance with it was limited to an occasional picnic lunch which she and Crispin took with them from the ranch and ate at a rustic table facing the sea. The shack was overhung with bougainvillea and one side of it was almost completely open to the ocean, giving at one and the same time a sense of seclusion and a sense of space. Only a fringe of palm trees at the water's edge broke the great expanse visible from the sheltered cove where the shack stood; and the peaceful lapping of the waves, soft against the sand, made the only sound that could be heard. Idling away an afternoon there, Eunice came nearer contentment than she did at any other time and place.

"Why, Ruth married," Crispin said, pouring iced pineapple juice from a thermos jar and appraisingly selecting a sandwich. "Surprisingly enough she married, and what is more surprising still, she married very well—one of our leading sugar planters. They live on Maui in a beautiful house with a gorgeous view—it faces full on Haleakala. It was a fine place to start with and Ruth's done wonders with it, especially in the way of landscape gardening. She's clipped two great mango trees to form a curved enclosure from which you get a vista of the valleys and mountains. She's veiled a fountain in the lanai with vines. And she keeps a great chalice filled with dazzling white hibiscus at the base of a snowy statue. It's all tremendously effective."

"It must be. I wish I could see it."

"There's no reason in the world why you can't. I know Ruth would be perfectly delighted to have you visit her, if you'd care to go there. You ought to plan to take in the Maui Fair, when you do. According to the circulars it's 'one of Hawaii's finest illustrations of community effort.' Actually, it's as typical an expression of American life as you'd see in Springfield or Syracuse or anywhere else you might choose to go. Ruth and her husband would show it to you with great pride. They'll have exhibits of everything there themselves, from live stock to vegetables."

"Vegetables?"

"Yes. The vegetable show is one of the most striking features of the Maui Fair. It's held in a large barnlike building completely transformed by the beauty of its decorations and the profusion of its exhibits. *Ti* leaves are suspended in a series of fringes from the ceiling, pineapples are arranged in golden pyramids, and jars of honey are built up into amber tiers. You couldn't possibly stand unmoved before all the

300

artichokes, bamboo shoots, gourds, ginger, lily roots, okra, peppers and kohlrabi. Not to mention the avocados, breadfruit, jackfruit, guavas, cumquats and mangosteens———"

"Crispin, you better stop, unless you can produce some more lunch. My mouth is beginning to water."

"It would water all right if you saw the papaya and persimmons and pomegranates and star apples and rose apples and tamarinds and passion fruit at the Maui Fair. Why don't you telephone to Ruth? You can fly over to Maui now, you know, in less than an hour. Transportation's changed a good deal since you were in the Islands ten years ago."

"It doesn't seem possible that it's been ten years, does it? Yes—I would like to see Ruth. I was always very fond of her. What's her name now?"

"Jameson. Mrs. George Jameson. You'd know Ruth would have a plain substantial name like that, wouldn't you, if she ever did marry? Not that it seemed likely to anyone. Her husband is that Scotchman I told you about before—the one who used to turn out the lights and set the clocks ahead—He's certainly changed his habits now. He fell for Ruth hard and her romance was a nine days' wonder in the Islands. She's even got a couple of very cute kids—a boy and a girl. We'll ask them all over here if you like. Perhaps you'd prefer that to visiting her."

"No, I'd like to go to Maui— You know I didn't get there before. I'd especially like to see the volcano with the silver sword plants growing in it. They must be very lovely and mystical. You don't think, if I went there, that there'd be any danger———"

"Any danger that you'd run into Edith? Not the slightest. She's somewhere over on the other side of the world. Siam, I believe."

"Did— Is she married too?"

"No. At least I've never heard that she was. And I imagine I would, if she were. Through Ruth, that is."

He began to gather up the remains of their lunch, stowing it neatly away in the English tea basket they had brought with them, and he spoke with the same unconcern he had always displayed in referring to Edith. But he went on talking about her.

"Your troubles with Edith were short-lived, weren't they? Perhaps you remember I told you they would be, if you didn't make an issue out of them. You might have saved yourself so much trouble, Eunice, if you'd only listened to me then. Just as you'd save yourself an equal amount of trouble if you'd listen to me now."

It was the first time since she had come to Molokai that he had spoken of his suit, even indirectly. Eunice, her eyes

301

fixed on the ocean, parried with a touch of archness alien to her characteristically grave mood.

"I might listen to you now, if I knew why you gave me such good advice before. What made you feel so sure that Edith wouldn't menace me for long?"

Crispin's answer came unhesitatingly. "Because I know the type. She can't be content to bewitch, though she has everything it takes for that. She wants to dominate, too, and she hasn't got either adequate brains or adequate character. Didn't you discover, after Francis had fallen for her, that she wanted to control him completely, that she'd hardly let him out of her sight?"

"Yes——"

"And didn't he turn on her when she began to do that?"

"Yes. Yes, he did. I hadn't thought of it that way, but it's so."

She abandoned her contemplation of the ocean and looked at Crispin with awakening attentiveness. He continued to talk like a man convinced of the soundness of his views, and outlining them without either indecision or emotion.

"Well, don't make the same mistake again, Eunice. There's an old saying that you shouldn't underestimate your antagonist. But if you're a woman and your antagonist's only an inconsequential rival, it's better to underestimate her than to overestimate her."

"But how can a woman be sure, Crispin? That her rival is inconsequential, as you put it?"

"Very easily. Merely by retaining a modicum of good sense and good judgment, even if she is in love."

"And you think I didn't, with—with Francis?"

"No, never. Not just in the case of Edith, but throughout your married life. At least all appearances point that way. Not that I'm likely to quarrel with your lack of judgment, my dear, since it's brought you back to me. But I hope that in my case you'll be wiser."

"What do you mean, in your case?"

"You didn't suppose, did you, Eunice, that you were the first woman in my life?"

For the first time she flinched. Up to that moment, every thing he said had been bearable, and some of his remarks had given her helpful understanding and a sense of liberation and relief. Now he was coming close to the one subject she had declined to consider, even by herself. She answered falteringly.

"No—not exactly. That is—I heard rumors about you when I was here before. But they were too fantastic to be true."

"Nothing is too fantastic to be true, especially in Hawaii

If you're coming to live here, that's a fact you'll have to accept."

He said it without equivocation, as he had said everything else. Eunice persisted in her evasion.

"Yes. But that wouldn't effect us, would it?"

"I don't know. I'm beginning to wonder. In fact, I've been wanting very much to talk to you about it. Because it might be better for both of us to thrash it out now, rather than later on. And this is a good place for it, as well as a good time. We're not likely to have any inopportune interruptions."

An expression of faint amusement crossed his countenance. It was under control almost immediately. Nevertheless, Eunice had seen it, and was immediately conscious of a jarring note. She herself had enjoyed the sense of seclusion which the shack gave her. But it had not previously occurred to her that Crispin had taken her there primarily because he did not want interference. It was one thing for her to find Jerry's society, at times, slightly superfluous; it was quite another for Crispin to take definite steps to see that there was no such superfluity. Soon he would be past the point where he did not want interference and would have reached the place where he would not brook it. But it was not clear to her, at this advanced stage, what she could do.

"From the turn this conversation has taken," Crispin was saying, "I think that perhaps a logical way to begin the next part of it would be by asking how much you mind about Edith, as far as I'm concerned?"

"*As far as you are concerned!* You mean that you really were in the cave with her?"

"Oh, that!" Crispin's look of amusement returned, unveiled this time. He laughed, and his laughter seemed to imply that the incident was of very little importance. "No. Edith did meet Francis in the cave. She had a hunch you might look for her in her room. So she bribed Suki to put a wax figure he knew I had, that we'd used sometimes for amateur theatricals, in her bed. Then she made good her escape. Not that she needed the figure after all. She knew a short cut, and even after you caught her in the cave—which she didn't count on—she got back to the ranch before you and Guy did. On the otherhand, Francis rode around the longest possible way and got back long afterward. I suppose now you'll always feel it was unforgivable that Francis lied to you about this particular episode."

"Of course I shall. Of course it will make me doubt everything else he's ever told me as the truth."

"I think you're going pretty far to say that. I shouldn't be the least surprised if it were the only thing he ever did lie you about. I'm certain, for instance, that he didn't know

Edith was going to take the same boat you did. And as to what may have happened since then, with other women—well, that's an entirely different story. I don't see how he could help lying about the cave. As a matter of fact, I think he and Edith were very adroit about the whole rendezvous. And of course I unconsciously played into their hands by staying all day at the mill."

"Then if you *weren't* in the cave——"

"Good God, Eunice, do you need to have everything explained in words of one syllable? How do you suppose Edith knew her way to the cave, short cuts and all, if she'd never been there before? How do you suppose she dared to swim around and take a man into the water with her if it wasn't all familiar ground? I wasn't in the cave with her the day you caught her. But I'd been there with her dozens of times before. Edith was a saucy little piece, but there's no denying she was the nearest approach to a nymph when I first met her that I've ever come across, even in this land of magic. I was infatuated with her once myself, with her witchery and her wantonness, just as Francis was. Then she began to bore me—just as she began to bore him. So I made a substantial settlement on her and told her to take herself off. Of course I didn't mind having her come back occasionally, provided she didn't stay too long. And I didn't care who else she took on, if it amused her to fool around."

"You mean that Edith was your mistress, long before she and Francis——"

"I can't understand why you didn't guess, Eunice. I can't understand why you didn't know all along."

"Did Francis know?"

"Of course. He treated her like the light of love she was. You didn't think he'd sinned against her innocence, did you? I've reason to believe I was her first lover. How many she's had since, I don't know. I've been too much occupied myself to waste much time guessing."

"With other mistresses?"

"Eunice, you must have known all this before. It can't be a surprise and a shock to you now!"

She had sprung to her feet, shaking off the appeasing hand which Crispin had laid on her arm. Her voice was vibrant with rage and horror when she spoke to him.

"And if I stayed here with you, that's what I'd become, isn't it? Another mistress! To be bought off when I bored you. Placated with a 'substantial settlement!' Told you wouldn't mind having me come back, as long as I didn't stay long!"

"Eunice, stop talking like that! Don't compare yourself to an empty-headed little golddigger like Edith, who never had any background! You've got breeding and character and in telligence and wealth of your own. You know you'd never bore me, you know there never could be any question of buying you off. My whole concern would be to keep you here — It is to keep you here! You know I'd be glad to marry you, if you were free. But you're not. So how could you stay here except as my mistress?"

"As your friend! As your companion! We talked it all over! You told me yourself I wouldn't be bound in any way!"

"We are friends, Eunice. We are companions. That's what you missed with Francis; it's what you've never missed with me. You never will. You told me Francis said that to you himself. He's been very just and very generous — much more than I'd have been in his place. He knew we'd be lovers if you stayed here. He told you that too, didn't he? Perhaps he didn't spell it all out, the way you seem to want. Perhaps he didn't say we'd be married lovers if you divorced him and unmarried lovers if you didn't. But that's what he meant. He knew that love would be inevitable. So did I. Why should I have bothered to bind you with promises? I was sure that in time you'd come to me anyway!"

Suddenly he put out his arms and caught her to him, pulling her close, holding her closer. All the dormant desire within her woke at his touch. For an instant she could not suppress it, and in that instant Crispin sensed her response. Then he felt her struggle in his embrace, straining to free herself as the inevitable recoil came and her longing changed to loathing.

"Let me go! Don't you dare kiss me! Don't you dare try to keep me!"

"Of course I'm going to kiss you! Of course I'm going to keep you! Now I know you want me, do you think I'll ever let you go? Don't refuse me, don't resist me! It only makes everything harder for us both!"

"But, Honor, how could Jerry have known I needed him? How could he have heard me call him? How could he act as if he were just passing by and naturally dropped in to join us?"

"Jerry had known you needed him for a long time, Eunice. You said something to him on shipboard, didn't you? Of course I don't know what. He never told me. But after he knew, he acted. He's kept as close to you as he could, ever since. In every way. He heard you call him because he wasn't far off. I mean, in actual distance. He *was* passing by—it *was* natural for him to join you. He was hunting, as Crispin had urged him to do, and he decided to use the lodge, which Crispin suggested also. Let's be glad he took our host at his word, even if that was the last thing that was expected

Crispin played straight into Jerry's hands—it's the only stupid thing I ever knew him to do—but as a matter of fact I think Jerry would have heard you anyway. No matter how far off he'd been. I think he would have come to you from the other side of the island. You see, I have unbounded faith in Jerry."

Eunice had asked the same questions and Honor had made the same answers a dozen times within the last two days. Now they were no longer on Molokai. They were on a boat again, but this time Honor was not taking it. She had only come to say good-by to Eunice, who was sailing alone. In another week she would be back at Evergreen, and she would be alone there, too. Unless Francis would let Noel come back to her. She wondered whether she could bring herself to beg that he should. She did not feel certain. The only thing of which she did feel certain was that she was going back to Evergreen to take refuge and that no man should ever enter her life again.

PART VII

"Neither Can Floods Drown It"

~~~~~~

Chapter 25

EUNICE WAS fond of rainy days. There was a restful quality to them, and a healing one, which she did not find in others. But this September day was different. It had rained all the night before, and all the day before that. The earth seemed drenched to its very foundations.

About noon, Mem telephoned from his own farm to say that the meadow road was covered with water. The message was not unexpected, because when he had come over that morning, he had told her that the water was rising, and he did not know whether he would be able to make Evergreen again that day. He suggested that she might call in one of the neighbors, and she had replied that she would, at the last moment, if it were necessary. But Noel had told her proudly, several times, that he thought he could manage alone whenever he had to. This might be a good chance to let him try.

"Mebbe you're right," Mem answered. "I swan I never saw a young 'un take hold better'n Noel does around a farm. Just like a Hale. He's gettin' to be the spittin' image of his grandfather, too, as I recollect his looks. Well I'll be goin' along, if there ain't nothin' more I can do for you. Just take a look at that water! I ain't never seen it so high in the fall of the year."

"No, Mem, I never have either. But I doubt if it goes up much higher. And don't worry about Noel and me. We'll be all right."

Without concern, she had heard him shut the door leading into the shed behind him, and three hours later, after his telephone call, she still remained undisturbed. She turned from the telephone to the stove where a savory stew was simmering. She had become a very good cook and she enjoyed the concoction of dishes. The housework at Evergreen was so light when she and Noel were alone there that Sue came in now only for the heavier washing and cleaning.

Eunice did everything else herself. She was glad of the occupation it afforded.

The stew was doing well. She added a little more onion to it and chopped up cabbage and green pepper for coleslaw. Then she sat down in the old rocker which she had never removed from the kitchen and took up her knitting. She made all Noel's socks and sweaters and sports suits for herself. She had become apt at this also, and she took increasing pleasure in all kinds of fine needlework. She embroidered napkins; she hemstitched sheets; she made her own underwear and blouses entirely by hand. It kept her fingers busy, and though it did not completely control her thoughts, it tranquilized these as it had in the Singapore hospital years before.

She had never needed to ask Francis if Noel might come back to her. She had found a letter from her husband awaiting her on her return from Hawaii. He felt that Noel's school year should not be interrupted again, he said; the little boy would start North when ever she gave the word. She had lost no time in doing this, and he had been with her all winter, except for his Christmas and Easter vacations which he had spent at Retreat. Now he had been with her all of another summer and had begun school once more. He had long since ceased to question her and seemed to accept his parents' separation as an established fact, without undue curiosity or undue grief. He always departed happily when he went South; on the other hand, he seemed quite contented in Hamstead. His disposition was even, though it was not especially sunny. Eunice took untold comfort in him.

She rose and looked at the stew again, then went back to the rocker and her knitting. If she could only have taken the same sort of comfort in Francis that she had in his son, if only he too could have been dependable and trustworthy, how different her life would have been! But Francis could never be stabilized. Even now, while he left her so unmolested, while he revealed such generosity regarding her claims to their child, the reminders she had of him were still disturbing. And these reminders were constant. In replying to his letter about Noel's return, she had first written briefly, almost tersely, saying how glad she would be to see the little boy; then in a spirit of bitter self-accusation, she had penned a postscript longer than the original letter, telling Francis the whole story of her struggle with Crispin. Her husband's answer had come by return mail. He was mighty sorry to learn that anything had happened to startle or annoy her, he wrote reassuringly; but he hoped she would put the thought of it behind her and not blame herself for what had happened. Or Crispin either, for that matter. An episode of that kind might take place almost anywhere and under almost any circumstances, and who could blame a poor devil for trying to get away with as much as he could when he was desperate? The only point was, he ought to know when he could not get away with anything, and in that respect Crispin had shown rather poor judgment, since one look at Eunice should be enough to convince a man of average intelligence that it would be impossible in her case. But after all, no harm had been done, thanks to good old Jerry, who was certainly canny when it came to smoking out trouble; and if she would not fall into her old error of making mountains out of molehills, she would soon forget all about it. As far as he was concerned, he was glad she knew the truth at last about the only lie he had ever told her, though on general principles he agreed with Virgin's theory that "a good lie well tole an' well stuck to is better den de trufe tole an' took back." Aside from this one point, the details of what she had said were vague in his mind already, and as he had torn her letter up, they probably would keep on getting vaguer all the time.

The whole tone had been as tender as a light caress offered with a happy smile to heal a hurt; and after that, she had heard from him in one way or another every week. Sometimes he wrote her a long newsy letter. He told her, for instance, that Millie's baby, a girl, had been named for her grandmother; the baby was doing finely and she was just as cute as she could be. Apparently Francis was determined that the topic of Millie should be approached without self-consciousness. He also wrote Eunice that since Honor had sent Melissa out to meet her lover so publicly—*The Tryst* had been a tremendous success—the ghost seemed to be laid; at all events, he had slept in the guest room several times himself, and nothing had happened. What was more, he had opened up the little secret chamber beside it for good and all—he thought Eunice would really be very much pleased with the effect of it, if she could only see it. Apparently the topic of the ghost was another one he had decided must henceforth be treated in a matter-of-fact way, for he went on to relate that Blanche had confided to him that once in his father's time she had surreptitiously sent for the Baptist preacher to come and lay the ghosts at Retreat. The preacher had come in the side door backwards, his coat upside down and inside out, reading the Bible from the bottom of the page up. None of this had done any good, Blanche added woefully; but now Honor had succeeded where everyone else had failed. Of course that was Honor's way.

Francis also wrote that good old Doctor Daingerfield had died, and that though the whole county had mourned, no one had been so deeply affected as Doctor Tayloe, who had broken badly under the blow. It was a mercy that Peyton was taking hold so well as his assistant; otherwise they might have lost Doctor Tayloe too. There were no more mint-julep parties at Barren Point; these were held at Retreat instead. Purvis had won another very important prize; it was beginning to look as if he might score a real success as a naturalist. Mamie Love had more beaux than either Bella or Bina had ever achieved; it was a problem how she would ever choose among them; but Francis had seen her digging with a little stick on the garden path, her head bent, while one of these callow youths talked to her very earnestly, and Francis had observed that such poking around often denoted serious consideration of a proposal. The negroes supplied various additional news items. The flies had been very bad that year, and Blanche had explained they were the souls of bad people sent back to plague other bad people; if this were the case, Retreat must be a den of inquity, judging by their number— but that would be no news to Eunice! Blanche was not feeling so well; she said the trouble was that she had the high pressure blood and change of life in the eyes. Violet, however, was in fine fettle; she had married Elisha instead of Malachi, from down Warsaw way; there had been gun shots on the wedding night which Francis had rather feared might have been fired by the discarded suitor. But Blanche had come in and told him they were only discharged at a dog who was "bailing" the moon and presumably disturbing the raptures of the newly wedded pair. They were not going to keep house by themselves just yet; they were living with Blanche who had given them the last feather bed on the place as a present. Apparently they were delighted with it and finding it quite adequate. The wedding feast—wine and cake—had been served in the kitchen at the big house.

Francis's communications did not always take the form of a newsy letter. Sometimes he sent instead a brief financial statement that spoke for itself. Retreat was solvent again now, and there were even some months when the balance sheets showed a margin of profit. He also sent her, without annotation, the specifications for rebuilding the broken dam which he had shown her the first time she visited Retreat, and which she herself had never been interested in restoring. The specifications included not only a plan for concrete reconstruction and another for the scientific restocking with fish, but also drawings for a grist mill and a small power plant, a rustic bridge and a couple of cabins. Occasionally, instead of a letter of any sort, Eunice received a shipment of the products, such as preserves and ham, which were now a standardized success. They all had trade names, but Francis himself referred to them as the "Fruits of Fielding's Folly."

There was nothing about his attitude to suggest that Retreat was an appropriate name for his place any more. Instead he seemed to be triumphantly asserting that, in the last analysis, he had been able to gather figs from thistles.

There was still an element of surprise in everything he did. During the summer and early fall, golden melons and purple grapes had come to Evergreen with lavish regularity. In September there were chinquapins, which Eunice tried to cook as she had learned to do at Retreat, boiling them in a skillet placed over fresh coals; but somehow they did not taste the same. In November, a bigger box than usual arrived, and Eunice decided that Francis had sent her a winter's supply of home-grown foodstuffs. Instead, when she opened the box, she found it full of Osage oranges. She was startled and shocked by this poignant reminder of her first meeting with her husband and she realized that the dispatch of the box had marked an anniversary. She set it out in the shed, but she found she could not bear to throw the oranges away. She took them from their coverings and arranged them in bowls; their pungent odor filled the house. They were not good to eat, they were not good for anything, as Francis had told her in the beginning. But they were arresting to look at, delightful to smell, and fascinating to touch. She could not leave them alone.

Eunice's letter thanking Francis for the Osage oranges was very restrained. Usually she succeeded in writing to him in a way which was detached, but agreeable; this time she was afraid she might say too much. But her formality did not seem to daunt him in the least. At Christmastime, it was holly that came, and in the spring, box after box of the early flowers she had learned to love: hyacinths, Lent lilies, snowdrops and Johnny-jump-ups; and later on, clove pinks, Persian lilacs and sanguinaria. A flower garden had never been a feature at Evergreen, though Eunice followed her grandmother's custom of planting a few hardy annuals in rows—sweet peas and sweet William, nasturtiums and petunias. She picked them regularly and arranged them carefully; they sufficed to give an inhabited look to the house. But they did not constitute a garden.

She tried not to think of the garden at Retreat as she sat in the kitchen at Evergreen, knitting and rocking, and occasionally glancing out at the fast-falling rain. By now the African daisies would be blooming in Virginia, the calendulas and ageratum. None of these grew in Hamstead. There were a few straggling tiger lilies flanking the clapboards at the front of the house, but Eunice could never look at them without thinking of the masses that ran riot at Retreat along the edges of the dark woods, making a broad brilliant border and penetrating past the fringes of the trees. It was beyond these masses of lilies that the copperheads sometimes lurked. There were no snakes in the groves at Evergreen. There were no lilies, either.

It was increasingly difficult to escape the realization that safety was somewhat colorless, just as seclusion was somewhat monotonous. A lack of suffering represented a lack of experience, and the apathy that came with this was joyless as well as painless. Inconsequentially, Eunice hoped the mint-julep parties at Fielding's Folly were as successful as those at Barren Point had always been. Mrs. Tayloe had confided the secret formula for the juleps to Eunice, but the old lady told it to very few persons; it was probable that she considered Mrs. Fielding too scatterbrained to remember it, and in that case the drinks would never taste the same— She could visualize the dam surrounded with pink laurel and reflecting tinted water lilies in the quiet depths which had again been plentifully restocked with fish. She had always found it a place of peace and beauty; it would be intriguing to find it productive also. She wondered who was to live in the two cabins under construction— She also wondered what Melissa's room looked like, now that sunshine filtered through it and the curtains and counterpane on the tester bed were soft and spotless— She thought there would be a great satisfaction in naming a child for its grandmother. Abigail Hale Fielding would have been a beautiful name. And how Noel would have loved a little sister——

The kitchen door banged, and Noel himself came into the room. His mackintosh was dripping.

"Gee, but it's raining hard. School's dismissed. There isn't going to be any session this afternoon. It was fun coming home. The puddles are as big as pools. Some of the boys went wading in them."

"Isn't it too cold to go wading?"

"No, it isn't cold. But it's pouring down dogs and cats. It's a queer rain. I'm sort of glad I don't have to go out in it again."

He shed his outer garments, hung them up carefully to dry, and went to wash his hands. Dinner was a comfortable, companionable meal. The rain falling on the roof and against the windowpanes, though it was coming down harder all the time, still made a sound that was soothing rather than disturbing. It was only after dinner, when the dishes were done and Eunice decided to finish the ironing, that she discovered the electricity had gone off.

The row of little candlesticks which her grandmother had always kept on the front hall table still stood there; Eunice had a sentimental attachment for them, and besides, they were useful in an emergency; the electricity in Hamstead had never been dependable during storms and freshets. But candlelight, much as she loved it for beauty and companionship, was impracticable for housework. She cast a hasty glance at the four old lamps also prepared against emergency, in the pantry; they were trimmed and filled, and they would last the night out—possibly two nights; but the disused kerosene can itself was almost empty, and the water on the meadows was now rising so fast that she could see a change every minute. She tried to ring up her nearest neighbor, knowing that Mrs. Manning would be glad to help out, provided she was supplied herself; but the telephone, like the electricity, had gone dead.

Eunice sat down and turned matters over in her mind for a few minutes; then she went to the foot of the stairs and called to Noel, who had gone to his room to tinker with his meccano.

"Come down here, will you, darling? And bring your rubber boots with you——"

"All right, Mother. Just a minute."

It was characteristic of Noel that he did not protest or argue or even question her. She heard a clinking sound such as might be made by strips of steel if they were stacked together, and knew that he was putting his meccano in order before he left it. Even as a little child he had taken good care of his toys instead of banging them about and destroying them. Now he was beginning to treat tools with the same consideration; farm implements would last for a long time in his hands. There was no delay, either, while he rummaged about for his rubber boots; he knew exactly where to find them. When he came into the kitchen, he already had them on.

"The electricity is off and the telephone isn't working, Noel. We haven't much extra kerosene in the house. I'm afraid I'll have to send you for some."

"All right, Mother. I'll try the Mannings first, shall I? And then go on to the Marlowes and the Grays if I have to. Or to the village."

He took the can from her and went out of the house, whistling cheerfully. She watched his sturdy little figure until it disappeared from sight among the pines. The falling rain and the mist which had begun to rise from the valley obscured it before it disappeared entirely; Eunice could not remember when such murkiness had enveloped the landscape. There was an eerie quality to it, and though she sat down again and tried to occupy herself, first with reading and then with knitting, again she was uneasy. Finally she rose and moved restlessly from one window to another, staring out into space. When she reached the old buttery overlooking the barnyard, she saw the cattle were uneasy too. They were not standing quietly under the dripping eaves according to their habit on a rainy day. They were circling about, tossing their heads and stamping, and the mournful noise of their lowing came to her through the stillness.

She had no rubber boots of her own, but she put on her overshoes and her raincoat and went out herself. Tightly as she had buttoned up her collar and fastened her hood, the rain penetrated her coverings and ran down in a rivulet under her clothes. It was this, she felt sure, that gave her such a sensation of shivering as she threw her weight against the heavy barn door and pushed it open. The cattle rushed past her, stampeding their way to shelter. By the time Noel returned with the oil, the cows were all in their stanchions, the calves in their pens. He had not been gone long, for Grandma Gray, with characteristic providence, had oil enough and to spare in the house; she had filled his can and another, which she loaned him, and had insisted that he should have a glass of milk and some sugar cookies before he started back to Evergreen. Otherwise he would have returned sooner. Now, still without curiosity or protest, he prepared to milk.

He had never done it all alone before. He was gentle and familiar with the cows, and his presence was soothing to them now. But he was not adroit enough to work rapidly, and twelve were too many for a little boy to handle in any case. Eunice knew that he would be tired and hungry when he came into the house and she had supper ready for him. In spite of Mrs. Gray's generosity, she thought it wise to conserve oil, and she was so unaccountably weary that she wanted to conserve her strength as well. Therefore she set the table in the kitchen, covering it with one of the old red-and white-checked clothes. It looked cheerful and warm under the shaded student lamp, and she tried to make her greeting to Noel gay also.

"This is fun, isn't it, darling, being here by ourselves? It's so quiet and cozy inside, we can forget all about the storm."

"Yes, Mother. But the wind is coming up. Can't you hear it howl?"

"I can hear it if I stop to listen."

"I can hear it anyway," Noel said soberly. "Not that I mind— I think it's the lamplight that makes everything seem so cozy. I like it. The glow over the table and the rest of the room dark. And I like having supper in the kitchen. But I think it would be even more fun if Father were here with us. Because he'd joke about the wind. You and I don't joke the way Father does."

"There's nothing to joke about in the wind, is there, Noel?"

"No-o. But I think jokes are nicest of all when nothing does seem very funny. They help."

Eunice did not answer. Noel washed his hands at the sink and began to bring hot dishes from the stove. Then he slid into his seat at the table, picking up one of the fringed napkins that matched the checked tablecloth and spreading it out over his knees with care. He looked even tireder than Eunice had expected, and he ate silently, without real heartiness. The milk and sugar cookies might account in part for his lack of appetite, but not wholly. The walk in the rain must have been a hard one, and the milking harder still. But like the sugar cookies, they could not account for everything.

"Do you miss your father, Noel?" Eunice asked suddenly. She did not do so voluntarily. The words were wrested from her, because she could not stand that look of patient weariness on her little son's face another instant. His answer came quietly, but with inescapable intensity.

"Yes, Mother, I do. Don't you?"

She sat looking at him, unable to say anything in return. The wind was howling so fiercely now that she would have been obliged to raise her voice, to scream almost, in order to make herself heard above it. Noel had not screamed, and yet she had heard him; but that was because she had known what was coming. Noel did not know what she would say, and she could not shout how she felt about Francis above the storm, she could not whisper it, even to herself, unless she took time, a great deal of time, and there was no time at all now. A terrific crash clove through the silence, and she leaped to her feet, thankful that she could act more quickly than she could reason in a crisis.

"A window has been blown in somewhere. We must get the opening closed before the house is flooded."

She snatched up the lamp and a pillow and she did not pause to think, now, whether she was screaming or not. Noel was more thoughtful than she was.

"The wind will blow the lamp out, Mother, if a window's fallen in. But there's a flashlight in the table drawer here, and I have another in my room."

The climbed the stairs together. The wind was rushing through the hallway with fiendish force, and Eunice could not shield the lamp from it, though she tried with one hand while she clung to the banister with the other. The lamp went out with the suddenness of a shot, and when she set it down on a step, it was swept away and fell in splinters on the floor below. She locked her arms through Noel's and

315

went on, groping her way by the beam of his flashlight. But the jagged glass still clinging to the frame pierced the ticking, and a flurry of feathers filled the air, leaving only a limp sack behind them. Eunice reached for the cardboard box which had held the meccano.

"That isn't heavy enough, Mother. I'll go down to the cellar and get some boards. If you're not afraid to stay alone. Here's the other flashlight."

He knew that she was afraid, though she had tried so hard to hide her fear. But she shouted to him that she was not, and he left her crouching behind the bed where the wind did not strike as fiercely as it did in the middle of the room. There was suction from the fireplace as well as the window, and between the two she could hardly keep her feet. She moved just in time to avoid a great chunk of plaster which fell with a heavy thud from the ceiling. A coarse powder rose, filling the air as the feathers had filled it a few moments earlier, choking her throat and nostrils with its dust. When Noel came back with the boards, she was coughing so hard that she could no longer shout to him, and she could barely hear him, though she knew he was calling to her more loudly than he had before.

"I have the boards. If you'll hold the flashlight so I can see, I'll nail them up."

Noel drove the nails in carefully. The boards would hold after he got them placed. And presently they would go from room to room, closing the dampers in the fireplaces. Eunice said this to herself while she held the two flashlights as steadily as she could and Noel did his work. But before the first window was boarded up, a second one had fallen in. He left her again, despite her protests, and went down to the cellar for more planks.

"Don't go, Noel. I don't want to be separated from you."

"But, Mother, we must do what we can to save the house. This must be a hurricane. You said you weren't afraid. And I'm not."

She did not try to stop him after that, and she did not try to move any more. She knew there was no sure shelter anywhere, and no safety. Noel might be hurt on the stairs or in the cellar; but he was quite as likely to be hurt if she kept him by her side. The Valley which had seemed to her the last abiding place of peace was now possessed of an unknown fury such as had never visited it before; the house which had been the stronghold of generations was rocking on its foundations. She sobbed, not because she was still frightened, for fear seemed to have left her, but because she could not receive, unflinchingly, this ultimate blow. More than her confidence had been swept away by the hurricane.

Above its raging, she could hear the still small voice of her own conscience, speaking words which her grandmother had quoted in the last hours they had spent together.

"'Pride goeth before a fall and a haughty spirit before destruction.'"

Eunice laid down the flashlight and covered her face with her hands. It did not matter what happened now. Even Noel did not matter, because in her anguish she had forgotten him. She remembered only Francis—Francis whom she had abandoned because he was weak and she was strong, because he was sinful and she was righteous, because she scorned the decadence of his household and gloried in the permanence of her own. Francis, whose bride she had been, whose son she had borne. Francis whose charm had imprisoned her and whose passion had illumined her beauty. He had promised her splendor, and this he had given her, only to be reproached because he had not given her everything else as well. He had told her of his faults and failings in the beginning, and she had brushed away his confession as trivial because she had been so sure she could change him; and when the change had not come to pass she had reviled and deserted him. Even when he had repented his sin and abandoned his sloth, she had hardened her heart against him, and in her vain search to find a substitute for his love, only the intuition of a friend had saved her from erring past forgiveness herself. Now her own implacability had come to a culmination. If this were indeed the end of everything, if she were to die tonight in the holocaust that overwhelmed her, the sharpest sting that death brought with it would be the knowledge that it was now too late to lock her life in her husband's again——

"Mother, where are you? I've brought more boards, but I can't find you."

Noel called her a second time before she answered him. Then she made a supreme effort. Reaching for the flashlight, he turned it toward the door, struggling to her feet as she did so. The tears were still rolling, unrestrained, down her desolate face. But her voice came through to her son, controlled and clear.

"I'm here, Noel. I waited for you right where I was. Didn't you know I would, darling?"

It was when they were boarding up the third window that they saw the red light on the horizon. The pines showed black against it while they still stood. But one by one they fell, until the skyline was all aglow and made a smooth curve upward without the piercing points of timberland. Noel stopped hammering to look at it.

"How could a fire start in all this rain?" he said. He asked

317

the question wonderingly, not as if he were frightened, but as if he were puzzled and interested. Eunice tried again to smother the fresh fear that was mingled with old pain in her heart.

"One of the first trees to go down may have fallen over a wire. You know the telegraph poles go across the hills."

"Yes, I know. I didn't think of that— The fire couldn't spread, could it?"

"No, it couldn't spread. Of course it couldn't. But trees may come down almost anywhere. I've thought, once or twice, that I could hear them falling around the house. I couldn't be sure though, the wind made so much noise."

"It isn't as loud now as it was, Mother."

"No, it isn't as loud now. Listen! Does that sound to you like a tree? Or is it just a blind blowing past?"

A mighty force seemed to be wrenching all growth from the flooded earth around the shaking house. As vividly as if darkness had not enveloped them, Eunice seemed to see the green sod overturned and the brown earth, veined with stringy roots, rolling about it. She knew that where trees stood above the sod these were like twisted ropes instead of shaggy string. The sound which came with their downfall was one of slow ripping and tearing, followed by a sudden crash and ending with shuddering echoes. As the sound grew louder and closer, Eunice put her arm around Noel and held him to her heart.

"If the trees fall over the house instead of away from it, they'll crush us, won't they, Mother?"

"They won't fall over the house. There aren't many more to fall—where they can hurt us. The last one we heard must have been Grandma's blue spruce. The others are all farther away."

"Grandma's blue spruce? The one she loved the best of all?"

"Yes, her own tree."

"Perhaps it couldn't live without her, Mother. Perhaps, when she died, it wanted to die too."

"Perhaps it did, Noel."

"She might have wanted the tree herself. I don't see why a tree couldn't go to heaven."

"I don't either, Noel."

"But she wouldn't want the whole place to perish just because she died. She wanted it to last. She believed it would. That's why she called it Evergreen. Isn't it?"

"Yes. And we won't let it perish. We'll save it somehow. In the morning, when the light comes, when the storm is over we'll go out and walk through the groves. We'll make plan for planting more pines. Strong little new ones."

They sat down, side by side, on the floor. Eunice's arm was still around Noel, and his head was on her shoulder. He had held it up for a long time, but now it was beginning to grow heavy, and it drooped. Eunice knew that he was utterly spent with weariness, that soon he would be asleep, and that the rest of the night she must keep vigil without his help. He was already half submerged in slumber when he roused long enough to ask a sleepy question.

"Mother?"

"Yes, Noel?"

"If you're going to plant pines, won't you need a man here?"

"I can manage, Noel, with you and Mem."

"No, you can't. Not with just a boy and a cripple. You need a real man."

"It would make everything easier, if we had one."

"Then hadn't you better ask Father? He would be so happy if you'd let him help——"

When daylight came at last, the sun came with it. The darkness which had seemed so interminable was dispelled not by a dull dawn but by beams of lambency, shining through the slits of the boards which Noel had nailed across the window frames. The wind had gone with the last tree, as if in its errand of destruction, it had destroyed itself. The rain had changed from a torrent to a downpour, from a downpour to a light fall, and from a light fall to a gentle dripping which gradually ceased altogether. Eunice had not heard the rhythmic pattering of drops for more than an hour when she saw that the sun was shining. An immense quietude had occupied the interval.

She and Noel were not far from the bed. Without disturbing him, she managed to reach first for a pillow and then for a quilt. She laid him gently on the floor and covered him. Then she slipped her shoes off silently, and rose.

It was a painful process. She had been sitting still for so long that she was cramped and stiff, and her shoulder, where Noel's head had rested, was very lame. Pain shot through her as she pulled herself erect and began to walk, picking her way over the feathers and between the pieces of broken plaster and past the dead birds that had been swept down the chimney to the hearth. Besides the window frames which Noel had boarded there was still many which he had not been able to reach. She went into her own room and looked out from one of these.

The radiant sun was gilding a scene of utter desolation. The earth around the house was strewn with shattered glass and fallen bricks and splintered shutters. The grass had disappeared. In its place was the overturned sod which she had visualized so vividly in the darkness—this and the roots of the trees which lay, pitiful and prostrate, on the sodden ground. The permanence of Evergreen had perished with its verdure.

Eunice stood at the window and saw it all. She did not sob again and her eyes were unblinded. In the night there had been moments when she was thankful for the scant mercy of the darkness, because then she could not bear to see. Now she could. She saw destruction and salvation together.

She took off the clothes that she had worn through the night, and went under the shower. She came from it tingling all over, and put on clothes that were clean. Then she went down to the kitchen, built up the fire, set the teakettle and the coffeepot on the stove, sliced bread for toast, broke eggs for an omelet. When everything was in readiness for Noel's breakfast and her own, she took a clean piece of paper from a drawer and began to write a message on it, so that this too should be in readiness when the wires were repaired and she could send it.

"There has been a hurricane in the Valley," she wrote, after she had set down the address. "Noel and I have not been hurt but we have lost our pines and we need you very much to help us restore the ruins. If you will come to us it will make us both very happy. Afterward we will all go back to Fielding's Folly together. With all my love—Eunice."